NAUTILUS

A MODERN SEQUEL TO *20,000 LEAGUES UNDER THE SEA*

7 Oct. 2015

For Dennis -
with all best b-day
wishes for fair winds -

PJC

aka Shaw

NAUTILUS

A MODERN SEQUEL TO *20,000 LEAGUES UNDER THE SEA*

PETE SHAW

Fireship Press

Nautilus by Pete Shaw

Cover design by Christine Horner

ISBN: 978-1-61179-359-8 (Paperback)
ISBN: 978-1-61179-360-4 (e-book)

BISAC Subject Headings:
FIC028010 FICTION / Science Fiction / Action & Adventure
FIC031000 FICTION / Thrillers / General
FIC047000 FICTION / Sea Stories

Address all correspondence to:
Fireship Press, LLC
P.O. Box 68412
Tucson, AZ 85737
info@fireshippress.com

Or visit our website at:
www.fireshippress.com

For CL, with love.

"He and his two companions did not then perish in the maëlstrom, in the midst of which the Nautilus was struggling?"

"They escaped, and a book has appeared under the title of Twenty Thousand Leagues Under the Sea, which contains your history."

"The history of a few months only of my life!" interrupted the captain impetuously.

—Jules Verne
The Mysterious Island, 1874

Prologue

Mid-summer, 2021

The twin-engine bomber, a vintage 1941 Luftwaffe, rounded the northern cape and powered in low over the shore. It appeared to be a fully restored original from the Second World War, not a modern copy. Someone had gone to a lot of trouble. Someone with, for all practical purposes, unlimited credit. To Serengetti, even though it was coming to end his life, it was magnificent.

Larsen yelled at Serengetti to lie flat on the ground, then lay down next to him, covering them both with the white sheet he carried in his pack.

"Now you know why I carry this sheet around the Arctic. We just became a harmless patch of snow."

"You know, it still appears to be coming straight for us," Serengetti observed. "Are you sure this trick worked in World War II?"

"Yes," Larsen said resolutely. And then, less resolutely, "But of course, the Germans didn't have thermal sensors in 1941."

"In that case," said Serengetti, as an intense wave of nausea spread through his stomach, "we're going to be killed." There was no time to ponder the irony: as a boy in Parma, Serengetti had built a plastic model of this same aircraft. The elongated fuselage of the German bomber veered offshore slightly, and then aimed toward the two explorers on the snowfield. Well, Serengetti thought, it has, after all, been an interesting life.

* * *

As Head of the Anthropological Directorate of the United Nations Educational, Scientific and Cultural Organization (UNESCO), Akagi Kurosawa arrived at his office in Tokyo each morning anticipating headaches. Kurosawa operated in a world where every resource had long since been commodified, where global warming had surged the rising ocean across every low-lying Pacific atoll, and where the pressures to move at least a sizeable percentage of human population off planet were becoming more intense every month. This competition for space, for resources, for access to off-planet geographies, had led to a cascade of funding for Kurosawa's Directorate, more credits that he had ever been able to muster early in his career as an officer and rising director in the old national science bureaucracies.

Yet each morning his world grew increasingly unmanageable. Few science bureaucrats enjoyed the professional longevity Kurosawa had established over four decades, but in a new world dominated by the episodic, by the freakish and the bizarre, it was increasingly difficult for a talented man with a well-thought-out plan to remain on a tight schedule, even with a surfeit of funding.

The continuous fissuring of the transnational economy, especially since the global climate shift of 2017, had created a bewildering array of economic alliances, all of which affected UNESCO. Corporations and chopped-up nation-states, economic exclusion zones, powerful cities combined with former military units, all of these and more were the result of a transnational human mass culture once based on the generation of corporate profit, now focused on base survival. The old systems of military and political unions between nation-states, partnerships lasting decades, seemed laughably antique now. It was true that a few kings, dictators, presidents, and prime ministers still remained—including those who served as more or less benevolent leaders of the U.N. But they were figureheads, kept in place to reassure the masses that something resembling stability still existed. But stability, as Kurosawa well knew, was a thing of the past, and the future held but one option for cultural survival.

The Directorate maintained a sophisticated intelligence apparatus in an attempt to keep pace with the activities of their economic and political rivals. From constant monitoring of Glöbnet reports and from direct human and satellite surveillance, they knew the results of various archaeological expeditions of European Union universities even before the expeditions returned from the field. And they kept tabs on the somewhat bizarre activities of two ideologically opposite but equally venomous rogue forces, Artifact Protection Enterprises (APE), and Écologie Maintenant (EM). The latter was an anti-globalization cell, one that had acquired several surplus diesel submarines. These subs patrolled shipping lanes, sinking the odd transnational tanker. One of these subs had even launched an unsuccessful torpedo attack on one of Kurosawa's research vessels, apparently in the belief that it represented the efforts of the transnationals to exploit global resources and then fly away, leaving the earth an ecological ruin. Kurosawa had gone to great lengths to ensure that such attacks were not repeated.

Of even more immediate threat were the activities of the treasure hunters of Artifact Protection Enterprises, an organization of extra-governmental parasites who were raiding Kurosawa's sites, killing off his field teams, and selling artifacts to the highest bidders on the internet black market. No one in the Directorate knew just how this crime syndicate had come together, but there was little doubt what held it together: the profits to be made on cultural treasure.

Most believed that APE was the brainchild of a criminal of obscure origins known only by the code name of Elgin. Its headquarters were variously rumored to be located in a Bavarian mountain fastness near the village of Berchtesgaden, on an island somewhere in Indonesia, or buried in cyberspace in some Russian server. Elgin himself, some argued, was merely a mafioso assassin with a refined taste in Italian archaeological treasures, be they from 2,000 BC or from the Second World War. Or perhaps he was a descendant of the man who robbed Greece of the treasures later known as the Elgin marbles.

In addition to these constant troubles, there were the usual distractions, cross border raids by fifth-gen National Socialists flying reconditioned Dorniers over his paleo site in Brazil. These rattled his archaeological teams and, worse, reawakened interest on the Glöbnet in racial questions, something he hoped to avoid at all costs. American spy satellites were also a nuisance, and Kurosawa lamented the inordinate amount of time he wasted responding to requests for field data from his favorite oxymoron, American intelligence.

As a result of these multifarious distractions, Kurosawa found himself in a strange position. He had all the funding he needed to carry out archaeological investigations, but his teams were under constant assault by raiders from APE, occasional zealots from EM, and spies from Washington. And the archaeological sites themselves were rapidly disappearing, both from raids by treasure hunters and from rising sea levels. He was under tremendous pressure to produce results, with fewer and fewer options for obtaining those results.

In the summer of 2021, Kurosawa was particularly interested in any results from a small archaeological expedition he had dispatched to an obscure island in the high European Arctic. Anticipating these results, he sat in his office, the very model of a confident, post-modern Head of Directorate. And he had no doubts that he was the man to control it.

One: In Northern Mists

The Spitsbergen Islands, late summer, 2021

A thick mass of cloud shifted across the summit like an army in retreat. Serengetti had never climbed this mountain before and he reached the summit with some difficulty. When finally he stood atop it, breathing heavily, he couldn't see the mass of crumbling metamorphic rock beneath his feet for the fog. Instead, he could reach out his arm and see his hand disappear into the white cloud, as if he were a spirit, moving quietly between worlds.

Loose grey scree lay along the steep upslope from the ridge. Visibility was just good enough to allow him to see the rock: jagged where it had broken in recent times, rounded and weathered where it had fallen in some ancient upheaval. He had, in fact, been on this island once before, but then only for a one-hour shoreline reconnaissance. Now, the weight of his backpack had inflamed his lower back. The pain would only be temporary, he knew. He thanked his stars for that; he had always recovered quickly from any injury and in his youth had never missed a single day of schooling to the various illnesses, viruses, and bacterial infections that had plagued his classmates.

Without his GPS and the sonic signals from the directional transponders flooding into his console, he would be completely lost. The high Arctic was nearly always hidden behind thick curtains of mist. For more than twenty years he had been shouldering these curtains aside, rediscovering archaeological sites left behind by the earliest explorers of these cold islands, from the Norse to the Heroic Era of polar exploration in the late nineteenth-century. From the catalog of polar archaeological sites he had surveyed, from Svalbard in the north to Cape Adare in Antarctica, he could recall each survey, the detail of each artifact, each explorer's hut on a rocky shore or whaling wreck under a frozen bay. Now, as he coordinated the final surveys of the most remote islands and waters of Svalbard, he sought to wrest the last archaeological secrets from them and from their deep fjords.

There had been so many gray summits, so many mornings like this that his memory had ceased to distinguish between them.

When one was green, getting experience was what mattered. One joined expeditions to anywhere, in search of anything, just so long as one submerged the awful green of youth in the river of experience. Expeditions, degrees, scholarly papers, books, lectures, year after year of washing the green from his body, his vitae was now painted with the deep blue of authority. For more than twenty years he had explored some of the most remote geographies on earth, searching for one more artifact, one more site, one more whisper from mankind's history of humanity's need to explore and exploit.

Lately, he had felt himself changing from explorer to businessman, selling his scholarship, living from one consultancy to another. Small amounts of time had to be balanced atop smaller budgets. Colleagues required politicking. Boards required mollification, appeals, results, over and over again. Transpac's old diesel submarine, the *Philippe Tailliez*, brought back into service for intensive sonar surveys of Paleolithic migration sites along the Continental Shelf, drained away more and more of their budget. Then there was the remotely operated unmanned blimp, on near-constant summer patrol in those parts of the Arctic they could not survey directly, which required a small air force to keep it flying.

During each new field season, he realized, these brief moments alone on remote summits became fewer, and his enjoyment of them more fleeting. After all these years he had succeeded in scouring away the green, but he had also lost much of the simple, sensual joy of fieldwork in remote places. At thirty-nine, there were times he would give anything to be green again, to erase all of the hard-won knowledge, and replay the blank tape of youth.

* * *

Behind his enormous polished rosewood table, Akagi Kurosawa sat like a white-haired Glöbnet news anchor. Arrayed before his somber presence were twenty-three computer displays. Technicians would arrive later in the morning to install the next four high definition television screens. Armed with those new HDTs he would possess continuous coverage of all of the major excavations currently underway in Java. With the touch of the keypad on his arm, Kurosawa brought in real-time satellite video feeds from every cultural site under his jurisdiction, which had just been extended to beds VII through XIII at the early Java Man sites. There, secure dating of *H. erectus* presence in Asia had just been rolled back three hundred thousand years.

Kurosawa was an anthropologist who thrived on questions surrounding the origins of humans and their spread across extreme and remote geographies like the stony islands of the Arctic and backwater harbors of the Pacific. It was the mission of his Directorate to study the myriad cultural problems inherent in the announced United Nations enterprise of organizing a human colony somewhere in the solar system. By uncovering the secrets and successes of past settlements, they hoped to safeguard the most important future settlements of all.

The U.N. had recently decided that forms of human culture—based on what were seen as successful past societies—were to be transplanted from earth to several destinations throughout the solar system. For a half century, the great University of Hawaii anthropologist Ben Finney had studied how Polynesian culture had radiated out from an Asian source, to found new and diverse cultures throughout the Pacific. He had extrapolated this knowledge into hypotheses on the course of human migrations into space. The challenge for the U.N. was a complex one: decide the nature of the originating, homeland, culture.

The instructions from Kurosawa's UNESCO board were to excavate any site or fund any experiment that might provide data to evaluate the crucial question of what combinations of cultures were best adapted to colonize space. It had long since ceased to be "How would we transfer people to remote destinations?" and had become instead "What is the character of the culture that will originate on earth, but diverge on some distant geography?" Will it be tribal or band level, or state level, or corporate? Will it be organized primarily for resource extraction, like some Arctic mining company town, or based on a small-scale social group?

In the eyes of Kurosawa and his Board, it had boiled down to this: how to migrate off-planet, preserving the diversity of human experience and culture that the 12th World Anthropological Conference had deemed essential for human cultural development? It was a question so fantastically complicated that it was worthy of his considerable imagination and intellect.

Kurosawa and his deputy, Australian industrial archaeologist Ellen Archer, led a cadre of intent young staff assistants who monitored the screens 24/7. In several shifts, they collated scientific reports from the Directorate's own expeditions, and searched archival collections around the world for clues to where new sites might be found. It was demanding work, but at that moment, Dr. Archer was not available to assist him with the Java excavations. Kurosawa had sent her to Russia on various archival research projects related to decommissioned nuclear vessels reported lost in the Arctic. This particular project was of profound interest to Kurosawa, and he had been personally monitoring its progress.

He considered these matters while tending the Balinese clown fish in the circulating seawater tropical fish tank that dominated the center of his office.

* * *

Out of the white mist, a large, indistinct form began to materialize near Serengetti. Reflexively, still trying to catch his breath, his arm went to his side, gloved fingers entwining the grip of a .357. They had issued him a 9mm pistol and a flashmaster, which blinded any animal within twenty meters, but he rejected them in favor of his old service .357. His sidearm had long been phased out, but he had asked for an exemption as a Chief's prerogative and, to his surprise, it had been granted. In the Arctic, one required stopping power, and the Glock 9mm did not possess the kick to stop a large bear. The scattered remnants of the Arctic bear population could still be encountered in these remote islands, especially in the odd summer when the shrinking polar pack pressed far south, and he had never forgotten—how could he?—that he had once been surprised in his sleep by a big one. Having escaped with a minor mauling, he had vowed never to be surprised again.

As he approached the shrouded form it slowly took shape as his friend, colleague, and field guide, Bjorn Larsen, and he relaxed his grip. It never ceased to impress him how the Arctic could so completely conceal things just meters away. Conversely, on rare crystalline days, it could make the very distant loom close.

Far the better climber and athlete, both in bed and out, younger by three years, half a head taller and twice as strong, Larsen had reached the apex first and was waiting for him. He looked ready, if it were necessary, to ascend another thousand meters. Larsen greeted him, then looked at the console bolted to his arm cradle, tapped a few buttons, and after a moment decided it was safe to punch up the three polarsats. As the reading came in, he listened to the familiar labored breathing of his friend.

Sucking in icy air in huge draughts, Serengetti asked slowly, in Norwegian, "What do you have?"

"You are late, as usual," Larsen replied, ignoring the question.

Serengetti looked around, his imagination wandering from the present to the glorious improbabilities of the archaeological Arctic past. The mist had begun to thin, as sunlight along the horizon filtered in wide arcs onto the summit.

If one saga of the Arctic fascinated them both more than any other, it was the flight to the North Pole of the airship *Italia*. They had searched for the remains of this airship wreck for years now. Just before noontime on the twenty-fifth of May 1928, an Italian airship returning from a magnificently daring expedition to the North Pole suddenly became heavy and started to sink toward the ice-razored sea. The dirigible had fought into the teeth of a biting wind almost as soon as it had left the airspace above the Pole. By the time the airship began to sink, the forty-three-year-old captain, Umberto Nobile, had been at his station for more than sixty hours without sleep. The pole was thirty hours behind him, and that after a twenty-hour flight from his hangar at Kings Bay, Svalbard. Renowned for an almost superhuman endurance, he was nevertheless close to the breaking point. He thought that perhaps one of the gas valves on the top of the airship had become frozen in an open position, allowing precious hydrogen to escape. Nobile sent his chief rigger aloft to check on the valves. Perhaps it could be unstuck and the airship brought back into trim. Nobile ordered the engines full ahead and the elevators up. They would, he hoped, fly their way out of the crisis.

But the airship, half the size of a battleship, did not respond. It continued to fall. They were almost home—just three hours away from the airship hangar at Kings Bay—when the *Italia* hit the ice pack and scraped along its jagged edge for a hundred meters. Nobile was dragged over the ice as the control car twisted apart. Something smashed into his skull. The crushing pressure of the car grinding into the ice snapped his right leg, then his right arm. When he came to, Nobile was lying on his side, his face in an icy pool of his own blood. His eyes turned upward to see his airship, a huge open gash where the control car had been, lift back into the air and drift off somewhere to the east. He saw plainly the large black letters: *I T A L I A*. When the severed hull disappeared into the mist, six of the sixteen-man crew were still on board. None were ever seen again.

Nobile assumed that his own death was only minutes or hours away. Instead, he lived on for a half-century, to the age of ninety-three, condemned to relive the helpless shock of seeing his airship and the six men on board vanish into oblivion. Two others of the crew died before they could be rescued. Then the Norwegian explorer Roald Amundsen, who flew north to find Nobile, was himself lost at sea. As designer and builder of the airship, as well as leader of the expedition, Nobile felt the burden of responsibility.

The search for the *Italia's* remains had drawn Serengetti to the Arctic more than twenty years earlier, as a young petty officer on board an American icebreaker. When he met Larsen years later, he learned that his obsession was a shared one. Larsen knew the history of the flight as if he had been on it, the design of the airship as if he had drawn it, the biographies of the crew as if they were his. Their Arctic offices looked out over the *Italia* monument, and both had long ago memorized the words and names on its simple rusted metal stanchion:

Caddero Per L'Alta Causa
Della Conoscenza Umana
Alessandrini
Arduino
Caratti
Ciocca
Lago
Malmgren-SV-
Pomella
Pontremoli

Even now, nearly a century later, no one knew why the airship had crashed. The ship had hit the ice less than fifty kilometers from the spot where Serengetti and Larsen now stood. It had taken nearly five years of planning, grant writing, and permit applications, but Serengetti felt that once and for all they were closing in on the cause of the wreck of the *Italia*. Four years earlier, he had discovered a tiny section of one of the *Italia's* tail fins, washed ashore on a rocky shoreline in the nearby archipelago of Franz Josef Land. He had assumed that he would quickly find the remainder of the wreck, and had suffered through a depressing winter when he had not.

"Where the hell are we?" asked Serengetti. Even in the cold air, he could feel his palms sweating inside his gloves.

"According to this console, which never works properly up here, we're within twenty millimeters of the summit of Foynøya."

"That's close enough," Serengetti replied. "I think if we search northeast from here we may hit it. We've only got one last day to find it, then it's back to Kings Bay, with one more week on board the *Quest*. After that, it's back to Oslo for the long winter."

Nodding his head, Larsen indicated the islands around them. "Here they have the long winter," he said. "In Oslo, it will rain."

Serengetti pulled his gloves off and tapped his console. He studied the console closely, and a slight smile came across his face.

"There," Serengetti said. "I have the hull of the *Italia*. Bearing NNE, 7.248 kilometers offshore. Metal composition matches exactly the fin I found in Franz Josef Land. We can launch the Autonomous Undersea Vehicle from the eight-wheeler and check it out, probably get the survey done in a few hours."

As Serengetti recalibrated his console instruments, Larsen heard a soft electric whine off in the distance. "You've been firing microbursts to the navigation satellite haven't you?" he said.

"I've been recalibrating our position while we've been having this nice chat."

"That's what I thought," said Larsen. "I think our friends have followed us."

"Don't be ridiculous," Serengetti protested. "There's not an APE probe within a thousand kilometers of this rock. There's never been a site attack this far north. And UROBs can't operate this far north."

"Look," Larsen answered, pointing to his console. "The beacon is out."

The directional beacon, an essential part of hardware on board their Arctic all-terrain eight-wheel vehicle, had suddenly ceased to function. So had the relay that allowed them to access the AATV's onboard computer. The vehicle was parked at the north end of the island below the four hundred-meter high cliff on which they now stood. Whatever had disabled their transport was now very close. And before they saw the Unmanned Remotely Operated Blimp, they saw through the thinning fog black smoke coming from their burning transport on the beach.

"Look at that low cloud," Serengetti said, pointing to a remarkably circular cloud rising rapidly from the shore.

"I see it," said Larsen, unshouldering his rifle and looking through the scope. "I thought you said one of these things couldn't operate this far north."

"Everyone makes mistakes in their dissertations."

They didn't wait for the UROB to reach their position. APE UROB's were equipped with state-of-the-art global positioning, along with real-time digital video transmission with better resolution than the human eye. The APE tech controlling this particular blimp could track the two explorers anywhere on the face of the earth. They had been under surveillance the whole time.

Both men shut down their consoles, switching them into sleep mode. A UROB was effective but slow, and it would now spend precious minutes searching the scree along their last known track. They headed in the opposite direction. But it was a relatively small island, and the UROB controller knew it as well as they did.

Every archaeologist knew that Artifact Protection Enterprises didn't like to be held up in its pursuit of treasure, especially since very few unplundered archaeological sites still existed. The market waiting for them had so intensified since 2017 that an artifact like the remains of Nobile's airship—the last and greatest undiscovered artifact in the polar regions—was worth several hundred million credits on the black market. Even so, there had never been an attack this far north. Raids at equatorial sites had become commonplace, but the Arctic had been left alone. Until now.

UROBs were not only unsurpassed mobile continuous surveillance platforms, they were also directional beacons for Artifact Protection's real muscle, the APE Air Force. A UROB alone was a nuisance. A UROB guiding a reconditioned Ju .88 with its two

7.92 mm forward firing machine guns was lethal.

"You really need to keep up on the APE page on Glöbnet," Larsen said as he led them around a series of granite boulders the size of two-car garages. Serengetti, breathing heavily again, paused briefly to get his bearings.

APE had made no secret of its scorn for the UNESCO's archaeological survey teams. A dynamic German Ph.D. fresh from a post-doc at the Ballard Institute had disappeared in a New Guinea mangrove only six months earlier while collecting data for a multi-scaler GIS of the exploration sites there. His body was never found. Disposing of Serengetti and Larsen, two of the Anthropological Directorate's best contract surveyors, on an Arctic island where they might not be found for years, if at all, would increase the value of the black market by four or five per cent overnight.

"You've been here before, haven't you?" Larsen asked Serengetti.

"Just once. Routine helo landing. Only stayed about an hour at the southeast shore looking for..."

"I know, looking for caches," Larsen finished the sentence. "Was there any kind of valley down there?"

"Just a small one. The pilot brought us in through it. Crazy Russian bastard. Did a wall crawl on the way out that scared the hell out of me."

"Didn't your mother tell you not to fly with strange Russians? Anyway, you should see a Norsk pilot do it. Was there any ice?"

"*Oh, ja.*" said Serengetti. "The valley is about two kilometers from here. Why?"

"Never mind." Larsen said, as they heard the growing whine of the UROB's electric motors. "Come on. Let's go. Now! And for Christ's sake stop saying '*ja.*' You're not Norwegian and this isn't *The Heroes of Telemark!*"

* * *

One of Kurosawa's predecessors had coordinated biomedical research on downed B-29 fliers during World War II. Much of the research was innocuous, the usual racial comparisons and cranial measurements; typically pedestrian, nineteenth-century stuff. But there had been the more medieval variety as well. The removal of organs, including and especially the brain, from living POWs, was routine. American fliers aware of their fate used their service pistols to kill as many approaching Nippon citizens as possible, saving the last bullet for their own brains. They were usually the commanders of the aircraft, men who understood—or had been briefed—that they would receive no quarter in surrender. He'd read too many of the reports catalogued in a secret walk-in safe/archives in the sub-basement. But that was after Kurosawa had already spent time in the U.S., where he had completed a post-doc in maritime anthropology at the University of Pennsylvania.

Kurosawa liked Americans, at least those not engaged in snooping about his activities, even though they were much too violent for his taste and tended to forget their history almost as quickly as they lived it. As a result, no one connected his first name with the queen of the Nipponese flattops, the flagship of the Air Fleet. He himself disassociated as possible, always using "A. Kurosawa" for his journal publications. In fact, he could not recall a single individual, Nipponese or otherwise, who ever called him by his first name. He was glad he didn't have to go back to the U.S. and look his colleagues there in the eyes after what he'd read.

That Director had survived the war. Even as similar German "physicians" were killed by the Soviets or went into long and eventually permanent exiles in Paraguay, that Director had been promoted to head of the science research establishment. He had enjoyed a productive career until he died in his sleep in 1971.

Kurosawa himself was particularly troubled by cruelty, carelessness, and waste. His Directorate bioengineers cut open the brains of rodents and the living hearts of fin whales all the time, especially now that the quota of science catch whales had been lifted. He had visited one of his coastal research laboratories where they studied human interaction with the maritime environment. Some of the physiologists used sharks. To his disgust, fully eighty-three per cent of the sea creatures were dead before they even got to the laboratory, mostly due to careless handling by the collectors. He didn't say anything to the staff during his visit, of course. That would have been impolite. But he knew the figure was eighty-three per cent. He had stood on the dock and looked through the slats of the collections tank. So many dead sharks. He had ordered an immediate review and study of this obscene mortality rate. As Kurosawa later discovered, no one before him had ever bothered to ask.

Just as bad, to Kurosawa's scientific mind, none of the supposedly world-class scientists he had working for him had chanced to ask how those dead eighty-three per cent skewed their experimental results. He had yet to read a scientific paper with an abstract that began, "of the seventeen per cent of the animals that survived the collection and processing ordeal, this limited sample gave these following results…"

How did they know whether the remaining seventeen per cent was indicative of the population as a whole? It wasn't, but science usually did not acknowledge such methodological niceties. Cut out the brain of the aircrewman who hadn't blown his brains out already and use that as the norm. Kurosawa shuddered. Well, at least he had revised those imbecilic procedures. But he didn't like to contemplate them at length. And what he least wanted to contemplate was the dread question of what his Directorate would have done if Nippon had actually won the war. He now possessed the global reach his predecessors had envisioned in 1935. Unlike his predecessors, his grasp was every bit the equal of his reach, and his conscience weighed heavily every time he evaluated his responsibilities. Nevertheless, his path was clear, and he was determined to follow it to its logical end.

To clear his mind of the nightmares of misguided racial programs, he did what many busy Nipponese executives did to relax: he played miniature golf.

In Nippon, miniature golf wasn't the silly little summer vacation pastime it had been for a hundred years in the old U.S. None of that sink-the-ball-in-the-cute-squirrel's-mouth. This was miniature golf treated with the respect and professionalism it deserved: a bonsai approach to golf. Kurosawa had organized his Directorate into squads that competed with great zeal for the Director's Cup. It had become such an obsession that many of his bureaucrats spent their spare time away at the Rising Sun Mini-Strokes course five kilometers from the Directorate. Wives, children, home life be damned, this was mini-golf.

Kurosawa himself was at near-professional level, having recorded one round where he sank seven holes-in-one out of eighteen. But he was forever tripped up by the thirteenth hole at Rising Sun, the dreaded Revenge-on-Fat-Boy. Computers recalculated the angles of the side bumpers, not with each player, but with each player's stroke, so that the hole changed with every shot. A good miniature golf player depended on each hole remaining the same, so that a mental picture could be drawn of it, angles memorized, correct stance filed away. But the thirteenth hole changed all that. It had stored each player's style and previous play of the hole in its computers. When the bar code on the player's sneakers activated the hole and the yellow ball popped up to the tee, it processed how the player had attacked the hole the previous twenty times, and changed the course accordingly, chaotically, eradicating the utility of previously played and remembered shots.

Kurosawa was thinking, as he often did behind his desk, of the thirteenth hole at Rising Sun Mini-Strokes when a mild tone, like a pebble dropped gently into Lake Fengshui, issued from screen number six. He glanced at his notes. That would be the Nobile site in northeast Svalbard. Automatic data feeds to the screen recessed into his desktop told him that an unidentified flying object had just entered air space over Site Number Six. Kurosawa's data feed came from two HDT transceivers positioned by the team at the start of the expedition, one atop Foynøya, the other directly at sea level and covering their landing area, their camp, and the area around their all-terrain vehicle. The HDT transceivers were equipped with radar and an acoustic beacon receiver, the latter scanning a series of Long Baseline beacons placed on the seabed. These operated equally well surveying archaeological grids as they did detecting submarines (including UNESCO's own contract submarine, the *Philippe Tailliez*, in the area), while the radar scanned the skies for any aircraft entering the protected airspace. The radar usually picked up unmanned Glöbnet heliceivers snooping near UNESCO archaeological sites for a scoop on the latest field discoveries.

There was definitely something wrong. The camera near the landing area showed black smoke pouring from the Arctic all-terrain vehicle, and Larsen's team from Oslo was nowhere to be seen. Kurosawa touched his computer screen and the view switched to the HDT transceiver atop the island, 400 meters above the HDT on shore. He immediately called his Chief of Staff.

"Excuse me, please, Ms. Higginson."

"Yes, Dr. Kurosawa."

"Can you switch to screen six and find out why an unidentified UROB is over our site?"

There was a moment's pause, as Higginson called up the requisite screen and site, then another moment as she split the screen and scanned mock-up diagrams and specs.

"It looks like APE," she said at last. "But they've never had one that could operate in the Arctic, nor one equipped with what look like thermal sensors in the gondola."

"Exactly as I was thinking," said the Director. "Where is the *Philippe Tailliez* right now?"

Higginson checked another screen. "About twenty-five kilometers south, surveying near Behouneck Point."

"Order the *Tailliez* to power up and rendezvous at Foyn Island immediately. Also, would you be so kind as to inform the on-scene coordinator on board the *Tailliez* of this development and have her stand by. This may be only a scout in advance of something more problematic. Tell her that assistance will be required."

* * *

Captain Ingvill Jørriksen of the research submarine *Philippe*

Tailliez let fly with a satisfying string of hard language. She was used to exercising at least a moderate amount of control over the course and speed of her own vessel. These constant changes of course and assignment by UNESCO bureaucrats in Tokyo were beginning to wear on her. This latest change of assignment held the promise of danger, and as a prudent captain she avoided danger to her sub and crew at all costs.

As a girl, she had role-played such scenarios, usually just after watching American naval movies. Many times she had rerun videos of *The Enemy Below, We Dive at Dawn, Torpedo Run*, and her favorite—the best submarine movie of them all—*Run Silent, Run Deep*. She had always admired the straight-talking American sub commanders, like Glenn Ford and John Wayne, who never put up with any BS. But, truth be told, she had always found Clark Gable the most convincing—and far and away the most handsome. Years later, when she finally made rank in the Norwegian Navy and boarded the *Kobben* as its commander, she realized that submarine captains, at least the coastal patrol captains she knew—and certainly the captain that she believed herself to be—were more like the thoughtful Gable than the bellicose Wayne.

In her stateroom on board the *Philippe Tailliez*, she had had just enough room to build from scratch three models of historic submarines. Growing up along the waterfront of Bergen amid a forest of masts and rigging, it was the occasional visit of a submarine that had most fascinated her. When most girls went to the mountains to ski and play with boys she, feeling herself hopelessly uncoordinated and unattractive, studied coastal navigation. While ambitious young women at university studied economics, she studied the sonar patterns of whales, dolphins, and Russian submarines.

Even as she believed herself completely unappealing to men, the long-limbed Jørriksen had distinguished herself with the ultimate phallus, the attack submarine. For more than two decades, she lived with smooth shapes that simulated hard cocks: the submarines themselves, of course, but also their torpedoes, the spokes on the propulsion controls, the levers of missile controls. The relative absence of direct sexual harassment from the men of the crew or fellow officers Jørriksen ascribed to her own unattractiveness, rather than gallantry on the part of the men. She rose rapidly in the officer corps. The Royal Norwegian Navy had been the first in the world to appoint a woman as skipper of a submarine. After Solveig Krey, Jørriksen was the second Norwegian to command a submarine and the second woman anywhere in the world with such a responsibility. So she had a special fondness for the German-built, Norwegian-modified *Kobben* class on which she had served for so long. After twenty-two years, there was hardly a deep, narrow fjord in Scandinavia in which she had not hidden at periscope depth.

The *Kobben* itself had been her first command and, like all of NATO's coastal subs deployed to patrol cultural protection zones around the world, hers was an all-female crew. When a sister boat of the *Kobben*, the *Kunna*, was brought out of retirement as a civilian archaeological survey submarine and renamed the *Philippe Tailliez*, she had put in for retirement and then immediately applied for and received the job of commanding officer. Her new civilian job allowed her to indulge her passion for undersea exploration.

Increasingly, however, these archaeological patrols were funded less and less by UNESCO science grants and more and more by UN paramilitary operational budgets. Her new executive officer, Karenna Johansson, was a recently retired lieutenant commander in an elite branch of the Swedish special forces, the Attack Divers, a fact which served to intimidate Jørriksen. The fact that this new X.O. was whip-cord lean and muscular, to say nothing of darkly attractive, obnoxiously outgoing, and apparently fearless, made her the very opposite of Jørriksen.

The captain's new orders were to meet the Transpac field team at Foynøya, then standby to render any assistance. Fine, thought Jørriksen. If Tokyo was going to fiddle with her command of her submarine, then she would take whatever matters into her own hands as she thought fit. She gave Commander Johansson a separate set of instructions. Johansson would be put ashore at Foynøya to clear whatever threats she might encounter. It would be good,

Jørriksen thought as the *Tailliez* maneuvered into position, to get the commander ashore for a few hours, and not have her panther-like presence looking over her shoulder.

* * *

The blinding fog that had hidden the UROB from Larsen and Serengetti now returned to conceal them as they retreated to a small snowfield on the southern slope of the island. The UROB wasn't very large, and the APE knew how to camouflage, so it melted into the environment. Larsen had once seen a completely clear gasbag used in Moroccan desert, an especially amazing sight because the gondola was also molded in clear plastic. The only visible parts were the wiring of the HDT transceivers, making it look like a giant Portuguese Man-o-War soughing across the desert, ready to sting him. Which it nearly had. In the Arctic—a new APE foray field—the camouflage scheme was a completely white gas bag made of non-reflective polyethylene, invisible against the glacier where it had no doubt been hiding. Larsen cursed himself silently. It was his job to anticipate these kinds of intrusions. Born in Oslo, but raised in the Arctic, he should have seen it coming.

They scrambled quietly and quickly, not knowing if the UROB was equipped to hear their movements. If it had thermal sensors, their silence wouldn't matter. On the UROB's controller's screen, their warm bodies would stand out like inflamed red eyes against the cold gray background of the permafrost. They reached the upper slopes of the snowfield and Larsen reached into his pack and pulled out what looked like a white bed sheet.

"Quickly," he said in Norwegian. "Get under this."

Serengetti dove to the ground and Larsen huddled close beside him, pulling the white sheet over their bodies and packs.

"You always carry a spare bedsheet around with you?" Serengetti asked quietly.

"Shut up," the Norwegian said in English. "You never know when it will come in handy after the husband has left for work."

It was the old trick of an Arctic warrior. Two heavily equipped soldiers, caught in the open, under attack. Their only option was to hide, to become an anonymous patch of snow. They were now indistinguishable, especially from above. The whine of the UROB began to fade, and Serengetti took a long cold breath. Then came a distinctly different sound, from the south, and steadily intensifying.

"That's what I was afraid of," Larsen said.

"Sounds like the UROB has blown an engine."

"That's not the UROB," Larsen said. "You're the aerospace expert. You tell me what it is."

Serengetti listened to the deep-throated sound as it roared closer to them from somewhere out of the south.

"I know what it sounds like," said Serengetti after a moment. "But APE isn't so desperate that they have to operate a Jumo engine up here."

"Only if you want to kill people and have fun at the same time."

"In that case, we're not in a very good position," said Serengetti, his heart thumping in his chest like a leather mallet against a bodhran. "Because that sound could only be made by a Ju. 88."

"Twin-engined bomber?"

"Yes. And if it's fully functional, it's got a nice bomb load to go with its machine guns."

"My great-grandfather evaded a German patrol with a sheet like this once," said Larsen. "During the Second World War. I never thought I'd have to do it."

"Reach in my pack," said Serengetti, "and take out my rangefinder."

Larsen handed Serengetti the monocular and resigned himself to death. Then, just as he looked out from under the sheet, the Ju. 88 suddenly exploded.

Serengetti was blinded by an orange fireball just offshore. Larsen, his eyes shielded by his glacier glasses, followed the flaming metal debris as it plunged almost in slow motion into the ice-studded water. Serengetti tried to regain his eyesight, to scan the crash with his rangefinder.

"Christ!" he found himself almost shouting. "A fuel line must have given way."

"With a little assist from A. Kurosawa," Larsen said, pointing down to a dark mass emerging from the depths of the deep channel near the shore. At that moment, the long black mass of their old diesel research submarine *Philippe Tailliez* shouldered aside the icy water and broke through to the surface of the fjord.

"What in hell is the *Tailliez* doing here?"

"Delivering an angel. You know," said Larsen, "the Germans weren't exactly welcomed the last time they invaded Norway. You'd think they'd learn their lesson."

"German aircraft," said Serengetti, regaining his senses and his sight. "But I doubt a German crew. And since when has my research submarine had short range missiles on board?"

Larsen scanned the cliffs around them, looking for something.

"Well, if you attended board meetings once in a while, you might learn a few things. Besides, you might own it, but Kurosawa pays all the bills." He fixed Serengetti's monocular on a brief gleam of metal several hundred meters away. At the same time, Serengetti watched as a small z-boat from the *Tailliez* made its way shoreward.

"She must have landed from the sub before the Ju. 88 got to the island," Larsen said.

"Who?"

"Come on. Let's go thank the woman who took that RBS ashore and cleared away that .88."

"I wish I could see what you're talking about," said Serengetti, rearranging his clothes, shouldering his pack, and feeling the rock of the island under his feet once again as he made his way off the snowfield and onto the scree.

"You need better eyesight," said Larsen. "There's more than one reason why they always pick me to lead these expeditions."

Several minutes later, they stepped over the gunwales of the z-boat and seated themselves deep in the bow. Larsen then began speaking rapidly in Norwegian to the driver, who twisted the throttle handle and backed the z-boat off the rocky shore. The inflatable cut toward the looming form of the *Philippe Tailliez*.

Near the young blonde crewmember driving the boat was an older, dark-haired woman who was quickly and professionally stowing an RBS 90 anti-aircraft rocket launcher into a hard case. Larsen nodded to the older woman, whose jaw remained impassive but whose eyes conveyed volumes.

Serengetti, in the flush of excitement over surviving the attack, began talking rapidly and nervously. But Larsen had ceased to listen. He was too busy trying to fend off all that the silent woman was saying to him.

* * *

Lieutenant Commander Karenna Johansson was once again fascinated by her own avidity. There was something in her psyche that she had never been able to control after intense field exercises. Only this had not been an exercise—she really had blown that aircraft and its crew from the sky. That crew—all men most likely—would never breathe again, never fly again, never fuck again. The thought of what Johansson had just done shot like lightning through her brain and sent a cascade of blood to flush between her thighs.

Ever since her early days as one of the very first women members of Sweden's elite *Kustjägarna*, she had known that the aftermath of combat, even simulated combat, brought out strange reactions in her comrades. She had seen her share of fire-fights, and in the shock-like aftermath had looked away as hard-bitten, intensely-trained men fell to the ground, the taut muscles in their young legs suddenly turned to noodles, had listened to them cry for their mothers like little boys. It had surprised her at first, entering this male-dominated clan, that there was no shame in this. In fact, their training officers had told them to expect it as a natural reaction to the experience of intense close-in fighting.

Johansson had seen such reactions often during live-fire missions along the Swedish coastline. Her unit was trained as a shock force for amphibious assault operations. Enemies for a thousand years had tried to exploit the vulnerability of the Swedish coast. It had been the job of her unit of *Kustjägarna* rangers to train to throw invaders back into the sea. If an opposing force was already ashore, then Johansson's unit was to take the shore back—in the most rapid and violent way possible. In compensation for their small numbers, their weaponry included machine guns, Carl Gustaf Recoilless rifles, anti-tank and anti-material 84mm rockets, and Mark 19 grenade launchers.

After her assignment to the elite unit of the *Attackdykarna,* the Attack Divers, she had been trained to mount attacks on enemy shipping from two-person infiltrator submarines, raid buildings, and sabotage enemy installations. Her personal specialty was the weapon she now stowed, the RBS 90 Anti-Aircraft Missile System. It was a vast improvement over the earlier and heavier RBS 70, which took two rangers to haul into position. She had become expert at humping this newer and lighter and more lethal weapon over glaciers and across shingle. She could be in position and ready to fire in a matter of seconds, instead of the minutes the old 70s had taken. She was too much of a professional to make a point of it, but this particular operation had been easier than shooting down a target drone. The Ju-88 flew low and slow, and she almost felt guilty at how simple it had been to clear it from the fjord.

Even so, it had been a bit of a hard climb to get into position, and one never took anything for granted during such operations. She could feel the adrenaline coursing through her. Her body seemed to hum. Johansson's own personal reaction to the combat shock she now felt was different from most of her male counterparts, who drank hard, or laughed too loud at stupid or crude jokes. On the other hand, after a particularly intense field exercise, she experienced an almost uncontrollable need to fuck. And she now focused that desire on the blond, bearded Viking named Bjorn Larsen who conveniently presented his towering body before her.

Two: West Fjord

Late summer

The marvelous saloon, still flooded with light, had been carefully closed. The iron door leading on deck was then securely fastened in such a manner as to prevent even a drop of water from penetrating to the interior of the Nautilus...

...at the water line, were two large stop-cocks communicating with the reservoirs employed in the submersion of the vessel.

The stop-cocks were opened, the reservoirs filled, and the Nautilus, slowly sinking, disappeared beneath the surface...

The powerful light it gave forth lighted up the translucent water... At last this vast effusion of electric light faded away, and soon after the Nautilus, now the tomb of Captain Nemo, reposed in its ocean bed.

—Jules Verne
The Mysterious Island, 1874

The sub lay quietly on the surface. They had showered and changed into fresh clothes from their permanent lockers on board the *Philippe Tailliez*. Captain Jørriksen requested they meet in her private mess. Serengetti slid across the bench seat to his usual spot at Jørriksen's right elbow. He could feel the sub gently rise and fall with the slight swell. Then the swell gradually decreased. They must be submerging. Soon the movement of the sub ceased altogether and he felt the equanimity of the depths.

It had not been a simple matter to acquire a mothballed submarine and convince funding agencies to operate it exclusively for archaeological reconnaissance. Albert Falco, pilot of Cousteau's famous *soucoupe*, or diving saucer, had suggested it as early as 1960. Bass had used similar arguments to get the submersible *Asherah* built two years later. But after two brilliant field seasons in the Mediterranean, *Asherah* had been drydocked for lack of insurance.

Even when most of the great U.S. nuclear submarine fleet had been mothballed in the late 1990s, no one in the science bureaucracy listened when Boyington proposed a sub-bottom profile of the paleolithic migration routes between Java and Australia along the Wallace Line. Serengetti finally surveyed the Wallace Line, that strange ocean divide that separated the biology of Asia from that of Australia and New Guinea, in 2015. In what was supposed to be a shakedown cruise for the *Philippe Tailliez*, his team of maritime archaeologists and submariners from Hawai'i, funded by what was then called the Anthropological Institute in Tokyo, discovered sixteen paleolithic sites. Three sites pushed human migration to Australia back to 120,000 years BP. This was exciting news, soon overshadowed by the discovery of two additional prehistoric base camps, one located north of Melville Island, the other near Bali. These finds sundered the archaeological community, for they seemed to suggest that *Homo erectus* had built rafts and sailed them to Australia as early as 325,000 BP, and that the famous speciation cleft marked by the Wallace Line was the result of self-directed human activity.

Lastly, most surprising, and by far the most difficult to demonstrate to anyone's satisfaction: stone tools, weapons, and bone cut-marks at the two sites pointed toward a titanic maritime struggle between two distinct groups of human ancestors around 40,000 years ago. This first of all naval wars was apparently waged between *Homo erectus* and early modern humans, *Homo sapiens*. The war had continued for several generations, as our own direct ancestors pursued on outrigger canoes and destroyed the last remnants of *erectus* culture on earth, leading ultimately to the extinction of *erectus*, and to the global primacy of the larger-brained *sapiens*. These discoveries seemed to demonstrate once and for all the global maritime nature of human culture.

Serengetti was invited to Oslo to curate a new maritime anthropology exhibit at the Kon-Tiki Museum, and he convinced Kurosawa that the *Tailliez* should return with him, to begin a new survey of both historic and prehistoric exploration sites in the Arctic. Thus, in the spring of 2018, together with Larsen, Serengetti formed Transnational Polar Archaeological Consultants, or Transpac, and the *Tailliez* took up a large part of the *kai*, or wharf, beneath the Akershus fort on the Oslo waterfront. In this, their fourth season in the Arctic accompanied by the venerable icebreaker, *Polar Quest*, Larsen and Serengetti had surveyed great swaths of the north coasts of Svalbard, Novaya Zemlya, and Franz Josef Land. Until today they had surveyed in peace.

An hour later, as they studied charts of the area, the door to the mess opened and they were joined by Larsen and the same compact, dark-haired woman who had packed the anti-aircraft missile launcher on board the z-boat. Serengetti noticed the quick glance she shared with Larsen, and suddenly, without any real reason, he felt envious. He noticed that when she sat down, she held a tiny prism in her hands, turning it slowly, deliberately, to catch and refract the dim light of the mess. She herself seemed suffused with a kind of glowing light all her own.

"The advantage of this machine," he heard the Captain saying, "is that we know where APE are, but they don't know where we are. If they are going to start making trouble in the North that is no small consideration."

Serengetti, whose thoughts were shifting incongruously from the heat of Bali to the missile woman, snapped out of his reverie. "So when was the Treaty of Spitsbergen rewritten to allow us to bring anti-aircraft missiles into the archipelago?"

"It wasn't," said Jørriksen. "At least not officially. The demilitarization of the islands is still intact. We have a minor administrative exemption from the governor to carry the anti-aircraft weaponry, along with our anti-bear weaponry."

"You've got to be kidding!"

"Look," interrupted the dark-haired woman. "I wouldn't complain. If we hadn't arrived when we did you'd be a smudge on that cliffside right now."

"Dr. Serengetti," said Larsen formally. "I don't think you've met the *Tailliez'* new executive officer, who reported on board last week. *La meg presentere* Lieutenant Commander Karenna Johansson."

"*Det gleder meg å treffe Dem,*" Serengetti said in his most formal Norwegian, by way of apology. "I am very pleased to meet you." His formality, however, which was reflexive whenever he met someone new, was not well received. When he held out his hand to the commander, it was ignored.

"*Hyggelig,*" she said curtly, using the Norwegian word for 'delighted,' even as she seemed less than that. Serengetti let his hand drop. The woman was so clearly competent that she was just short of ferocious. That quality made her dark beauty even more attractive. Serengetti thought that she looked more like a Greek than a Swede. Worse, he thought gloomily, she almost certainly shared some secrets with Larsen, who, as usual, showed barely a trace of emotion. Maybe that was part of his attractiveness to women and men alike. When they couldn't faze him, most surrendered to him. It was an emotional equilibrium Serengetti knew to be forever beyond him. For the moment, it was enough to be alive. He was on board his own submarine, old as it was, after a scalding shower, comfortable in blue jeans and a gray sweat shirt over a black turtleneck clean and dry from his locker, with his favorite coffee mug between his fingers.

"Well," said Serengetti, after a long drink from his mug. "You just killed a very big bear with that missile. Do you think it was flying from the APE field in Franz Josef Land?"

"Probably," said Jørriksen. "We weren't tracking it; *Polar Quest* was. So was Kurosawa's office, which alerted me three hours ago.

We arrived in time to set the commander ashore near your last reported position. A shore party from *Quest* is cleaning your base camp now. We'll transfer you to her in one hour."

"I thought you were surveying much farther south."

"We were," said the Captain, without further explanation.

"Can't we get back to Wellman station on the *Tailliez*?" asked Serengetti. He was not particularly fond of extended cruises on board the *Quest*, a small, spoon-bottomed, constantly rolling icebreaker. On the *Tailliez*, cruising fifty meters below the surface, it was easy to forget, in all but the most horrific storms, that there was such a thing as an ocean surface in constant motion. Almost as he thought this, he felt the submarine moved by surface swells, and knew they were nearing their rendezvous point with the *Quest*.

"The dock at Kings Bay is under repair, so we're putting in at Tromsø for two weeks for refueling and repairs," said Jørriksen. "Then we're off on a survey of paleolithic sites in the Bering Strait. We'll be back in Oslo for the winter on October fifteenth. We may even have the sonar data ready for the world meetings in Stockholm in November."

"Stockholm in November," mumbled Larsen. "Terrible. Terrible. Can't the Swedes schedule these things at a better time? Or meet in Rome? Christ, I'd settle for Amsterdam."

Almost before they had time to finish their coffee, the gleaming red icebreaker *Polar Quest*, less than half the length of the *Tailliez*, came alongside the submarine. Serengetti and Larsen tossed their sea bags on board the z-boat, motored to the open hatch of the *Quest's* cargo bay, heaved their bags into the hold, and jumped across. After they had been welcomed on board, Serengetti turned around to wave good-by to his colleagues on the sub, only to find the *Philippe Tailliez* had already vanished.

* * *

The Wellman-Andrée-Riiser-Larsen Research Station was not grouped amongst the other international research stations on the southern shore of Kings Bay at the Arctic science village of Ny-

Ålesund. It had been built more than two kilometers further east, as if self-conscious of its status as the only social science research station in the high Arctic. It lay just beyond the memorial to those who had died in the *Italia* disaster, built along a shallow inlet near the bed of an old narrow gauge mining railroad. To the archaeologists and historians who for ten years lobbied with their respective national science bureaucracies to have it built, it was often called by its appropriately combative acronym: WARS. To Serengetti, for whom it was both field station and home away from Oslo, it was simply Wellman Station.

Wellman Station was also the last station to be built during the old national regimes, funded in large part by the former National Science Foundation in Washington, through its Office of Polar Programs, as well as by the Royal Academy of Sciences in Stockholm, and the Cultural Ministry in Oslo. Reflecting this multi-national funding base, it was named to commemorate the first aerial explorers of the Arctic: the Swede Salomon Andrée, a patent clerk from Stockholm who tried to reach the North Pole in a hydrogen balloon in 1897; the American journalist and polar explorer Walter Wellman, who led five polar expeditions from 1894 to 1909, and in 1907 flew the first airship in the Arctic; and the great Norwegian aviator Hjalmar Riiser-Larsen, who piloted the airship *Norge* over the North Pole in 1926. Unlike the Wegener Station, built by the Germans for upper atmosphere research, or the Dirigible *Italia* Station, built by the Italians and dedicated to glaciology, or the Gino Watkins Station, built by the British as a center for biodiversity research, the Wellman Station was designed by social scientists to study human adaptations to extreme environments.

Since its dedication in 2013, the station's research had centered on a comprehensive survey of archaeological sites related to human migration and exploration, especially sites now located under the sea, on the continental margins. To accomplish this mission, Wellman Station possessed one facility—a submarine dock, located in the shallow channel near the old rail bed—found at no other high Arctic research station. Two EU research submarines—first the *Hergesell* and later the *Prince Albert of Monaco*—had berthed in this channel. Now the *Philippe Tailliez* based its circum-arctic summer sonar surveys at Wellman Station, but the late summer of 2021 had been set aside for routine dock repairs at Kings Bay.

The *Polar Quest* tied up at the old cement dock leading to the main science village at Ny-Ålesund. Serengetti left his surveying gear and sea bag on board. During the rough cruise from the North East Land to Kings Bay, Larsen had consulted with Wellman Station and it had been decided that they had time for one final sonar survey before the arrival of winter in the middle of August. They had two days at the station, while the *Quest* reprovisioned, to decide where they would concentrate their efforts.

After picking up a stick to wave over his head for protection against the nesting terns, Serengetti left the dock and went into town. He walked down Main Street, past the preserved wooden barracks built for the coal miners a century earlier, converted to conference rooms and beds for visiting scientists. Behind the one-story wooden houses, an area had been circumscribed in twine by the field biologists, to study the trampling effect of reindeer hooves on the permafrost.

Serengetti angled to the central village square to pay his respects to the sad old bust of Captain Amundsen. He spoke in low tones to the Captain, as he always did when returning from the field. For good luck he patted Amundsen's shoulder, careful to avoid the caked bird shit that dribbled in frozen streams down from the Captain's fur hood onto his grand bulb of a nose. It was the fate of all famous explorers to be memorialized in bronze, only to be left out in the cold and shat upon in perpetuity.

After a dinner alone, he walked through a light mist to the mooring mast, still standing nearly a century after Amundsen and Nobile had left from it en route to the pole on board the *Norge* in 1926. The clear carbon fiber reinforcement that had stabilized the structure in 2012 was barely visible now, nearly ten years later. The plaque at the base of the mast had received its annual polishing, and the raised lettering stood out in bold relief:

AMUNDSEN-ELLSWORTH-NOBILE
TRANSPOLAR FLIGHT
1926
HONOURING A
GLORIOUS ACHIEVEMENT
OF HUMAN
ENDEAVOUR
TO ROALD AMUNDSEN
LINCOLN ELLSWORTH
UMBERTO NOBILE
AND THE CREW OF THE AIRSHIP
NORGE N1

The need to memorialize in the Arctic was an impulse nearly as strong, it seemed, as the need had been to mount the expedition in the first place. At the very bottom of the plaque were words that appeared to have been the target of an erasure attempt: *"THIS PLAQUE WAS PLACED HERE BY THE ITALIAN AIR FORCE.*" Serengetti continued on his way, thinking that he should write a deconstructing monograph on polar memorials. The *Norge* plaque would be his first case study.

He crossed the field between the mast and the old mining access road. Looking back at the new airstrip, the two new radars for upper atmosphere research began to fade from his view, and looked like crescent moons on the horizon. As he crossed the wooden bridge over the channel that separated Wellman Station in the east from the science village to the west, he noticed the tents of the Eurotouristas, the only artificial colors in the landscape. They were encamped close enough to the village for access to a hot meal, and far enough away to pretend to be enduring an expedition to the real Arctic.

Several years earlier, one unarmed group that called itself Friends of Arctic Animals had pitched their tents across the channel. When a polar bear ambled into their camp one morning, one of the fathers bravely placed himself before the others, saying he would deal with the situation. The bear promptly picked the man up in his jaws. He carried the brave human to a floe in the bay and ate him in front of his family. After that, the Friends confined their advocacy to a spiffy web site, but not before raising the funds to erect a small monument to the brave father on the western side of the channel. The ceremony had been protected by a well-armed security force from the mainland, flown in just for the occasion.

Serengetti continued to the middle of the bridge, where he entered the rickety WC and relieved himself into the stream below. On the eastern side of the channel, past ancient slag heaps from the mines, he glanced at a recumbent reindeer a few meters away, and crossed over to a footpath leading to Wellman station. Serengetti entered through the backdoor and took off his boots in the mud room, a necessity appended to every structure in the muddy Arctic. The building was quiet, and in his stocking feet he climbed the three flights of stairs to his office.

* * *

The three-story museum and research station was built of wood and glass, with an overturned-boat-shaped roof. The bulk of the building's interior was an open plan, with museum spaces and an artifact conservation laboratory occupying the expanse from floor to roof. The primary exhibit was a German He.111 recovered from Advent Bay in 2008 and restored to its deadly wartime aspect. Nearby were coal scuttles and sections of aerial tramways from the mines, and a quarter-scale replica of Andrée's balloon hangar, based on the model in the Andrée museum in Gränna, Sweden.

Serengetti's own space looked less like an office than a library that had been subject to carpet-bombings. Reference books, zip discs, reports, sheafs of unfinished manuscripts, all were piled in whatever free space had been available at the moment. Most of the remaining space was taken by a disorganized collection of science fiction in several languages, including a prized first edition of Jules Verne's *Vingt Mille Lieues Sous les Mers* found in a tiny Parisian bookshop during a brief tryst there years before. The only clean and organized space was the single long shelf that held his own books, three copies of all four of them. All but one had obscurantist scholarly titles, starting with his doctoral dissertation written at Hawai'i: *Prehistoric basalt mines of the South Pacific as surveyed with element-SAR from space station Inishi-1: Indicators of transitionary post-Lapita migratory routes.*

He looked out the window at the intensifying snow over Kings Bay. He was a long way from Oahu. Beyond the books were the only two artifacts in his office: a basalt axe blade from Samoa, and a Point Revenge arrowhead, a copy of the original taken from the grave of Thorvald Eiriksson in Labrador twenty years earlier. During his first canoe expedition to the sub-Arctic, he had stumbled into the camp of Helge Ingstad, a ninety-seven-year-old Norwegian explorer. With no other prospects, he'd stayed to become part of the small team that later that summer discovered Thorvald's grave, the first European to die a violent death in the New World.

Four HDTV screens were arrayed on the credenza behind his desk. One showed him the continuous Glöbnet feed from the Andrée launch site on Danskøya, another the thermal data from the abandoned mining village of Pyramiden. The third screen was his everyday laptop, mated with a secure server that connected with Tokyo. A voice message from Larsen suddenly appeared on this screen, telling him that the survey team would meet in the second floor conference room at 8:00 the next morning.

The fourth screen, his favorite, showed him a continuous view of the Oslo waterfront, from a Glöbnet webcam mounted on top of the Aker Brygge. It was still dark in Oslo. The clock on the east tower of Oslo's City Hall, the Rådhus, illuminated by the lights of the harbor, showed that it was almost three in the morning. Only four hours to sleep, Serengetti thought. In Oslo nothing stirred, not even the hundreds of boats at their moorings. How many times had he wandered those streets at this time of night, alone along the waterfront, in the only city in the world in which he had never once felt fear, not even after Breivik? His terrace apartment there was just outside the city, and he had a sudden longing to return to it, and hike the trails of the nearby forest of Nordmarka.

He wandered through the tiny kitchen to his small bunk. Heavy curtains blacked out the constant daylight of the high Arctic summer. It was ridiculously easy to lose track of time where daylight lasted from April to October. Even in Oslo, three thousand kilometers to the south, summer daylight would arrive before four in the morning and last nearly until midnight. Serengetti did not keep a regular schedule during the summers, preferring to free cycle, working until he was exhausted, then sleeping until he woke up. He opened the clean duvet on his bunk and collapsed within it. He was soon asleep.

* * *

The bunkside alarm forced Serengetti awake. It was seven-fifteen in the morning. Time to shower and make coffee before the staff meeting. Still he lingered in bed. Flipping on a light above his head, he picked out his copy of Paul Bowles's *The Sheltering Sky* from the recessed bookshelf on his left, and started to read. By the time he put the book down, an hour had passed. He arrived at the meeting thirty minutes late.

"Management and study of archaeological sites in extreme environments has occupied my entire professional life," Kurosawa was saying over the HDTV. "It was the research of this Directorate that developed the ability of the U.N. to manage extraterrestrial sites on many of the same principles."

The floor-to-ceiling HDTV in the light blue conference room gave the impression that Kurosawa, leading this meeting from his office in Tokyo, was floating in space, a god uttering his pontifications. Larsen was writing something in his field notebook. Serengetti cradled his coffee mug.

Serengetti had never met Kurosawa in person. On screen he appeared to be a slight but commanding man, with a strong, deeply-lined face and a bass voice. No matter what time of the day or night these conferences were scheduled, Kurosawa's voice always impressed him, always an octave lower than anyone else's.

"In order to gather continuous data on the condition of sites in extreme environments, we developed continuous surveillance of our global cultural treasures, obviating past reliance on time-limited human presence at such sites. Data gathered from such uninterrupted long-term surveillance have answered many of the questions archaeology only guessed at in the twentieth century. For this, we can all take justifiable pride."

Serengetti wondered why he hadn't slept in late; no one would have noticed his absence, especially with Larsen there to answer for him. But Directorate funding for the 2022 surveys was still under review. He didn't want to take anything for granted.

Serengetti opened his console and logged onto a site offering private islands for sale. Dreaming of owning an island in the middle of a northern lake was one sure way to pass the time during these interminable meetings. These meetings rarely transcended the obvious. Kurosawa was ticking off a list of priorities for research stations in the Pacific, all out of his area of expertise. There were a lot of projects, and many of them would be expensive.

"That is why," Kurosawa continued, "given the recent events in Svalbard, we have reevaluated many of our priorities."

The mention of his area pricked Serengetti's ears. Given the new APE activity this far north, continued funding for U.N. research was assured. They might even get an increase over last year's budget. As Serengetti leaned over to whisper this thought into Larsen's ear, he heard Kurosawa clear his throat and continue.

"I consider it advisable to curtail further surveys, and to concentrate on a new and vigorous analysis of the data we have at hand. I will therefore recommend to the Directorate board that we shift completely to remote monitoring of our polar and extraterrestrial sites by 2023. This will, of course, mean the discontinuation of funding for next year's surveys by the *Tailliez*, and leave just enough funding for two weeks of surveying this current season by the *Polar Quest*."

Serengetti looked up suddenly. He glanced at Larsen, who

remained impassive. The solid wooden floor underneath him felt as if it had suddenly turned to sand. Without funding from the Directorate the *Tailliez* would be mothballed, perhaps scrapped. His team would be disassembled and scattered. He felt his face flush with blood, his ears burn. His career was over.

* * *

"Well, where do we go from here?" Serengetti asked Larsen as they walked from Wellman Station toward the dining hall in the science village through a low pall of mist.

"Well, we have two more weeks to wring out of the *Quest* before the winter. And then, who knows? There's always the Pacific. You have a lot of colleagues there."

"The hell with the Pacific. I don't want to go back to the Pacific. I spent ten years sailing from the Bering Strait to Cape Adare. I had to spread the ashes of my stepchildren across the damned Pacific. No thanks. I want to stay in the north."

Larsen let it drop. Instead he asked, "How much leeway do we have with the *Quest*?"

"I doubt we can get very far around the islands at this time of year," Serengetti replied as they approached the bridge. "We might get as far as South Fjord. We've never tried to survey the Dutch whalers there. Why?"

"During the meeting I had an interesting e-post from a friend in Moscow. It seems she's found a diary in the old Soviet polar archives written by a young girl who lived at Pyramiden during and after the war."

"We've been monitoring Pyramiden for fifteen years now."

"I know," Larsen said. "But this diary mentions that the girl and two male friends hiked north across Dickson Land to Vestfjorden."

"Vestfjorden? That's got to be at least fifty kilometers away."

"Yes, across mountains several thousand-meters high. In her diary, she writes that they stole a camera and were pretending to be spies for Mother Russia. Apparently, she was an innocent. The boys, however, had other ideas."

Serengetti felt a sudden sickening in his stomach, for the second time that morning. "They always do," he said morosely.

"But that's not the interesting part, at least not for us. When they arrived at Mount Petermann they were looking down at the West Fjord from an almost vertical cliff 900 meters high."

"Good height to take an aerial photograph from," said Serengetti, thinking suddenly that he didn't care about a goddamned thing.

Larsen put his hand on Serengetti's shoulder and stopped him as they crossed the bridge. He uncovered his console and stylus.

"Apparently, you idiot, the young woman had the same idea. Here's the photograph."

Larsen placed the stylus on one corner of his console and a grainy black-and-white image appeared. To Serengetti, it looked like any one of hundreds of photographs of Arctic fjords he had seen. With one exception.

"They would have been the first people to visit that area since when?" he asked.

"I thought you might ask that, so I checked," said Larsen. "There was a Swedish mapping expedition led by Dunér and Nordenskiöld in 1865."

"1865," Serengetti said slowly, trying without much success to regain his interest. "1865. And there's no record of the Swedes wrecking a ship in the West Fjord in 1865?"

"None," said Larsen. "What's more, I don't think that's a ship. It looks more like the outline of a submerged submarine."

"If it is, it's got to be a U-boat from the war. It must have been supplying a weather station. Nobody's ever reported this?"

"The Russian girl was raped and killed by her two male companions on their way back from West Fjord. The Soviets impounded her diary and camera, then suppressed the whole incident. My e-post friend got a hold of the diary earlier this week, and since she knew I was working up here, let me know about the details, along with the photo."

Serengetti leaned onto the bridge railing. A small trickle of glacial run-off wended under the bridge. He followed with his eyes as it made its way to the bay. He didn't care about a damned German sub. Kurosawa's announcement had blasted him, although he felt a flicker for the young Russian girl, pretending to be a spy, off on her first great wilderness adventure, only to be raped and murdered. It brought back his ex-wife's opinion that men and women are different species altogether.

"I still don't see how this helps us," Serengetti said at last. "They were probably just lucky enough to catch a sub putting an automatic weather station ashore. It must be a station that has somehow been overlooked. The sub wouldn't have stayed there more than twenty-four hours for fear of being spotted and bombed by the British. And even if we find a weather station in the West Fjord, who cares? The Germans put seven meteorological stations ashore in Svalbard during the war. Who's going to care about one more?"

"Think, man. *Think*, for Christ's sake! The Germans never reported placing a weather station in Vestfjorden."

"They didn't report killing six million noncombatants either," said Serengetti, suddenly exhausted. He started to walk toward the dining hall. "But they still managed to get it done."

"There's more," said Larsen. "The photo wasn't taken during the war. The young woman was killed in 1954. That sub is dead in the water."

* * *

Serengetti stopped again.

"It can't be," he said. "Brendan McNally's history of German naval operations in the north makes no mention of a sub wrecked in Svalbard. Selinger's article on Arctic weather stations says nothing about a station anywhere in the entire Wijdefjorden. A U-boat could have wandered into the Wijdefjord after resupplying the station up to the northwest, in Liefdefjorden, but that station only operated from late '43 to the summer of '44."

He started walking again, and Larsen followed.

"Maybe it was a British or U.S. sub spying on the Soviets. Maybe a mobile listening post. Whatever it is," Serengetti said, "it's not the *Italia*, and that's what we were funded to find this summer. Goddamnit. We were so close. Now APE probably has the *Italia*, and I'm out of a job. Kurosawa isn't likely to care that we found the wreck of one of his old Axis partners."

"Tread lightly on that. He's pretty sensitive about the war."

"So am I," said Serengetti bitterly. "Since when are you and AK such good friends?"

"Since his deputy, Ellen Archer, sent me this photo this morning."

"What!?" Serengetti stopped once again and turned around. He couldn't help but notice the smirk on Larsen's face. "You son of a bitch. Do you have to screw every woman I introduce to you?"

It was said as much in jealousy as anger, and both knew it. Serengetti had often dreamed of that strangely intense Australian face, so perfectly blonde, and yet there was something just slightly off about it, something that he couldn't identify but which nevertheless made her all the more attractive.

"You're still not following me, you ass," said Larsen gently. "Before Ellen sent me this, she already knew it was important. Last night, on the pretext of giving us some preliminary data for our last survey of the summer, she had the Directorate image Vestfjorden from the Thor-15 satellite."

"But Kurosawa just told us that we had a couple of weeks left on the *Quest*, and then we were through. There's nothing else he wants surveyed."

"Well," said Larsen evenly, "we'll just have to restart your failed career, because Kurosawa was lying. Thor-15 got a clear shot at Vestfjorden last night. Whatever that girl saw in the fjord in 1954 is still there. AK thinks it's extremely important, but even he's not sure what it is. All that crap about cutting our funding was meant to throw APE off our tails."

"And you knew about this all along?"

"No," said Larsen. "Well, not all of it."

"Jesus Christ," said Serengetti. "Have you checked Tromsø?"

"Not yet," said Larsen. "But my guess is that when we do, the air photo archive from the 1930s will show the sub was there then too."

"Not good enough. It could still be German. They could have been making mischief there as early as 1935."

Serengetti looked up at the summit of Zeppelin Mountain, now visible through the clearing sky. He knew he should feel immense relief that all his hard work had not been in vain. But all he could think of was the Russian girl: she had saved his career by losing her life. After being raped. Then it suddenly struck him that she had also saved the *Philippe Tailliez* from the cutting torches, and a wash of enthusiasm began to rush through him.

"You know," Serengetti said, "the West Fjord will freeze over soon."

"I know," said Larsen, leading Serengetti toward the village. "That is why the *Quest* has been ready to leave since eight o'clock this morning. We're not eating in the hall today. We're going straight to the ship."

"I really wish you'd clue me in about these things in advance."

"I would," said Larsen, "but you need a sustained level of stress to perform at your peak. At least that's what AK thinks."

"AK better cut this crap," Serengetti said as they walked through the square. "Or else the next time I'm in the Pacific I'll start an excavation of the Bataan death march camps. Then we'll see how AK likes stress."

Serengetti detoured slightly to pat the shoulder of Captain Amundsen. He said a few quiet words to the bronze bust, but the rising wind distorted his words and Larsen heard only odd phonemes and sibilants.

* * *

Twelve hours later, *Polar Quest* chugged past Gråhuk, the Gray Hook, the northernmost point of the peninsula separating Woodfjorden from Wijdeforden, the Wide Fjord. Like many locations in the Arctic, it was a victim of the simple, if not simple-minded, nomenclature of the gazetteers. Larsen and Serengetti stood at the bow of the icebreaker as it cut through the crystalline Arctic water. As the gray Devonian shales and sandstones that gave the Hook its name slipped by, it was easy to imagine that the entire archipelago could have been similarly described. The Gray Islands. Here substance turned to shadow, and shadows vanished with the remote sun.

The mouth of the fjord was more than twenty kilometers wide. One hundred kilometers south it split into a large eastern branch, which some geographic genius had named East Fjord, Austfjorden; and a smaller, western, branch, the West Fjord, or Vestfjorden. The *Quest* was making for the Vestfjorden at ten knots.

"Fotherby visited the mouth of this fjord as early as 1614," said Serengetti, still trying to make sense of their mission. He almost had to shout to be heard over the engines and the water pushed aside by the *Quest*. "He named it after Sir Thomas Smith, a patron of Fotherby's and many other Elizabethan adventurers. The British continued to call it Sir Thomas Smith's Inlet, even after the Dutch had renamed it Wijde Bay. Pettersen mistranslated the Dutch and called it White Bay."

"Go to bed," Larsen said with sudden impatience. "Get some sleep. We still have more than a hundred kilometers before we reach Vestfjorden. Might as well be fresh when we get there."

"You coming?"

"No," Larsen said, gazing off at the gray hills of ancient rock. "I want to enjoy the view for awhile.."

Serengetti retreated through a hatch, climbed down the ladder, and reached his tiny cabin near the chain locker at the bow, where he lay awake thinking of his very first survey in these islands.

After several days of mist and gloom, Serengetti took a break from mapping the whaling station at Pentrap Point to lash small logs of driftwood to two larger logs and make a raft. On a calm morning he waited for high tide, then he climbed on board and poled his way across to Bird Island, a small moss-covered hill in the corner of the harbor.

On Bird Island he found a whaler's grave. He crossed himself before opening the two wooden boards covering the coffin lid. They parted easily, and he looked inside. Bones and a bit a fabric were all that remained. He crossed himself again—he hated skeletal work—and closed the coffin.

He hiked the short climb to the top of the hill and found an abandoned trapper's hut, decades old. Inside were the remains of a stove and an empty whisky bottle. He sat on the ground next to the stove in the tiny hut and wondered what sort of man spent a winter in such a place, with no sunlight, no daylight, a thousand kilometers from the North Pole and a light year from a warm human body.

Not a young man, he decided. Someone who had seen enough of the world to know that he could do without it—except for the transient merriment provided by the whisky. The solitary trappers fascinated him. He remembered the story of one man who had hidden himself from the Allies when they evacuated the entire human population of the archipelago during the war. Only when the last ship departed did he emerge from his hiding place in the adit of a mine, high on the side of mountain. He was the only human being within an area of more than 60,000 square kilometers. Completely alone, while the rest of the world was at war. He was a man Serengetti sometimes envied.

* * *

Ingvill Jørriksen envied no one's solitude; she had perfected her own. Alone in her stateroom, she enjoyed her time to herself and the new orders from Tokyo. These directed her do what she did best: patrol a deep wide fjord while hiding from and observing a single surface vessel. That the surface vessel was the *Polar Quest* troubled her, but she assumed it was part of some coordinated mission to be revealed in due course, and thought no more about it. Once the sub's course, depth, and speed were set, the Captain retired to her quarters and took up the sharp blade she used to shape the balsa wood submarine model she had just started.

She was trying to make this third model as perfectly as she could, not least because the wreck of this particular sub lay in her home harbor at Bergen. In 1931, the Australian explorer Sir Hubert Wilkins had attempted to drive a submarine called the *Nautilus* under the ice north of the Spitsbergen islands all the way to the North Pole. During leave time, Jørriksen had attempted to learn more about this proposed Austrian expedition, but other than a brief newspaper clipping, there was nothing.

A print-out of the particulars of Wilkins' *Nautilus* occupied the wall in front of Jørriksen's work table. The O-class submarine used by Wilkins, the *O-12*, had been built in 1916 by the Lake Torpedo Boat Company in Bridgeport, Connecticut. It was fifty-five meters long, had a normal compliment of twenty-nine submariners, and could reach speeds of eleven knots submerged, fourteen knots on the surface. Decommissioned, June 17, 1924. Placed in reserve, Philadelphia Navy Yard. Wilkins signed a lease for the use of the O-12 on February 1, 1931, at a cost of one dollar per year.

As she carved, the Captain would glance up occasionally, refreshing her memory of more facts:

—Modifications to *O-12* made at Mathis Shipyard in Camden, NJ.

—Boat stripped of military armament, fitted with the latest scientific research equipment.

—Changes made to the superstructure to allow operation beneath the ice.

—Snowstorm briefly halts expedition while still on Delaware River.

—Entering New York Harbor, Assistant Radio Engineer Willard I. Grimmer falls overboard and drowns.

—March 23, *O-12* at the Brooklyn Navy Yard. Christened *Nautilus* by Wilkins's wife, in presence of Jean Jules Verne, grandson of the author of *20,000 Leagues Under the Seas*.

—Test runs, various locations off New England coast, including a thirty meter dive off Block Island in Long Island Sound. Expedition two months behind schedule.

—June 13: starboard engine cracks a cylinder in mid-Atlantic. Port engine soon fails. S.O.S. call made. *Nautilus* rescued June 15 by U.S.S. *Wyoming*. Towed to Queenstown, Ireland, then Davenport, England for repairs.

—August 5: *Nautilus* leaves Bergen after picking up scientific officers and equipment.

—August 19: *Nautilus* encounters the ice.

—August 22: *Nautilus* tries to submerge but the diving planes have been carried away. Wilkins tries again on August 31, filling all four ballast tanks and diving beneath a meter of ice.

—September 8: *Nautilus* arrives at Longyearbyen in Svalbard

—Storms en route to England force Wilkins back to Bergen, where the *Nautilus* is towed out and sunk in the fjord on November 20, 1931.

As she made several long, sloping incisions into the balsa, Jørriksen thought of how she might have responded to the many crises faced by Wilkins. Perhaps she could have used the machine shops of the coal mining company in Longyearbyen to fashion new diving planes; she almost certainly would have sought new engines in Bergen before attempting the cruise north.

Jørriksen found herself in such deep concentration that it took two messages from the conn before she responded.

"Jørriksen."

"Kaptein," called out the conn. "*Polar Quest* has just turned into the West Fjord and dropped anchor."

"All stop," ordered Jørriksen immediately. "Hold our position here. Silence on board. I'm on my way."

Jørriksen put down the blade and the block of balsa. In her stocking feet, she silently made her way to the bridge.

* * *

The *Quest* had arrived in Vestfjorden a bit ahead of schedule. Larsen commenced the survey and decided to let Serengetti get some more sleep. Three techs were seated in front of two screens as Larsen paced the small survey room.

"I've picked up strong readings for some kind of steel alloy. The way it's reflecting, maybe a double steel hull." The sonar technician turned to see Larsen's reaction.

"Background noise?" asked Larsen.

"I don't think so. It matches the coordinates from our Thor-15 data."

"Size?"

"Pretty big; about the size of a World War II LST. Did Eisenhower and Monty make an amphib landing up here?"

"Dammit," Larsen exhaled. "Somebody better go tell Serengetti."

When Serengetti arrived ten minutes later, still dressed in the coveralls he had been wearing the night before, he glanced over at the depth sounder, then at the sonar. "Five fathoms," he said. "No wonder the Russian girl saw it from the cliff. It's nestled in a small cul-de-sac just inside Cape Petermann."

"We're moving the *Quest* over top of it right now," said Larsen. "We can't stay for very long. An American satellite comes over the pole in about four hours. The contact is on a submerged ledge, lying about due north-south."

"Have you put the ROV in the water?" asked Serengetti.

"We will as soon as we're on top of it. And I just got the air photo from Tromsø. Whatever this is, it was here in 1935."

"It doesn't appear to be broken up," said Serengetti. "I still think it's got to be German."

"It could be a wreck that drifted into this bay and snagged on an underwater obstruction," said one of the techs.

"Which would mean that it had been abandoned further up Wide Fjord."

"Exactly," said Larsen. Serengetti took his eyes off the depth meter long enough to look at Larsen's magnetometer read-out.

"ROV-1 is in the water," said the visual data tech, Sam Kahana, a recent School of Ocean and Earth Sciences and Technology (SOEST) grad from Hawai'i on his third research cruise with Transpac.

"It's definitely a sub," said the sonar tech. "And it's roughly seventy meters long."

"That's it," said Serengetti. "Definitely German. Prototype Type VII, maybe. It must have been on some kind of geographic expedition, one that was never recorded."

"A military expedition," said Larsen.

"Possibly," said Serengetti. "It would explain a lot. Type VII's were what? Sixty-three meters?"

"Sixty-seven meters," said Kahana. If chances came up to demonstrate his encyclopedic knowledge of undersea exploration history, the Hawai'ian seldom let them pass by. He liked nothing better than showing Serengetti he knew more about his specialization than did Serengetti himself.

"I think you want to take a look at this," Kahana said suddenly. The ROV had arrived at the site. As Serengetti and Larsen collected themselves behind his screen, the tech maneuvered the submerged probe over a silvery-green metallic surface.

"There!" Kahana called out.

Now the other two techs switched their screens to the visual display.

"That's a porthole," said one, transfixed.

"And it's lit from the inside," said Larsen.

"My God," said Serengetti. He bent down and spoke barely above a whisper to Kahana. "Have you ever seen anything like this?"

"No," said Kahana, almost grudgingly.

"Neither have I," Serengetti said.

"I only find 'em," said Kahana. "You have to analyze 'em."

Serengetti straightened and looked over at Larsen, who was watching the screen and stroking his beard. Larsen caught his glance.

"Don't look at me," said Larsen. "One thing is certain. Your U-boat hypothesis just went to hell."

The visual display continued to reveal the same smooth, silver-green metallic skin of the submarine, broken at regular intervals by what appeared to be portholes faintly lit from the inside.

"This is like no submarine I've ever seen," said Serengetti.

"Shit," said Kahana, as the ROV suddenly collided with what looked like the conning tower of the sub.

"Back off. Back off. Stop there," said Larsen, pointing to a spear-like protrusion from just forward of the conning tower. "What do you make of that?"

"Now, one of those I *have* seen," said Serengetti. "Dick Gould studied a mid-nineteenth-century wreck of a British naval vessel in

Bermuda that had an armored bow like that. H.M.S. *Vixen*. That's a battering ram."

"On a submarine? No sub in history has ever had a battering ram," said Larsen. "Besides, it looks more like a spear than a battering ram."

"Not strictly correct," said Kahana, suddenly on familiar ground. "The U.S. Revolutionary War submersible *Turtle* had an arm fixed to it—as did the Confederate *Hunley* during the American Civil War. They used them to attach explosives to enemy surface ships."

Serengetti alone stayed silent, staring at the screen. He took over Kahana's chair and began guiding the ROV himself. A small flange of metal caught his eye. It seemed almost a decoration of sorts, the work of a naval craftsman, a signature of a very different age.

As he watched, an impossible explanation began to take shape in his mind. He looked more closely. Something wasn't where it should have been—like Conan Doyle's strange case of the dog that didn't make a sound in the night.

As the ROV continued toward the bow of the wreck, he noticed one more such embellishment. It was an ornate escutcheon, incised in the hull. It was not large, and he had to maneuver the ROV close, until it nearly banged into the silver-green skin of the hull. He twisted a focus knob and twenty thousand pixels per centimeter rapidly resolved onto a small, elegant, capital letter "N."

"Jesus Christ," he said to himself.

Over the "N" was the arc of a phrase in Latin: *mobilis in mobile*.

After twenty years of sifting the world's past, of seeking surcease of sorrow in scientific rationality, he knew with a sharp certainty that the impossible was indeed possible. He lost control of the ROV, which swam off into the depths of the fjord. Kahana called to him to correct the ROV's course, but it was as if Serengetti had lost his hearing. He had to go outside the control van, onto the deck of the *Quest*. The bitterly cold clear air nearly burned his lungs. A few moments later, Larsen came out to find him.

"Are you okay?" Larsen asked.

"I'm fine," Serengetti said at last. He was looking up at the cliffs around the fjord, trying to puzzle out the height from which the Russian girl had taken her picture so long ago, but he couldn't focus his vision. Finally he looked at Larsen.

"I know what submarine that is," Serengetti said quietly. "Or maybe I should say, I know *whose* sub that is."

"And?" asked Larsen.

Serengetti didn't answer. Instead he looked up again, trying to focus on the high cliffs. He had been left alive. And now he knew why.

"The problem," he said, looking back at Larsen, feeling his breath taken from him along with his sight. "The problem. The problem is that no one is going to believe it."

"Why not?"

"For one thing, it's not the *Italia*. For another, it's not even supposed to exist…."

"What in hell is that supposed to mean?"

"It means," said Serengetti. "That we just discovered Captain Nemo's *Nautilus*."

"I think you have lost it," said Larsen. "But I have no explanation for it either, so we'll have to inspect her."

"My thought exactly," said Serengetti. "And we need to be ready to spend a few days here."

The wind seemed to be blowing more sprightly.

"We need to get the *Quest* out of Vestfjorden as fast as possible," said Serengetti, "and we've got to shut down the operation," said Serengetti. "If the American satellite catches us here, the game is up."

"The game?" Larsen repeated.

"Don't you see?" said Serengetti, loudly enough so that Kahana could also hear. "We've been set up. That can't be what it seems to be down there. The *Nautilus* exists only in a book. A novel. It can't be real. So whatever it down there was put there to trap us here. The photos, the sat data. It's all fake. They didn't get us on Foynøya, so they're trying to trap us here, in a fjord nobody's explored in a hundred and fifty years. By the time they find our bones, another hundred years will have gone by."

"But we have to go down there. We have to see what it is," said Larsen.

"Did you say *Nautilus*?" said Kahana. "Last I knew, the *Nautilus* was still moored at the sub museum in New London, Connecticut. Unless you're talking about that sub found by the NUMA team in 2003. The one they claimed was a 19th century *Nautilus*."

"Different one," said Larsen, trying to find a suitable lie. "Serengetti has a hypothesis. He thinks it might be the sub Wilkins tried to take to the pole in 1931. If it is, we need to survey it without the *Quest* here, so we don't give away the position to APE."

"Can we have just one more hour?" asked Kahana. "Wasn't Wilkins' *Nautilus* scrapped after that expedition?"

"Allegedly scrapped," said Larsen, trying to change the subject. "The American satellite is over the pole in three hours. *Quest* needs to be long gone by then."

"That's right," said Serengetti. "We can't survey the sub with the *Quest* here. Too easy to spot from space. Sam, tell the other techs we're shutting down because we've located the target and that's enough. The *Quest* leaves for Kings Bay in five minutes. Larsen and I will stay behind. We'll get dropped on shore from the z-boat with our lo-tanks and dry-suits. We'll take a look; either it's Wilkins's *Nautilus* or somebody's idea of a very big practical joke."

Kahana hurried back to the control van to begin reeling in the ROV. Larsen scanned the shoreline with his rangefinder, trying to scout a landing spot. When he did, he called the bridge and told them to get the z-boat in the water.

"Lo-tanks, huh?" Larsen said. "So you're not convinced."

"On the contrary," said Serengetti. "I know what it is. But if *Quest* goes back to Kings Bay and lets out the word, we're fucked. There would be no way to protect the greatest underwater archaeology site ever discovered."

Three: The Maelstrom

> *The Maelstrom! In the midst of our terrifying situation, could a more frightening word have reached our ears? Were we in those dangerous waters off the coast of Norway? Was the Nautilus being dragged down into this abyss…?*
>
> *—Jules Verne*
> *20,000 Leagues Under the Sea, 1870*
> *Anthony Bonner translation (1962)*

Three hours later, as *Polar Quest* steamed north at ten knots, an American intelligence satellite was coming hard over the North Pole at slightly more than 1,600 kilometers an hour. Since leaving Serengetti and Larsen behind in Vestfjorden, the icebreaker had covered about twenty-five kilometers. In six hours, it would clear Widjefjorden; ten hours after that, it would moor back at the pier at Kings Bay.

The satellite covered the 900 kilometers from the Pole to the mouth of Widjefjorden in less than thirty-four minutes. Less than three minutes after that, the synthetic aperture radar (SAR) on the American satellite picked up the movement of the *Quest* and sent an optical record to a tracking station in Iceland. From seven hundred and fifty kilometers up, continuing its polar orbit, the ultra-high resolution cameras of the satellite clicked out a rapid series of images of both branches of the south end of Widjefjorden. Then the satellite continued on its inexorable diurnal course toward the equator, Antarctica, and around the bottom of the world.

On the shoreline of Vestfjorden, Serengetti huddled with Larsen under his white sheet. Larsen studied his console. At precisely 0905, he counted to thirty, then threw the sheet aside.

"It's gone over," he said, glancing upwards as if he might see the satellite high overhead. "The American polar satellite has a daily orbit. It won't be back until tomorrow morning. It's likely that AK saw to it that they didn't get anything anyway. The fog is rolling in, too. That will screw up their visual data."

"AK doesn't even know we're here," said Serengetti.

"Yes he does. I told him before we left the *Quest*."

"I wish you'd tell me about these things once in a while," said Serengetti. "You're wrong, in any case."

"*Jo?*"

"I've seen that satellite's data before. The National Imagery Center will have already identified the *Quest*. My guess is that a note has already been sent to AK at UNESCO, asking him just what the hell is going on up here."

"In that case," said Larsen. "We don't have much time. Let's get on that wreck."

* * *

Near a boulder the size of a control van a few meters from the edge of the fjord, their gear bags were stacked to simulate a small pile of stones. As Larsen unpacked their drysuits, Serengetti walked along the shoreline.

When he did not find what he was looking for in one direction, he turned around and walked back, past their small camp, and along the shore toward the inner part of the fjord. Before he had gone two hundred meters, he found it. It was off to his left, up on the shingle, and covered by some small pieces of driftwood. Carefully he lifted the smooth gray lengths of wood to reveal a collection of similarly sized stones. They had been carefully placed to form the letter "N."

"So you were here," Serengetti said to no one. He lost himself in contemplation of this linguistic evidence of human presence on the grim shore of this remote fjord. *Where did you go from here? How many of your men survived? If you died, did your men bury you somewhere nearby, under a pile of Arctic rocks, chinked together to shield your body from the desecrations of wild animals?* His concentration was suddenly violated by a sensation unmistakable to fieldworkers in remote environments.

Eventually, nearly everyone who travels alone in the high Arctic experiences the chilling, atavistic sensation of being stalked by something much larger. For an archaeologist, lost in thought on a remote and uninhabited shore, contemplating wispy notions of human evolutionary patterning, the realization that one is being silently analyzed as a potential food source comes as a sharp blow. Serengetti knew that a polar bear was exactly behind him, perhaps less than five meters away. Worse, in the flush of the stunning excitement over the discovery of the wreck, he had inexcusably wandered down the shore without his sidearm.

Whoosh! A blast of bear breath scattered all bird life on the shore. Serengetti stood immobile, scanning the shore for a refuge. There was none. He felt the powerful presence move closer to him, and from the corner of his eye saw that it was an enormous white form. A large male. If he's more hungry than frightened, thought Serengetti, I will be dead in less than two minutes.

Paralyzed by dread, he heard another huff from the bear's mouth, this time more of a groan than an aggressive exhalation.

"Don't move," he heard Larsen say softly over his console, causing Serengetti to jump slightly. "It will take a moment for the drug to kick in." He allowed himself to turn slightly, and caught a glimpse of the bear as it collapsed with a thud on the stones of the shingle. One hundred meters away, Larsen emerged from behind a small boulder with his tranquilizer rifle over his broad shoulder. Serengetti felt his knees give way beneath him, and slowly he settled on the stones. The bear lay motionless less than three meters away. Larsen jogged up.

"Once again, I save your miserable life. You really need to stop these aimless walks."

Before Serengetti could respond, Larsen noticed the stones arranged on the shore. He left the bear and stepped over to them.

"N," he said to himself. "N. So, Professor Herr Serengetti, your hypothesis gets more possible, *yes*?"

"Yes," said Serengetti, looking first at the bear and then at Larsen standing over the arrangement of stones. "And thank you for not saying *'jo'*."

* * *

They stepped into their dry suits, black with a single yellow stripe running from the right shoulder to the right wrist, another from the right armpit to right ankle, and continued to inventory their gear. Larsen, four inches taller and seventy pounds heavier, waded into the fjord to attach their regulators to the scuba tanks tethered to shore with a short painter.

Serengetti, his back damaged by a score of field expeditions over two decades, sat propped against a rock on shore. He was still shaken. Looking at his console, he tapped away with his stylus, glancing around occasionally as he should have done while walking down the shoreline. He scanned several different pages, until he found what he was looking for.

"What are you doing?" asked Larsen, returning from arranging their tanks. "I mean, besides sitting down while I carry all the gear."

"Looking for the 1998 Butcher Oxford translation. Here it is."

A small flat voice on his console said: "Downloading a full-text e-Book of *Twenty Thousand Leagues Under the Seas*. Butcher translation." The voice then said that twenty credits had been deducted from Serengetti's Eurobank account; if he downloaded any additional books in the next ninety minutes, he'd receive a twenty percent discount on his order.

"Can you get *Swedish Wives at Play* for me?" asked Larsen.

"I could, but I don't think you'd get much detail on a ten centimeter console. Besides, I thought you didn't like Swedish women."

"In the right leather, they are all appropriately edible."

"Buy it yourself. Otherwise, I won't be able to charge this book off to my grant."

"I don't think AK will mind," said Larsen. "Did I hear her say *Seas*? I thought it was *Twenty Thousand Leagues Under the Sea*."

"Everybody does. At least everybody outside the French-speaking world does. But that's not Verne's title. *Sous les mers*, Verne wrote in the original French. *Under the seas*. Only Butcher got it right. And right now, since my French is weak, I need somebody I can trust."

"I read it in Norwegian when I was fifteen."

A moment later, a tone sounded on Serengetti's console, and he stood silently, scrolling quickly through the text. Larsen noticed that his friend's hands were shaking.

"You found something?"

"Maybe," said Serengetti. "They really might have ended up here. At the end of the novel Verne leaves open the possibility that the sub might have escaped, or at least he offers some possibilities for where it might go. *'From now on who could say into what part of the north Atlantic basin the* Nautilus *would take us? And always traveling at such speeds through these northern mists! Would we go to Spitsbergen or Novaya Zemlya...?'*"

"You work on the literary problems," said Larsen impatiently. "I will get us ready to dive."

Larsen strode back to their gear moored in the shallows and waited for his partner. Tiny castles of ice drifted slowly in the fjord. In another three weeks, this entire valley would be blanketed by two meters of snow, and an implacable skin of ice would layer much of the fjord. Only for these few short weeks of high summer did the ice and snow relax its grip on the valley and the fjord. It was, Larsen thought, an excellent place to hide for a century and a half.

By the time Serengetti had found what he was looking for, Larsen was lying on his back, floating on the surface of the fjord, as serene as if he were on a Caribbean holiday. Serengetti walked slowly into the water, checked the seals on Larsen's suit, helped lift the scuba tank onto his back, then attached his Mark VII helmet. Serengetti then sat himself down in the icy water of the fjord. He put on his own gear as Larsen reciprocated in checking the thin rubber seals. When they were both properly suited, Larsen tapped his console and opened the communication channel with Serengetti's Mark VII.

"Well, where to?" asked Larsen.

Serengetti, suddenly hot in his drysuit, looked up to the high cliff where the Russian girl had taken the photograph, but it was obscured in fog. It was the moment of a dive when all he ardently desired was to forget details and plunge downwards. Still he looked back down at his console. They had more than enough air for such a shallow dive. His rangefinder, depth gauge, and transponder receiver all checked out. The sonar readings from the sub were so strong that it was hard to know where to start. If this really was Verne's *Nautilus*, the only way to prove it was to gain entry.

"If we descend here and swim north-northwest, we'll hit the hull just forward of the engine room. If I'm right, an airlock chamber will be waiting for us. It will be open."

* * *

Transformed by the water to one of Jacques-Yves Cousteau's archangels, Serengetti descended along a sharp slope, hovering over seaweed-covered rock. He was entirely comfortable here, in an underwater landscape as familiar to him as the bays and harbors of his native Maine. Perhaps that is why he felt so comfortable with Larsen as well. They grew up on opposite sides of the same North Atlantic shoreline. A message in a bottle dropped into Serengetti's adopted home waters of Soames Sound might wend its way into the Oslo fjord three months later. Long before he had ever met a Norwegian or learned Old Norse, he had rigged a square sail on his expedition canoe and cleared Soames Sound on early summer mornings as if he were Eirik the Red himself. Now, through his body woolens and the rubber of his drysuit, he could feel the cold of Arctic fjord water.

They descended to a flat sand-covered shelf about fifteen meters down. Through the clear water, about twenty meters away, down a gradual slope, they saw a dark wall of greenish-silver metal. They could see where the hull tapered back to a point where an enormous screw hung off the shelf like the hand fan of a giant. Toward the bow, about ten meters forward of a massive diving plane, a great luminous metallic circle, like a green eye, stared back at them. It was an awesome sight, as terrifying to Serengetti as if he were seeing a one-hundred meter long squid, casting baleful glances at insignificant humans nearby. It took just a few moments to flipper the remaining distance to the hull.

They stopped less than a meter away, close enough to reach out their gloved hands and touch what their minds told them should not be there. Serengetti held himself back, and when Larsen lifted his arm to touch the skin of the hull, Serengetti shot out his own hand and pulled Larsen back.

"What did you do that for?"

"If this is what we think it is, and Nemo really did jolt a tribe of Papuans off the *Nautilus* hull with an electricity field, it might still be dangerous. Anybody who would casually electrocute a primitive tribe might have left the house alarm activated against unwelcome visitors."

Serengetti took from his gear bag a small current meter and gently touched the tip to the greenish metal. No current. But he felt instead a clear and unmistakable vibration. Emboldened, he put the current meter back in his gear bag and reached out his hand. He immediately felt a surge of vibration through his fingertips and pulled his hand back in surprise. Then he rested his palm against the hull; the vibration raised the hairs on the back of his neck, even in the wetsuit.

"It's okay," he said, but Larsen, watching, had already begun to caress the port flank of the submarine. Serengetti looked down at his console, zipping through the e-book version of Butcher's translation of *Twenty Thousand Leagues Under the Seas*. "Let's take a look at the entire hull first, before we think about boarding her. This wing above us must be the aft diving plane. If we go just forward of it, we should find the airlock."

They swam slowly aft along the narrowing hull, pausing to study the perfectly-formed rivets that held the great curved steel plates together. Serengetti took out his electronic calipers and discovered a pattern of a large rivet every sixty centimeters, with a smaller rivet every twenty centimeters in between. Approaching the screw, they moved over a slight separation, where the greenish-silver steel of the main hull gave way to the bronze screw shaft. Then they were swimming between two of the enormous bronze screw blades.

"Hold this," Serengetti said, placing the end of a measuring tape at the base of one of the screw blades. He filled his lungs with a bit more air and ascended to the edge of the blade, flipping the tape over the top of the blade. The screw hung off in space, as if the undersea machine had been merely parked temporarily on this sandy shelf. It seemed ready for its next command. Serengetti looked at the tape and entered some figures into his console.

"Three meters exactly."

They swam under the screw assemblage to see how the sub sat on the bottom and to measure the great steel rudder. The main bulk of the hull, supported by a keel that ran from the rudder to as far forward as they could see, rested in sand. The keel cut a neat path into the shelf, balancing the sub nearly perfectly upright. Serengetti repeated his measurements, this time asking Larsen to stay at the top of the rudder as he let a bit of air slip from his lungs, reduced his buoyancy, and descended to the spot where the rudder bit into the sand.

"Let me guess. Three meters exactly."

"Yes" said Serengetti. "Whoever built this machine had a metric imagination. The screw is six meters in diameter. Let's move toward the bow, over the top of the deck."

Serengetti placed his measuring tape at the very tip of the screw assemblage, then drove a meter sonar stick into the sandy bottom about five meters perpendicular to the aft of the sub. Returning to the screw, he followed Larsen back up to where the screw assemblage met the green-silver hull. They swam along a slightly upwards curve for approximately twenty-five meters, until they touched upon a platform about twenty meters long. The platform appeared to be an extended conning tower, encircled by a waist-high railing, with a pilothouse at the forward end and a raised hatch aft. Lifting themselves up and over the aft hatch, they came face to face with a porthole. It was lit from the inside, but all they could see inside was a dimly lit ladder leading downwards.

Larsen focused his camera and tried to shoot down into the hatch, but all he captured were some hazy images of a dark passageway. Serengetti had another location on his mind. He swam forward of the hatch, feeling his way along the platform until he arrived at a point midway between the aft hatch and the pilothouse. He searched along the floor of the platform until he found what he was looking for.

"Come here. Look at this."

"I don't see anything," said Larsen, hovering over the deck.

"Exactly," replied Serengetti. "Just like the dog in the night. This is a bolt-down pin for a boat. The submarine's metal launch or dinghy. If we're looking at what we think we're looking at, this is where, according to Jules Verne, the French marine biologist Pierre Aronnax, his assistant Conseil, and the Canadian harpooner Ned Land unbolted the metal dinghy and escaped into the maelstrom off the coast of Norway. The dinghy that should be here is gone. We're looking at what's left after the last cruise of the *Nautilus*."

"And how do you propose to prove that?" Larsen asked.

"I don't know. Not yet anyway. I want to go to the bow and finish measuring the hull before we try to get inside."

* * *

They continued forward to the pilothouse, a diamond-shaped steel turret about three meters tall. Small convex lenses, about the size of a man's head, protruded from the two aft-facing sides of the diamond. A thin layer of marine growth made it difficult to see anything through them. Maneuvering themselves along the deck, past the corners of the diamond, they reached the forward end of the pilothouse. There, two enormous convex lenses, glowing with a dullish light, stared back at them.

Serengetti wiped his gloved hand along the surface of the portside lens to clear away the obscuring algae. Larsen hovered near the edge of the starboard lens, having found a small break in the marine growth along its edge. The Norwegian slowly turned his entire body sideways, aligning his sight with the length of the break. He hovered motionless, feeling along the edge of the lens for a firm grip amongst the rivets that attached the lens to the pilothouse.

Serengetti paused to rest his arms, and in that moment felt a familiar sensation of being an intruder. As he sought to gain entry to the private world of another human being, he had once again to suppress his qualms against trespassing. He had been born in Italy but moved as pre-teen to a coastal town in Maine where one's fence marked the edge of the known universe. As a child, he would no more cross the stone wall of an ancient field and venture into another's property than he would accept rides from strangers. Boundaries were not just protection for your world, they protected privacy for the world that existed on the other side. As an archaeologist, he had learned to ignore such feelings—almost.

Unlike anthropologists working with living informants in living societies, archaeologists were trained to develop emotional detachment from their subjects. Dry bones, even bones showing obvious evidence of violent death, were ultimately abstractions. He recalled once being mesmerized by a researcher describing the fate of a small child, whose skull showed evidence of being smashed in with a rock while the child was still alive. The researcher's tone was flat, analytical, appropriately yet almost perversely clinical. Sickened, Serengetti had found himself mentally adrift, imagining himself intercepting the marauder's rock-filled hand in mid-swing and, like Superman, sending the attacker reeling backwards, over a cliff, tumbling down to a dusty death. But no Superman had appeared to save the child, who had suffered her fate, according to the researcher's radiocarbon dates, somewhere between 1150 and 1225 C.E. Serengetti had felt the blow almost physically, across nearly a millennia. He could never quite muster the detachment of the forensic teams. It was infinitely more appealing to immerse oneself in the details of human creation, to study all the varied craftsmanship of human technological ingenuity on shipwrecks and aircraft, on remote trapper's huts on now-deserted polar islands. It was a delicate balance: to keep the objectivity required for measurement while not abandoning the sensitivity essential to analysis. In 1956, after years of careful searching, the great Swedish underwater explorer Anders Franzén had located the wreck of the royal ship *Vasa*. The warship had capsized off Beckholmen in Stockholm Harbor almost as soon as she was launched in the summer of 1628, after a voyage of little more than a thousand meters. The royal ship had become the coffin of pauper sailors. As Serengetti thought of those doomed sailors, he cleared a space in the lens large enough to see into the *Nautilus*, and another thought came to him. What if this was more than history's most notorious submarine boat? What if they had just stumbled upon a tomb, a monstrous underwater tomb?

* * *

Peering into the pilothouse, Serengetti gained his first real glimpse into the interior of the machine. Given his absent-minded thoughts about the *Vasa*, he was momentarily stunned to see a pair of eyes staring back at him.

"Very funny," he said to Larsen, who had managed to clear away a large swath of algae from the starboard lens and mug Serengetti through it.

"It is a beautiful pilothouse," said Larsen, admiring the polished wood of the deck and wheel spokes, the curved yellow brass tubes and what looked like electricity relays. "It reminds me of the wheelhouse of my uncle's old wooden trawler. Only with more advanced technology."

"Stop making jokes."

"Who's joking? You've never been on my uncle's trawler. Spending money was like contracting a fatal disease for him. I think he still uses blocks made by his great grandfather. Knocked me on the head with one when I hauled a net too slowly as a boy."

To Serengetti, the impression was more of a museum exhibit, of gleaming yellow brass speakers and an engine order telegraph set against a flat blue background of steel. He could imagine the feel of the grains of the well-polished wooden spokes attached to the brass wheel. He suddenly wished that Captain Jørriksen was with him. A professional submariner could make sense of the tangle of instruments and levers far better than he. Even in his drysuit he began to feel cold, and he shivered as he continued to scroll through page after page of text on his console, searching for clues.

"It really is a beautiful piece of work," Larsen said again. "Almost like a model-maker's vision of what a nineteenth-century submarine should look like."

"There are so many contradictions in this text, it's hard to know where to start," said Serengetti, not listening to his partner. "If Nemo wanted to lead a rebellion, why did he abandon his best piece of war-fighting equipment here in this dead-end of a fjord?"

"Maybe he found a better piece of equipment?"

"Smart ass. But how would you make sense of this? Verne describes this machine as making its maiden voyage in 1867-68. Yet Nemo shows up again in *Mysterious Island*, as some disaffected Indian royalty named Prince Dakkar, dying of old age in 1869, and talking about how the voyage of the *Nautilus* took place sixteen years in the past. And he was there on the island with the *Nautilus*. But here it is, right here, at the bottom of Vestfjorden."

"What if we assume that all that was merely a distraction? Everybody who reads Verne knows he throws around a lot of nonsense. What if he did it deliberately?"

"Red herrings," said Serengetti.

"Herrings?"

"An old murder-mystery term for a calculated misdirection, an off-putting clue," said Serengetti. "Who knows. Maybe he went mad." Madness was one of many areas of human experience where archaeology provided little purchase. "He could have been unbalanced by seeing all this. Frightened of its power or potential as a weapon. Maybe he wanted to write about it but was afraid to reveal too much?"

"Maybe Nemo was pursuing him?"

"I don't think Nemo pursued Verne, but it's an interesting possibility. It's more likely that whoever Nemo was, he wanted some kind of witness-scribe to record his movements, to testify to his power. But even those movements are crazy. He was all over the earth, and I don't think it was simply to take Verne on a global underwater pleasure cruise."

"If Nemo drove Verne mad, we'll never find out what happened—unless he left a logbook behind."

"If Verne himself was Aronnax, or some kind of composite of Aronnax and Conseil—and this machine was capable of the kinds of maneuvers he wrote about—then he would have been correct in believing that every navy in the world would have been out to either sink her or steal her. The real question is, how was it concealed all these years?"

"You know the answer to that as well as anybody," said Larsen, pushing himself over to the port side lens. "The Arctic is the best place on earth to hide something. This fjord is covered with ice for nearly ten months out of every twelve. As best we can tell, other than that Russian girl, and whoever left this boat here, it wasn't visited, much less explored, after 1865. Whoever piloted this boat here either knew this fjord well, or made a very lucky guess at a hiding place."

"Or a very desperate guess."

"No one ever ventures very far into the Widjefjorden, much less all the way here to Vestfjorden. Until the two degree greenhouse temperature elevation of 2009, it was almost continually blocked by ice. We'd have to check the meteorological data in Tromsø, but I would almost be willing to guess that the summer of 1868 was colder than normal, and that this fjord was covered by ice maybe for the whole summer."

"You think they were pursued here?"

"No. If they'd been pursued, someone down the line would have let the word slip, and this boat would have been found. My guess is that they came to rest here because it was the one fjord on earth where no surface vessel could follow them. Once Nemo entered Widjefjorden, he effectively locked the door behind him."

* * *

Swimming steadily forward, they felt their way along the forward surface of the sub, descending toward the bow by pulling themselves by hand along a thick raised steel ridge, a sort of vertebral column. Along one side of the ridge Serengetti reached out to stop Larsen as he slid downward. He pointed out the small escutcheon he had seen from the control van on the *Quest*.

"*Mobilis in mobile*," said Larsen. "My Latin is not what it used to be."

"It means 'Mobile in a mobile element,'" replied Serengetti, running his fingers over the letters incised into the steel. "Or changing in a changing medium."

"That could have a lot of meanings."

"And probably did. As they approached the South Pole, Ned Land called Nemo a 'superman.' It would have taken a kind of superman to conceive of a machine like this."

"No," said Larsen. "An ordinary man could conceive of it. But to build it? Now *that* would have taken a superman. But as you know, supermen have been out of favor in my country for some time."

"But imagine what it would be like to control a vessel like this!"

"Control. That is the right word. Supermen eventually lose all control."

"One man alone, in control of his own destiny. Absolute freedom of operation."

"Don't get too carried away. It took us six years to defeat the last horde of supermen, in 1945," said Larsen. "My great-grandfather's home was burned to the ground by retreating supermen."

Twenty meters from the pilothouse the raised ridge along which they pulled themselves flared out in four directions to form the enormous spike of the bowsprit. Serengetti swam to the forward end of the mighty construction, feeling along its surfaces for the imperfections, the scrapes and evidence of collisions and disasters. He ran his gloved fingers along a particularly deep gash in the metal.

What produced you? he wondered. The keel of the *Moravian*? The bilge of the *Scotia*? The warship that attacked the *Nautilus* as she returned from Nemo's pilgrimage to the wreck of the *Vengeur*?

"Here is your battering ram," said Larsen.

"Yes," said Serengetti, running his hand along the instrument of death. "Incredible, isn't it? Like the work of an avenging angel. Wait here for a moment."

Serengetti descended to the sandy shelf beneath the wreck and placed a sonar stick under the very tip of the spike. Once activated, it searched for the other stick he had emplaced at the stern.

"Seventy meters," he said.

"And what does your Butcher have to say about that?"

"It matches exactly. It can only be the *Nautilus*, and yet how? It's like scuba-diving through a dream."

"Or a nightmare," said Larsen, as he too ran his hands along the knife-edged weapon that formed the wreck's bow. "The nightmare of a machine built to puncture steamers and antique wooden warships."

"Both of us have seen hundreds of sites where stuff survived where it wasn't recorded to have survived. I wrote a paper on that very topic, but the editor at *Deconstructing the Arctic* rejected it, of course. Let's move aft and see if we can't find the door to this thing."

Both men descended to the surface of the shelf and began swimming slowly along the underside of the submarine. They had not gone very far when Larsen looked up to see the bottom of a large circular metal plate. He motioned for Serengetti to stop and straightened himself. Pulling himself upwards, he let his body angle alongside the circular plate, with his flippers balancing on a short ridge of metal. Reaching his hands upwards, he found only smooth metal above him. The surface vibrated gently under his touch. Serengetti launched himself upwards and, using Larsen's extended body as a measuring stick, saw that the metal disc was more than twice his size.

"The porthole to the study?"

"It matches the description in the book," said Serengetti, using keywords to rapidly search the text. "Glass panels held in place by copper frames. That's what should be on the other side. But I doubt if it is really glass. Or copper, for that matter."

"One thing is for certain. With this layer of growth on this plate, without removing it somehow, this porthole will never open again."

"Probably exactly as intended."

Larsen allowed himself to fall away from the disc, and returned slowly to the sandy shelf, where he continued moving aft along the port side of the vessel. Serengetti lingered for a moment at the edges of the disc, then followed. They felt their way along the hull until Larsen again slowed, pointing upwards to a massive diving plane. The plane was oriented to the horizontal, and as such fit neatly into a massive shield at its forward edge, like a second cutting tool to match the spear at the bow.

"Well, now we know what happened to the diving planes when he sawed through all those surface ships," said Larsen. He tried hanging from the leading edge of the diving plane, tried to pull the plane downward. He only succeeded in pulling himself upwards.

"So there are at least three weapons on this boat," Serengetti said. "The bow spear and the port and starboard diving plane sheaths."

Larsen let go his grip on the diving plane and settled back to the floor of the fjord. As he continued aft, he was brought up short by something underneath the boat. It appeared to be a curved metal plate that had somehow peeled away from the rest of the sub, as if swung on a hinge, or as if it had been opened by a giant can opener. Larsen felt a sudden and huge disappointment. While swimming along the topside of the boat, looking into the pilothouse, he had dared to hope that it might really be intact, that what they had seen in the dry pilothouse was more than a solitary pocket of trapped air. Now he saw that the sub was almost certainly a wreck. He tapped Serengetti, who was still studying the diving plane. Serengetti's eyes widened, and Larsen knew that he shared his disappointment.

Instead, Serengetti squeezed Larsen's shoulder as hard as was possible through his bulky drysuit.

"Incredible," he said. "They really did abandon ship."

"More likely they all drowned, and we'll find them all inside," said Larsen.

"I don't think so."

* * *

Almost involuntarily, Serengetti pushed himself away, using Larsen's shoulder as a springboard. Rapidly he kicked toward the small plate of metal attached by a hinge to the sub. He could feel his blood suddenly pulsing in his head, and he was no longer so cold. He swam carefully underneath the sub, fully aware of what would happen if the vessel rolled. He felt drawn to the hinged plate.

He covered the twenty or so meters in just a few seconds, and even that seemed too long. When finally he grasped the edge of the hinge and swung himself headfirst underneath the plate, he became confused, not knowing which direction was up. He had entered a small compartment, entirely dark. Searching his belt, he groped for his handheld Q-light. He switched it on just as Larsen joined him.

"So I guess this is not a rent in the hull?"

"No," said Serengetti. "It's an airlock. And if I'm right, this is where the crew of the sub exited and entered the sub while it was submerged. They would seal themselves in this chamber, flood it with water at the same pressure as the water outside, then open the hatch and float out. We should be able to reverse the process if we can fill it with air from our lo-tanks and close it. If the inner hatch can be opened, we might get on board."

Larsen felt huge elation with the knowledge that the sub had not been wrecked and filled with seawater. An inveterate rationalist, he did not expect to find more than a stripped-down submarine beyond the airlock chamber. But so far everything he had seen was so strangely familiar that he was beginning to believe that the impossible might really be true.

Without having to say a word, they simultaneously turned the outflow valves of their Mark VIIs, and the loud hiss of escaping air filled the chamber. Serengetti pointed his Q-light along the top of the compartment until he found the hinge he was looking for. It attached to the movable airlock hatch about fifty centimeters below the overhead of the chamber.

"We won't be able to put more air into this chamber than the space above that point," he said, pointing to the hinge.

As the bubbles of air pushed their way upwards and sloshed against the ceiling, a small air pocket began to form. As they vented more air from their tanks, the pocket grew larger, until they could almost entirely lift their helmets clear of the water. Larsen then shut off his valve, flipped himself upside down, and searched the bottom of the airlock hatch for a way to close it. On the forward wall, his hands found a hatch lever. He tried to maneuver it to either side, but it was frozen.

"What do you think if I try to force it?"

"It can't hurt," said Serengetti, closing his own valve. "And it might tell us something about how the rest of the vessel operates. Is there any directional indicator?"

"My guess is that it would have to be pushed outward when the chamber is empty, and pulled inward when someone returned to the sub."

Larsen removed his flippers and let them drift downwards, out of the chamber, and onto the floor of the fjord below. He anchored his feet against the far wall of the chamber, and pushed outward until his shoulders came to rest on the wall nearest the lever. Then he reached down and, using his upper body strength, tried to pull the lever up. When nothing moved after ten seconds, he loosened his grip.

"Try pushing it forward now," said Serengetti. "Then pull it back again"

Larsen did so, and heard an uncomfortable sound which he first thought was his biceps tearing.

"It's working" said Serengetti. "The hinge is moving!"

"You'd think that with all this technology they'd have found a way to keep the door from sticking."

"I don't think it was designed to be used once every century and a half."

Then Serengetti started to feel a cold sweat as the airlock door began to close on them, shutting out the fjord below. He had a momentary view of Larsen's flippers, laying askew on the sand beneath, then all he could see was a solitary spot illuminated by his Q-light, with a tiny sliver of light coming from the opening of the compartment. He immediately reopened the vent on his tank, and the level of water in the chamber began to drop again.

"Stop there," he told Larsen. "If we close it all the way, we may never get out."

As Larsen relaxed his grip, he loosened the vent valve on his tank, and the water level in the chamber dropped even further. When it had dropped to the level of the open chamber door, he shut off the valve and began to remove his Mark VII. Serengetti watched as Larsen removed his helmet, closed his eyes, and took a short breath. He exhaled and then gathered in a larger breath, letting it out slowly.

"Well, Herr Professor, should we knock and introduce ourselves?"

* * *

As he removed his own Mark VII, Serengetti studied the circular hatch latch. A century and a half had covered it with a fine, whisker-like layer of Arctic algal growth, while the near-freezing polar seawater had retarded almost all traces of disintegration in the metal. It seemed as strong as the moment it was forged. It probably was. He looked at Larsen.

"Okay, I'll try," said the Norwegian.

Larsen clasped both sides of the circular latch and braced his feet along the small ledge that served as a platform for divers exiting and entering the hull. But when he tried to turn the wheel, it spun madly around, and Larsen almost lost his grip as he slipped from the platform.

"It would have been nice if they could have put up a sign telling which bearings they had greased and which they hadn't."

"They didn't need any signs," said Serengetti. "They probably didn't plan to return."

Larsen opened the hatch and stepped across the threshold into the inner airlock chamber. Serengetti followed, and as soon as his boots touched the metal floor of the inner chamber he felt the slight vibration of a generator through his soles.

The inner chamber lacked the high humidity they had felt when they filled the outside chamber with air from the lo-tanks. The interior of the small gray chamber was lit by dim green lights. Did they seem to pulse slightly?

The inner chamber was itself sealed by another hatch, and when Larsen opened this, they stepped through into a short narrow passageway. Two more hatches, left and right, led … where? Serengetti tried to orient himself to the plan of the submarine according to the novel.

"Before we go much further, we need to find some plans," Serengetti whispered. "This boat is going to offer up a thousand questions. The answers may be found in some archive. Or, they may never be found. According to Verne, Nemo consigned his logbook to the sea in a sealed box, like a message in a bottle. It could have been lost or destroyed. Or washed up on a shore where no one could read it or grasp its significance. Used it to start cooking fires, like the Gnostic Gospels were in Egypt. It could have circulated around the polar basin for decades, only to wash ashore on an uninhabited island where the box rusted and the pages were slowly dissolved by salt water and air."

Larsen thought of a German light bulb he'd once seen one the shore of Jensen Lake. A fragile glass bulb, carried to an Arctic shore a hundred kilometers from the nearest lamp, it had survived forces that could kill a man in seconds. Yet it had survived. And so might Nemo's logbook. He knew it existed; he felt it in his guts. It would be found somewhere, and they had to be the first searchers and the finders, just as they had been the first to find the sub itself. Finders and keepers.

Serengetti was lost in the image of Nemo's metal box, sealed, perhaps with Bulgarian beeswax, rusting on some anonymous stretch of shingle, as the weak polar sun faded the spidery script of his increasingly mad writings, a treasure dried and desiccated.

"Try that one," Serengetti asked, pointing to the nearest

left hatch. When Larsen spun the wheel, the hatch responded by swinging loosely back at him.

"The sub must be canted slightly to starboard."

Serengetti peered through the hatch into what looked like a small uniform locker compartment. Large hooks hung down from poles mounted along one wall, while a waist-high railing had been bolted to the other wall. A single uniform remained, and it appeared remarkably similar to the dry-suits worn by Serengetti and Larsen. The helmet attached to the neck of the suit seemed oddly similar to their Mark VIIs. Only the small compressed air tank hanging from the back of the suit made the difference obvious.

"Unbelievable," said Serengetti. "Come here and look at this. A Denayrouze and Rouquayrol diving suit. State-of-the-art, 1864. Sold to navies all around the world. With this, someone from the sub could have stayed underwater for an hour at this depth. That may explain why they grounded the sub on this shallow shelf. It would have given them plenty of time to get their men and gear to the surface, through a hole in the ice. What a beauty! I've dreamed of seeing one of these ever since the first time I read the novel. Cousteau probably got the idea for the aqua-lung from this very same invention."

"And there's only one here."

"Which means one of two things. Either they carried a spare, or someone was left behind," said Serengetti, hoping for the former.

"Well," said Larsen, turning to look Serengetti full in the face. "How does it feel to have discovered the most famous submarine of all time?"

And for the first time, Serengetti felt the magnitude of his burden. Extraordinary claims require extraordinary evidence, said a famous twentieth century scientist named Carl Sagan. The artifact was only the beginning. He was starting to shiver. Standing inside the largest artifact he'd ever explored, he felt that, like all artifacts, it was trying to speak to him, but what was it saying?

"We have the evidence," Serengetti said finally. "But will anyone believe us?"

* * *

If ever there was a time for precision, it was now.

"We need to conduct a preliminary survey of the whole boat before we leave," said Serengetti, reaching into his gear bag to extract what looked like several plastic bags.

"Your scene-of-crime kit?"

"Yes. Take off your boots and gloves, and put these on. From here on, we can't leave a fingerprint. This boat must be preserved intact, no alterations."

Larsen removed his rubber gloves and boots and placed them alongside Serengetti's discarded gear. He stepped into the plastic sock coverings Serengetti handed him, then forced his large hands into a pair of thin rubber gloves.

"You might think about carrying gloves big enough for a normal person's hands next time."

"Your hands are anything but normal."

Larsen shrugged. "So you are convinced that this really is the *Nautilus*?"

"I am convinced," said Serengetti, "that Verne's novel was not entirely science fiction. Its relationship to the actual undersea voyage that took place in 1867 and 1868 is uncertain. That's what we need to find out—and it may be impossible. We know this much: we have found a submarine that looks like the one described by Verne, a sub that has been on the bottom since at least 1935 and probably a lot longer than that. Beyond that, who knows? Who built it, when, for what purpose—those are all unanswered questions. And, of course, if Verne actually took a ride in this thing, how close was that voyage to the one he describes?"

Serengetti slipped rubber gloves over his own slender fingers and pressed his palm against the wall of the passageway. He felt the same gentle vibration through his hand that he still felt through his feet. *Where is the engine room?*

"What sort of generator stays on-line for a century and a half?" he asked.

"I don't know. A good one. But whatever it is, it's right on top of us. What does your Butcher say?"

Serengetti scrolled through the translation, nothing from Verne's narrative seemed to make any sense: mining coal on the sea floor; using coal to heat seawater to extract sodium; combining sodium with mercury to create a battery called a Bunsen pile. All to generate the electricity that gave the sub both its motive power and the light for its salon and quarters, mess and galley, the light for Nemo's famous study.

"It's all gibberish," said Serengetti. "None of it makes any sense. Coal, sodium, mercury, Bunsen piles."

"Sounds like a lot of bullshit to me. Nineteenth-century guano."

"It may be exactly that. But why?"

"I have an idea."

"Yes?"

"Suppose Verne or Aronnax-Verne actually went on this vessel, took a voyage, saw the technology, and understood exactly none of it?"

"Given the fact that, at the moment, you and I are baffled, it's not such an indictment of Verne. We have the whole twentieth century behind us, and he had it all in front of him. He could have been trying to describe things no one had ever seen before."

"And doing a terrible job of it?"

Yes. Verne-Aronnax would have been as unprepared as a novice anthropologist on a first visit to an unknown tribe—like Malinowski his first day amongst the Trobriand Islanders, a strange white man in a strange dark land. Absolutely nothing would have been familiar: not the language, not the technology, not the undersea environment. Nothing. Serengetti partially understood these problems; they were not insurmountable. He himself had more than once been that strange white man. Verne was trying to write without access to a technological dictionary. What frustration—which led to invention.

Or consider the problem from the point of view of the sub's captain. An unwanted visitor, even a highly educated one, could never understand more than a fraction of his technology. It was far beyond the most fantastical dreams of an untrained observer like

Verne—a former law student! Nemo would even have had trouble explaining his applications to an engineer from the Sorbonne or the École Polytechnic Francaise—even if he had wanted to share his discoveries and knowledge. With the voluble but scientifically illiterate Verne, Nemo must have spoken as an adult speaks to a small child. He would speak like Dr. Seuss.

"Let's open this hatch," said Serengetti, "and see if we can't find out where this hum is coming from."

* * *

As Serengetti and Larsen stepped through the next hatch, a brighter green light flashed below them. The sudden light took both of them by surprise.

"Jesus Christ!" cried Serengetti. But when nothing else happened, he let out a long breath.

"Never seen track lighting on a timer before?" Larsen chided, but he had also taken a step back when the long strips of green light came on.

"Does this sub have *motion sensors* to conserve power when no one is using a particular room or chamber?"

"Since we are standing in an impossibility, that is a funny question."

"It would explain how its energy is conserved, but not where the energy came from in the first place, nor how they managed to keep the sub on "sleep mode" for nearly 150 years," said Serengetti.

"Do you smell that?"

"It's like sulphur, only not as strong. Aronnax mentions smelling something burning as soon as he entered the engine room, and Nemo claims it is a by-product of the sodium being extracted from seawater."

"Here," said Larsen, pointing to a ladder leading to a kind of abbreviated catwalk above them. "I think your answer is up there."

As they went up, the green light at their feet was replaced by an almost flowing blue light overhead. Larsen ascended the short ladder to a narrow catwalk and motioned for Serengetti to follow. He saw that the blue light came, not from a lamp, but a large clear tube. The pulsing blue material inside the tube seemed to flow like glacial ice around a mountain. It wavered and danced, until finally the particles in the blue stream coalesced around a sheet of perforated metal at the aft end of the clear tube. A blue flame, at once frozen and yet still burning.

Several smaller, box-like metallic constructions were arrayed forward of the tube, toward the bow of the submarine. Both clear and metal tubes linked the metallic constructions with the large clear tube that held the flowing stream. The whole assembly took up ten meters along the narrow catwalk and appeared to be a single functioning unit. The one exception was a larger box that appeared to be a turbine, attached through a complex series of gears directly to the screw shaft.

"Just off the top of my head," said Larsen, "I would say that coal and salt water are not big factors here."

"My god," said Serengetti, transfixed. He stared into the flowing blue stream of particles, which seemed to perform a dance for him. "I've seen something very similar to this before."

"*Yes?*"

Serengetti nodded. "It looks like the jet of gases produced by the plasma spectrometry machines at the archaeology lab in Hawai'i. We used super-heated argon gas to create spectra of metals we'd excavated at different sites, to analyze their composition. But the color of the stream was a much lighter blue than this."

Serengetti moved his fingertips toward the clear tube in which the dark blue particle stream danced. It was cold to the touch and seemed to be many centimeters thick. If this was the engine of the *Nautilus*, it was indeed—as Pierre Aronnax had speculated—a revolutionary one, capable of generating a continuous stream of electric power for more than a century.

"The stream is being drawn into that metal grid there. It looks like some kind of gathering valve for the…the…whatever this plasma stuff is. Maybe just keeping the lights on for 149 years, in some kind of standby mode, has kept the motor running," said Serengetti. "It's certainly enough to keep the deck plates of this sub humming, which might be why we didn't see much algae on the hull. Who knows? Maybe one of the Arctic biologists at Tromsø can tell us. I didn't measure any current from the hull, but then I'm not sure this is even electrical."

"So you think we should announce this right away?"

"Absolutely not. We don't even know what we're looking at yet. What would we say, anyway? We've found Nemo's *Nautilus*? Well, at least that's what we think it is. But maybe not. We could call this a fusion engine; maybe we'll get some grant agency to build us a brand new building in downtown Oslo: The Larsen Centre for Fictional Submarine Studies. Maybe they'll even let us out of the asylum long enough to attend the dedication."

"Okay. Okay. Enough. I get the point."

"As a wise old archaeologist once told me: two artifacts is a pattern; one artifact is only noise. Until we find something to corroborate this one artifact, all we have is a lot of noise."

"Archaeologists have an amazing ability to make the exciting boring," said Larsen. "Give me Errol Flynn any day."

"If this was *The Sea Hawk*, no doubt we'd already be fighting off a boarding party of cutthroat Spanish privateers. Or rather, you'd be fighting them off, while I guarded the wine cask."

"Alan Hale you're not."

"Yes, well, I doubt Alan Hale could lay down a sonic underwater grid," said Serengetti, looking closely at the forward edge of the clear tube. "This tube has to be fed from some kind of reservoir, but I can't seem to find any kind of feeder valve."

"Maybe there is none."

"Hmm, hmm," Serengetti consulted the text. "Right here, Nemo tells Aronnax: '*my* electricity is not the commonly used sort, and that is all that I wish to say on the matter.' He also openly doubts whether anyone will ever be able to figure out exactly how it works. "

* * *

"There's your intake valve," said Larsen, pointing out a small aperture near the bottom of the tube. As Serengetti watched, a thin jet stream of blue particles seemed to enter and coalesce with the material already circulating within the tube.

"But what *is* this stuff? Whatever it is, my console is not reading anything beyond this tube. All my sensors seem to be blocked."

Larsen, opting for direct observation, had already climbed underneath the tube and was examining it from the bottom up. He now noticed two different intakes, the one at the bottom of the tube, and another running from the starboard side of the tube. The starboard intake was also clear, but the flowing blue particles moved in a smaller, more focused stream. He followed the clear starboard tube as it led first to an apparent valve, and then to what appeared to be some kind of reservoir hidden behind the bulkhead.

"Wherever this smaller tube leads to, my guess is that there is where you will find the source of these particles."

"Since this bulkhead separates the engine room from the double hull, the reservoir for this material may be built into the double hull."

As Serengetti continued to study the large clear tube, Larsen walked back to the other areas of the engine room. As he approached one of the metallic boxes, he sensed a barely perceptible increase in the vibrations beneath his feet. Placing his hands on the box, he confirmed his suspicions.

"Here is the generator," he said. "It might be slightly out of alignment, which is causing this hull vibration. It looks like some kind of turbine."

"And it's connected to what looks like a generator, one that is feeding current into the clear tube," said Serengetti, moving over to join Larsen. Larsen had left the turbine to study a large plate fixed to the hull of the submarine and connected to the turbine.

"Maybe it's not the turbine that's out of line, after all. The connections between the turbine and this place seem to be causing all the vibration."

"The turbine is generating both heat and vibrations, along with whatever power it is feeding into the electrical generator. My guess is that whoever designed this engine sought to get rid of the turbine's heat through that plate attached to the hull, which acts like a radiator."

"It is possible," said Larsen. "But what is powering the turbine? This silent little woman back here?"

Larsen stepped into the farthest forward section of the engine room, where a small cylinder the size of a lo-tank stood bolted to the floor. The small tank radiated neither heat nor vibration. Both Serengetti and Larsen inspected the tank, finding only one connection leading to or from it, and that connection led directly to the turbine.

"Here is your power source," said Larsen. "But I'll be damned if I know what it is. I used to break down the turbine on my uncle's trawler, but a turbine connected to a clear tube connected to this tank thing? I've never seen anything like it. What speeds does Nemo claim for this engine?"

"I haven't found that yet," said Serengetti, tapping his console with a stylus. "Here: he says that this engine can turn the screw at 120 revolutions per second, which must be a misprint or misstatement. He has to mean 120 revolutions per *minute*."

"Who knows? Without seeing this thing in action, who can say what it might be capable of?"

"If that six meter screw can turn at 120 revolutions a second, it would push this machine at, what? About ten thousand kilometers an hour?"

"Something like that. But it all sounds like nonsense."

"McHargue might know. Nemo may have refused to communicate in any meaningful way with Aronnax. His whole tone is patronizing."

"That would put him in the same category as most university professors. Who is McHargue?"

"Wilson McHargue is an old friend from Hawai'i, and one of the best underwater engineers in the world."

"Maybe we need to consider another possibility," said Larsen. "I am just wondering. Whoever built this…"

"Yes?"

"Even though he stopped here in 1868, maybe he was not from the nineteenth century at all."

* * *

"Okay, Captain Blood. I'm open to suggestions."

"I wish I had some," said Larsen, "Except to say that at the very least we need someone who knows something about plasma physics and submarine engines to look at this one."

"I know. I've been thinking about that. At some point we need to go see Wilson McHargue. If he's in Bermuda, we can be there and back in a day. He's the only person I know who might have a clue about bizarre undersea propulsion systems. He was the main tech at SOEST when I was there. Kahana was one of his acolytes. But we are a long way from having enough data to show him."

"Couldn't we e-post him from here? Do you have a clear channel?"

"No. And I'm afraid it might be intercepted or corrupted en route. But I can send him some data on a secure line from Wellman Station."

"Well, given the fact that by the time we get back to Kings Bay it will probably be snowing, a hol in Bermuda sounds very nice."

"A week in Bermuda is a holiday; a few hours at Wilson's would amount to cruel and unusual punishment, especially if he's cooking. I roomed with him for a semester in Hawai'i; I know. Anyway, we need to look at the rest of this boat before we can do anything."

"You better get some images for him if you want to go to there," said Larsen, stepping off the catwalk and climbing back down to the main deck.

Serengetti fished out a small underwater digital camera from his gear bag and attached it to his console with a short length of fiber optic cable. He pressed one of the three buttons on the camera, and swept the lens around the engine room. As he did so, high resolution images appeared simultaneously on his console, where they were stored as insets to his site plan. After sweeping the room, he selected individual components of the engine and gathered five second clips of each. When Serengetti was satisfied that he had enough to show McHargue, he stowed the camera and followed Larsen back to the catwalk.

"Can you open that forward hatch?"

"Yes," said Larsen, emerging from underneath the catwalk with his usual blank expression. "Captain Blood can do anything."

Four: Time and Chance

"It is not new continents that the earth needs, but new men!"

—Jules Verne
Twenty Thousand Leagues Under the Seas, 1870
William Butcher translation (1998)

The Offices of the Anthropological Directorate of UNESCO were located on the seventh floor of the Wang Wing of the Gates Complex in Tokyo's Technology Park. Ellen Archer's office opened onto a narrow private balcony, from which she had an oblique view of the harbor. Several times she had asked to be moved to an office at the other end of the building, where the view was straight down to the water. Each time she had been denied. She liked to work with the balcony door open, to feel the cool breezes that sometimes surged up in the mornings and evenings. It was a preference that put her at odds with the building's strict environmental controls—which bothered her not a whit. Generally, she took what she needed. Late at night, after a typical fifteen-hour day, she would shower, change into her favorite silk robe, and take tea on her balcony. Sometimes a vodka.

Kurosawa had just left her office. Larsen's brief communication from Vestfjorden had staggered them both. There were a thousand things to do, much of it outside her ken. She was responsible, however, for the multifarious details of on-the-ground operations. Her people planned, permitted, and equipped dozens of field teams.

If an operational detail was overlooked—a rare occurrence—the chain of command, and the blame, led to her desk.

As AK's deputy, Archer oversaw a key sector of the directorate, one that had dozens of field teams working in precarious situations all around the globe. More than a few of these expeditions had rewritten human history and prehistory. She had organized and led sixteen different field expeditions, going back to her undergraduate days. At the age of twenty-one, entrusted by her major professor at Canberra with the leadership of an oral history project along the Sepik River, she had quickly learned the fate of the unprepared. One of her charges, a young student from California, wandered into the rain forest without his console and was never seen again. Two other researchers, both of whom had failed to take their prescribed anti-malarial prophylactics, contracted the disease and had to be sent home. One of them died. Archer herself spent six months after the expedition recovering from the prostrating infection of a stomach parasite. She learned from her mistake.

In the intervening ten years, there were few swaths of territory in the Southwest Pacific she had not personally explored. Her report on the cultural genocide carried out in the transnational copper mines in the Sepik had generated international outrage in '16. Her experiences had led her to develop the concept of "cultural quarantines," which sanctioned placing regions of anthropological or archaeological importance off limits to corporate devastation, in return for permanent interest-free credits. AK appointed her as a special consultant in 2018 when the Solo River area in Java became the first area placed under a cultural quarantine. It had been only a few short steps—too short for the liking of some—from that slot to the office adjacent to AK's in Tokyo. She was already being talked about as the most likely successor to AK, if and when the old man ever retired to his favorite mini-golf course.

The two had developed a symbiotic work relationship that served both well. Other than for golf, AK did not like leaving his office even to walk in the park's Japanese garden; she, on the other hand, began to climb the walls if confined to her office for more than a few days. As a result, he entrusted her with his most important foreign assignments.

Instinctively, without knowing much about the Arctic, she had felt that the diary and the photo that she had found in Moscow were important. Larsen had proven it. This discovery was the result of her own hard work, her years of training, of deciphering and then feeding the right materials to her teams in the field. She trusted her instincts (after checking them against AK's) in evaluating and protecting such finds. She knew how fragile discoveries were. It would not be long before APE or EM or the Americans found out about Larsen's discovery, but by then AK would be certain the artifact was under protection. Otherwise, it would be obliterated by political and military forces far beyond the containment of their directorate.

Thank the gods that Larsen was there at the outset. Bjorn Larsen. At the sudden thought of him, she closed her eyes and enjoyed a brief shiver of memory. Enormous hands on her small breasts. Kinky-silly office lovemaking in three languages. Her laughter when he had asked if she was more multi-orgasmic than multi-lingual, or vice-versa. His heart-breaking smile when she invited him to find out.

"Cruel woman," he had said, trying to make a joke. "Or is that redundant?"

Instantly she had answered, "Intelligent man," returning his electrifying glance. "Or is that an oxymoron?"

A slight tone from her primary desk screen abruptly called her back from the balcony. Her trip bag, always packed and ready for international jet travel, was still on the couch in her office, where she had left it after returning from Moscow. Even before he had received confirmation of the find in West Fjord, AK had asked her to be prepared to travel to Europe on a moment's notice. She, *she* would be in the heart of the affair.

* * *

Serengetti and Larsen found an empty passageway before them.

As Larsen opened the hatch, they stepped from the engine room through a watertight bulkhead. Their movement into the passageway activated a set of green track lights. Closed hatches indicated four compartments on the port side, two on starboard. These hatches were sealed with what appeared to be watertight rubber gaskets. Small circular ports were fitted into each.

"These must be the crew spaces." Ever since they had come aboard the submarine, Serengetti had been measuring each compartment with the sonar sensor on his console. By placing it against the first corner of any space they entered, precise sonar measurements for that space were automatically entered into the SiteMaster v.6.3.1 software in his console. The technique had proven rapid and efficient on large sites, like the whaling station at Grytviken and the airship hangars of Lakehurst. His console told him that this narrow passageway was ten meters long.

Through the ports in the first two hatches they saw cabins with several levels of sleeping racks. Serengetti counted twelve sleeping racks in each, arranged in two stacks of three bunks each on either side.

"Blue and white striped duvet," said Larsen. Some of his favorite moments were spent between just such coverings, which were like comforters sown into their own rough cotton sheets.

"Apparently, nobody has come up with better bedding in a century and a half."

Each bunk was neatly arranged, with small bookshelves against the wall of each. Six narrow standing lockers separated each stack of three bunks. At the far end of each cabin was a wash basin beneath a mirror, and what looked like the speaker of an intercom system. They tried to turn the handles of the hatches, but they would not move.

"Clean, efficient, literate," said Serengetti, straining his neck to see further into the cabins. "Just what you'd expect of a crew under Nemo's command. I would love to find out what they were reading. I can't quite make out any of the spine titles, but one looks like *Madam Bovary*."

"Clean and efficient perhaps, but literate is not what I expect of sailors," said Larsen, pointing to a small, elegant bottle partially filled with a golden liquid. "But women are another matter. If I didn't know better, I'd say that was a bottle of perfume. I count twenty-four bunks." Like a sailor, he was trying to figure the vessel's compliment. He asked Serengetti to look up how many men Aronnax might have noticed on board the sub.

"Verne dodges how many men it took to run the sub. He never saw the control room. He only says that the hatch was closed, so Aronnax could never get any idea how many men were required."

"Maybe Nemo's crew was composed all of women? Maybe Aronnax couldn't bring himself to acknowledge that such a machine could be run by a crew of women? Just think, Nemo and twenty-four women. No wonder he left the world behind and took to the ocean."

"Somehow I don't see Ned Land being overcome by a couple of women. Besides, Arronax did see several different male crew members."

"Ned Land was a sailor," said Larsen, very much enjoying this line of thought. "They wouldn't have had to force him to do anything."

"No," said Serengetti, sighing. "As a nineteenth-century officer and a nineteenth-century novelist, Nemo and Verne would have felt themselves far superior to the submariners running this vessel. If they respected privacy, it was because they were uninterested in those they considered socially inferior to themselves. Don't forget the Papuans. Nemo electrocuted the Papuans from the surface of this submarine."

Forward of the portside crew area was a similarly sized mess. Through the window in the hatch, Serengetti noted eight neat place settings. Three watches of eight submariners apiece, he thought. Beyond the mess a smaller room housed a galley. Beyond that, a common head.

When none of the hatches leading into these areas opened easily, they moved to the hatch at the far end of the passageway. The handle spun easily; it opened onto a large mess area.

"Care for dinner?" asked Larsen, as he stepped through the bulkhead and into the dining room of the *Nautilus*.

* * *

This was the largest space they had seen on the vessel.

Serengetti's sonar read-out told him that this dining area was exactly five meters in length. The measurement corresponded to Aronnax's description of the room as being fifteen feet long.

"You might have eaten in here with the officers," said Serengetti. "I'm an old chief. I would have been back in the passageway mess with the NCOs."

This was officer country. Six place settings. Were selected officers invited to dine with Nemo, much as Captain Ahab dined with Starbuck, Stubb, Flask, and the three harpooners on the *Pequod*? Or was the vessel run on social rules of its own, apart from western naval traditions? Each chair was backed in a kind of red leather, embossed with a gold "N." Like the plain wooden table, each was bolted to the deck.

Unlike the crew's mess, the dining room service had been stowed away in tall oak dressers at either end of the table. Through the windows of the dressers Serengetti saw that each white porcelain plate was imprinted with a similar "N." Over the top of each "N" was the inscribed semi-circle of "*Mobilis in mobile*".

"He liked European seaports," said Larsen, admiring a rather small painting of a dock-works. If he were to guess, he would say it had been rendered in Holland by a Dutch master. As a boy, Larsen had messed around a dozen yards just like this one. The mud banks near such yards were playgrounds of abandoned dinghies and rotting wharf pilings. How many times had his own skiff been transformed into a Viking raider as he leapt ashore from its grounded bow to drive a boat hook through an Irishman's skull? By his early teens he had permanently stowed his boat hook/spear in order to reorganize his skiff into a floating research platform. With his uncle he had built an observation platform on the bow, where an old microscope and a series of notebooks had served as his private mobile marine laboratory. On endless summer afternoons, he had recreated himself as a new Fridtjof Nansen. As he looked at the details of the painting, he thought that he would have much in common with the mariner who had hung such a painting in the dining area.

Serengetti noticed how brightly the indirect overhead lighting glowed off the porcelain. The dishes were stacked in neat piles, and the drawers of the dresser were similarly arrayed with tableware. It could be the neatness of a female crew, he thought, but then any chief steward worth his rating would run exactly the same kind of impeccable galley. He found himself wondering whether they should go back into the passageway and force open the door to the galley. Serengetti felt an intense sugar crash coming on. He pulled a small glucose pill from his bag and placed it under his tongue. Was there really such a thing as jam made from holothurians that would tempt any Malay? Did Nemo in fact offer Aronnax a jam made from anemone?

"You might not want to tell Jørriksen about this," said Larsen. "She might demand a private mess as big as this one on the *Tailliez*."

The mention of anyone learning of this discovery, along with the glucose jolt, snapped Serengetti back to his mission.

"Jørriksen is about the only person I'd trust on board this submarine. Imagine the catastrophe if *Nautilus* fell into APE hands. Forget APE. How about EM? They would take up right where Nemo left off, only they would trawl the oceans looking to sink whaling vessels. I think we need to let AK know we've found a sub, but as far as the exact nature of it—what would we say? We need to get more answers before AK and his bureaucrats get to make a decision."

Larsen said casually, "You are probably right."

"Look at this," said Serengetti, studying the hatch on the opposite side of the dining area. "It looks like some kind of double hatch. This is the first one of these we've seen."

As Serengetti scrolled through his Butcher, Larsen began to turn the latch, first on the inner and then the outer hatch. As the second hatch came free, Larsen pushed it back to reveal the most wondrous room he had ever seen.

* * *

They stepped, tentatively, into Nemo's library.

Much of what they had seen up to this point was a technological puzzle. Not this. It was a collection of much the world's history, natural history and art history, in many of the world's languages—everything the world had known about itself in 1865. Serengetti remembered reading this scene in the novel and imagining himself in this very place. Twelve thousand volumes still rested on Brazilian rosewood shelves.

To assemble such a library required an unusual individual. Such an individual, Serengetti thought, would have to possess not only extreme wealth, but the obsessive intellect of a master collector. After letting their eyes wander around the shelves from a distance, they moved into the heart of the great library.

"Kanksje," said Larsen, feeling his own equilibrium tottering. "Now we are not inside a book."

They were struck dumb. Serengetti admired the bindings of the great publishing houses of the world. These were all placed on barred shelving designed to keep them stowed in the event of any rolling or pitching. A dark blue leather sofa curled the length of the chamber, broken only by a brief passage to the hatches, at their feet, a deep green rug embroidered with an enormous "N." There was greatness here—and great ego as well.

"Look at these volumes: Cuvier, Agassiz, Maury, all first editions, in English, French, Spanish, Swedish, Russian … and what is that?" asked Serengetti.

"I don't know," replied Larsen. "Maybe Chinese. I don't know any Oriental languages."

"These ridiculously odd catalogues of world treasures," said Serengetti, scrolling rapidly through the Butcher. "Massive collections of books by anti-Darwinists. Lists of books and paintings. Nemo's lust for enumeration always struck me as strange, even for the nineteenth century."

"Perhaps he had Asperger's Syndrome," said Larsen. "Look at this."

It was a copy of Bertrand's *Les Fondateurs de l'Astronomie Moderne, Copernic, Tycho Brahé, Képler, Galilée, Newton,* published by Hetzel in 1865. It rested on a circular mahogany reading table. This was the book that had allowed Aronnax to date Nemo's last contact with land. Serengetti leaned down to look at it closely, without touching it.

"Incredible," Larsen said simply. "And more than extravagant. It's as if Nemo assembled an Alexandria library."

"Here," said Serengetti, reading from his console. "'These are my last memories of life on earth, which is dead … as far as I am concerned.' Why would someone who had turned his back to the land want to carry all of its books with him?"

"Maybe we should look in here," said Larsen, opening a large ornate hatch leading from the forward side of the library. He looked into the room, and then back at Serengetti. "Captain Nemo awaits us in his private study."

* * *

The same green light seen throughout the passageways, like that diffused by the green glass shade of a banker's lamp, glowed as they entered the salon. Both men shivered, as much from the cold air as from the icy imponderables of what they still couldn't believe fully, even as they moved within it.

"Nemo's study," Serengetti breathed. After 150 years, the engine still hummed through the deck plates beneath their feet, as if the motive power of this mightiest of all vessels were purring in its sleep. He had a sudden remembrance of snuggling under his stepfather's arm, watching Kirk Douglas as Ned Land plotting his escape from this very submarine.

"*Ja*," said Larsen slowly, rolling his Norwegian into a low long trough, even as Serengetti sighed. Serengetti half-expected to hear James Mason admonishing a transgression into his private study. Or maybe welcoming them with that inscrutable combination of hospitality and hostility he displayed to Pierre Aronnax.

"You're the expert on the history of Arctic exploration," was all Serengetti could think to say. "How did this boat get here?"

"Arctic history, yes. Arctic literature, no. But you said, on the beach, that in the climax of the novel the *Nautilus* is racing toward Spitsbergen," replied Larsen, using the name commonly used for Svalbard both in Verne's time and throughout much of the twentieth century. Spitsbergen, the place of sharp mountains, was how most of the world referred to these islands, despite Norwegian insistence on Svalbard, the Old Norse name.

"Yes," said Serengetti, scrolling through the Butcher. "Here. After the encounter with the British warship in the English Channel, Nemo went crazy. He headed for the Norwegian coast and raced north along it. Aronnax wonders if they are headed for Spitsbergen. Then Aronnax, Conseil, and Ned Land escaped, just as the sub was sucked under by the maelstrom. And the maelstrom is off the northern coast of Norway, more than a thousand kilometers south of this fjord."

Larsen had been born on the same island near Oslo where four of the world's greatest maritime museums housed the *Fram*, the *Gjøa*, the *Kon-Tiki*, and the Oseberg viking ship. He had grown up with a powerful and detailed comprehension of ships and the sea, and had traversed most of the watery globe in nuclear ships, scows, catamarans, and submarines. But this vessel was completely outside his experience, an unaccountable wonder, rooted in a fiction. He had never been terribly religious. To him, bread and wine were, in the end, bread and wine. Yet here he was aboard a machine his intellect told him could not exist; his rationality was totally confounded.

"I am Norwegian," said Larsen. "I have heard of this maelstrom a time or three."

"So how did the *Nautilus* wind up a thousand kilometers north, under the ice of a remote fjord in Svalbard?"

"Perhaps we are thinking too hard," Larsen said. He was trying to account for all the various meanings of maelstrom. The Norwegian language is really two languages—Book Norwegian and New Norwegian, both official, both regularly revised for each generation. A language for scholars. There were also regional dialects, for populations had been separated by high ranges and deep fjords for a thousand years. One built a road in Norway only at tremendous cost. You could not travel very far without an almost impassable mountain stopping you, or a fjord barring your way. If a road extended for more than a few kilometers, it did so over a bridge or through a tunnel.

"It would be the first time we were accused of that," said Serengetti flatly.

"I mean, what if the story happened exactly as told? If Aronnax, or Verne—whoever—was thrown free of the sub in the maelstrom, he would never have known that it survived. Then, if Nemo's voyage ended here in Vestfjorden, if, say, his engine was not functioning properly, he and the crew would have been forced to abandon ship and hike across the islands. Whether they were outlaws or outcasts, the result would have been the same. There were no settlements of consequence on the islands in 1865, and few visiting ships to hitch a ride on. They would have been completely cut off from the rest of the world. Their frozen corpses are probably buried up there, or eaten by the bears."

"If you're right," said Serengetti, "they may have been trying to escape the navies attempting to pursue them, only to succeed too well."

* * *

"Look at these paintings. My God. Raphael. Da Vinci. The monk by Velazquez; the nymph by Correggio… are these originals?"

Serengetti switched from scrolling through the text to tapping on the keyboard with his stylus. He typed in RAPHAEL.

"Okay. Okay. Yes. Here it is," he said in a rising voice. " 'For it was a veritable museum…all the treasures of nature and art…a wash basin made out of a giant clam.' "

"There's no giant clam wash basin in this room," said Larsen slowly walking around the library.

"A Vernean embellishment perhaps," Serengetti said, suddenly looking up from his console. "But the rest of it, it's all here. There's Nemo's pipe organ, the one he played Scottish melodies on."

"Do you think it's okay to sit down?" Larsen asked.

"In my considered archaeological opinion, no," replied Serengetti. "Who knows what fiber evidence we might disturb?"

So Larsen continued to stand. But he stroked his reddish-blond beard and was soon lost in thought.

"He was a collector," said Larsen, looking at a village fair scene by Rubens.

"Yes and no," said Serengetti. "He was a rebel. But he wasn't a destroyer. At least, not on this submarine. It's a cultural Noah's ark. He wanted to carry an entire civilization away with him. Or restart civilization somehow, on his own terms."

"You are getting way beyond me," said Larsen, as he watched the light fade from Serengetti's eyes. Serengetti seemed to be sharing a remote and sad understanding with Verne's Captain No One. Then he noticed that Serengetti was looking at a small bronze plaque attached just above the door to the salon. The plaque was inscribed: "*Nemo me impune lacessit.*" Larsen spoke it aloud, and his voice seemed to bring Serengetti back from a faraway place.

"But my Latin is old," he said.

"It really is his submarine," said Serengetti. "*Nemo me impune lacessit*. No one attacks me with impunity."

"'These are my last memories of life on earth, which is dead,'" Serengetti said quietly. "Does that mean he had found somewhere else that, for him, was alive? Or at least not dead; a place he needed a submarine to reach, a permanent undersea haven."

"The Pacific?"

"Maybe," said Serengetti. "He turns up again in Verne's *The Mysterious Island*. But if his machine is here, I don't think he went back to the Pacific. 'The earth is dead,' he said. So where was he going?"

"*Jeg vet ikke*," said Larsen, whose own eyes began to brighten. "I don't know. But something else just came to me."

"*Hva*?" Serengetti asked in Norwegian.

"In Norwegian," he said at last, "the word '*maelstrom*' has two meanings: it can be the "deadly whirlpool" off the Lofoten Islands: which is clearly what Verne wanted his readers to believe. But it has another meaning: 'dangerous current.'"

"A dangerous current that carried the *Nautilus* to Svalbard and Vestfjorden."

Serengetti absorbed this as he looked around at the hundreds of nineteenth-century expedition reports, beautiful things, and at the natural history specimens, the art.

"If Verne's use of the word had a double meaning, maybe it was his way of coding what had actually happened. Maybe he wanted people to think the sub had been destroyed off the coast of Norway, in the North Sea."

"Maybe a triple meaning," replied Larsen, listening to and feeling the hum of the engine. "Who knows what he was thinking of?"

"Dangerous current."

"*Yes.*"

"The engine."

"That would be my guess."

"If that's true, he was referring not only how the sub got here, but to the motive power of the submarine itself, this apparently unlimited engine still operating after 150 years. Or his warning to the world about its potential misuse. Who knows, maybe the novel was a part of Nemo's ultimate plan...whatever that was."

"Verne did not write books for children," said Larsen, raising himself up until his six-foot-four frame stretched nearly halfway to the overhead of the study. "He was clearly an intellectual. Maybe all the bad information in the book was his way of writing a warning to the world, or protecting it. Fool around with this technology at your peril." Larsen looked directly at Serengetti for the second time since they boarded the sub. "Because it destroyed Captain Nemo."

It took a moment before Serengetti was able to think this through fully.

"Of course," he said, when the meaning hit him. And with it a new and intense feeling of insecurity washed over him. "And it will destroy us, too."

* * *

"What if Nemo did escape to the Pacific?"

"If he did, then, somehow, word got back to Verne, who wrote *The Mysterious Island* to let the Captain know he knew."

"Or maybe to warn the world that Nemo was still alive," said Larsen.

"It may be so; it may be so. If I recall *Mysterious Island* correctly, Nemo was alone on the *Nautilus* when it descended for the last time. The sub was intact, its interior lights still glowing, just like it is here. The 'mysterious island' was halfway around the world from this fjord, yet the two places were connected. I think this compartment in particular we need to leave alone. I want you to take the camera and record everything."

"O.K.," said Larsen, taking up the tiny digital video recorder and slowly capturing a visual catalog of the museum. Serengetti moved back into the library, where the 12,000 volumes again nearly overwhelmed his senses. He had always believed that one could learn the essential identity of anyone—Hitler, Ramses II, Virginia Woolf—by studying their library; but how to understand the personality behind this particular collection? Which of these 12,000 volumes, or what combination, was the key to Nemo's mind? Or delineated his covert intentions? Serengetti felt adrift. A thought came to him, an old quote from Paul Valéry: "A man alone is in bad company." He couldn't decide whether the quote applied more to Nemo or to himself.

The array was staggering. History, poetry, political economy, an impressive collection of fiction. There was also a heavy emphasis on the natural and physical sciences. He walked over to one section that seemed to hold the bulk of the works of Baron Alexander von Humboldt, including the famous self-published and unfinished *Kosmos*, in which Humboldt attempted nothing less than a complete catalog of the entire physical world. *Eureka*, Edgar Allen Poe's 1848 treatise on meta-astrophysics, dedicated to Humboldt, was shelved, appropriately, next to *Kosmos*.

He touched the Poe through the frustrating bars, and immediately drew back as the barred shelving started to move downwards into long recesses set into the edges of the shelves. In a few seconds, every volume in the library was freely available. When his breathing had returned, Serengetti merely mumbled "Well done, Captain," and continued his examination.

There was a lot of physics, almost all of it completely lost on Serengetti. He noted a book on gyroscopes and another on the refraction properties of water, both written by Léon Foucault. Next to these were monographs by worthies such as the chemist Henri Sainte-Claire Deville, on the process for separating aluminum from aluminum ore. Three volumes of Michael Faraday's *Experimental Researches in Electricity*, published between 1839 and 1855, as well as his *Experimental Researches in Chemistry and Physics*, published in London on 1859, seemed to have been thoroughly consulted. Looking inside the latter, Serengetti noticed a marginal notation, written in a dense script he could not understand, on one of Faraday's papers concerning electromagnetic induction, electrochemistry, and diamagnetism. But the marginal notes were unlike those of a student, underlinings of key points. Instead, passages were scratched out and handwritten notes inserted between the lines, as if the inscriber knew more about these physical forces than Faraday.

Beyond these works were a succession of tracts and field studies published by a parade of French anti-Darwinists such as Henri Milne-Edwards and Jean-Louis-Armand de Quatrefages. Many focused on the study of obscure marine invertebrates. One volume, written in French and beautifully bound in red leather, described a descent into the sea off the coast of Sicily made by Milne-Edwards and Quatrefages together in 1844. Whoever had assembled this enormous library, it seemed obvious that the nineteenth-century war between religious and rational views of nature had dominated his thoughtful hours.

On another shelf were a host of works by the U.S. naval commander and inventor of the electric torpedo, Matthew Fontaine Maury. These included editions in several languages of his influential *The Physical Geography of the Sea*. This path-breaking oceanographic work described the world's oceans as being criss-crossed by great salt water "rivers," vast currents that circulated the globe with the same kind of power as the great continental rivers. Serengetti stopped at a page describing the effects of ocean currents and the drift of objects thrown into the sea. He noticed that one lengthy paragraph had been encircled by a wide and jagged line—as if Nemo had been slightly drunk, or had been responding to his Maury while the submarine was rolling in a surface swell.

What did it all mean? The scientific references would take years to sort out. Serengetti felt his spirits flag. Never before had he confronted an archaeological situation beyond his training. He needed a squad of PhDs from a score of disciplines. Such was the circumambient strength of Nemo's knowledge and intellect. Twenty years of reading Arctic history and combing the base camps of Arctic explorers had not prepared him for this. He remembered the weather-beaten British meteorological station in Antarctica where he had found a small reference library left behind when the station was abandoned in 1960. With the exception of a few Hammond Innes novels and some scattered popular magazines, that library had little besides oversized bound volumes of wind pattern charts and a forlorn assortment of weather almanacs. This submarine library was entirely different: it appeared to be an attempt to fathom the chief aspects of human evolution, culture, and science. How could one human being encompass this much learning in one brain. Almost forlornly, Serengetti turned his head to search the many shelves of poetry, of history, and of fiction. Perhaps Nemo had concluded that science alone could not produce all the answers.

* * *

A long blue line of uniformly bound volumes contained works of Homer and Aeschylus. Somewhat incongruously, a copy of Dickens' *Bleak House* was tucked in amongst the ancient Greeks. Why not? They understood obfuscation and delays as well as the Brits. But everywhere else, there was order: Serengetti sensed pattern. A few other nineteenth-century novelists, including Cooper and Dumas, *pere*, occupied their own shelves. As a native of the New England coast, he was drawn to the collection of Melville. There were heavily scored editions of *Omoo* and *Typee*, what appeared to be a first edition of Melville's desperately cynical novel, *The Confidence-Man*, as well as an almost unreadable copy of *Moby-Dick*, its pages scrawled upon almost to the point of violence. Page after page seemed to have triggered an agitated response in its reader. *"He tasks me; he heaps me; I see in him outrageous strength, with an inscrutable malice sinewing it. That inscrutable thing is chiefly what I hate... I'll chase him round Good Hope, and round the Horn, and round the Norway Maelstrom, and round perdition's flames before I give him up."* Serengetti was quick to notice that a double stroke of ink had been slashed underneath "Norway Maelstrom."

It was almost comical. Anyone who ever sailed the northern coast of Norway knew full well that the legendary destructiveness of the maelstrom was almost entirely mythical. It was a kind of minor coastal whirlpool, one that might have thrown a Viking longship off course and perhaps temporarily trapped an ill-captained whaling vessel, but have had little effect on a submarine. Yet it had clearly fascinated Nemo, if only in a metaphorical way. At that moment, Serengetti wondered if Nemo had laid out a gigantic puzzle—scientific, literary, philosophic, and geographic—in this library, and dared anyone to try to solve it.

Serengetti noted that Aeschylus's *The Persians*, a work written nearly five hundred years before the time of Christ, was out of place on the neatly arranged shelves. This volume, one that described the Athenian naval victory over the Persian Empire, had been placed at the end of a huge collection of the works of Victor Hugo. When Serengetti removed it from the shelf and opened it, he noticed more indecipherable margin notations. They were not merely appreciations of memorable passages. Rather, they seemed to be an attempt to rewrite the story; the annotator seemed to have been a combatant in the struggle: "I am the man, I suffered, I was there," as

Walt Whitman had put it. Was Nemo imagining himself as an ancient Greek, engaged in mortal combat with Darius and his Persians? Was he trying to find an heroic model for his own life story? Or was he simply engaged in a search for a historical precedent to his own terraqueous struggle? Whatever the truth, it was clear that this library had been his lifeblood. These books were not for decoration; they had not merely been read; they had been intensively analyzed. A number of them—poetry, physics, history—looked as if they had been clawed apart, every word sifted through the fine mesh screen of Nemo's intellect.

But to what end? If Nemo forced Serengetti to pursue him not only across a global landscape but also through an impenetrable literary maze as well, the archaeologist would have to give up. Nemo—no one—was everywhere and nowhere, like God. It was one thing to explore a mythical submarine in an isolated Arctic fjord, or even try to track down a man hidden away on some remote Pacific base. Those were the sort of geographic challenges Serengetti felt prepared for. But what if that man could disappear into history as well? There were, perhaps, six million pages in this library. On which one, or combination, had Nemo had written the key to his identity? If Serengetti were forced to play this game, not only around the globe but across five millennia and in a dozen different languages, he would certainly lose. *Narrow the search*, he thought.

It occurred to him, as an archaeologist, to look for a pattern in the contents of the library. Perhaps, like some prehistoric stone altar, its meaning was in the arrangement of the stones, and not in the content of the ritual. Yet as he looked more intently at the rows of multi-colored bindings, nothing came into focus. Nemo's system of color-coded bindings, not to mention the scattered first-edition bindings, seemed hopelessly arbitrary. Generally, history was separate from poetry, poetry from mechanics, mechanics from expedition reports, but that would be the case in any library.

Serengetti then noted that the works of various authors—Stendahl, Moliere, Goethe—were grouped together. Except when they weren't; how often? he wondered. Hugo's work took up almost an entire shelf, as did Dickens (excepting *Bleak House*); but Balzac's seemed to be speckled randomly about, even though their bindings were uniform. He noticed that there were clusters of volumes by Sir Walter Scott in widely separated places, high and low, fore and aft. Then there was the isolated Aeschylus volume. Were there others that had been misshelved? Serengetti walked slowly around the perimeter of the library, attempting to construct a mental picture of the titles from all the various languages in his mind. If there was a pattern, perhaps he could find where it was tentative, or broken.

He remembered how his Uncle Harry, a bibliophile and a scotch drinker, had, in a fit of inebriated lucidity, reorganized his 5,000-plus volume collection by color: red Mailer with red Austen, green Joyce with green Marquez, blue Shakespeare with blue Chekov—pairings that made Harry's long-suffering wife conclude that Harry was only drunk north by northwest. He looked at the leather couch for permanent indentations of a man's weight. On the port side of the library, in the aft corner, he noticed such a depression. He bent over the couch and searched the shelves behind it. Then he saw something else.

A tiny volume was set by itself. It was a small green book, enclosed by bookends made from two rough pieces of brass, perhaps the casings from an old clock. Gold lettering on the spine of the green volume announced that the book was a Harvard University Press edition of Xenophon's *Anabasis*. He knew nothing about it, not the author nor the subject. Was it history or science, fiction or poetry? Noticing the slight scuff marks on the shelf where *Anabasis* had been retrieved and replaced, Serengetti's rubber-gloved hand prised it free.

* * *

He opened it slowly, as he had the other volumes, in case it contained notes, or perhaps a letter, but nothing tumbled out. The slim, musty volume had been closely read; the margins were covered with notations in that same script Serengetti could not decipher. Printed on the verso pages was what appeared to be the original version of *Anabasis* in Attic Greek. The recto pages contained a translation into English. As he turned page after page, it became obvious that this was a volume its owner had wrestled with on numerous occasions. Phrases in both Greek and the English had been circled or underlined, and the margins were studded with notations. In a few spots, parts of the text had been crossed out, and lines written into the spaces between the lines. The reader, apparently, had disagreed with the translation and had substituted one more to his liking.

But what was this story? What relevance did an ancient Greek text have to this literary submarine? Without noticing the passage of minutes, Serengetti violated his own instructions to Larsen and took the *Anabasis* to the dark blue leather sofa and sat down with it. It had to mean something, he thought, yet it was all so obscure. Ancient history, modern technology. A book set off from the others, one augmented by a nearly continuous interlinear commentary. Was this small piece of ancient literature the Rosetta Stone for Nemo's brain?

As Serengetti flipped the pages of the book back to the beginning, he read a few lines of introductory text written for this 1840 edition by a Harvard professor named Caldwell. According to Caldwell, Xenophon had been another of the classical world's warrior-poets, a philosopher, historian and statesman. Born in Attica around 430 B.C., at the start of the ruinous thirty-year war between Athens and Sparta, his Athenian family was rich, and Xenophon and his friends had studied with Socrates. Early on, Xenophon had joined an elite branch of the Athenian cavalry. With his anti-democratic bias, he had thrown in his lot with conservative revolutionaries who had seized power, briefly, when Xenophon was nearly twenty, and again when he was twenty-seven. Most of his youth and early manhood had been devoted to overthrowing the Athenian democracy. When the democrats triumphed in 401, Xenophon fled. His bitterness deepened two years later with the execution of his old teacher Socrates. A few years later, Xenophon was called a traitor by the government and banished.

It was after this that Xenophon embarked on a great adventure. As one of an army of Greek mercenaries, "The Ten Thousand," he joined an expeditionary force raised by the Persian prince Cyrus the Younger, in a campaign against Cyrus's brother, the King of Persia, Artaxerxes. Cyrus marched his vast army, including "The Ten Thousand," through the western reaches of the Persian Empire, to a place near Babylon called Cunaxa. There, four hundred and one years before Christ, Cyrus and his Greek mercenaries entered into a pitched battle against the well-disciplined armies of Artaxerxes: as many as a million foot soldiers and horse cavalry, men with slings, javelins, shields, and bows, locked in a death struggle. When Cyrus finally caught sight of his hated brother, he lunged at him, thrusting a javelin through his breastplate. But Artaxerxes was only wounded, and at the very moment Cyrus struck, one of Artaxerxes's personal guards pierced Cyrus's face with a javelin. In the fighting that followed, Cyrus was killed. He was found later, with eight of his personal guard lying dead across his body.

It was several days before the rebellious army comprehended that Cyrus had fallen. The Greek mercenaries, including Xenophon, were now cut off, leaderless and a thousand miles from home. On the morning they learned of the death of Cyrus, heralds from the King also appeared, demanding that the Greek mercenaries surrender their weapons and appear before the King to beg for mercy. It was then that Xenophon, barely thirty years old, stepped forward and addressed his comrades.

* * *

Xenophon the Athenian said to his fellow Greeks: "At this moment, brothers, we have no other possession save arms and valour. If we keep our arms, we imagine that we can make use of our valour as well, but if we give them up, we will certainly lose our lives. We should not give up the only possessions we have. Instead, we should battle the King for his." Hearing these few words, the stricken Greek army elected Xenophon leader.

It was clear enough that the quote meant something to the owner of the library. It had been underlined, and both the Greek and English texts had been slightly modified, as if to capture nuance.

The new general's first order was that the army should burn its supply wagons, thereby permitting the men to take paths not open to the beasts that pulled the wagon trains. Next, the tents, being of no use either in fight or forage, were put to the torch. Lastly, all baggage save those articles necessary for war or eating and drinking were ordered abandoned, so that the largest number of men could be put into the battle lines, and the fewest used to carry the army's baggage. If any man grumbled at leaving belongings behind, Xenophon reminded him that their opponents carried much treasure, and if the Persians were vanquished, all of it would fall to the victors. At the thought of their opponents acting as pack servants for soon-to-be liberated treasure, Xenophon's men revived.

Over the next two years, Xenophon led the survivors of the Ten Thousand through hostile territory, native attacks, and desperate food shortages, from the valleys of Mesopotamia to the Black Sea. While on the march the army found itself in common cause. But when they reached the shores of the Black Sea, unity began to erode. Xenophon came upon a beautiful natural harbor, with ample resources, and a vision of a utopian city came to him. He asked his men to join in building his dream of paradise. But for the first time since he had rallied and saved them, his army rejected his vision and opted instead for the long march to their Aegean homes.

Here, as Serengetti read, *Anabasis* became almost wistful, full of longing and regret, as if a great chance for a new and better life had been lost. There was discord between those men who believed they should build a new life in a new and fertile land, and those men whose only desire was to return to their old homes in Greece.

Xenophon himself was divided between the luxuries of the Persian land and his duty. In the end, he returned to Greece and eventually retired to his estate at Scillus, near Olympia, there to write the history of "The Ten Thousand" and to try over the later decades of his life to make sense of all the carnage and courage and beauty he had seen. Yet even this small peace was denied him. Xenophon was sixty years old when the Thebans invaded Peloponnesia and captured his estate near Olympia. Ten years later his warrior son was killed in a skirmish. As he witnessed the destruction of Sparta, the aged Xenophon wrote with longing for his beloved estate at Scillus, and the utopian visions of his unfounded city on the Black Sea.

Serengetti closed the book and rubbed his eyes. His mind was suddenly cloudy: an uncomfortable feeling akin to ennervation or a mild hangover. He knew that many polar explorers had been subject to strange dreams and nightmares. Exploring Franz Josef Land in 1898, an American named Evelyn Briggs Baldwin dreamed that he had come across the survivors of the Andrée balloon expedition to the North Pole. Later during that same expedition, Baldwin dreamed that he had watched as his long-dead younger brother slid down the glacier that he himself had crossed earlier that day. Even the great Nansen was not immune to strange visions. During the first winter of his epic three-year expedition to try and reach the North Pole between 1893 and 1896, Nansen awoke in his bunk on board the *Fram* in a temporary panic. Searching through his memory, he realized that he had dreamed that he had in fact reached the North Pole. As he confided in his journal:

"I had a strange dream last night. I had got home. I can still feel something of the trembling joy, mixed with fear, with which I neared land and the first telegraph station. I had carried out my plan; we had reached the North Pole on sledges, and then got down to Franz Josef Land. I had seen nothing but drift-ice; and when people asked what it was like up there, and how we knew we had been to the Pole, I had no answer to give; I had forgotten to take accurate observations, and now began to feel that this had been stupid of me. It is very curious that I had an exactly similar dream when we were drifting on the ice-floes along the east coast of Greenland, and thought that we were being carried farther and farther from our destination. Then I dreamed that I had reached home after crossing Greenland on the ice; but that I was ashamed because I could give no account of what I had seen on the way—I had forgotten everything."

Perhaps the dreams and visions were due to the change of diet, the meals consisting of walrus meat and coffee, or the eternal daylight of summer and the unrelieved darkness of winter that played tricks on the mind.

Two words from the Caldwell introduction stuck in Serengetti's mind. The translation for "Xenophon" was "the Stranger." Serengetti carefully replaced the *Anabasis* on its shelf. *Xenophon. Nemo. The Stranger. Nobody. The Avenger. Ahab. The Madman. Arthur Gordon Pym. The Maelstrom. A Dangerous Current. A Man Alone.* Serengetti used his stylus to write these words onto his console. He heard Larsen in the study, changing one data tape for another and placing the one into a sealed bag. It would later be placed in a small waterproof container for the short ascent back to the surface.

This book, of all the works in Nemo's library, had a special place. But what was the foundation of his undeniable fascination with *Anabasis*? Nemo had been interested in, perhaps obsessed with, the story of Xenophon. He also had a deep fascination with some of the greatest minds of Europe—except Wallace, Huxley, and Darwin. If Nemo were interested in a complete catalog of human knowledge, why had he so ignored Darwin? Had he taken personally the Darwinian earthquake that threatened notions of a higher human calling, the rational cataclysm that had placed all humanity in the mud alongside the worm and the rat?

* * *

Serengetti rose from the marvelous leather sofa and walked toward the science shelves. He pulled off the English-language edition of Maury's *The Physical Geography of the Sea*. He flipped through the book and saw passages bordered by the reader's pen, as well as other sections bordered and crossed out. One in particular seemed to have aroused the dismissal of the Captain: "The sea, by the circulation of its waters, doubtless has its offices to perform in the terrestrial economy; and when we see the currents in the ocean running hither and thither, we feel that they were not put in motion without a cause. On the contrary, we know they move in obedience to some law of Nature…never so far beyond the reach of human ken…"

So many of the pages were covered with annotations that it seemed as if Nemo had been commissioned to write a new edition of Maury. The corrections amounted to a full-scale refutation. The note he now read in the margin was a terse protestation against Maury's implicit attribution of the fairness of Nature and humankind's ability to comprehend the design of that fairness. The note read: "There are only two states of so-called 'Nature:' consciousness and death. The former state imposes law, the latter allows a final release from the tyranny of law."

Serengetti felt at once that here, at last, he was reading the private thoughts of Nemo. There could be no mistaking the existential anguish in this voice, the belief in the manifest unjustness of life and the leveling justice of death. Or was it exasperation at human inability to grasp underlying meanings?

A few pages after the disputed Maury quote, Serengetti read another section, and again this part of the book had been heavily scored and annotated. It described a trick of ocean currents that had been reported in 1712 by the ship *Phoenix*. A privateer out of Marseilles, the *Phoenix* had chased down a Dutch ship as it cruised through the gut separating Tariffa and Tangier. With one broadside, the *Phoenix* sent the Dutch ship to the bottom. Or at least the captain of the *Phoenix* thought he had. A week later, the wreck of the Dutch ship washed ashore off Tangier, more than four leagues to the west from the point where it had gone down. Scattered along the coast were crates of brandy blown out of the wreck. Reading this, Serengetti saw the scrawled notation next to it: "No grave is permanent."

As he read this vignette, Serengetti remembered the brandy bottle he had seen on the sideboard. He looked up now to see it again. He walked over and bent down to look at it more closely. A set of snifters rested nearby, covered with a fine layer of golden dust. He had expected more dust, but concluded that its absence had to do with the high pressure and low temperature on the sub. The bottle looked like a hundred others he had excavated from early eighteenth-century sites in New England and South Africa.

He slowly uncorked the bottle; it was still half-filled. Brandy? He dared not drink, but refrained only with great reluctance. Just one golden swallow, he thought. Was this brandy from the Dutchman that drifted off Tangier more than three hundred years ago? Nemo had used the *Nautilus* to obtain fabulous works of art for his study. Had he also availed himself of the chance to scour the oceans for other treasures—like Dutch brandy? Doubtless.

Feeling guilty as a child, Serengetti quickly replaced the cork in the bottle, fearful that Larsen would enter the study and catch him in mid-swallow. Yet the temptation to imbibe a draught of 300-year old brandy, to drink from the same glass as the Avenger, was hugely compelling. Instead, he pulled his own spare digital video camera from his bag and made a quick sweep of the entire library. Then he removed the small video disc and sealed it in a separate watertight pouch. Now he wanted nothing so much as to rapidly conclude this survey, and return to his office at Wellman Station to study the disc in detail. Better still, he should head for the Special Collections Library at the University of Oslo, where he could compare the two collections.

Next to the Maury volume were several scientific as well as popular volumes authored by the nineteenth-century Harvard zoologist Louis Agassiz. Serengetti pulled his *Principles of Zoölogy* from the shelf, opened it, and noted immediately opposite the title page a circular frontispiece diagram of the distribution of the principal types of animals, their order and longevity within the layers of the earth's crust. From the "Reign of Fishes" to the "Reign of Reptiles" to the "Reign of Mammals" and finally to the "Reign of Man," the diagram expanded outward in concentric circles. These circles contained hundreds of species. Some, like the "Ammonites," had risen with the fishes and died with the reptiles. Others, such as the "Canoids," were represented by a spear-shaped time on earth, the spear point driven into the time of the fishes, the spear blade spanning the time of the reptiles, and a spear shaft progressively thinning throughout the reigns of the mammals and man. Serengetti noticed underneath the cephalopods, the subclass of "Nautili." Alone amongst the mostly uniform shapes of the various time spans, the Nautili were distinctively tapered at each end: the unmistakable shape of a submarine.

* * *

Next to Agassiz's *Principles of Zoölogy* was a volume of travel writings co-authored by Agassiz and his second wife, Elizabeth. It was entitled *A Journey in Brazil*, and as Serengetti flipped rapidly through it he saw that it contained a fairly standard nineteenth-century description of a combined scientific/pleasure cruise along the Amazon. But it also contained a remarkably racist appendix on the "Permanence of Characteristics in Different Human Species."

In this almost concluding appendix, Agassiz recounted his field research along the lines of research being conducted by anthropologists around the same time. He made a special point of describing his careful measurements of the relative distances between the breasts of human females of Indian and of African descent. He concluded that while Indian women have breasts spaced far apart (a distance "nearly equal to the diameter of one of them"), on the other hand "in the Negress they stand in almost immediate contact." Agassiz made no mention, of course, of having compared such data with the distance separating his own wife's breasts, or the breasts of any other white European women. Serengetti thought that such a study, undertaken in Paris, or better still, in Scandinavia, might be the basis for a rewarding sabbatical proposal. Potential titles came to mind: "Radical Breast Volume/Diameter Contrasts: Hemispheric Divergence." It was the first notion during this survey of the *Nautilus* that brought a smile to his face.

Agassiz went on to speculate about what happened when Indians mated with Africans, or Africans with whites, or whites with Indians. Agassiz was keenly interested in this stuff, which had the effect of denying his contention that these human groups were different species. Of all people, Agassiz should have known that modern humans were not different species. An Eskimo could mate with a Bushman as easily as could a human from Manhattan with another from the Bronx.

The larger question was whether or not Nemo had subscribed to any of this racist nonsense. “Don’t forget the Papuans,” he had told Larsen. Should he himself be remembering that episode now? But as he thumbed through the book he saw something. The title page revealed that *A Journey in Brazil* had been published in Boston by Ticknor and Fields. At the bottom of the page, Serengetti stared at the year of publication: *1868*.

According to Verne, the *Nautilus* had been destroyed in the maelstrom in late June 1868. They had not made landfall at any time earlier. If that were true, how did a book published *after* the *Nautilus* had been destroyed find its way into this library?

* * *

There was little time left. Serengetti glanced at his console to check how long they had been on board the submarine. Almost an hour and a half. Larsen told him that AK wanted them off the sub quickly. If they were to get back to Kings Bay in time for a late flight to Tromsø and then to Oslo, they had to leave now.

His visit to the library had given rise to the suspicion that the *Nautilus*, magnificent as it was, was perhaps the first, tantalizing piece of a greater mystery, but to solve that mystery, he first must identify it. “More brain,” he moaned. “I need more brain.” The presence in the library of *A Journey in Brazil* suggested that the maelstrom was the beginning, not the end, of the mystery of Nemo’s whereabouts.

Their work would now separate into two tracks. Once they left the sub, the site would be placed under an antiseptic protection cordon. Serengetti expected that several remote cameras would be mounted both on board and around the submarine, and at least one autonomous undersea vehicle would be placed on continuous patrol around the site. The other track involved research, and lots of it, in archives around the world. And that was his speciality. Once word of the discovery leaked out to Glöbnet, pressure for access to the submarine would be sharp and the debate about its future white hot. Vandals would be afoot. Serengetti wished to stay as far from that heat as possible.

He felt a distinct chill at the thought that Nemo was still here, alive, hidden, perhaps observing, but still aboard. He felt a tap on his shoulder.

"Jesus Christ!" he shouted at Larsen. "Will you let me know when you are around, goddammit!"

"Well," said Larsen, his gear shouldered, "unlike you, wasting time looking at a lot of books you could just as easily scan in Oslo, I have catalogued the entire study, and have enough data for the next four cultural resource conferences. Let's get off this thing and get out of here. I'm looking forward to my three days off to read up on Verne."

"Sorry," Serengetti apologized, feeling like an idiot at having gotten completely lost in a well of speculation.

"Find anything interesting?"

"No," Serengetti lied. "Just your basic nineteenth-century cabinet of curiosities."

"OK, then," said Larsen. "Let's go. Kurosawa will be wondering what is taking us so long. And my long weekend is waiting."

* * *

Serengetti collapsed his console and strode aft. These discoveries had transformed the image of Captain Nemo that he carried in his literary memory. He was no longer the one-dimensional Avenger, bent on a calculated course of destruction. Nemo was now strange and new, complex, an alien anthropologist intent on grasping the roots of the human condition. What if Nemo were a time-traveller? Or What if Nemo had actually been there on the plain at Cunaxa the day Cyrus was fatally wounded?

Perhaps, Serengetti thought, Nemo was rewriting history itself. Crazy idea. And yet, as he looked around, he found himself surrounded by nuttiness. If Nemo had been there when Cyrus was annihilated and Xenophon led the retreat of "The Ten Thousand," had he played a part? Or merely been a witness? Was he correcting Xenophon's account because he had been a participant and had a different, sharper, memory? Or, was he Xenophon himself, doomed to constantly remember and revise a kaerotic event that had occurred two thousand years ago?

Could it be that Captain Nemo was not only a man ahead of his times, but behind as well? Had he grown so frustrated that, at the last, all he could accomplish was a final global dash, madly obliterating everything in his path? As Serengetti felt the deck plates of the submarine vibrate beneath him, he considered again the notion that Nemo might possess the ability to travel back and forth through time. If so, was this the machine that transported him through loops of time? He remembered the accordion page in *Anabasis*, covered with impenetrable symbols and algorithms.

The *Nautilus* as a time machine! What if they surfaced from this brief visit to Nemo's private world and found themselves several thousand years in the past, or in the future? Serengetti felt himself short of air. He wanted nothing more than to retreat from this submarine quickly. As he made his way toward the airlock, he began to fear that it might be locked.

An otherworldly aspect to Nemo now began to crowd out all other mental images. The Captain began to take on the aspect of a zephyr, invisible and yet subtly felt. If Nemo could travel through time, then he was still alive! And if he was still alive, where was he right now? *Mobilis in mobile*...

Five: Ferry Reach

He piled upon the whale's white hump the sum of all the general rage and hate felt by his whole race from Adam down; and then, as if his chest had been a mortar, he burst his hot heart's shell upon it.

—Herman Melville
Moby-Dick, 1851

Serengetti woke when he sensed a change in the timbre of the high-pitched engines. During the flight from the Arctic, then the overnight in Paris, and then during the long trans-Atlantic flight while Larson had slept, Serengetti had been preoccupied with thoughts of the *Nautilus*. They had no absolute understanding of what they were dealing with, nor any real understanding of where the discovery might lead. What was certain was that the artifact would soon be revealed, and then all bets were off.

They were now forced to play hide and seek, much as Verne's fictional submarine captain was forced to hide this machine during his round-the-globe voyage a century and a half earlier. For Serengetti, whose only political instinct was to keep far away from politics, it was essential that they understand the esentials of Nemo's invention before squabbling bureaucracies laid claim. Once the site became known, they would lose control of it.

The early morning flight from Paris was arriving in Bermuda in mid-morning, Paris time. Larsen was already up, comparing the color of the ocean around the hook-shaped island with the color of the Oslo fjord. There was really no comparison, he thought, between the profoundly blue seawater in the north and the shallow turquoise ocean here. Some of it was worse than light blue, consisting of an almost light-green algae-tinged muck. This was an ocean from a child's kindergarten watercolor. Light blue ocean, light blue sky. If I went to a waterfront bar here, he thought, more likely than not I'd find a light blue liqueur to match the sea and the sky.

The other passengers were also just coming awake, entertained by a particularly stunning French model doing stretches on the cabin-front video screen. She looked in her early twenties, an elegant, impossibly prettier copy of Deneuve, in short hair and sandals, seated on a dock at some resort in Bora Bora. He felt an aftershock in his groin. She reminded him of the woman he would see when he returned to Paris.

Larsen hated the tropics, and he shuddered when a blast of heat and humidity hit him on the tarmac. A slight breeze off the ocean soon made the abrupt change from the high Arctic almost tolerable. In less than twenty-four hours, they had gone from an ice-filled fjord at eighty degrees north to a semi-tropical archipelago in mid-Atlantic. Larsen's stomach felt uneasy; he had no desire to travel any further south or west. At the terminal, Serengetti introduced Larsen to Wilson McHargue. Larsen was immediately unimpressed, but hid it artfully. Bodily appearance counted for a lot for Larsen, and it was hard to see how this slovenly, near-sighted, fat man was going to help.

"Wil was a friend of mine at the School of Ocean and Earth Sciences in Hawai'i," said Serengetti, making the introductions.

"It's a pleasure, Larsen. Saw your broadcast from the South Pole. That was good stuff," said McHargue.

"Thank you," said Larsen stiffly.

"So tell me, Wil, how is Janet?" Serengetti asked.

"Better than ever. We divorced a year ago when she couldn't stand the place, or me, any longer. She's already remarried on the mainland and happier than ever, best I can tell."

"I'm sorry to hear that. I really liked her. And how did you pad your vitae enough to land a tech job at the BI?"

"*Senior* technician, if you please," said McHargue. "Iwas lucky. I had always wanted to get back here. Did I ever tell you that my great-great-grandfather is buried in the old Royal Navy Cemetery on the other end of the island? Maybe if we have time we can ride down there and I'll show you around the graves. The old family cottage is still in the family, and the last uncle who wanted it died three years ago. Anyway, the chief engineer at the BI was ready to retire, and then the senior tech was hired away by the ocean technology program at Portsmouth, England. So I sort of fell into it. You should see the wine cellar—dug four generations back. And the library. You'll love that. Take a major hurricane to blow me out of here now. We have a nice little coastal research vessel to test the new probes, so I'm never far from home. And I have a little cabin cruiser of my own moored over in Mullet Bay. I heard Sam Kahana is working with you guys now?"

McHargue lead them to his tiny natural-gas van. "You hungry? When I got your message I thought you might want some chow when you arrived, so I went out back and buried a chicken in the *imu* an hour ago. It's lunchtime in Paris, so I thought you'd like something substantial. I like to cook it about two hours, so it should be good to go just after you've settled in. I would have put in a pig, but pig takes a lot of time."

"Buried a chicken?"

"Polynesian delicacy, Bjørn." Serengetti said. "Don't worry. It's a hell of a step up from mackerel in tomato sauce. Although I wonder how you got an *imu* past the zoning board."

"Religious exemption," said McHargue. "I convinced them that a Scotsman who'd lived in Hawai'i for ten years would suffer egregiously without his *imu*. And if you don't like it, we've got plenty of wine to drown our sorrows."

* * *

"When I got your message last night I have to admit I was shocked," said McHargue. "The wreck of a nineteenth-century sub would be extremely rare, although not nearly as much as I thought it would be initially. There were several European attempts to build sophisticated subs in the nineteenth-century, and I thought it was entirely possible that one of them could have been sent on some crazy-assed secret expedition to the North Pole, or to find the Northwest Passage. It would be just like you to find it some place nobody else had thought to look."

McHargue drove out of the airport and turned right onto Kinderly Field Road. To the left was Longbird Bridge and the way south to the main parts of the island group; to the right was the road to St. George's across Swing Bridge and to St. David's via Swaiwell Drive. Serengetti looked across Ferry Reach to try to get a glimpse of the Ballard Institute, but it was hidden behind a wall of dense foliage.

"You know, I took that course with old Kleindienst at Hawai'i on the history of ocean technology, the one everybody avoided because the old man was all but retired and still reading his graduate school notes from about a million years ago. But I needed a requirement and was desperate so I took it. Well, through no fault of Kleindienst, it turned out to be really a great course. I spent hours in the Still Archives reading nineteenth-century engineering reports. I got out my old notes last night and went through them, then surfed a few nuances. Do you know where Landskrona is in Sweden?"

"*Ja*," said Larsen. "It is down on the southwest coast, just across the Öresund from Copenhagen."

They passed Swing Bridge and turned left onto Swaiwell Drive. McHargue continued talking as they maneuvered quickly along the narrow roads towards St. David's. The van turned right at the hospital and continued out toward the easternmost points of land in the islands. They soon passed the eastern end of the airfield, heading toward Well Bay.

"Well," said McHargue. "Did you know that they built a submarine there in 1882? Pretty good one, too. It was called the *Nordenfelt 1*. When you asked me to compare the data you sent me with that of other nineteenth-century underwater propulsion systems, the *Nordenfelt 1* naturally came to mind. It's a bit later than 1865, but the technology would not have changed drastically in the intervening fifteen years or so. I rejected any similarities with Fulton's *Nautilus*, which he tried to sell to the French Navy in 1800, or the *Hunley*, the *Intelligent Whale*, or any of the other hand-cranked submarines from the American Civil War. The only other subs that might have influenced the design of whatever it is you surveyed were Holland's, like the *Fenian Ram*, or the *No. 1*. But Holland's boats ran on small, Brayton four-horsepower petrol engines, and had a limited range. Here we are."

McHargue's family cottage rested at the top of a gradual slope overgrown with sea grass and wildflowers. He boasted that it was the last unmanicured lawn in Bermuda. The van turned into a drive made up of compacted sand and crushed shell and labored up the slope. Serengetti noticed a rusting yellow Schramm tractor in an open field a few hundred meters from McHargue's cottage. The tractor had long since come to permanent rest, but was still attached to a petrol-powered generator trailer it had once pulled. The front wheels, almost completely obscured by weeds, were buried deeply into the field. The seat was broken and canted forward at a crazy angle. The engine cowling had likewise collapsed, although the generator seemed as if it might yet have some life in it. Like a great sea turtle, defeated in an attempt to return to the ocean after laying its eggs on the beach, the Schramm had given out with a groan and died, never to move again. McHargue pointed to it with evident pride.

"My grandfather's," he said. "My father had the presence of mind to leave it where it was the day my grandfather died. Now, instead of an eyesore I'd have to pay somebody to haul away, it's a local cultural icon. I thought you'd appreciate that, Paul. Our land extends just beyond the Schramm, but it's so ugly that nobody wants to build near it, so it effectively extends our land another hundred meters. And now it's been declared a historic monument from the mid-twentieth century, so nobody can touch it! Even get a tax break by leaving it right where it is and allowing it to rust in peace." McHargue cackled as he ushered them inside the cottage to the guestrooms.

* * *

Once he had stowed his overnight bag, Larsen joined McHargue at a small hut set along a brief garden path behind the cottage. The cottage itself was a single story of airy rooms that opened onto a trellised walkway facing east toward the ocean. A kitchen, dining room, living room, and two bedrooms made up a west wing, while the east wing, facing the ocean, comprised a single bedroom connected to a library and a study. A weary sailor had designed this cottage, Larsen thought, one who wanted nothing more than to retire to his ocean-facing study and consult his nautical breviaries amid the morning fog and warm afternoon breezes. Both visitors appreciated it at once, and envied McHargue his cozy solitude.

The door to the library was open, and Serengetti walked over to peer inside. He immediately felt at home. Walls filled with books, around a large freestanding globe; long dark tables piled with charts and engineering sketches; a single thin screen carefully mated to and concealed within an oversized desktop. Apart from the secure computer dock, one could imagine Commodore Maury, or even Captain James Cook emerging from just such a library. One long table appeared to have been recently swept clear, all modern accoutrements replaced by a stack of two-volume nineteenth-century expedition reports. But before he could see which they were, McHargue called him out to the small hut behind the cottage, where the engineer had dug his *imu*.

When Serengetti reached the hut, Larsen was already devouring a piece of roast chicken McHargue had torn from the bird on the coals. Serengetti, a vegetarian, took the offered roast *kumara* tuber and a glass of wine and sat by the coals. McHargue was already back on the case and took up his thread of the conversation.

"The *Nordenfelt 1*, built in northern Europe, was a fairly sizeable boat, almost twenty meters long. But what interested me most was the engine room."

"Anything resembling what we saw during our survey?" asked Larsen.

"Not so much the substance as the form. Basically, the *Nordenfelt* *was* an engine room. There wasn't much room for anything else."

"But our boat has a fairly small engine room," said Serengetti. "At least compared with the rest of the machine." They had not told McHargue anything about the forward half of the sub, about the dining room, the library, or the salon.

"You never do listen to a thing I say," said McHargue. "You might have finished that lousy dissertation of yours a lot sooner if you had. I said that the form is different, but I think the substance might be similar."

"So you think that we might have a refined version of the Swedish sub *Nordenfelt*?" asked Larsen.

"Finally," said McHargue. "Someone who listens to me. How did you ever get hooked up with Serengetti, anyway?"

"Someone has to keeping him from walking off the cliff."

"Right. Now look. I had a little conference this morning with a friend in Stockholm, a former student of a student of Franzen's, now the lead tech in the underwater exploration section at the Technical Institute. He found a copy of the *Nordenfelt's* deck plans in their archives, and that thing was just stuffed with machinery. There were boilers and, more important, a steam accumulator with a heat exchanger on the bottom. As steam from the boiler was forced through the coils of the heater, it transferred its heat to the water in the accumulator, which was then pumped back into the boiler. This superheated water was stored in a steel reservoir. The superheated water could then be fed at low pressure into the main boiler, where it turned to steam. The schematics look a bit like your images, but your engine takes up about one-tenth the space as the double steam engine on *Nordenfelt*."

Larsen looked despondently at Serengetti. They had hoped that the engine they had surveyed was revolutionary. He was also irritated that Stockholm now knew something was afoot. There were few things that could rattle a Norwegian; being upstaged by a Swede was one of them. And now McHargue, a recognized expert on undersea engines, was telling them that all they had seen was an elaborate steam engine. Serengetti, munching his *kumara*, looked incredulous.

"You're telling me that what we have on this sub is a steam engine?"

"Absolutely not," said McHargue. "I said the form is similar, and it is. But the engine on the *Nordenfelt* took three days to power up. They had to light the fires in the harbor and then wait seventy-two hours before they could put to sea. I know damned well that your engine is not powered by steam. In fact, if it's what I think it is, it wasn't designed for underwater propulsion. And it's broken."

He had Larsen's attention now.

"What's more," said McHargue, swallowing a sizeable gulp of wine, "it hasn't even been invented yet."

* * *

"What? That is absurd!" protested Serengetti. "What do you mean, hasn't been invented yet? We just looked at the thing. I sent you images from the engine room!"

"That's right," said McHargue. "And that's all you showed me. You pulled this chicken shit before with me, Serengetti, when you found that B-29 between Necker and Nihoa. Now cut the crap. I want to know exactly where you found this sub, and I want to see the whole record. I'm not a fucking grad student. And I don't have to put up with this crap. I'm the senior tech here. This ain't SOEST."

Serengetti had to this moment been enjoying his roasted sweet potato. He had drunk a glass and a half of some icy and dry white that McHargue had provided. Now it all went sour in his stomach. As much as he liked McHargue, he knew McHargue loved to talk. Once McHargue got word, the whole underwater community would know about it within two days. On the other hand, he was out of options. Nobody—certainly nobody he knew—knew engines like Wilson. It was going to come out sooner or later, so it might as well be now. He glanced at Larsen, who suddenly did not seem to be bothered by the situation at all. He was working on his third glass of wine.

Serengetti inhaled deeply.

"We think we've got the *Nautilus*."

"Goddammit, Paul. Stop shitting me. It reminds me of the time you and George Han…"

"Wilson, will you shut the hell up for two seconds," said Serengetti, almost yelling. He took out his console, placed the small silver disc into the expansion slot, opened a file, then turned the console and showed it to McHargue. "What do you think that is?"

"It's a library. Looks like an old mansion library. Looks like *my* library."

"Exactly," said Serengetti. "Only it happens to be on board a submarine, in ten meters of water, sitting at the bottom of a fjord in Svalbard. Larsen and I were on board less than twenty-four hours ago. See that time code? 1015. We surfaced yesterday around noon, and flew here immediately. That is the library of one pseudonymous Captain Nemo, a.k.a. Prince Dakkar, when last seen alive."

"Well I'll be damned," said McHargue. He rearranged his bulk around the *imu* and seemed to plunge into some private well of thought. Conflicting emotions battled for advantage across his imagination. Then, with a conclusive shudder, he poured the last of his wine over the coals. "So he wasn't a visionary after all—just a journalist. You fellows finish the second bottle over there. I've got a lot of work to do."

And he got up and walked toward the open door of his library.

"Where are you going?" called Serengetti after him.

"Give me two hours," he said. "Then we'll go over to the BI. Do you mind if I invite the old man to join us?"

Serengetti was about to shake his head no when Larsen called out, "Not at all."

"Good," said McHargue, "because I think we're going to need his help."

* * *

"I think Verne was a lot smarter than people gave him credit for being," said McHargue as they drove across the Swing Bridge and turned left toward the Ballard Institute. "Everybody knows that he's considered the father of science fiction and all that. There are so many places where he writes about stuff that might have seemed futuristic in the first part of the twentieth century and prophetic in the latter part of the twentieth century. But I've always felt that it was possible that he was *way* ahead. I think the reason he may have seemed a bit silly at times is more our fault than his."

"Our fault?" said Serengetti. "Why?"

"Because in my view we still don't understand what he was writing. I don't think he was writing popular science for dummies, as many have supposed."

"So you're saying that instead of not understanding what he was seeing, he really knew more than he wrote?"

"As usual, you managed to say it as only an anthropologist can. But yes, that's about it."

"Look, Wil, you're the only person I trust who knows about advanced ocean engineering. What do you see in these images?"

"Well, I think you are right to consider the problem from Verne's point of view. Maybe the reason there are so many different drafts of his novel is that he was trying to find the right lexicon, the best words to describe engineering that we in our time still haven't figured out. Here we are."

The Ballard Institute for Undersea Exploration in Ferry Reach occupied four separate and distinct buildings. Two were rather conventional concrete laboratory spaces, designed more to withstand hurricanes at the lowest possible cost than to appeal to any refined architectural aesthetic. The main building could have doubled as the backdrop to an accurate film adaptation of Hemingway's *To Have and Have Not*. Breezy, open, white-clapboards and blue shutters, with a wide and inviting veranda, it had been built along an early twentieth-century design to serve as the estate of a turn-of-the-century e-baron. When the baron lost his fortune in the collapse of '17, the estate was given over to a land trust, which in turn offered it as the location of a marine exploration institute. The most famous undersea explorer in the world had been persuaded to move his headquarters there and gather other undersea mavens around him.

The fourth building, a great modernist structure that served as the conference center and auditorium for IMAX films and JASON projects, contained an undersea garage, large enough to berth the nuclear research submarine *NR-3*. It was from this berth that the first autonomous undersea nuclear vehicle had been launched on its around the world cruise in 2019. The global reach of these manned and unmanned undersea technologies at the Institute had made it the foremost design and testing center for the undersea exploration vehicles of the twenty-first century. McHargue parked his van in a space near the conference center, and ushered Serengetti and Larsen inside.

McHargue strode down the main corridor with the familiarity of someone both at home and in charge. He paused at his office long enough to find his laser projector, then showed his guests into the second conference room. Before Serengetti could admire the view over Ferry Reach in the distance, McHargue pressed a button and green curtains closed over the oversized window.

"The Director said he would be down to see us, so grab a drink from the refrigerator and make yourselves comfortable." With that, McHargue disappeared for a moment, saying he needed something from his office.

The door to the conference room opened and the director of the Institute entered. Serengetti knew him only via a brief meeting in Honolulu many years earlier, and since then he had aged considerably. Dr. Robert D. Ballard must be nearly eighty by now, Serengetti thought, yet he carried himself with such assurance and aplomb that it was difficult to credit him with so many years.

His undersea discoveries had made him the equal of Cousteau or Franzen. After locating a wreck from the Franklin search in the Northwest Passage in 2010, he had turned his attention to China's fourteenth-century *Star Raft* fleet, which he had discovered off Sri Lanka in 2011. Semi-retired since then, his influence was nonetheless still felt throughout the maritime community. He was both loved and hated, respected and feared. A legend.

Serengetti was stunned when the Director recognized him instantly, calling him by his first name. Ballard introduced himself to Larsen, then took his seat at the back of the long oval conference table.

* * *

McHargue returned from his office wearing a pressed white shirt and a light blue tie. He looked completely different. His khaki pants were sharply creased. Wilson's casual friendliness over lunch was gone, and Larsen noted that he carried himself in this room with the magisterial *gravitas* of an Oxford dean. This was the McHargue whose reputation preceded him at conferences, whose brilliance Serengetti had referenced on the flight over. Larsen recognized at once that here was a formidable intellectual presence, someone Larsen could respect.

McHargue stood at the lecturn, his face lit by a small reading lamp. In the subdued light of the small conference room, he focused his laser projector on the wall-sized screen at the front of the room.

"Good afternoon, gentlemen," said McHargue, nodding to each of them as if he had just noticed them for the first time. "Let's get started. While you fellows were en route from Svalbard, I worked out some equations. After you arrived, and you confirmed some of my suspicions about your find, I spent the last two hours trying to understand if the physics were possible."

Larsen had taken out his console and was tapping onto it with his stylus. McHargue immediately drew him up short.

"No wireless transmissions from this room," he said abruptly. "If you need secure communications we can provide them after the meeting." Sheepishly Larsen holstered his stylus. Serengetti had leaned back into his chair and crossed his right leg over his left. The Director looked on with focused eagerness.

"At one point in the novel, Pierre Aronnax wonders how electricity could possibly act with such power, wonders where did Nemo's almost unlimited energy come from. I think I know. The reason it took me a while to put my thoughts together is that the kind of engine that exists on the putative *Nautilus*, the one in the Arctic, was not developed until the 1960s."

"But you said it hadn't been invented yet," said Serengetti.

"Yes, that's true. It hasn't. What I think we're looking at is an ion engine, and there is no such thing as an ion engine for an undersea vehicle. They were designed in the 1960s as an alternative to nuclear-powered and liquid fuel-powered spacecraft engines."

Once again, he had caught Larsen's attention, but it was Serengetti who spoke.

"Spacecraft engines?"

"Yes, but the one on your sub was designed and built by someone who only had access to materials available in 1865. He knew what he wanted, but the execution fell a bit short."

"It's still working after 150 years," Serengetti protested. "I wouldn't call that a failure."

"It failed because it didn't get its skipper where he wanted to go. An ion engine requires an ion source, obviously. Early experiments used cesium as the ion source, but the cesium tended to erode the ionizer. Whoever built your engine knew that, and opted for a different source of gas. My spectral analysis of your images pretty much narrows it down to xenon gas."

Serengetti started at the mention of the element. He tried not to show his shock, but he felt his face flush, as if a town crier had just announced his favorite sexual fantasy to all the assembled villagers. The word associations from a day earlier—a day that now seemed a year earlier—flooded in. The Stranger. Xenophon. Now xenon. Linguistic happenstance, or…? Vaguely, as he pondered the coincidence, he heard Larson and McHargue continuing the conversation.

"So that's what we saw in the chamber," asked Larson.

"Yes, but that's only half of it. I don't think the ion engine was used to drive the sub, at least not underwater. It's more likely that a small steam generator powered the actual drive shaft. The ion engine would have been used to provide the power to keep the lights on, to get oxygen from seawater, as well as all the other operations Aronnax couldn't puzzle out."

"So why does he go to all the trouble to build such an elaborate engine just to get his oxygen? Isn't an ion engine a bit complex for that?"

"The engine itself has many uses. As for how it works, xenon gas, collected from the atmosphere, is bombarded by electrons. The resulting xenon ions are drawn toward high-voltage grids and spewed out behind the submarine through a directional nozzle at great speeds."

"How great?" the Director asked.

"Perhaps as high as 100,000 kilometers per hour," McHargue replied. "This glowing blue stream of xenon ions would provide low-key yet constant power, as well as acceleration, for months, even years."

"How about a decade?" asked Larsen. "A century?"

"Theoretically there is, for practical purposes, no limit," said McHargue. "None. Assuming a sizeable reservoir of xenon and a low drain on power. I would have to look directly at the layout of your engine, but from what I've seen, it's operating at only a fraction of its power."

"You can't run a submarine at 100,000 kilometers per hour," Larsen said matter-of-factly. "You'd be around the world in fifteen minutes."

"Exactly," said McHargue. "Twenty thousand leagues would have gone by pretty quickly."

"You're saying that the design is correct, but the engine is not providing all the energy it should?" asked Larsen.

"Essentially, yes," said McHargue. "That is why I say it may be broken somehow. It is a phenomenally efficient engine by our standards. But our current standards are miserable."

* * *

Serengetti understood very little of this. He had run ICP-AES scans on materials recovered from archaeological sites around the Arctic. But the Inductively Coupled Plasma Atomic Emission

Spectrometry he used was an old technique, somewhat out of favor, little used since Boyington's study of the hydrogen residues at the Wellman site nearly a quarter of a century earlier. Larsen, on the other hand, almost immediately sensed the implications of what McHargue was trying to say.

"But how would one get xenon gas one hundred and fifty years ago?" Larsen demanded.

"Ahh, " said McHargue. "I sent out some discrete feelers on that very subject before you arrived, and got an e-post back late this morning from Fridtjof Haraldursson at Reykjavik. He did his graduate work forty years ago with Siggurdsson at the University of Rhode Island, and he said that in the late 1970s they measured several undersea gas vents off Iceland. One of them vented *almost pure xenon gas*. It was the only place they observed such a phenomena in the Atlantic, although another expedition found a similar vent off Gabon. The only other places where similar vents were ever reported were from a few undersea calderas in the Pacific."

Larsen started at the mention of Iceland, but said nothing.

"Where in the Pac?" asked Serengetti.

"Several were found off Java. And one, you'll be interested to know, was found on the back wall at Molokini."

"Molokini! Does Zeke know about that?"

"Zeke found it," said McHargue.

"Who is that?" asked Larsen.

"An old friend from SOEST," said McHargue. "Zeke is kind of a canoe-builder, mystic, and maritime anthropologist who knows just about every bit of Pacific lore and legend. Did his dissertation on the spiritual symbolism of Molokini for ancient canoe builders. We used to complain that he had an unfair academic advantage over us *haole* because he was able to get his data telepathically from his ancestors."

"You know of this Molokini?" Larsen asked Serengetti.

"I've been there a time or three. But you know I've never drifted the Back Wall. And Zeke found a vent there. Damn. So Nemo could have had, in effect, an undersea xenon gas station?" asked Serengetti.

"I think it's very likely," answered McHargue. "And I think the reason we haven't heard about it before now is that it exploded sometime in the nineteenth-century."

"Krakatoa," said Larsen. "1883."

"That would be my guess," said McHargue. "But I don't think he parked his sub off Molokini. If he had, maybe the monarchy would have struck an alliance with him and sunk the first Dole Fruit Company ship that tried to moor at Aloha Towers."

"Nemo would have been dead almost twenty years by then," said Serengetti, although he mentally crossed his fingers.

"So where was he going before he died, eh?"

The four of them were momentarily silent, marooned in private thoughts. A line of light laced through a gap in the conference room curtains. Serengetti looked absently through the gap, beyond to the turquoise line of the waters of Ferry Reach. It was Larsen who finally broke the silence.

"Can you provide us with all the data you have on these xenon vents? Location, intensity, and so forth?"

"You thinking of tracking Nemo around the globe?" asked McHargue, with a barely suppressed smile which Larsen ignored.

"Something like that," Larsen said. "And I come back to the point. You can't drive a submarine 100,000 kilometers per hour under the seas."

"Right," said McHargue. "Either Nemo had absolute mastery over the ion engine, so much so that he could control it more finely than any kind of digital control we possess now. Or…"

"*Ja*, of course," said Larsen suddenly. It made perfect sense. How had he not seen it earlier?

"What, for Christ sakes?" demanded Serengetti impatiently.

The Director spoke, startling them all. It was only the second time he had said anything during the meeting.

"Captain Nemo, or whoever he was, was not aiming for Molokini; he had a different destination entirely."

Six: Diamond Head

In the early morning of the twenty-ninth day a group of eleven long black birds with handsome cleft tails flew by on a foraging trip from their home island, which lay somewhere beyond the horizon, and Teroro noted with keen pleasure that their heading, reversed, was his, and while he watched he saw these intent birds come upon a group of diving gannets, and when those skilled fishers rose into the air with their catch, the fork-tailed birds swept down upon them, attacked them, and forced them to drop the fish, whereupon the foragers caught the morsels in mid-air and flew away. From their presence it could be deduced that land was not was not more than sixty miles distant, a fact which was confirmed when Teura and Tupuna, working together, detected in the waves of the sea a peculiar pattern which indicated that in the near distance the profound westerly set of the ocean was impounding upon a reef, which shot back echo waves that cut across the normal motion of the sea; but unfortunately a heavy bank of cloud obscured the western horizon, reaching even to the sea, and none could detect exactly where the island lay.

—James A. Michener, Hawaii

Serengetti waited in his seat on board the transpacific shuttle until all other passengers had departed for their vacations in paradise. As queasy feeling rumbled through his gut. Nearly ten years had passed since he had left the Pacific, for what he'd hoped was the last time. Now the *Nautilus* had forced him to return, while Larsen returned to Norway to coordinate the protection of the *Nautilus* site. Serengetti was returning to Polynesia, where one could almost smell the colors of the landscape, and touch the sounds of the conversations in the shops. The sunsets were unnerving in their incandescence.

Anyone watching him as he slept and read his way across the Pacific would have seen nothing more than an unremarkable man in his late thirties. Had they glanced at his console, they would have found an eBook of Jules Verne's *The Mysterious Island.* Serengetti had downloaded a copy of the book and read it e-cover to e-cover during the twelve-hour flight to Honolulu. It was impossible for him not to relate to the five Union prisoners, attempting a daring escape in a balloon from the disastrous siege of Richmond, only to be swept westwards by a freak storm, all the way to a landing on an uncharted island in the Pacific.

On the very first page, Serengetti had been brought up short as Verne described the escapees' balloon, caught in an enormous and swirling column of air: "turning round and round as if seized by some aerial maëlstrom." A century and a half later, Serengetti was also being drawn unwillingly westward over the Pacific, in search of that same island. But much more than that, he was troubled that the conclusion of the novel had offered no certainty regarding Nemo's fate. The iron door leading on deck fastened so that no water could penetrate to the interior of the *Nautilus*. Two stop-cocks were opened, the reservoirs filled, and the *Nautilus* allowed to sink, with Nemo still on board, *in extremis*, even disabled perhaps, but very much alive, a morose and unsuccessful old revolutionary. He might have escaped, and with him the *Nautilus*.

As he read, it occurred to him that he might take advantage of this unexpected trip to the islands. He would see Zeke, of course, but why not stop by the Still as well? On a whim, he sent an e-post to Dr. and Mrs. Krauskopf, dear old friends and archivists at the Still Maritime Archives in Honolulu. This wizened old couple, steeped in maritime lore, had catalogued expedition reports for fifty years. Their mahogany repository held the largest collection of Pacific exploration narratives in the world.

Serengetti had first met them almost twenty years earlier when, on a month-long leave, his wife and his two stepchildren had met him in Hawaii. Even though his stepchildren were both gone when he had returned to Hawaii to study, Dr. and Mrs. K for some reason had thought they were still alive, and still small. Perhaps that was not so unusual after all, thought Serengetti; that was how they always returned in memory to him.

His message to the Krauskopfs asked if they would be there that night. He went on to ask if they knew of reports about early expeditions in search of rare gas vents, or military bases. Had they read *The Mysterious Island*? They were perhaps the only people besides Zeke who might be able to help him find references to Nemo's gas stations in the Pacific, or offer clues to Verne's place in Nemo's plan—was he agent or mere messenger?

Several hours later, Serengetti moved a bit shakily off the aircraft and into the wide open-air walkways of Honolulu International. His senses came instantly alive to the smell of warm salt air and some of the more than 7,000 different species of plants in the islands. There was a paucity of plant species in the Arctic, few of these had flowers, and fewer still any fragrance; he felt blasted by the assault of color and odor.

By the time he reached the concourse, most of the passengers who had departed before him had already rushed off to the parade of solar trolleys that snaked down Ala Moana Boulevard to the beachfront hotels at Waikiki. A few of the passengers who were going on to Tokyo and Hong Kong, or Jakarta or Sydney, made their way to the showers and massage rooms where they could recuperate and rest before the long flights to those distant terminals. As for Serengetti, he had made arrangements to meet the Krauskopfs at the Still Archives that evening, but he found anticipation difficult.

After a while, he walked almost absently to the public bus stop and took the first solar carriage to Aloha Towers, where he got off and began walking toward the Maritime Center, but when he felt the Pacific breeze on his face he stopped. Closing his eyes for a moment, he inhaled deeply as he remembered the first day he had taken his stepchildren to see the ocean here. He looked around, suddenly and awkwardly afraid that he might be recognized. He was wearing a tan bush shirt with shoulder epaulette straps. On the left sleeve, over the small pocket that held the tiny disc of library data, he had stitched a small circular patch. The patch was decorated with a polar bear and an antique airship, the twin symbols of Wellman Station, more than fifteen thousand kilometers away on almost the exact opposite side of the earth. Irrationally, he imagined one of the hundreds of Chinese tourists in their Hawai'ian shirts suddenly pointing at him, shouting "Look! Look! There is the explorer who discovered the *Nautilus*!" He clapped a hand over the patch and walked away from the Maritime Center.

He had a deep-seated feeling that he should not have come.

* * *

Kurosawa was staring at one of his HDTVs, the one that broadcast a continuous feed from a Glöbnet webcam mounted atop Aloha Towers in Honolulu. As Kurosawa watched, Paolo Serengetti seemed to hesitate as he walked toward the Maritime Center. Kurosawa followed these movements with intense interest. Serengetti was supposed to be returning to Europe from Bermuda. Instead he appeared to be headed for the Maritime archives. When the archaeologist veered away from the archives building and began walking toward Chinatown, the Director sighed. Time was critical, and one misstep could prove disastrous.

Having reviewed Larsen's messages, Kurosawa, for reasons of his own, was now convinced that Nemo had assembled his submarine on either Lang or Verlaten islands in the Pacific. The exact location of the initial construction, however, was of no great concern. Both islands had been blown off the face of the earth by the eruption of Krakatau in late August of 1883. It was Kurosawa's hypothesis that Nemo, knowing that his construction base was fundamentally unstable, had searched for a new base, most likely somewhere in the Arctic, at a place that was accessible to him, yet difficult for others to find or reach.

Unlike his field team, Kurosawa was only mildly surprised by the identity of the submarine. Many years earlier, during his graduate studies, he had been one of four first-year students invited to a lunch with a scientist famous for her theory of human social evolution centered on female-dominant coastal societies. As interested as Kurosawa had been in her thesis, he found himself paying more attention to the heavily-lined corners of the woman's eyes. As she recited the well-known outlines of her ideas, he noticed that she did so with scant enthusiasm, like a politician who had given the same speech several dozen times too often. She ended her weary soliloquy by telling the assembled graduate students that, after a long career in academia she was convinced that nothing ever really happened. Theories were vapors, conferences were ego-fluff, and at the end of fifty years of research she felt no closer to a solution to the problems of human evolution than when she started. With that she rose from the table, remarking as she did so that the food served at the luncheon was inedible, that she was extremely tired and had a long flight back to Jo-burg, and that she did not care to answer any questions.

Recalling that long-ago lunch, Kurosawa thought of the submarine his team had just found in the Arctic, and how he had spent the preponderance of his own long career learning that eventually almost everything happens, including, often, the unforeseen, and, occasionally, the unthinkable. Aberrations dropped like acorns. No one, not Archer nor any of his other deputies knew about the POW reports in the sub-basement. Those damning reports alone could spell the end of Kurosawa's Directorate and its long-range mission. And that was hardly all. None of his deputies were aware that it was this same Directorate that had hidden the Peking Man fossils from the Allies after the war.

Nor was it likely that any of them would ever learn the true reason why Kurosawa would have little trouble believing that Jules Verne's *Nautilus* might be more than a fiction. The sub-basement held another report, and this one had been passed personally from Director to Director for nearly a century now. Kurosawa was the only person alive who knew of its existence. That report was the basis for every action Kurosawa had taken for the past forty years.

In 1920, an old, powerfully-built sailor dropped dead after a bar fight in the Japanese port of Sasebo. Amongst the meager personal effects found on the body were a gold pocket watch engraved on the outside cover with an ornate letter "N," and on the inside of the cover with the phrase "Mission 46." A small photograph found in the sailor's wallet showed a dozen sailors and their captain. The men were standing just forward of the conning tower of a strange-looking submarine boat, and this submarine in turn appeared to be floating under an iron archway emblazoned with the same letter "N" as that on the watch.

The circumstances of the foreigner's death were just suspicious enough to warrant a local autopsy. The report of that examination, along with the sailor's personal effects, found its way to the predecessor agency of Kurosawa's Directorate. The photograph was eventually dated to 1865, but it was sixty years before one of Kurosawa's own geographic specialists identified the area in the background as Verlaten Island in the southwestern Pacific.

As unprecedented data flowed into his secure monitor from Larsen's console in the Arctic, Kurosawa had feared explosive revelations from the submarine's library, but Serengetti's report struck him as rather pedestrian. According to Serengetti, the library contained a large collection of standard nineteenth-century expedition reports, some classical literature, and some period novels. There were no primary records, no logbook, no engineering papers, and no letters. All in all, thought Kurosawa, a considerable relief.

Kurosawa had feared, since the first report from Larsen, that the submarine might hold essential papers that could reveal the design behind the genetic experiment the Directorate had been conducting for over a century. He worried that Serengetti, who had considerable experience in the Arctic, might uncover any such material. It was for this reason that Kurosawa had tried to eliminate him two days earlier as he explored Foyn Island. It was too great a risk to keep him around as the Directorate closed in on the *Nautilus*. It was simple bad luck that Captain Jørriksen had decided on her own accord to put Commander Johansson on shore and had saved the doctor.

According to Serengetti's meager findings, there was nothing on board the *Nautilus* that need trouble Kurosawa now. No references to the band of twelve immortal explorers and their leader who had built the submarine, nor evidence of their places of origin, nor, most importantly, any evidence of the uniqueness of their bodies. No mention of Mission 46, which Kurosawa had long ago decided was both scientific and extraterrestrial in origin. Nothing that Serengetti might let slip to an inconvenient list-serv. Kurosawa's own primary mission was still a secret, and he intended to keep it that way.

Kurosawa turned his attention to more immediate matters. The message he'd so eagerly anticipated had arrived from Captain Jørriksen. The past twenty-four hours had been the most intense of his life, and the next day promised to be more so. Kurosawa tapped a brief message of reply, and attached a detailed set of orders that he had drawn up hours earlier. There was no more to be done now. He would have to live with the result, one way or another. He went out to his balcony and sat behind his spotting scope. Soon he was studying the junks in the harbor, intrigued by the sail rig of one of the smaller coastal junks in the ocean beyond his window. The sun was just beginning to set, the ships in the harbor casting long, wavering shadows. At length he decided that the junk's mainmast was hewn from the heart of a chestnut tree. He turned the focus ring of his spotting scope to look more closely at the silk fan-shaped Chinese sails and guessed that they had been stitched by hand, probably in a shop in Hanoi where such work was still performed at reasonable rates. Kurosawa continued to study the junk as he considered his next move.

* * *

Serengetti continued to hurry away from the Maritime Center, walking northwest, towards Chinatown. He couldn't shake the feeling that he was being pursued, being watched. Yet each time he looked around, no one was there.

As a student, there had been a small Chinese café and shop near the Yong Sing restaurant where one could eat cheaply and drink huge amounts of native coffee mixed with chocolate and cream. Few tourists knew of it, and it was the one significant place on Oahu that he had discovered on his own during his graduate student days. Not even Zeke Warner had known of it, so Serengetti had a special feeling for the place. He had even forced himself to learn a few words of Mandarin, just so he could offer a greeting to the owner in his native dialect. As a result, he had always beenmade to feel welcome there.

At the corner of Merchant and Alakea he was stopped by the traffic light. As he waited for it to turn, he felt again that sense of dread: someone was watching him, following him. He waited for a moment, then turned suddenly. No one was there. When he turned back again, he saw a white-haired old man approaching him. Serengetti felt the awkwardness of someone trapped on a corner as one of the stateless approached.

Ever since the buyout, the numbers of stateless had grown, which placed increasingly greater pressure on limited resources, especially water and electricity. Water had long been strictly rationed in the peripheral states. There was even talk that the New British Empire would soon begin to ration access to both electricity and bandwidth. The old, consoleless man who approached Serengetti was almost tottering, and though it was a very warm evening he wore a knit cap tilted crazily on his head. Before Serengetti could move away the old man spoke.

"Can you help me?" he asked.

Serengetti pretended to not hear him.

"Please help me," the man repeated.

Serengetti ignored him, wishing the traffic light would change so he could cross the street and retreat to his favorite hole in the wall. He could see the sign for the Yong Sing. He was almost there.

"I am disabled," the old man continued. But Serengetti averted his glance as best he could. He caught only a brief glimpse of the stateless man's gray eyes.

"I need food."

Serengetti rolled his eyes, and looked straight ahead. Finally, the light changed and Serengetti hurried across the road. Behind him he heard the old man's pleas.

"I have a blood clot in my head and a pacemaker in my heart."

As he reached the far curb, Serengetti realized that he could have given the old man the half sandwich he'd brought with him from the airport bar. Quickening his step, he reached the shop and hurried through the door. He did not hear the man call out to him one last time: "Maybe, then, I can help you?"

Nothing was familiar. The low paper lights he remembered with such fondness, the quiet corners, the darkness, all were gone, replaced with garish, flowing neon. Where he remembered a certain dignified quietude, there was now the general noise level of a nightclub. An earnest, middle-aged Asian was engaged in a hopeless attempt at karaoke, a heavily inebriated and hoarse travesty of Sinatra's effortless "Stardust." His discovery, Serengetti thought sadly, had been discovered. And ruined.

"Where is Mr. Lee?" Serengetti asked the bartender in Mandarin. When the woman shook her head, he asked again in English.

"Mr. Lee? Is he here?"

"You mean the old guy who used to own the place?"

"Yes, is he here?"

"Sorry. He died years ago."

Serengetti thought he might as well stay for coffee, but the bartender told him the coffee maker was broken. He thanked her and left the shop, glancing around as he did so. The stateless man was gone. Serengetti walked quickly back toward the Maritime Center. He now wanted nothing more than to get through his two meetings and return to the West Fjord.

* * *

It would be imprecise to say that Dr. and Mrs. Krauskopf had not aged, Serengetti decided. They were a few degrees more stooped.

Was their skin now the texture of parchment? Nevertheless, they were still functioning, still moderately robust and alert. He had entered their special collections room, where they were engaged in a lively discussion with a visiting researcher. As Serengetti signed the guest book, he heard them expounding on a 1920s expedition to the Big Island in search of a rare species of butterfly.

The Krauskopfs had been reading and cataloguing scientific reports for decades. They had collected expedition reports as a hobby almost from the moment they had met in 1962. Their annotative knowledge of these reports was the equivalent of the scribblings on the card catalogues of the largest extant marine library collections: irreplaceable. When the doctor had retired from his practice three decades later, they'd moved to Honolulu. There they donated their entire collection to the Still Maritime Archives. Despite the mixed reaction of the Board of the Archives, they donated their time as well. Three days a week, they could be found in the mahogany room that they had paid for themselves, lovingly tending their rare books the way some retirees tend flowers.

This room had not changed a mote since his last visit. It was crammed with polished, dark brown bookcases with glass fronts, surrounding an elegant hexagon table where Dr. and Mrs. Krauskopf held court. Every time he had visited as a doctoral student, they had made certain to tell him that this table had been brought to the Pacific by none other than Captain William Bligh himself. They had rescued it from oblivion in Samoa, removed seven coats of paint, lovingly restored it, and added it to this room overlooking Honolulu Harbor. On one wall were a series of hand-colored prints of now-extinct Pacific birds, and in one corner the framed Nobel Prize in physiology awarded to von Schatzhausen in 1937. This room was both the sum total of their lives together and their gift to the Hawaiian people.

When the other researcher had taken her butterfly report to a reading table in an adjacent room, Serengetti announced himself.

"Doctor!" said Mrs. K, smiling as if she had awaited his arrival for months.

"How are you, son?" asked Dr. K. A retired surgeon, Dr. K. never felt obliged to refer to a mere Ph.D. as "doctor."

"I've been well," Serengetti lied, wincing slightly when they asked after his children. He explained the reason for his sudden visit. He needed an obscure piece of information, and he didn't have much time. He wondered what might happen to the ventricles of their ancient hearts if he told them about the library he had so recently explored. His request triggered a flood of references.

"Of course," said Dr. K. "You've no doubt read that the U.S. government wrote several reports prior to the Second World War about the possibility that two nineteenth-century submarine bases existed in the Pacific. We have one of the only surviving copies."

Serengetti nodded. He had never heard of this, but he hated to appear stupid in front of the Krauskopfs. Mrs. K was already up from her wooden chair, searching the stacks behind the sitting room for the precise archival box.

"Yes," she called from the stacks. "There were oblique indications in these old reports that the U.S. Navy knew of the existence of such antique bases."

"By the way," said Dr. K. "Have you sent us all of your reprints?"

It was almost an accusation. There was never any charge to use these archives. The *quid pro quo* was that you had to send copies of your scholarly articles if you wished to return. Serengetti lied that he had, making a mental note to do so.

"Do we have a current picture of you on file?" asked Mrs. K, arriving back at the table with a gray archival box cradled in her arms.

"Um, no. But I'll make sure to get you on as soon as I get back to my office."

"Here you are," said Dr. K., taking the report from the box and searching through it. "Here, here, here, here. Here it is. The Navy never found these suspected bases. But apparently both the U.S. Navy and the Imperial Navy believed that the other knew where they were."

Serengetti was not interested in World War II history. He tried to change the subject.

"Is it possible," he asked, "that these bases could have been located on volcanic islands, and destroyed before anyone could find them?"

"If they were located anywhere near Krakatoa, they might have been destroyed when it exploded," said Mrs. K.

"Did I ever tell you that this table came from William Bligh himself?" asked Dr. K.

"You're kidding," was all Serengetti could think to say. He was getting a touch impatient.

"Yes, and it took forever to get it here from Samoa, where we found it in a second-hand bookstore. I recognized it right away. Only six-sided desk outside of England, I said. Has to be rare."

"Let me ask you," said Serengetti, hoping against hope that he might get somewhere quickly. "What can you tell me about any expeditions that might have looked for sources of rare gases in the Pacific? I'm wondering specifically about xenon gas."

"Well," Mrs. Krauskopf said, not missing a beat. "It is well-known that xenon is named for the Greek word for stranger. It is a rare gas that was first extracted from the atmosphere by Ramsey and Travers in 1898."

These facts were anything but well-known. It was possible that Serengetti was talking to two of the only people in the world who still retained such lodes of knowledge inside their own skulls, who did not rely on the hope that all information was invariably to be found in some Glöbnet database.

"Wasn't that the same series of experiments when they also isolated from the atmosphere neon, krypton and radon?" Dr. Krauskopf queried.

"You know, I believe that is exactly true," his wife replied. "And these were critical for establishing—"

Serengetti interrupted again. "You say this was done in 1898? There is no record of xenon gas being isolated before 1898?" "Well, that is the first time it shows up in the literature," said Mrs. K., matter-of-factly. As any scientist knew, if it wasn't in the literature, it had no cognitive right to exist, or it never happened. Take your pick.

"But you know these nineteenth-century scientists," said Dr. K. "They might have found it twenty years earlier and just not gotten around to publishing. Who knows? Maybe one of them was too busy collecting butterflies, or flying hydrogen balloons, or playing Mozart, and didn't get around to it.

"I'll tell you, not like today. Not like today," Dr. K. said, shifting his bulk by grasping his cane with both hands and sort of half-pole-vaulting his bulk to the other side of his large leather armchair. "These young scientists today don't know diddly-squat, and they rush to publish what they don't know before their competitors do. And their competitors usually know less than diddly."

Serengetti might have enjoyed engaging them in a conversation on the current state of scholarly ethics, but he didn't have much time to spare.

"Is it possible that a terrestrial source for xenon gas exists?" Serengetti asked.

"You know," said Mrs. K, "now that we are talking about it, yes. Yes. Gabon has been mentioned, but in the Pacific I seem to remember something about a report of an expedition to the islands near Java, written by Iverson, I believe, in 1856. He mentions that one of his researchers measured several different reactive gases on the flanks of Krakatoa, as well as on several outliers where gases previously unknown to science were detected."

"Wasn't that the same expedition where they found the vent creatures 150 years before the Alvin Group found them?" interrupted Dr. K.

"I think you are thinking of the results published in an obscure German journal from that same year," corrected Mrs. K. "They were later translated and published in the *Silliman Journal* at Yale. You know, that is a fascinating story. It seems that none of the 1970s team of Americans could read German, and—"

"I want to thank you so much," Serengetti said, interrupting the interruption. "I'm very sorry, but I have to meet Dr. Warner in two hours on the Big Island. As usual, you have been a godsend. Thank you so much."

He had learned nothing. It had been a long shot, anyway. Maybe the meeting with Zeke would be more productive.

"Wait," said Dr. K., as he read from the end of the report Mrs. K. had found in the stacks. "You've missed the best part of the story of the submarine base report from before the war."

Serengetti stopped himself with difficulty.

"Yes?"

"Yes," said Dr. K. "According to this report, as early as 1933 the U.S. not only suspected that there was a base right here, on the flank of one of the islands, but they were convinced that the Japanese had a similar report and knew the exact location. The U.S. apparently believed that it was only a matter of time before the Japanese attacked and claimed it for themselves!"

* * *

Serengetti stopped short. He sat down again.

"Let me understand. You're saying that the Nipponese attacked Pearl Harbor because they wanted an undersea base for submarines that was supposedly constructed in the nineteenth-century!? But that is absurd!" said Serengetti, even though, as he spoke these last words, a familiar queasiness began to crawl back into his stomach.

"I know," said Dr. K. "Ridiculous, isn't it? Of course, that was not the only reason for the attack, but from this point in time it is impossible to know how large a part it played in their calculations."

"And just who did this report claim was building a submarine base here in the nineteenth century?" Serengetti asked, speaking softly and cheerfully and forcing himself to appear as uninterested as possible.

"No one knows," replied Mrs. K. Her face, as he had always remembered it, wore a mask of completely objective innocence.

"Ah!" said Dr. K, suddenly brightening. "Maybe it was Captain Nemo!"

And then they both laughed at this fictionally plausible-factually implausible explanation. When Serengetti realized that he was being conspicuous by not joining them, he tried to laugh too. But he felt an electric jolt, a sharp surge of adrenaline to his heart. He looked into the reading room, to make sure the women researcher was not listening, but she had turned around and was listening to them intently. She was laughing, too. Christ, thought Serengetti.

"So," he said, after waiting for an appropriate moment. "If no one has ever seen this Japanese report, where in the world did the rumor ever start that such a base ever existed?"

"Actually," said Mrs. K. "Dr. K is not being entirely silly. As you read while you were flying here, Jules Verne wrote of a Pacific submarine base in *The Mysterious Island*. And then, about five years ago, when ms4 was found, and that margin notation was found about the Italian engineer…"

"ms4?"

"Yes, the fourth manuscript," answered Dr. K. "The fourth manuscript of what?"

"Of the novel, of course," said Mrs. K. It was like trying to hold a conversation with a stereo. Serengetti was about to give up when Dr. K answered.

"*20,000 Leagues Under the Seas*, of course," said Dr. K., and he gave his wife a lightening-quick frown as if to say, 'They simply do not train these people anymore.'

"There had always been talk that Jules Verne wrote four separate versions of *20,000 Leagues Under the Seas*," continued Mrs. K., almost as if talking to an idiot. "But ms4, the final version, disappeared, and was all but considered a myth until it was found five years ago."

Serengetti felt himself on the edge of either absolute clarity or total insanity. He could tip either way. The room seemed like it was beginning to rotate.

"This fourth manuscript. You say it had a notation in it about an engineer?"

"An Italian engineer, yes, named Tizzoni."

"And he visited the islands when?"

"I don't remember all of the details," said Mrs. K. "But I seem to recall that there was no date. There was simply a notation in Verne's hand that a real submarine base existed, in the islands, in the 1860s."

"That's right," said Dr. K. "Now I remember it too. And this Tizzoni. Bold, fascinating man. Used a primitive diving suit around the islands in an attempt to find the place, but never did."

"He then gave up," said Mrs. K.

"Is there anything else known about this Italian?" asked Serengetti.

"Only that the search for this base became something of an obsession with him." This from Mrs. K. "Supposedly, ms4 contained hints that there was a third base. Which makes some sense, since Nemo said that he set up his workshops in the middle of the ocean. And 'workshops,' plural, means there may even have been more than that, even though he only mentions one deserted island."

"A third submarine base? Here in the Pacific?"

"Yes and no. Yes, there was a third base, and no, Tizzoni never found it. Because it wasn't located in the Pacific."

"Do you remember where the third base was *supposed* to have been located?" Serengetti was now half-sitting, half-standing at the edge of his chair. This was why he had come. He was ready to run from the room once he possessed this knowledge.

"No," said Mrs. K., and Serengetti slowly deflated back into his chair. It was getting late. He had to go. Dr. K was himself now having trouble keeping his eyes open. The lids fluttered briefly and then closed. "But then we haven't been able to travel for many years now. So we never had a chance to look at the manuscript ourselves."

"Where is it now?" asked Serengetti, getting his notes together and rising to leave.

"In the Verne Archives, of course," said Mrs. K. "In Paris."

"Paris," Serengetti said, and stopped. His gaze was suddenly far away. The organizing, Ph.D. part of his mind tried to put the pieces together, but they flew apart. Another mental discipline was required. An Ouija board perhaps. He needed to consult the mystic half of Zeke's mind right away.

"Thank you once again. It has been wonderful to see you both again."

"Don't mention it," said Dr. K., suddenly rousing himself with a cursory snort. "Just remember to send us your reprints for our files. It's been five years since the last. I assume you are still publishing? And a current picture. And not one of those hot-dog digigraphs either. Are your kids here with you? Here, here's a few credits for the ice cream stand outside. Treat them for me."

Serengetti took the money. There was little use in explaining. He thanked them both again, and hurried out.

"A wonderful fellow," Dr. K. remarked after Serengetti had left. "Not like the crum bums who run *this* place. Can't even get a credit from them for environmental controls."

"He used to be generous with his reprints, too," added Mrs. K. "But you know, I think we might have him confused with Dr. Serrano from Mexico City."

"Serrano. Serrano. He's the high altitude man, right?"

"Yes, he organized the 2007 pre-Incan high altitude archaeological excavations that seemed to indicate a dental connection with the Mexica around 1,200 AD," stated Mrs. K.

"Right. Right," said Dr. K. "That was the same expedition that isolated the myocardial proteins in the human coprolites, I think." He paused as she nodded. Then he added, "Did he send us his reprints?"

* * *

Serengetti's flight from Oahu landed at Kona International Airport on the Big Island. On the flight over he'd had just enough time to send his thoughts on ms4 to Larsen. He suggested that they meet in Oslo; better yet, Paris. But once he disembarked, his focus abruptly shifted. Zeke Warner and two young Hawaiians were waiting for him.

"My God, is it good to see you," Serengetti said as he grasped Warner's massive hand.

"Aloha, Dr. Serengetti," Warner replied with a wide smile. "I want you to say hello to my sons."

"My God," Serengetti said again. Was it possible? "These are your boys? Those same boys who swam with us at the Black Sand Beach?"

"The very same little brats. The last time you saw them, they were nine and twelve."

Serengetti looked at these two young men. The seventeen-year-old was taller than Serengetti and almost as powerfully built as his father. The fourteen-year-old was only slightly smaller. Both were handsome, friendly, only slightly awkward. As the boys turned to lead him from the waiting area, sharing some private joke and jostling each other back and forth, he felt his smile tighten almost imperceptibly. What would his stepson have looked like now, as a twenty-six-year-old? A grown man. But Benjamin had died thirteen years ago. The rush of the years hit him. Had it really been thirteen years? As the boys loaded his two bags into a natural gas van, Serengetti felt old. They drove about thirty miles north along Route 19 until they reached Warner's home on Waipio Bay.

Through a stroke of good luck, the anthropology department at the university had assigned Ezekiel Warner to be Serengetti's student mentor. At most universities, this relationship usually amounted to a brief chat over coffee, a chance to pick up department gossip on which professors one might profitably study under, and which to avoid altogether. But Warner took to his role as mentor with the determination of a father teaching a son to throw a curve ball. In the late summer of 2011, when Serengetti had walked into the graduate student cubicles for the first time, he found a small, carved double outrigger canoe on his desk. Standing in the canoe were two figures, one tall and thin, the other large and round. The large figure was naked to the waist, and held a wide-bladed canoe paddle, while the slight figure was clothed in shorts and a tee shirt, and held a length of fishing line. The line trailed behind the canoe to a beautifully carved miniature turtle. On the turtle's back were painted the letters *Ph.D.* On the slight figure's tee shirt were painted the letters *U.S.C.G.*

The image was unmistakable. Warner, the navigator and canoe maker, would teach Serengetti to navigate his way into waters from which he could land the degree he sought. From that singular moment, the outsider, the orphan, was made to feel as if he belonged in the islands. But more than acceptance into a place, Warner saw to it that Serengetti would become a part of an ancient seagoing clan. Warner's clan traced its routes, through oral legends, back nearly a thousand years, to the first voyaging canoe to land in the Hawaiian Islands. His very name was an Anglicization of *wa'a wa'a*, the Polynesian word for canoe.

When they arrived, the boys piled out and ran for their consoles. Warner had bought them the new version of "Deathmarcher" and they had fought over it all day.

"Here we are," said Warner. "We set up a bed for you in the guest cottage. I thought that tomorrow we could sail over to Molokini and show you the site."

"Zeke, I'm sorry. I can't stay that long. I just found out that I've got to head back to Europe tomorrow."

"Impossible!"

"I wish it were. But if I don't get back there right away, I don't get funded next year." Serengetti would have liked to fly out immediately, but there was no convenient route back to Paris until the next afternoon. He knew that ms4 was waiting in an archival box on a shelf in Paris. He wanted to make certain that he was the first person to see it.

"Always in a rush. Well, let's get inside and see what Elizabeth has cooked for us. What do you say? One of these years you need to screw the funding and come back here and relax for awhile."

"Believe me, I have promised myself that for years now," Serengetti lied. "But I have to catch the 1700 flight."

* * *

Just after 1000, after the dinner dishes had been cleared away, Warner's wife went to bed and his two sons disappeared with his van, off to meet some friends for a late night party. Warner and Serengetti sat on the edge of a small porch off the living room, drinking beer.

They were too far away to hear any surf, but Serengetti could smell the salt air and almost feel the ocean surge as it broke along the shore on this northwestern-most corner of the islands.

"You're not afraid of the boys getting into trouble?"

Warner only laughed.

"This is the "Big Island," he said. "But it is still an island. There is nowhere on this island where I myself did not hide from my father. They know I would find them sooner or later. Besides, the sooner they grow up, the sooner I can retire!"

"You've never worked. How can you retire?"

"Ah, but there you are wrong. It is a full-time job to guide lost souls like you through the wild and unpredictable jungles of academia. I've been the graduate student coordinator for more than twelve years! And in that time, fifteen of my personal charges have finished their doctorates and flown away. You, of course, flew the farthest."

"Zeke, I saw Wilson this morning in Bermuda." Was it really only this morning? The take-off from Europe now seemed as if it had occurred about a million years ago. And in just a few hours he would be on his way back, with a crushing jet-lag hangover.

"I know. A few hours after I received your e-post saying that you were coming, I got an e-post from Wilson."

Jesus H. Christ, thought Serengetti. Wilson and his big mouth. Goddammit! Was there anyone left in the world who did not now know what he and Larsen had found in the West Fjord?

"He mentioned your visit, and then asked me to send him everything I had on the vent at Molokini. Seems like a strange combination of events: your visit to the BI; Wilson's request for the vent data—especially since he wasn't very clear about why he wanted it. Something about comparing it with a vent site in the North Atlantic."

Amazing, thought Serengetti. Wilson McHargue and discretion: almost an oxymoron.

"Do you have any idea what he's onto?"

"Yes," said Serengetti. There was no point in denying it. For all he knew, McHargue had already told him everything anyway.

"Look, Zeke, before I go into all this, I need you to tell me what's going on at Molokini. All Wilson knows is that you found a vent on the back wall, one that is giving off xenon gas. How did it happen?"

It had never been Warner's way to hold back anything that he knew of the Pacific, in part because the subject was so vast that he himself was learning something new almost every day. His own ancestors had sailed on these waters for thousands of years and never saw but a fraction of it. So he wasn't about to start treating his ocean like a lock-drawer of secrets now. Still, as he took a long pull on his beer, he looked Serengetti over. Serengetti, always five steps ahead of every other student. Thin, washed-out and weary now, he thought. Or was he?

"C'mon," Warner said at last, rising. "Let's go into the study. I've got something to show you."

* * *

The working table in Warner's study had been cut—one might say hacked—from a single plank of koa wood. Two small squares had been incised to make room for consoles, and along the back of the table, where it met the wall, rested a wide screen flat monitor. Light harp music played softly from a hidden CD player. The speakers were placed along long tiers of bookshelves, bookshelves that groaned under the weight of the journals of Wallis, Cook, Bougainville, Banks, Bligh, Darwin, Dampier, and dozens of others, along with the recorded legends of a hundred different islands. Serengetti admired again Warner's complete run of the field bulletins of the Bishop Museum. These landmarks in Pacific archaeology stretched back over a century, to the first field surveys by Kenneth Emory.

Warner retrieved a series of data tapes from one of the shelves and placed one of them into the console nearest the monitor. Instantly, the monitor showed Warner on board a moderately sized outrigger canoe skimming through the channel between two islands.

The camera must be mounted at the very point of the bow of the canoe, Serengetti thought, continuously recording the whole trip.

"That is the channel that separates Maui from Kahoolawee," Warner said. Serengetti thought he recognized it himself, but it had been a long time since he had had a chance to sail around the islands.

"I see you're not exactly exerting yourself during these research trips."

"Now you know why I give my sons so much slack. Already they're both better sailors than me, and my youngest can land an outrigger over the surf better than anyone I've ever seen. The oldest is an expert with knots. When they sail, it gives me a chance to sit back and observe. It's amazing how many coastal details I saw for the first time after they started to handle the canoe."

Serengetti watched as Warner's son navigated the canoe to within a few meters of the back wall of the dead volcano. He watched as Warner tapped his console, apparently searching for the right GPS reading. Then, at a signal, his oldest son dropped anchor. They were just above and nearly flush with the flank of Molokini's underwater caldera. Rather than enter the open end of the caldera, Warner had stopped on the opposite side, away from the fishing and tourist charters.

"Now for the fun part," said Warner.

Serengetti watched as Warner donned a liquid oxygen tank, flopped over the side, and descended down the exterior caldera wall. But instead of a long drift down the Back Wall, the anthropologist returned only a few moments later, surfacing at the ladder that hung from the foreward outrigger. Clambering back on board, Warner called to his younger son to unreel a tiny underwater camera, while Warner himself went into the outrigger's small cabin and sat down in front of a monitor.

"You suspected that there was a submerged *loko kuapa* here?" Serengetti asked, using the Hawai'ian words for a seawater fishpond. These prehistoric rock-walled enclosures were constructed to harvest the best-tasting fish for the chiefs. For all others, the schools in these fishponds were *kapu*, off-limits.

"Let me tell you," said Warner. "For ten years I've been diving on this wall, always within ten meters of the surface. It never occurred to me that I might want to look deeper. What for? Even during the Little Ice Age, the water level was not more than five meters lower than it is now. And there was no human occupation of the islands at any time previous to the Little Ice Age, so there was no reason to look any further down."

As they watched, the data tape showed the brilliantly colored marine life clinging to the back wall. Serengetti also noticed a persistent stream of bubbles moving to the surface, almost along the same track taken by Warner's remote camera as it descended. The camera dropped slowly along the wall, along the outer rim of the dormant volcano.

"Jesus!" shouted Serengetti. "What is that!"

An enormous green form knocked the camera from its course, then continued on its way. The camera swung crazily, then returned to its previous position.

"Whale shark," said Warner, enjoying Serengetti's reaction. "Harmless. Must be about fifteen meters long. I thought you'd like that. But he's only the sideshow. The main event is below."

As the camera renewed its descent, Serengetti studied the depth readings on the monitor. The camera was now below seventy-five meters, approaching what looked like a large underwater ledge, or shelf.

"There," said Warner, and the underwater camera passed ninety meters. Serengetti watched as the bottom came into focus.

"My God," was all he could think to say.

"Your God is different from my Gods," said Warner. "But my reaction was pretty much the same."

A curved, solid, and obviously artificial wall of rock rose at least five meters off the bottom of the ledge. At the center of the U-shaped enclosure, gas bubbles trickled from the vent.

"If that's a fishpond," said Serengetti. "It's the biggest one ever created."

"Yes," said Warner. "And it's nearly one hundred meters underwater."

"If that was built by humans..."

"A geochronologist colleague at SOEST estimated that sea levels would have been low enough for this dock to have been built—"

"It must have been at least 15,000 years ago," Serengetti breathed.

"The best minds from your alma mater, the honorable School of Ocean and Earth Sciences, estimate 16,450 years, give or take a generation."

* * *

Serengetti was dumbstruck.

"You've surveyed the whole structure?"

"For two field seasons now," said Warner. "What I'm showing you is the biggest discovery of my life. Unfortunately, I can't announce it yet because I don't have a clue what it is. I'm not about to push the colonization of my islands back 15,000 years without a damn good reason."

"My God," said Serengetti again. "It's brilliant. How far does this thing extend?"

"That's the most interesting part," said Warner, as Serengetti stood mesmerized by the images coming from the camera. "From this bow in that U-shaped end, to the opposite end of the structure, is exactly seventy-five meters. If this was built by humans, it was accomplished when much of the oceans were locked up in ice and sea levels were a hundred meters lower than today. Although, for the life of me, I haven't yet been able to imagine what the enclosure is for."

Serengetti could imagine it.

"Those bubbles," he said. "That is the xenon vent?"

"The very same. But that didn't really concern me. I let the geochemists study stuff like that. I am only interested in the wall. It's extraordinary, isn't it? It's almost as if someone had designed this structure in order to be able to harvest the gas. I know that sounds crazy. But so far I really have no solid hypothesis to account for its purpose. Until I do, everybody keeps quiet."

Earlier, with the Krauskopfs, Serengetti had wondered about the possibility of a submarine base in the islands in the nineteenth century. The possibility of a *prehistoric* submarine dock, a submarine dock constructed ten millennia before the Egyptians built their first pyramid, had not occurred to him. No wonder neither the U.S. Navy nor the Imperial Fleet could find the undersea base they sought and fought for. Even if they had managed to stumble onto it, the discovery would have meant little to them, and they would have been unable to exploit the enclosure or the xenon militarily. This base was of value only to someone with entirely different needs.

"Unbelievable," said Serengetti, as he stared at the bubbles making their way past the camera to the surface. Was it possible that Nemo had wandered the oceans of the world for tens of thousands of years? Or even longer? Twenty thousand biographies have been written about the single life of Napoleon. Serengetti wondered how one wrote the biography of a man who could live 20,000 lives? For the first time, he glimpsed the dimensions of his search. Suddenly, ms4 did not seem so important. Just another tile in a mosaic the size of Wyoming.

"You know," he said at last. "This may sound strange, but it doesn't seem crazy to me at all."

"You are one of the few people I trust with this information," Warner said, causing Serengetti to wince slightly. Trust. It occurred to him how much he had come to hate that word. The artifact in the West Fjord was taking its toll, and taking it rapidly.

"Since you are here, I want to know what you make of it?"

"Zeke, let me ask *you* something."

"Shoot."

"How long did it take before you felt confident, I mean really confident, that you could navigate to any spot in the Pacific?"

Warner laughed.

"No one possesses that sort of confidence. Any one who says they do is a fool. Or a genius! It took my ancestors 5,000 years to reach the limits of this ocean, and by most estimates there were still over a thousand uninhabited islands when they stopped exploring."

"But suppose this ocean were completely new to you. I mean, suppose your ancestors had not lived around its edge for a hundred thousand years before you stuck your toe in the water for the first time."

"You mean, if I had to learn it all from scratch?"

"Exactly."

"I don't know. It's a good question."

"And if you were trying to return to one single spot in this whole ocean? A single spot you had failed to mark somehow, or had forgotten its precise location?"

"Then you're talking about a very long time. Maybe forever."

"Forever," said Serengetti, ruminating on everything he had heard and seen since meeting with McHargue in Bermuda. There could be perhaps only one explanation for it all. And that explanation filled him with a horrible sadness.

"Zeke," he said finally. "You know Pacific mythology better than anyone I know. Can you think of any references to a person, to a people, a culture, even to a god or gods, someone who is lost and can't find their way home?"

Warner looked at Serengetti closely, and for a brief and unfamiliar moment felt himself wondering whether or not he should answer.

"As you know, Ta'aroa, the Polynesian god of the sea, looks after navigators when they are lost. I myself have had reason to appeal to him once or twice. But I expect that is not what you mean."

"Not exactly."

"Well, I would say that our places of refuge, our *pu'uhonua*, might be what you are getting at. These are sacred areas, thought to protect and to shelter those who are able to reach them in a storm."

"And these *pu'uhonua* were very different from *heiau*?"

"Yes, if only in scale," said Warner, not unmindful that Serengetti, like most *haole*, subconsciously or not referred to his culture in the past tense. It was not done maliciously, he thought, but it was there nonetheless. "Where a *heiau* is a ceremonial platform, the *pu'uhonua* can be an entire district, or the distance from a mountain to the sea. Its limits are set only by the will of the chief. It is a place of refuge during wartime."

"So they were only used as safe harbor during tribal conflicts?"

"No. They can be used at any time, by anyone who breaks the *kapu*. If you break the *kapu*, you can escape to the *pu'uhonua* and you will not be killed. But… you will have to stay there for a time, in order to placate the gods for your transgression."

"And once you had done your time?"

"Well," said Warner, smiling. "Then you are allowed to return home."

Serengetti thought all of this over.

"How about another beer," he said finally.

"Of course."

They made their way to the kitchen, then back to the porch, where they sat down with their beers. Serengetti looked up at the stars overhead, an infinite chart.

"Zeke, I have something to tell you."

And he gave Warner a hypothesis for that data at Molokini. He thought it unlikely that Warner would write it up any time soon. They stayed up until just a few hours before dawn, when jet lag finally caught up with Serengetti and he fell asleep on the rumpled settee on Warner's porch.

* * *

He was alone, hovering over a seamount, a pillar of volcanic rock rising thirty thousand feet from the sea floor. But the summit of this seamount had never developed enough to break the surface. At least, not yet. The 'summit' of this mountain was nearly twenty meters below sea level. He was fully suited in his scuba gear, motionless, hovering with arms outstretched, looking down at the summit. He was suspended halfway between the summit and the surface of the sea.

Slowly he rotated his body, like a human windmill, until he faced the surface. He could see where the sun struck the surface, and knew he did not want to go there. He had to stay away from the heat of the sun. Ezekiel Warner was on the surface, leaning over the gunwale of his outrigger, leaning over and looking down at him, speaking to him. He could see Warner's mouth moving, and though he could not hear the words, somehow they registered in his brain.

"...skimming across the strait between Oahu and Maui...explore a submerged dormant volcano caldera..."

And then Warner was gone, and he rotated his body again, as if his body was hinged to pivot on the very Equator itself. Where was his liquid oxygen tank? Were his lungs filled with liquid oxygen, so that he could descend freely? If he could only reach that platform down there, on the summit, only a few feet away. But as he tried to maneuver his body downward, a massive bubble emerged from one particular vent in the submerged volcano. It swept him upward, toward the surface. Even before he broke the surface of the sea, he was blinded by the poisonous gas vented from the volcano.

He found himself sitting at the end of a worn and slippery old dock, with his feet dangling into a warm ocean. Warner was seated next to him and they sat in silent admiration as two separate and distinct suns rose on the horizon. For some reason this did not seem strange.

"There are anomalies all over the sky," Warner said in his deep, friendly voice.

"But this is not my sky," he heard himself saying.

"If you always look for patterns, you will never see where the pattern is broken."

"But can the anomalies take you from one place to another?"

They kept on talking like that, speaking in profound but incomprehensible gibberish. One of the two suns raced across the sky faster than the other.

"Not a military weapon at all," he heard Warner saying.

"No, but a very good one." What on earth did that mean?

He was feeling increasingly frustrated. He could understand little of what was being said.

"Was the violence and frustration the inability to find his way back to this anomaly?"

Yes, yes, he thought. Perhaps he was looking at it all wrong. There had to be an undersea portal somewhere near New Guinea. But the island blew up. Now it made perfect sense. "Remember the

Papuans!" he shouted. "They are the key. If you must strike, then strike! Strike through the mask!"

Then he found himself on a wide boulevard, and someone wanted to speak with him about governments, transnationals, ultra-wealthy private collectors. And a submarine voyage to the second star on the right.

* * *

"We are the people of the canoe, navigators of the winter sun, the clan that waits for the west wind."

Serengetti had heard this once before, during a similar ceremony a few weeks after he had first arrived in the islands. Now, as the sun shallowed the eastern horizon, he stood facing that sun and listening as Warner recited the words again. Warner was honoring a close friend who had died in a recent diving accident.

Warner's two boys were there, quietly observing from the edge of the Warner clan *heiau*. They looked tired, and Serengetti wondered if they had even been to bed yet. He was tired himself, having had only a few restless hours of sleep. As he looked at the boys, Serengetti realized how many times like this he had missed. Zeke's family life was with him and ahead of him, while Serengetti's was buried in the past.

"We ask *Kupa'aike'e* to allow this young *wa-yana* to join us now, and to escort him into the presence of *Kuahuia*, where he will become one with *Ku*."

It had been a long time since he had listened to Polynesian ritual; even so, Serengetti found that it came back to him quickly, and he could follow most of what was happening. In its most basic form, Warner was asking the various forms of the god *Ku* to accept a deceased but fondly-recalled friend as one of the Warner clan, symbolized by the *Kupa'aike'e*, the god of all canoe-builders, and allow him passage to the waters of the seashore world, symbolized by the god *Kuahuia*. The whole ceremony was taking place in the presence of *Ku*, the god of the rising sun, the god of gods. It was a big request. Warner had referred to his deceased friend as *wa-yana*, which loosely meant "without canoe." In an oceanic world dominated by seafarers, no one was lower on the social scale than someone without a canoe.

It was difficult to know precisely where authentic tradition left off and revision began. Hawaiian traditions had been so completely obliterated by European merchants and American missionaries—to say nothing of inter-tribal warfare—that many forms had vanished by the late eighteenth century. Or at least they were thought to have vanished. Even now, hidden caves were being discovered showing archaeological evidence of complex ancient ceremonies.

When attempts were made at various sorts of cultural revivals in the late twentieth century, these were often fused with late twentieth century sensibilities. Trans-historical interpenetration, Serengetti thought. He therefore saw it as completely in keeping with tradition when Warner placed a tiny CD player on the edge of the family *heiau*, and the minute speakers issued forth a slow and meandering version of an old Beach Boys song, "The Warmth of the Sun."

Without a body to bury in the sand—a practice that had long been outlawed—Warner had instead burned a few of his friend's few possessions while Serengetti slept. The ashes had been placed in a small model of an outrigger, about a meter long, that Warner and Serengetti now carried out beyond the surf. Standing in the ocean up to their waists, Warner said a few more words, then smiled and nodded that it was time.

Serengetti raised the miniature crab claw sail, secured the rigging, and then stood back. A gentle breeze caught the sail and carried the outrigger rapidly out onto the ocean. Serengetti stood and watched it as it grew smaller and smaller. At last Warner touched his shoulder and they turned towards the beach.

As he tried to move towards the shore, Serengetti felt the Pacific surf sucking out, as if to try and pull him further out to sea. It seemed that the harder he tried to move shoreward, the more insistently the surf pulled him back. Halfway to the beach he stopped, his mind filled with the images of two small faces. He turned to look out to sea again. The ashes of his stepchildren had been spread on top of these same waters, and it now felt as if the remaining grit and tiny bone fragments that he had dispersed were clutching at his legs, pulling him towards them, towards the death world where they existed forever. Or, he thought with an even more intense sadness, were they were clinging to his legs, begging him to pull them away from death and back into his life?

When finally he regained the beach, he sat down heavily. The sun had risen clear and hard above the rim of the eastern Pacific.

It was time to leave.

Twelve hours later, Serengetti was on board the 1700 flight to Paris. Shifting his legs and feet around in order to find a comfortable attitude in which to sleep in the small seat, he could still feel a few grains of sand between his toes.

Seven: Hubris

"The whole day I was disturbed by sinister forebodings. That night I slept badly and, between my frequently interrupted dreams, I thought I could hear distant sighs and something like a funereal intoned psalm. Was this the prayer for the dead, murmured in that language I could not understand?

—Jules Verne
Twenty Thousand Leagues Under the Seas, 1870
William Butcher translation (1998)

Écologie Maintenant had become increasingly sophisticated in its eco-terrorism, even to the point of operating three diesel-electric subs almost as old as the *Tailliez*. Two of these had kept up an almost constant submarine patrol of the 500-kilometer "Ecological Protectorate Zone (EPZ)" around New Guinea for three years now. It was a quixotic venture; as every transnational knew, the vast majority of the island's mineral wealth had long ago been stripped. But it was fabulous public relations and went a long way toward raising money from a few remaining guilt-ridden citizens, even those who had burned up nearly all of the planet's resources while keeping the peripheral states alive on crumbs.

As the action front of some three dozen more mainstream and officially unconnected environmental groups, EM in recent years had cranked to a more lethal level its twenty-year war against globalization in the peripheral states, a war triggered in 2001 by riots against the old G-8 nations. It was generally agreed that a large bequest from a dying, remorseful petrochemical magnate had enabled EM to purchase the three retired *Challenger* Class submarines from the old Republic of Singapore navy, as well as an old diesel tender that kept them re-supplied at sea.

These subs began their lives as *Sea Serpent* Class submarines built for the Swedish Navy by Kockums. As fifty-meter-long coastal patrol subs, they had exceptional maneuverability and could, at need, be handled by a single submariner. As such, they had proved extremely effective in suicide attacks against undefended port facilities around the world. Four *Sea Serpent* subs had been modified for routine patrol work in the tropics, then sold to Singapore as the *Challenger* Class in the late 1990s. One had been destroyed in the stateless uprisings that swept Asia in 2019, and the other three were eventually retired.

These three retired submarines were now in the possession of EM. The *Freeport-McMoran Avenger* and the *Bophal Avenger* operated in tandem to sink any transnational shipping in the New Guinea EPZ. These two Pacific boats disrupted shipping between Tokyo and French Polynesia, and were still holding eleven EU diplomats hostage, demanding a complete ecological protectorate around the entire island of New Guinea.

Neither the EU nor the U.N. had much success keeping track of the third sub, which of late had been operating in the North Sea, sinking U.N. whale killers. No one in the U.N. was certain of its name, if it even had one.

It did. EM called it *North Sea Avenger*, its crew of four called it *NSA*, and it was now maneuvering its way slowly and carefully along a wide but shallow track leading into Andreeva Bay, an Arctic channel filled with scores of wrecks, industrial detritus, and a century of accumulated heavy pollutants. The sun had just come up, its meager light blocked by clouds of recycler plant effluviums.

The sub's commander, Josef Kutepov, knew this channel well from years as a Russian Navy officer. He ordered speed reduced and headed for the decommissioned Russian submarine base at

Zapadnaya Litsa, a port less than fifty kilometers from the Russian-Norwegian border. As the black market refueling dock came into view, Kutepov looked at the bleak landscape and breathed deeply of the sour fumes of home.

Kutepov enjoyed this duty. Most of the time, *North Sea Avenger* hid in filthy side channels, avoiding transnational patrols. Rarely had the EM home office been able to provide enough credits for more than a few days of fuel. But Kutepov knew many ways around such shortages.

Lack of funds meant that requests for EM missions arrived infrequently, but Kutepov took full advantage of each one. He counted seventeen non-operational nuclear submarines aground in the marshes along the channel. All had been split open, their missiles removed, then the halves roughly welded together. The sound of air pumps filled the fjord, noise from a forlorn attempt to keep the old hulks from sinking permanently into the marshes. His own former boat, *Barentsburg*, was one of six decommissioned nuclear subs, reactors corroding and spent fuel leaking, already at the bottom of Andreeva Bay. The water now gurgling past *North Sea Avenger* was black with oil and tar balls, and Kutepov admired the artistic swirls made by the pink goo that dribbled into the bay from a marsh creek.

His Executive Officer, a former French submariner named Alena Espadon who had signed on with EM because of her love of whales and her desire to sink whalers, appeared beside Kutepov wearing a breathing filter. She looked at the sludge adhering to the sub, at the abandoned salvage yards crammed with cannibalized submarines and rusted yard vessels, and at the low-grade uranium waste processing plant staffed by the same recyclers who sold diesel to *NSA* at black market rates.

"It's like navigating up the asshole of the universe," said Espadon.

"Oh no," replied Kutepov, passing along orders to moor *NSA* to a rotting refueling pier along the shore of Andreeva Bay. He glanced at his console, which showed him the balance available in his private account. The reimbursement for his last mission had just cleared, making him temporarily comfortable. He felt surprisingly well. "You should have seen it twenty years ago. Now *that* was a sight. This is nothing. It's Disneyland now. After we moor, see to the refueling. I am going to see some friends in town about a torpedo or two."

"Aye, sir," said Espadon, taking one last look around before going below. "Disneyland, *mon Dieu*," she wheezed through her mask. "Maybe after Heironymous Bosch butt-fucked the mouse ."

* * *

Once the *NSA* was moored to a pier in a side channel off the main bay, Kutepov hopped off the sub and into a decrepit harbor launch. There was no one on board but, as he'd expected, the keys were in the ignition. It took several turns, along with a hop or two onto the engine compartment, before the inboard spluttered to life and Kutepov drove to the black market pier.

Some people had experienced bad years. Kutepov had for most of his life endured bad decades. The decade that followed the Yeltsin revolution had been bad for the whole country. The decade after the destruction of the *Kursk* had been bad for the submarine service. The decade after he left the Navy had been very bad.

But lately—for the past five years, as Kutepov measured the concept of 'lately'—he'd felt his luck beginning to turn. Through revolution and tragedy, marriage and divorce, he had, like almost all of his colleagues, participated in a thriving black market. Kutepov dealt mostly in tobacco products: American cigarettes, Zippo and Colibris lighters, tins of Skandinavik pipe tobacco and Jeantet pipes, the occasional cache of Cuban cigars, and Dominican cigars—Cohibas, Partagas, and H. Upmann Churchills—disguised as Cubans. His Russian navy sub had been a familiar visitor to the Med, and he had made himself expert at parlaying old Soviet caps, coats, insignia, and the odd small arms cache into tobacco. In the bad old decades, when naval pay arrived months late if it arrived at all, a carton of Marlboros judiciously dealt often meant survival.

As a freelancer, Kutepov's side business was often his primary source of income. For the past five summers, profits were up and credits were again flowing to the northern ports as the winter ice melted earlier and earlier until year-round navigation became a relatively simple matter.

Two years ago, business had been so good that Kutepov had saved enough to purchase a block of flats along the waterfront on the outskirts of Murmansk. The decrepit collection of apartments became the foundation of his desire to leave the sea and go into semi-retirement in a refurbished double flat. There he could collect rents while reading Dostoevsky and Gogol over strong black coffee in the morning, and in the evenings, enjoy two large glasses of vodka with Messrs. Tolstoy and Turgenev. By the end of this emerging good decade, he reckoned, he would have left the sea behind to enjoy both his new wealth and his newer wisdom.

Then, a year ago, Kutepov had been presented with an offer too good to refuse: a freelance submarine command for a marginal eco-terrorism group at three times his old Navy pay. All for an occasional foray into EU waters to sink transiting whale killers. Simple work. Work that allowed him to liberally pad his expense account, all the time drawing closer to his permanent berth along the Murmansk waterfront. More than once since he took this job he had secured fuel for *NSA* at Andreeva Bay on the strength of his black market connections until the EM home office could provide reimbursement. With interest.

His primary financial strategy was to attack the whaling fleet with unarmed torpedoes. Three times he had entered EU waters and three times *NSA's* torpedoes had bounced harmlessly off whale killers. Attacking with duds was the best of both worlds: terrifying but relatively harmless to those he fired at, cost-effective for Kutepov. In one energetic raid a hundred kilometers into U.N. territory, Kutepov had plunked a few rusting minke fishers moored in Tromsø. No one had been killed; such raids underlined the limited range of EM's three old diesels, revealing their actions to be more symbolic than punishing. EM liked them for the headlines; Kutepov for his bonuses.

Duds were less than half the cost of live warheads. Besides, he reasoned further, live torpedoes were dangerous. In any case, they were increasingly scarce. He could charge the full cost of a live torpedo to his EM expense account, after practiced, elaborate explanations of the many technical reasons why a perfectly good torpedo might fail in real naval undersea combat.

One more mission with a dud torpedo, Kutepov calculated, would set him up nicely for retirement as a leisurely collector of rents in Murmansk. He was well on his way. EM had just requested another freelance job, paid in advance, with a nice little bonus paid into his personal account.

* * *

Ellen Archer settled herself deeply into a long, comfortable transnational-class seat/bed of a direct Airbus Sleeper 50 flight from Paris to Tokyo. A steward closed the privacy curtain against the other passengers angling their way by her node. It had been an eventful twenty-four hours, and from at least part of it she was pleasurably sore. Now she had a twelve-hour flight back to Tokyo, so she had changed into her light flannel travel pajamas and tilted her chair back until it formed a bed. Her meeting with Larsen had gone better than expected, both professionally and personally, and she had every reason to believe that the operational details would now go smoothly.

Less than eighteen hours ago, following up Larsen's tip from Serengetti, she had emerged from the Metro station at the Bourse and walked into the Bibliotheque Nationale de France on the rue de Richelieu. As she searched through the four different original manuscripts in the nineteenth-century special collections division, she once again thanked her parents, who had both insisted and paid for her to spend a year in New Caledonia during her undergraduate years. Her immersion in French language and literature, regularly reinforced, allowed her to zip through the first three manuscripts.

When she arrived at the fourth, she was reading a manuscript that had only recently been made available to the public. Classic scholars had relied exclusively on the first three manuscripts for their interpretations of the novel. Most had considered a fourth manuscript—which scholars had dubbed *ms4*—a will-o-the-wisp. Some considered it merely a story made up by Verne to add still more mystery to Nemo's tracks, if not obscure them entirely. Verne's son had let slip the existence of *ms4* in 1910, but the manuscript itself did not surface until more than a century later. In 2012, Lennon, researching his definitive comparative study of Verne and Melville, discovered *ms4* in a dusty carton of Verniana in a second-hand bookstore in Provincetown, Massachusetts. Rejecting Inishi-Sotheby's auction offer, Lennon had won the applause of France when he donated the manuscript to the Bibliotheque Nationale, where it joined the first three manuscript drafts of *Twenty-Thousand Leagues Under the Seas*.

When she'd looked up from her researcher's table, three hours and a half had passed. After lunch, she'd returned for another four hours. She had decided not to break for dinner, since the Special Collections room closed at eight o'clock in the evening, and she needed every minute. If he made his connections from Bermuda, Larsen would arrive at the Bourse around eleven, and they would have six hours together before she returned to Tokyo.

As it had happened, she hadn't needed all the time. An hour before closing, she'd found what she had been looking for. Unfortunately, it was not as revelatory as she had hoped. Archer discovered two margin notes in *ms4* that referred to a northern island called Beeren in one place, and Bæren in another. Did Verne mean Barren Island? And if so, where was it? Were Beeren and Bæren one and the same place? Or were they different locations entirely? There was an additional reference to an iron-reinforced undersea cavern on the northwest corner of this Bæren Island. Unfortunately, her Swedish was extremely limited, and she had only a tiny bit of German, so these Scandinavian references were for the most part lost on her. That was precisely why Kurosawa had ordered Larsen to travel directly to Paris from Bermuda, leaving Serengetti to waste time traveling to Hawai'i. There was not much time to get it right, and they had already used up most of it.

Archer had hurried from the Bibliotheque to the Bourse, and by ten-thirty had found her way on the Metro to the Etoile Charles de Gaulle station. In a sea of short, dark-haired Frenchmen, Larsen stood out almost jarringly, like a raiding Viking. She could see that he was pretending he hadn't noticed her, which only intensified her feeling of power over him. They greeted each other, and she tried to move to business immediately. He resisted. The sky had already darkened, and he pulled her beneath a plane tree and kissed her. He made her laugh by saying that he was only trying to blend them both into the background. No one took notice of amorous couples.

He surprised her by rapidly slipping his hand down the back of her jeans and raking a fingernail up from the small of her back. Her eyes rolled back in her head. "You can have anything you want," she breathed, and she had felt his heart leap. She waited for a moment as his large hand probed deeper, then stiffened and abruptly pulled away. "But first, I need you to translate some documents for me."

Archer grew up in a neighborhood with all boys. Afternoons were spent in a gritty field playing baseball and soccer, her skills as good if not better than the boys'. These games quickly changed to others when she reached puberty. Her unusual good looks and ferocity attracted not only the boys but the men in her small town. Able to pick and choose, she spent her weekends with the older men in secluded parts of the forest surrounding her town. She came to love every aspect of the forest, its moisture, its heat, its ever-changing scents, its darkness. She knew every creek, field, cave and crevice by her meetings with so many men over so many weekends over so many teenage years.

Among her many past and current lovers, Larsen stood out in many ways. Like her, he had no time for foreplay. She preferred that he tear off her clothes and drill into her like a jack-hammer. Jack hammer her into the mattress, dirt, sand, against the trunk of a tree, a drilling that caused her thighs to twitch and her pelvis to contract as if being gripped by a huge, invisible fist.

Larsen also had some annoying traits. She dismissed his gifts of flowers and dinners as a waste of time and sentiment. His need to talk about his feelings, and his numerous offers to stay hours or days with her after lovemaking, both were as unacceptable as they were unwelcome. She always put him off with a lie—she was packing and had to be off. She had no time. At times she blurted out the truth, just because it always felt better. She had too many things to do and he was now in her way. Besides, she would have him again later. At her convenience.

Later, in her room, as he switched from French to English with the impeccable ease of someone raised to speak five languages with equal fluency, he took her notes and brought them to a small circular table in the corner of the room. The references to a barren island immediately made sense to him. He explained where they needed to go, and between them they decided on a course of action. She appreciated his professionalism, for it matched almost precisely her own. The next hours passed like minutes, and before she knew it, she was sipping pinot noir as her plane sat on the runway, awaiting departure from Charles de Gaulle. As the wine took hold, she allowed herself to close her eyes, relax her shoulders against the back of her seat, and concentrate on how she could still feel him in her.

Kurosawa, she knew, would be immensely relieved at the outcome of her trip. By now, she thought, AK would have probes in the water and the *Philippe Tailliez* would already be underway. In the end, she was supremely confident, Kurosawa would followed their recommendations.

* * *

Even though the Anthropological Directorate in Technology Park had a perfectly comfortable dining area, one with high, wide windows that overlooked Tokyo harbor, and even though there was in addition to this large area a smaller executive dining room, Kurosawa preferred to take lunch in his own office. There, alone with his thoughts, he could tend his fish, admire his bonsai tree, and listen to music while sitting comfortably on his own private balcony overlooking the harbor. In the event of a situation somewhere in the world, he had his several HDTV screens. There was also a private elevator, installed on his order, one stop of which took him directly to the sub-basement vault. His imperturbability, built up slowly over the decades, was a big comfort.

Kurosawa weighed and calibrated each decision, those he had already made and those he would soon make, working through his checklist of scientific, political, financial, and personal considerations. Not for nothing had a recent profile in an anthropological journal called him the individual most noted for *sang-froid* in the anthropological establishment. The article went on to quote a revealing vignette from an old acquaintance. If he suddenly learned that the world was going to end in half an hour, the colleague said, Kurosawa would call each of his field teams to their consoles, and in his deep voice of authority spend about ten minutes giving them all the bad news. Then he would order them all to turn on their high-resolution speakers. Since they still had eighteen minutes and four seconds left, Kurosawa would announce that there was time enough left to listen one last time to the "Fantasia on a Theme by Thomas Tallis for Double Strings" by Ralph Vaughan Williams.

But even with such innate calm, he had to admit to himself that matters were worse. It was not only that Serengetti had been alongside Larsen when *Nautius* was discovered. He had then gone on, of his own accord, from Bermuda to Hawai'i, and introduced the added complication of ms4. Such fragments of knowledge could easily be pieced together by a creative mind. He had forestalled this possibility with Archer's trip to Paris. But, in the hands of a contractor whose loyalty was an open question, such knowledge was an obvious risk.

Kurosawa would see to it that it did not remain so for very long. He might even be able to arrange things to the Directorate's advantage. He usually did. Serengetti's knowledge of the submarine and ms4 would both soon become irrelevant.

Kurosawa considered the possibility that Serengetti had indeed uncovered something of interest in the submarine's library, and might be keeping it to himself. But he quickly put the thought from his mind. He had made clear to Larsen to get off the submarine after little more than a cursory search. Two hours was not enough time to gather more than the basic evidence needed to confirm Kurosawa's suspicions. Now he had proof at last that at least one and maybe more than one of the Verlaten submariners from Mission 46 had survived the destruction of the island. As had their submarine.

The body of that 1920 sailor had followed the autopsy report to Tokyo. Several additional examinations led to the preservation of the entire corpse, which by various estimates—the last made in 2003—had survived an existence lasting between 9,000 and 22,000 years! For the past half century, the Directorate had used nuclei from isolated tissue cells of the corpse to create a new kind of human being with this same enduring genetics. In 1985 and again in 1990, they had succeeded. Unbeknownst to anyone outside his own Directorate—and even there it was its most closely-held secret—it was with these two new enduring beings that Kurosawa sought to start a new world, apart from Earth. He had already seen to it. Even if something happened to Kurosawa, even if he did not live to see it, Ellen Archer and Bjørn Larsen would lead the first human colony on another planet. Akagi Kurosawa had played God.

He walked from his balcony to a small resting room off the side of his office. There he lay down on a thin sleeping pad. He expected Archer's report from Paris very early the next morning. It was time to get some rest. There would be scores more decisions to be made in the morning.

As he closed his eyes, Kurosawa thought of the mixture of elation and anxiety which he had experienced when those first images came through from Larsen's webcam inside the submarine. He had sought this artifact for so long that he almost felt an impulse to preserve it. More eminent scholars than he had failed in similar lifelong quests for such a discovery. It had been his premonition that this particular artifact would be found in the Arctic. It was he who had, against nasty bureaucratic opposition, pushed for the development of the vast array of new survey technology the Directorate now deployed. It was he who, alone, had had the foresight to link each of his field teams to a unified global data network and begin to see global artifact and migration patterns. And it was also he who—when each of his budget officers had implored him to cut off its funding—had kept the aging *Philippe Tailliez* afloat for one last great archaeological mission.

Kurosawa had prepared for this hoped-for success in many other ways, as well. Gods had to see to the bad as well as the good. He had learned long ago that a large science bureaucracy survived on the well-founded fears of a gullible public. In the old days, it had been enough to plant a story in the *International Herald Tribune*, or *Le Monde*, based on legitimate scientific data, and an increase in his budget was all but certain. In recent years, however, much more direct action had been required. To awaken a distracted public and pry loose diminishing amounts of tax largesse and transnational contributions, Kurosawa had developed an increasingly lethal symbiosis with several criminal organizations. His judicious financing of attacks on his own field teams by commandos from EM, combined with periodic attacks on individual scientists and heists of artifacts by operatives from APE, had generated the reactive budgets Kurosawa required for his primary mission to succeed. It was a dangerous balancing act, requiring a complex double, even triple, life, but Kurosawa had always felt up to the challenge. He would soon put many of those useful contacts to work once again.

Kurosawa knew well that each triumph brought with it a thousand stinging headaches, and he began to feel a fresh assault on his frontal lobes. The abandoned submarine was a big security problem, albeit temporarily, but for at least the start of the operation he had enjoyed the luck of the well-prepared. On the basis of the Thor-15 data, he had secretly ordered Captain Jørriksen to shadow the *Polar Quest* with the *Philippe Tailliez*, even as the icebreaker made its way south into the Wide Fjord. While the *Quest's* forward-looking sonar scanned the fjord ahead, the *Tailliez* followed silently in the ship's wake. When the discovery was made, Kurosawa was in position to trip down a series of options. As the *Quest* retreated from the Wide Fjord and made its way back to Wellman Station, only he and Jørriksen knew that the *Tailliez* remained behind, rigged for silent running, as Serengetti and Larsen made their dive.

There could be no doubt of the huge risk this gambit represented. But by treating the *Nautilus* strictly as a cultural protection issue, he had the authority necessary to run the operation without interference from any of the other directorates of the U.N., much less the Americans. On the other hand, it was entirely possible that the Americans had received enough satellite data from the West Fjord that they now suspected the nature of the discovery. He could easily picture Americans panting after the submarine. He might turn that to his advantage as well. But the Americans would not be able to respond before he himself had a chance to move. He was determined that his Directorate could and would handle the entire operation. And that meant removing certain obstacles, a bit of tidying up here, some tweaking there.

As these problems played across his mind, Kurosawa found himself feeling sharply wide awake. He got up from his sleeping pad and walked back into his office. Why not take care of several pieces of unfinished business before bed? He sat at his main console and tapped out a brief message to Serengetti, who would now be on his way to Europe. With Archer returning to Tokyo and Larsen to Oslo, he suddenly felt the urge to put Serengetti out of the way, once and for all.

He had asked Serengetti, "as one of my top contract archaeologists," (nice touch, that) to travel directly to Paris ("we'll cover all expenses, of course") to search the Verne Archives there. Now that he knew both the location and the identity of a lost submarine in the Arctic, Serengetti could be immensely helpful if he could spend some time there looking for answers in Verne's papers. It was something Serengetti would be planning to do eventually anyway. "Yes, yes, I know this will delay your trip back to Oslo and Kings Bay, but it will be a useful service." Mid-summer in Paris, high heat, heavy crowds, so many opportunities for tragic and inexplicable incidents.

Kurosawa tapped out another message, this to a long-time intermediary in Europe, to request that an APE agent be waiting for the doctor in Paris. No sooner had he arranged this when he felt that he was not covering his bases as well as he might. It occurred to him to order Captain Jørriksen to evacuate Lt. Cmdr. Johansson from the *Tailliez* for a special assignment. Then, in a coded message to Johansson, Kurosawa revealed that he had just learned that his contract archaeologist in the Arctic, Dr. Paulo Serengetti, was traveling to a meeting in Paris in order to sell Directorate secrets to a criminal syndicate. Kurosawa sent flight details, contact data, and a request to terminate this meeting in the usual manner.

* * *

On board the submarine *Phillippe Tailliez*, Lieutenant Commander Johansson was hastily stuffing a pair of jeans and a few extra pairs of socks and panties into a small weekend bag. She was agitated by the sudden mission, doubly so because she had only recently been introduced to the target. She had, however, been in the military too long to question such missions too closely.

Fifteen minutes before she was due to leave the sub there was a knock at her cabin and a petty officer relayed a message from the Captain that she wished to have a word with Johansson before she departed.

Johansson knocked at the Captain's open cabin and Jørriksen seemed perhaps too eager to see her X.O. off. The Captain was sitting at her small desk, slowly and carefully carving a block of balsa wood into the shape of a submarine. Johansson stood at the entrance and watched the chubby fingers flick the knife with a delicate expertise she would not have imaged possible, until Jørriksen, without looking up, asked her to come in and close the hatch behind her. Johansson was not about to share any confidences with the Captain, but she was curious nonetheless as she stood just inside the hatch.

"Sit down, Commander," said Jørriksen, still without looking up. "And switch off your console." Johansson found a slim spot on the edge of the Captain's bunk, stretched out her arm and clicked off her console. They sat this way for a few minutes, the only sound the quick slicing of the carving blade on the block of balsa.

"The helo will be here soon," Johansson wanted to say. But that would be breaking protocol. Instead she kept her eyes on the rapid movements of the knife blade. Knives weren't really her thing, but she nonetheless kept a professional eye on the blade.

"This is my twenty-third year on boats," Jørriksen said at last. Johansson said nothing. It had always seemed unnecessary to her to answer a senior officer if they had not asked a question, made a request, or given an order. "I must know every harbor in Europe by now. Especially the northern ports, which we have been in and out of these past five years. Know them as well as I know this boat."

The tiny cabin, occupied by the oversized, heavy Jørriksen, was beginning to become oppressive to the light and lithe Johansson.

"From your record," said Jørriksen calmly, "it seems you have unusual abilities on glaciers. A born commando."

Suddenly she realized why she had been summoned: Jørriksen had intercepted the message from Tokyo. Johansson watched almost in detached fascination as Jørriksen turned from her carving with speed and silence and thrust the edge of the blade directly into the block of wood.

"I appreciate it very much," the Captain whispered, still not looking at her X.O., "when my second-in-command keeps me informed of her orders."

Johansson looked at Jørriksen steadily, searching for any weakness or unsteadiness. She found none.

"Why does the Directorate want Paulo Serengetti dead, Commander?"

"I only know that they want him out of the way."

"Bullshit," hissed Jørriksen, turning to stare Johansson in the face. "Don't fuck with me, Commander."

"Tokyo says he's selling out."

"That is the biggest bunch of bullshit I've ever heard. I've worked with that man for fifteen years, Commander. He's like my brother. He doesn't have a greedy bone in his skinny body, unlike some former commandoes Tokyo has seen fit to place on board my submarine, where they receive coded messages and don't possess the courtesy to keep their Captain informed."

Jørriksen withdrew the blade from the balsa and calmly resumed carving the block of wood.

"Maybe their superiors should stop reading secure messages," said Johansson, rubbing her neck. She half expected the Captain to make a lunge for her, but dismissed the thought. In such close quarters, Johansson could disarm and disable any opponent, of that she was certain. "Captains don't have the luxury of respecting privacy when it comes to the lives of their friends and the safety of their boat."

"I'll remember that if they ever make me Captain."

"I don't have time to give you on-the-job training, Commander," said Jørriksen calmly. "I read your dossier in detail. You have a well-earned reputation with both mountains and men. Not being that type, I wouldn't have believed it myself, not until I heard it for myself when you slipped into Bjorn Larsen's cabin when he was on board."

Johansson wanted suddenly to spit, but held herself in check. She flushed despite herself, more in remembrance of that impossibly massive body maneuvering between her legs than from any embarrassment. It had, after all, been awhile since she'd done a man quite that large.

"Don't worry, Commander. It's a small submarine. And you do not, evidently, have much experience in silent service. The talent that you possess that I can make use of is your apparent ability to track human beings like so much prey."

Jørriksen then placed her carving knife on her desk, and tapped her console. "I don't know what Tokyo is up to, but I intend to find out. You have your orders from Tokyo, orders that in my experience make no sense and in my view are illegal in any case. We are explorers, not assassins. Tokyo is using us, and I'm determined to find out why and by whom. That bureaucracy is so full of wolves and vipers it will take some time."

"So you are offering me a new contract?"

"You might say that. I'm offering you a chance to get back on the right side. I'm giving you new orders. You will do whatever is required to protect Serengetti and our work up here. I'm not sure what is going on, but I do know that if someone wants Paulo out of the way it means he knows something that he hasn't told any of us yet."

Jørriksen seemed to be lost in thought for a moment. "Check in with the sub every day," she said at last. "And remember, if anything happens to him, I have friends in every port in Europe. And they're not as gentle as Mr. Larsen."

"I'll remember that," said Johansson, even though they both knew that an army would be required to track down Johansson if she did not want to be found. "Now, I've got to go."

"Commander," said Jørriksen.

"Yes, Captain."

"Do the right thing."

"I always do, Captain."

"Then go well, and I'll see you in a week."

It wasn't until Johansson was on board the helo for the brief flight over the sharp-sided mountains, gazing down at the brilliant blue water patches on the receding glaciers that separated them, that Jørriksen's comment about mountains and men hit her with full force. Apparently Johansson's legend had spread to the Norwegian Navy. It had been awhile since Johansson herself had thought about the glacier. She looked straight down at a particularly ice-blue water hole on the glacier below. The casual Arctic tourist might be mesmerized by its singular beauty. Johansson knew better.

It had already been a long exercise, and Johansson could see that the other four rangers of her unit were exhausted. Their mission was to scale an Alpine ridge and move into position to launch a surprise attack on a small target on the other side. The ridgeline was at 3,500 meters; they would receive no outside support; and they had to carry two M136 AT4 anti-tank weapons, as well as a Bofors anti-tank M3 system with a full suite of 84mm ammunition. They were given three days to be in position. At the last minute, their commanding officer added a World War II Bangalore torpedo, in ten separate sections, to their kit. The Bangalore added two lengths of heavy pipe to each ranger's pack.

By the first night, they had reached the foot of the glacier, a frozen river two hundred feet deep designed by the devil himself. For the next day, they laid thin titanium bridges across deep blue crevasses, supporting each other in the ascent. By the second afternoon, a storm front moved in, cutting visibility to zero, and putting the unit far behind schedule. At their final crevasse crossing, the officer-in-charge decided to forego the titanium and trust instead a narrow snow bridge in order to make better time. The first ranger had almost made it across when a span of the snow bridge gave way. The ranger fell onto an icy ledge ten meters below the surface of the glacier. His arm was broken, and Johansson watched as the pack with two sections of the Bangalore fell further into the crevasse, still attached by a lanyard to the screaming ranger's broken arm.

There was only one thing to do: get the metal bridge across and rig a winch to bring the man up. But as two other rangers tried to lower the metal catwalk into place in the howling winds, a deep rumble could be heard from above them. As they looked up, a tower of snow and ice rolled down upon them. The wall of ice slammed into the metal catwalk, carrying it downhill, along with the two rangers tethered to it. The OIC and Johansson clung to their ice axes as the avalanche rolled over top of them. When she finally came to, Johansson saw that the OIC was unconscious. She took charge of the mission immediately.

The detailed account of how she managed to rescue four men, each nearly twice her size, arrive at the staging point thirty minutes ahead of schedule, and then use the M136 AT4 to blow a hole in a dummy target, made her something of a legend in the Coastal Rangers. It led soon thereafter to her selection for the Attack Divers. She served with distinction for ten more years, leaving the AD in anger after being passed over for selection to the King's bodyguard unit.

The sudden recollection of the glacier made Johansson both cold and hot, and she began to crawl inside her own skin. She hated the thought of anything beyond her own control. Maybe a week in Paris was just what she needed.

* * *

As soon as he was certain that the helo bringing Johansson to Kings Bay was in the air, Kurosawa sent another message to Captain Jørriksen. He ordered her to lead a boarding party from the *Tailliez* to the *Nautilus*. Until he sent further instructions, they were to secure the site. He forbade them from entering any area of the submarine except the machinery spaces and the conn. Now he was tired, and it was time to sleep. He returned to his sleeping pad and, his consciousness suffused with the unfailingly erotic prospect of starting the world all over again, slept at last.

Twelve hours later, as the rising sun filled his office with light, Kurosawa read the report from Archer. The potentially flammable combination of Larsen and Archer together in Paris had excited him once again. Years of experiment, of trial and error, had gone into arranging this union. Not only had they worked together perfectly, but Kurosawa now knew where he needed to go. The whole complex operation was settling into place now, barriers had fallen away, and he allowed himself a smile of satisfaction. *It was the best feeling in the world!* And soon the world would be new.

He would have to contact Trondheim and get the AUVs away immediately to carry out his planned deception. Again, he congratulated himself for the foresight of investing in the new and faster autonomous undersea vehicles two years earlier. They were now on line, and he needed them right away. He furthered congratulated himself for his foresight in having control stations for these probes decentralized. He could control them from Tokyo, or from his Pacific station on Easter Island. Larsen had additional control stations at the Transpac offices in Oslo and the Wellman Station in Svalbard. At sixty-five knots, these AUVs could be on site in half a day.

There were personal confrontations ahead of him as well. Ellen Archer would be back in his office soon. Kurosawa would then be required to tell a series of lies to his most valued deputy, and that was a breach of trust he took extremely seriously. But there was no other way. If he was ever to use this unique woman to restart the world, he needed to shield her from the contents of the sub-basement. The discovery of the *Nautilus* offered him the perfect opportunity to test her loyalty, her discretion, and the ambit of her abilities.

The discovery of the *Nautilus*! How those words dripped! Above everything else, there was the reality of the *Nautilus*. He had found the artifact he had so long sought. discretion would be maintained until he chose otherwise. And now it seemed that his team had puzzled out the location of Nemo's Arctic base. Soon he would be rid of the greatest submarine in all history; and with it, the secret of its appearance in the oceans of the Earth.

It was true, he thought, that he himself wasn't so different from the explorers that had coursed the world's oceans in that submarine. And this thought filled him with both envy and resentment. They had been, one might say, a special band of biological anthropologists, and from wherever they had come, they had used Kurosawa's planet as a kind of laboratory, implanting different species of hominid over a span of hundreds of thousands of years. Kurosawa envied their capabilities; he resented that they had, in effect, created him along with the rest of humanity. For this reason he called them the scientist-gods.

Kurosawa did not know the ultimate reason for these radical experiments, but he was fairly certain *Homo sapiens* had not been the intended final design. Yet it was also apparent that some event had interfered with the introduction of the species to follow. Perhaps the submariners of Mission 46 had decided to stop the experiment? Perhaps they had looked at a Michelangelo Buonarroti sculpture and decided there was no more to be done.

Well, no more of their interference! thought Kurosawa. That experiment was ended, once and for all. And now, once the *Nautilus* was removed from the face of the earth, his own experiment, built on the genes recovered from Mission 46, would begin in earnest.

He took a deep breath and sent another message to the *Philippe Tailliez*. He was about to multiply the risks to both his Directorate and to himself. These were not decisions a career bureaucrat contemplated lightly. What he now undertook, he did with the full knowledge of the dangerous situation in which he was placing himself. He was about to turn the mission of his Directorate on its head, in favor of a new mission, one known only to a succession of men like himself. Now was the time. The culmination of a century of experiments was within his reach. The sheer wall of circumstance, chance, and error that he faced had but one slender ladder over the top, and he would take it.

On the basis of the data Larsen had obtained from the engine room, which his engineers had now analyzed, Kurosawa instructed Jørriksen and her engineers to work together with Tokyo and attempt to power up the *Nautilus*. This was by far the most complex message of all, and his fingers fairly trembled as he typed the words. If this worked, the ages would sing praises of glory to his honored name. If it did not, well, he would not contemplate failure. Still, he hesitated. He was about to go against his deeply inculcated bureaucratic ethos and turn upside down an entire career dedicated to the preservation of the world's greatest archaeological sites. He knew personally nearly everyone who was about to die. It was the biggest risk of his life.

Before he sent the message, Kurosawa reached into his vest and pulled out a gold pocket watch. He rubbed his thumb over the beautifully-engraved "N". Then, slowly, he typed onto his console two final sentences:

"To Commanding Officer, *Philippe Tailliez*. Request please that you have *Nautilus* ready for sea in twenty-four hours."

Eight: Bear Island

What lies beyond the margin of the world often sings to us with the voice of a siren, as if calling us into its embrace. We listen, we are lured, and finally we are seduced. The heavily scored margins on charts that I have observed over the years are testament to this predilection on the part of many seafarers. They are utterly bewitched by the prospect of continuing along one rhumb line until it reaches its farthest point. They want to find out whether its ultimate destination concurs with their idea of how the world really is.

—*James Cowan*
A Mapmaker's Dream: The Meditations of Fra Mauro, Cartographer to the Court of Venice

"*Nansen-Uemura 3* is away."

As Ellen Archer entered Kurosawa's office, she heard him speaking with the director at the Norwegian marine technology institute at Trondheim. These were the words she had waited impatiently to hear from the moment she made her initial report from Paris. A last-minute software problem had delayed the deployment of the unmanned AUV probes. Only now, twelve hours later, as Archer landed in Tokyo, had the problem had been solved and the autonomous undersea vehicles got underway.

"How soon can we have *No. 4* in the water?" she asked Kurosawa by way of greeting.

"*Nansen-Uemura 4* is away...now," replied the disembodied voice of the director in Trondheim instead. "It will take about forty-five minutes to clear the fjord, and an ETA twenty-six hours later."

Archer exhaled heavily, as if she had been holding her breath. They were behind schedule now, which left much to chance. Much too much. In twenty-six hours much could happen. It was too much of a muchness. Even as these autonomous nuclear undersea vehicles cut rapidly through Trondheim fjord at sixty-five knots and then blasted into the North Sea, she knew that this was only one part of securing the *Nautilus* site. All they could do was monitor the submarine visually while the Directorate labored to bring more human resources into the fjord. And getting a full team with logistical support would take days, perhaps. It was her work that led to the original discovery; and it was again her work in Paris that was leading them to Nemo's Arctic base. She had gotten a whiff of victory, but she could also sniff six ways to failure.

As she studied the screens relaying the images from the cameras on board the probes, they showed only blue water streaming past the AUVs. Kurosawa was asking the director in Trondheim about a project that Kurosawa himself had approved only a year earlier. A new and much larger probe was under construction, the *Amundsen 1*, which could carry on its back a separate remote undersea observatory to any spot on any ocean or any shoreline on the planet. The probe would then withdraw and return to its undersea base at Trondheim, while the observatory would be left behind, with its cameras and sensors fully engaged, sending data to an Inishi satellite parked in a stationary orbit five hundred kilometers up.

"*Amundsen 1* has been in testing for a month now," said Trondheim.

Kurosawa typed the coordinates for West Fjord onto his screen.

"Can we deliver the observatory here?"

Trondheim made a few hurried calculations.

"If we send it now, it could arrive in about thirty-five hours. It has only half the speed of the N-U probes."

"Good. Send it. Where is the *Blue Marlin* right now?" Kurosawa asked.

"On standby in Tromsø, awaiting orders,"

"How soon can she put to sea?"

"Moment's notice."

Kurosawa typed a set of coordinates on his screen, which the director in Trondheim immediately read on his. *Blue Marlin*, as AK well knew, was one of only three ships in the world capable of transporting the *Nautilus* on submersible decks. He had to at least appear to be covering all his bases.

"Can the *Marlin* be there in twenty-four hours?" The location, a spot off the northwest corner of Bear Island, was less than half the distance from Trondheim to the West Fjord.

The director looked at the coordinates on his secure screen, did a quick calculation, and said "no."

"Thirty-six hours, at the earliest."

"Fine," said Kurosawa. "Ask her to stand by."

As Trondheim disconnected, Archer impatiently asked Kurosawa where the *Philippe Tailliez* was.

"Right now, she is on her way to Tromsø to refuel," Kurosawa lied. But she's brilliant, he thought. It was the very question he himself would have asked.

"Don't you think we should turn her around and get her into the West Fjord right away?" asked Archer.

She tried not to show it, but she was incredulous that AK had not seen to this necessity already. With news of the discovery sure to slip, they had a massive security problem on their hands. And so far Kurosawa's only response had been to order three unmanned probes to the site; and these were half a day behind schedule. With its closed-cycle engines, which operated independently of oxygen, the German-built *Tailliez* could remain at sea for two weeks if necessary. There was no reason why it should not be on site right this very minute. For the first time in her relationship with the Director, Archer found herself entertaining doubts about his decisions.

"We need people on the ground," Archer insisted. "We can assume that word is already out. We can't wait and give APE a chance to board the sub."

"Except that we have no one on scene now," Kurosawa lied again. "Serengetti and Larsen are in Oslo. *Polar Quest* is back at Kings Bay refueling, and can put back to sea in twelve hours, but will not arrive back at West Fjord for almost a day and a half. Once Serengetti and Larsen get back to Kings Bay, in a day or so, we can get the *Quest* on the move again back to West Fjord."

Kurosawa would have preferred to have Larsen on board the *Quest* right now, but it couldn't be helped. Perhaps he could have the Directorate's Falcon waiting for him in Oslo, for a direct flight back to King's Bay. On the other hand, Transpac's Oslo headquarters were set up to monitor the new AUVs, and the ones heading for the West Fjord would find nothing but an empty space where the *Nautilus* once rested. Larson could unknowingly do that little misdirection job for him in Oslo. Yes, that might work.

"But we can get the *Tailliez* there in a few hours if we turn her around right now!"

"The *Tailliez* needs to refuel. The *Nautilus* has been in West Fjord for over a century and a half. It's not going anywhere. Besides, the bathymetric data from the *Quest* indicates that there might be a problem. The West Fjord may be too small for both the *Nautilus* and the *Philippe Tailliez*. We have no option but waiting for the *N-U* probes to arrive. And they will not be on scene for at least another thirty hours."

Archer was exasperated; her neck pulsed. "There is something else we need to think about," she said. She was uncomfortable even in bringing this up, since it might reveal to AK just how close she was to Larsen. But it was hardly a time for timidity. "Yes?"

"Larsen seemed to think that Serengetti was holding back something he found in the library."

"Indeed," said Kurosawa. This new sliver of data reinforced his already powerful desire to rid himself of the Serengetti nuisance. Satsifying that desire would be another in a series of wonderful feelings he had enjoyed lately.

"We might want to shadow his computer traffic."

"Is that really necessary?"

"I think it is," said Archer. "I think we also need to consider having a bodyguard follow him. APE has tried to reach him once. They are certain to try again."

"Yes, that might be appropriate," Kurosawa agreed. "Commander Johansson is scheduled for leave. I can ask her to look after him."

As for console traffic, Kurosawa thought that this was not an appropriate time to tell his deputy that he was already secretly monitoring all of the screens in his Directorate. The Stealthware v7.2.4 on his secure desktop offered him real-time images of any screen he chose to view. He was well aware of which employees cruised the e-bars during work hours, knew how many of them engaged in what varieties of cybersex during staff meetings. If he desired, he could follow each keystroke tapped by any member of his Directorate, engaging his sporadic voyeurism. He had even intercepted e-posts from two former partners of the Deputy. He knew things he should not know. He knew, for instance, the orgasmic scenario that most stimulated Ellen Archer.

The intricacies of Nipponese Shinju Shibari ropework her climax occasionally required was the last thing on Archer's mind at the moment. She was keyed up from her Parisian night, from her long, sleepless flight, and from the increasing tension over the security of what she now considered her site. Bouncing around her office for a day-and-a-half waiting for the AUVs to arrive would drive her crazy.

Kurosawa sensed this as well. "Look," he said to her as she watched the probes slice through the North Sea. "You've had a long flight. Get some sleep and meet me back here in six hours." And before she could protest, he added, "I want you to take on a special assignment, a demanding one."

* * *

Ellen Archer was furious.

It was now 0615 in the morning, and she had just left her early morning meeting with Kurosawa. All during the early part of this operation it had been her foresight that had provided each new leap ahead. Because of that, she had automatically assumed that AK would entrust the completion of the mission to her.

She had already made a mental plan of how she and Larsen would board and secure the *Nautilus* in the West Fjord. With that accomplished, the announcement of her discovery would be made in a live global broadcast over the Glöbnet. She would never admit it to anyone, but she had already thought of a title for the best-selling book she would write about how her prescience had led the Directorate to the site: *One Hundred-and-Fifty Years Beneath the Arctic Sea*. Perhaps, she had thought, generously but tentatively, she would even co-author the book with Larsen. It would give them another excuse to be together. She had already pondered what she would wear during the exclusive interview with Christiane Amanpour, the anchor of the Global Report. Perhaps she would even be interviewed while seated in Nemo's private study itself! She would have to think about her hair. And her jewelry.

But right now all she could think about was how angry she was at Kurosawa. It was becoming clearer with each passing hour that he meant to take from her all credit for the discovery, and she was livid. To make matters worse, he had fobbed a sideshow of a survey off on her. Near the end of their meeting, AK had tapped a new set of coordinates into one of his consoles, and one of the Nansen-Uemura probes had veered suddenly from its northerly course. He explained that it was now speeding east, toward Bear Island.

Bear Island! The location of Nemo's Arctic base! An undersea lair that would become as fabled as that of Grendel and his mother in *Beowulf*. A location that AK would have never even known had it not been for her brilliant, intensive work in Paris. For it was the reference that she had found to a Beeren or Bæren Island, an apparently casual notation within ms4 in the Verne Archives, that Bjorn Larsen had translated as the island the Norwegians call Bjornøya, or Bear Island. It was somewhere on the northwest corner of this small island of precipitous cliffs, located halfway between the north coast of Norway and the islands of Svalbard that, Verne had hinted, Nemo's submarine base was located.

But it was only a hint. And the "special assignment" Kurosawa had given her was to monitor *NU-4* as it diverted from its planned surveillance of the *Nautilus* in the West Fjord, to a needle-in-the-haystack search along the northwestern corner of Bear Island for the undersea entrance to Nemo's lair. Larsen was to be given the task of monitoring from Oslo the undersea probes as they arrived at the *Nautilus* site, a task she thought was hers by right.

Archer had been in the Directorate long enough to understand that one never showed disrespect to any proposal offered by AK, but this slight hurt. Had she not shown enough of her abilities to AK to earn control of the *Nautilus* mission? That thought—that perhaps she had not shown her true abilities—made her even angrier with herself than with Kurosawa. She wondered with some bitterness if this was not one of those dreadful moments when one hits the ceiling of one's career.

She tried to comfort herself. She felt an unaccustomed and almost desperate need to talk to someone. She thought of calling Larsen, but instantly thought better of it. She liked the balance of their relationship just as it was, and had no desire to change it in his favor. Although the more she thought of it, she realized that AK had tipped the balance himself. Larsen had, after all, just leap-frogged her in AK's eyes. And that thought made her ferociously angry at Larsen. How could she have been so stupid? She took a coffee mug an old lover had given her and was about to throw it across her office, but then put it down.

Instead, she got up slowly from her chair and laid down flat on her back. She placed her hands behind her head and intertwined her fingers. Then, with easy and methodical movements, she began the first of 126 ab crunchies. Each time she folded her torso off the floor and felt the sting in the muscles of her abdomen, she powered through the sting with thoughts of her mistreatment and a harshly whispered count. At the count of fifty, her thinking began to clear. After seventy-five, she began to consider her assignment. When she reached 100, she had identified several hidden consolations of her second-tier mission. By 126, as she collapsed and let out a deep and satisfied breath, Bear Island had become the most exciting project of her career.

Her probe would arrive at the island in a few hours. The two probes speeding underwater to the West Fjord, the *NU-3* and the *Amundsen 1*, would not arrive at the *Nautilus* site for more than a day. That gave her a potential advantage. On her main screen she watched as *NU-4* blistered its way through the North Sea. These new probes, she thought, were very fast. The *NU-4* was impressive. Control of the probe had been fastened to her console. In two hours, it would slow to a few knots, and she would gain manual control of the missile-shaped undersea probe.

If AK was going to take the *Nautilus* away from her and give it to the Viking, so be it. But there would be no doubt about who had discovered the base on Bear Island. Her fame was assured.

* * *

Noon. Tokyo. Ellen Archer watched the stream of bubbles in front of the *NU-4* begin to dissipate. She squeezed her coffee mug as a chime from her console informed her that she now had manual control of the autonomous undersea archaeological probe. She had reluctantly sent two e-posts to Larsen, who was back in his Transpac office in Oslo where he would monitor the West Fjord AUVs.

These e-posts were strictly business. Larsen had been able to access some bathymetric data for Bear Island, and in response to her first e-post, had been able to amplify his first translation of Verne's notation. Combining the two, he had been able to narrow her search to an undersea rift in the northwest cliffs. Archer grudgingly agreed that an appropriate depth would be about ten meters. She made the appropriate entries onto her console, and sat forward in her chair. In a few moments, the blue of the sea was replaced on her screen by the looming presence of the black undersea cliffs of Bear Island. She felt a cold *frisson* run from her medulla to her vulva. Her ego was rebounding.

* * *

In Vestfjorden it was 0300. Captain Jørriksen and her team of four engineers from the *Philippe Tailliez* were both exhausted and exhilarated. Tokyo had picked a truly cocked-up time to send her X.O. on leave. They had now been on board the *Nautilus* for nearly thirty-six hours, and Jørriksen was beginning to feel comfortable in the small, antique pilothouse. As she took in the boat's contours, she tried to memorize them so that when this mission was over she could build a fourth model for her stateroom shelves.

The four female submariners on her team had passed through four levels of awe and it was difficult to remember what aspect of the submarine had surprised them the most, even though the most interesting compartments of the submarine were off-limits. Tokyo had restricted them to the engine room and the pilothouse; the spaces on Nemo's boat available to her team, therefore, were only one-third of its total.

Working in concert with Tokyo engineers, her team had discovered a series of corresponding level tubes in both the engine room and the pilothouse. These apparently relayed speed and direction adjustments from the pilothouse, a lovely sort of engine order telegraph. When she moved a lever almost imperceptibly, her engineers relayed to her that the movement registered on the tubes in the engine room. After several such tests, Jørriksen, with great trepidation, moved one of the levers just a few centimeters. Almost instantly, a mellifluous whir could be heard. The single screw that propelled the *Nautilus* began to turn. Still since Bismarck was Chancellor, since a trice after Lincoln's assassination, since Stanley found Livingstone and the glory years of Queen Victoria, the massive blades again churned salt water. Chut-chut-chut…

Over the amazing day that followed, the Captain and her team determined the controls to be an annunciator for propulsion, several smaller levers for ballast, and large, bronze-spoked, wooden wheels for trim. They had now made several trips back and forth between the *Tailliez* and the *Nautilus*, lugging over survival suits, food, water, a waste disposal unit, and additional consoles. Captain Jørriksen had slipped her personal flask of Ketel 1 vodka into her gear bag. The only modification that had been allowed on the *Nautilus* was the addition of a submersible webcam mounted on a railing forward of the pilothouse. This cam and the one already broadcasting from the stern of the *Tailliez* would give Tokyo a real-time perspective on the submarine's transit.

Jørriksen set up a console in the pilothouse and coordinated communication between the subs. When that was finished, and she was satisfied that she could move the *Nautilus* out of the shallow fjord using the *Tailliez's* active sonar, she set a new watch schedule for the reduced crews. Five hours earlier, she had ordered the lock-out closed and pumped. An hour later, she told everyone off watch to get some sleep. They would need it. With a boarding party on the *Nautilus* and Johansson on leave, the *Tailliez* was reduced to a crew of twelve.

When the detailed orders from Tokyo arrived, Jørriksen allowed her crew—now two separate crews—to enjoy five more minutes of rest. She read through the orders twice, committing them to memory. Once on the surface, she was to cruise on the surface and trail the *Tailliez* at all times. Her speed was restricted to four knots. *Nautilus* was to remain a thousand meters astern of the *Tailliez*, allowing the *Tailliez's* active sonar to ping the fjords for possible undersea obstructions and surface bergs. If there was cloud cover shielding them from the polar satellites, she was to proceed north, out of the West Fjord, and then north to the mouth of Wide Fjord. If there was no cover, then they were to hide on the bottom of the Wide Fjord until there was. If all went well, they would clear the mouth of the Wide Fjord by midnight. More orders would be forthcoming at that time.

At 0305, she checked with the *Tailliez*, where the acting executive officer, Lt. Zöe Lindgren, was in command. The weather forecast from the *Tailliez*, the X.O. related, predicted moderate snowfall for the next twelve hours. Once she had passed on the orders from Tokyo, Jørriksen let out a deep breath.

"Okay," said Jørriksen to the *Tailliez*. "Let's go. Proceed as ordered."

"Proceeding as ordered, aye," responded the *Tailliez*. "The *Philippe Tailliez* is proceeding as ordered, ma'am."

A few moments later, as the *Tailliez* broke the surface, Jørriksen called her Chief Engineer and ordered her to blow the tanks.

The *Nautilus* shuddered briefly, and very slowly began to rise.

* * *

Captain Jørriksen had begun to decipher the imagination of the designer of this most famous of all submarines. This was the dream of every submariner who ever went to sea, to stand in this very pilothouse, to hear the flushing sound of the tanks emptying, to feel the heft of this infamous weapon begin to rise, to surface, as its commander.

The *Nautilus* surfaced into a gathering snow squall.

As Jørriksen searched for the details of the West Fjord shoreline, she considered the fact that she was making history yet again. She couldn't help but imagine the reception they would receive when they steamed into port! But where? Tromsø? Trondheim? Oslo? Maybe her hometown of Bergen! It would be the biggest celebration since Nansen returned from the north! But these vainglorious thoughts vanished when Jørriksen was confronted with three immediate problems.

"Engineering," she called. "We're down a few degrees in the stern."

"Conn, engineering, aye. Engineering is now trimming off."

As the boat came level, two unfamiliar and contradictory sensations overtook Jørriksen. She could see, yet she could not see. While the sub had been stationary on the bottom, she had not paid very much attention to the two oversized convex lenses that dominated either side of the pilothouse. Now, on the surface, she felt almost naked, as if anyone could look inside to observe her as she conned the sub. Even stranger, she was unaccustomed to being able to see out of a submarine without the aid of a periscope. It forced her to remember that the *Nautilus* was primarily a surface boat. It had been designed to watch, not listen, for nearly noiseless nineteenth-century sailing ships, as well as lumbering steamships, and then slice rapidly thought their undersides and send them to the bottom in splinters. Even had Nemo possessed sonar, it would have been of little use in searching for vessels whose motive power was the soughing wind. Her orders were to stay on the surface, and stay on the surface she would, but this pilothouse made her feel naked.

Her second thought was that, even with all of this newly discovered and unfamiliar visibility, she could see nothing. Absolutely nothing. The snowy sky outside the convex lenses had come right down to the surface of the sea. The white-out conditions were so total that her depth perception was lost. Visibility: nearly zero. As engineering trimmed the boat, she watched the moderate snowfall come straight and slowly down, absolutely straight down. There was not a breath of wind in the fjord. She found herself hard put to recall if she had ever seen such a snowfall as this. It was not at all heavy, just continuous, and in almost slow motion. The snowflakes alighted lazily onto the pilothouse lenses like small white butterflies. It was almost as if the *Nautilus* were being blessed. Jørriksen shivered.

Occasionally, through a pause in the squall, she could see a lone seabird in the distance as it swept down over the fjord. The gray birds were hard to distinguish from the gray sky. Jørriksen surveyed the fjord again and nodded to herself. It was time to get to work.

"*Tailliez*, Jørriksen."

"Conn, *Tailliez*."

"Let's take it nice and easy, shall we? Continuous positioning to my console. Conn follows in four minutes now. I want you to ping this fjord to death."

"Active sonar, aye," replied the *Tailliez*. "Jørriksen to follow in four minutes, aye."

"On my mark," called Jørriksen. She took a deep breath. "Three, two, one, mark."

"Jørriksen, *Tailliez*. The *Philippe Tailliez* is underway."

"Godspeed *Tailliez*."

"Godspeed, conn."

* * *

As the *Nautilus* trailed the *Philippe Tailliez* from the West Fjord and north through the Wide Fjord, about 250 nautical miles to the south the *Nansen-Uemura 4* probe controlled by Ellen Archer's console in Tokyo entered a narrow undersea channel on the northwest coast of Bear Island. The speed of these new probes was more than double that of the first two models, which even now were engaged in a laborious survey of submerged cave sites along a ridge of seamounts in the southeastern Pacific.

The size of that ocean made the intensive survey of undersea sites—caves, for example, where remains of human migrations might be found—a near impossibility. If the discovery of the *Nautilus* had come a few days later, the three probes now devoted to this mission would already have been on their way to the Pacific. Kurosawa's Directorate was engaged in a furious and complex race, not only to find and study those sites, but place them under protection from the APE and other criminal entities who would sell them to the highest bidder. Both the Directorate and those who sought to destroy it knew where the important action was to be found: on those now-submerged sites where humans had once lived, and where sea levels had risen since the last ice age.

The multi-beam sonar on *NU-4* picked a precise path through the channel, toward what registered as a gaping hole in the side of the island. Impatiently, Archer wished the cameras would see something, but visual data were always several hundred meters behind the sonar profiles. "Find with your ears, study with your eyes." Hadn't that been the mantra of the sonar techs on Kurosawa's staff? It was one of the strengths of AK's method that his top staff were trained to both operate the AUVs and interpret the data they collected. The person who controlled the autonomous probes on global survey missions was always the same person who interpreted all of the visual, magnetic, and sonar data. For AK, it meant tighter security and more reliable data analysis; it also eliminated the need for a tech to explain methodology to an analyst. For his top deputies, it meant hands-on control of all mission functions, instant access to data, and more personal satisfaction.

The data now streaming into Archer's console from *NU-4* showed that the channel was about fifteen meters wide and twenty deep. Given such a shallow bottom, Archer had shifted all three survey sonars to their highest possible frequencies, in an attempt to obtain the finest image quality. The high frequencies limited the range of the sonar sweeps, but what was important now was not range, but resolution. Her eyes shifted rapidly from the images on the main screen to the data strips along the bottom of her console, as she tried simultaneously to scan all of the parameters as they were relayed: ping number, speed, altitude, lat/lon, course, heading, pitch, roll, pressure, temperature, depth. All except the ping number were fairly steady now, as the probe made its way slowly through the channel.

If someone had managed to use this as a base for the *Nautilus*, she thought, they would have been forced to come in real slow, on only the calmest of days, as the *NU-4* was doing right now. Such a delicate passage would have to be executed on the exposed northwest coast of an Arctic island that enjoyed few sunny days. That would help explain why no one had ever found this undersea channel. Could it also be why Nemo had bypassed this base on his last mission? Had he tried to enter this channel and been forced back by a storm?

Bear Island was an arrowhead aimed at the jagged coast of northern Norway. High, flat mountains dominated the point of the arrowhead, and these fell almost vertically into the sea. Only twenty kilometers of land sloped from the point to the flat northern coast, and this limited space was pocked by more than 700 lakes. Polar bears and Arctic foxes patroled the island. A tiny radio and meteorological station was the only human refuge. On the east coast stood the ruins of an abandoned coal mine, the fierce northeast storms gradually pummeling its loading dock into the sea. Railway locomotives for bringing the coal from the adit of the mine lay skewed across twisted narrow guage tracks, their rusting boilers resembling miniature submarines.

Archer became so absorbed in peering at the visual data, trying to make out any details in the distance, that for a moment she was completely unaware that the magnetometer readings had gone off the scale. Not wanting to be irritated by the constant chiming of systems alarms, she had turned them all off in order to concentrate on the visuals. When finally she noticed the magnetometer reading, she did not need it anyway. The *NU-4* had found what she sought.

"At last," she whispered, turning on an extra set of lights that had been added for this mission. Her first thought was of the medal the Directorate would award her. And vindication. Never again would a mission be taken away from her, nor would she be upstaged by Bjorn Larsen. Or anyone else.

For a moment she thought that the structure looked like the ornate wrought-iron gateway to the estate of a nineteenth-century robber baron, something one might see on Bellevue Avenue in Newport. But as she adjusted the focus and maneuvered the probe closer to the top of the arch, she saw that it was more like the heavy and uniformly riveted crossbeam of an overbuilt railway bridge. And in the middle of the arch was a large and elegantly forged glyph, a symbol that was both simple and almost obscenely direct in its force. She forgot about medals and missions; she was in the presence of something very large: power and pride, the high and mighty. For a full minute, while she wondered what to do next, she kept the cameras focused on that lone symbol.

It was the letter "N."

* * *

After Archer had overcome her initial awe, she began to check each of the dozens of data dumps her console was receiving from *NU-4*. They were going to need all of this data, and soon. Once AK saw this, she was certain that he would order her to lead a field team to conduct a direct site survey, what archaeologists liked to call the 'ground-truthing' of remotely gathered data. There was obviously going to be a lot of truth to be found on the ground, or underwater, in this case. Carefully manipulating the joystick in front of her, Archer maneuvered the probe downwards, allowing the side-scan sonar to click off a precise measurement of the opening. Using Larsen's measurements from the West Fjord, she quickly calculated that both the *Tailliez* and the *Nautilus*, if they took it real slow, could enter this opening side by side. The door to Nemo's lair was thirty meters wide.

Before the *NU-4* penetrated the opening to the base, Archer instructed it to deploy a small tethered buoy, which shot to the surface. As the probe entered the cave, the buoy would transmit signals to the satellite that would, in turn, relay them to Tokyo. As soon as she drove the *NU-4* beyond Nemo's gate, she found that the sonars were recording a wider and a higher space. Beyond the entrance, the chamber opened into some kind of large enclosure. The magnetometer readings were still off the scale, and she began to see what looked like riveted catwalks and possibly some sort of dry-docking cradle.

Archer drove the probe into what the multi-beam told her was the apparent center of the structure. The probe was suspended about three meters off the floor of the cavern, in a space that she recorded as one hundred meters long by forty meters wide. More than enough room for what they had found in the West Fjord, and for the *Tailliez*, too, if it came to that. It was the kind of routine undersea docking structure like the ruins of the old First World War German base the Directorate had surveyed in the New Hebrides several years earlier, or the one built by the Russians into the granite of Mali i Cikes mountain where it touched the Adriatic in southern Albania. If this structure was similar to those, she thought, there would be little of great interest here, besides that single, spectacular letter at the opening. She had long concluded that military technologists, from whatever century, were generally huge bores. Big boys with expensive and deadly toys. And that thought made her, once again, feel a pang at the loss of the *Nautilus* mission. If there was anything sublimely interesting to be found during this whole project, she knew it would be on that submarine in the West Fjord. They all knew it.

The upward-looking sonar told Archer that another twenty meters of water lay above the probe. Beyond that, she was getting a different reading, possibly from a pocket of air. Whatever it was, it was about four meters tall. Archer directed the *NU-4* to maneuver to the far end of the structure and begin to rise. In a moment, the probe had reached a wall at the far end, and begun to ascend slowly toward the surface of the cavern's pond.

When the maneuver was complete, it took a moment for Archer to register the fact that the probe had stopped and was resting on the surface of the undersea cavern. All readings were now stationary. The altimeter showed that the *NU-4* was twenty-three meters off the bottom. The sonars were sending back the same continuous readings, so she shut them down. The magnetometer too. Her attention was now focused on the roving lens of the high-resolution camera, which swiveled slowly upwards like the baleful eye of a whale, and revealed something that made her jump back in her chair.

Someone was looking back at her.

"Bloody Jesus!"

She froze in her chair, heart pounding. Several people were looking back at her. Then she saw that they were all standing in odd, formal poses. She was looking at a clutch of statues, statues of classical figures, maybe Greek or Roman gods. She was not a classicist. This was incredible.

"AK," she called over her console. "I need you to come in here right now."

It was an undersea Pantheon. Seawater sloshed around the legs of the taller of these white figures, around the torsi of the shorter ones. The figures, more than a dozen and apparently marble, stood upright along some kind of ledge. Her mind was spinning. She thought she recognized one as Zeus, but she could not be sure. Perhaps it was Prometheus. Her thoughts were racing ahead to all of the things she would need to do now. She made certain that the high-resolution digital camera was still on-line.

"Record, you bloody son of a bitch," she whispered. "Just keep recording, goddamn you."

Of course, she thought. A man who retrieved cargoes of art and jewels from the bottom of the seas. What would he possibly do with such enormous statuary? He could not keep it permanently on board the *Nautilus*, so he established a sculpture garden here. But why only this classical stuff? She hollered through to the executive assistant's console.

"Ms. Higginson, are you there?"

"Yes, Dr. Archer. Is there something I can help you with?"

"Ms. Higginson, who do we have on the staff who is a classicist?"

"I'm not quite sure. Do you want me to—"

"Look, Ms. H.," said Archer. She felt herself hyperventilating. "This is really important. I need our best person, and immediately."

"Do you want me to also—"

"Goddamit, Ms. H! Just do it, please! I want someone on my console in five minutes who knows every pimple on every bloody Greek god's ass."

"Yes, ma'am," replied Higginson evenly. If Higginson was offended by Archer's tone, she did not express it outwardly. She had worked for academics long enough to know that they were more temperamental than racehorses. One gave them wide berth. Ms. H set about her assigned task, punched up a list of their classical consultants, and thought no more of Dr. Archer's tizzy.

* * *

On the third morning after their discovery in the West Fjord, Bjorn Larsen heard the urgent chime on his console as he was bolting it to his forearm. It was the first night he had slept in his Oslo apartment since before the start of the summer field season more than two months earlier. It had been very late when he arrived home. He had been asleep while Ellen Archer in Tokyo had made the remarkable discovery of the undersea Pantheon at Bear Island.

There were six e-posts on his console, two of them marked

urgent. Of the four others, two were either a solicitation to buy something or an inquiry about earning big, Big, BIG credits in his spare time doing some unremarkable e-tasking. He recognized one addressed from playagrl69, and containing a large attachment, as a crude APE attempt to inject the Directorate server with a virus. They had already been warned about this one—such warnings seemed to come almost daily now—so he deleted it immediately. The fourth e-post was yet another from a romantic entanglement, one he thought he had artfully dissolved. He also deleted that one without reading it—he had no time for such stuff this morning. He then deleted all of the others save for the two marked "urgent."

One was from AK, another from Ellen. After he had read the detailed instructions contained in the e-post from AK, he opened Ellen's. Maybe he had time for that stuff this morning, after all. He was momentarily deflated when he saw that it was all business, but when he read the contents he felt his pulse begin to hammer at his temples. "Damn," he said aloud. Wait until Serengetti hears about this! He and Serengetti had themselves visited Bear Island in the past, to map out the ruins of the old mining complex there. And all that time, as they shivered on the surface in constant wind and occasional snow flurries, on the other side of the island, *underneath* the island, lay this, this… place. Was it a base or an archive or a warehouse? Or all three?

When Archer had brought him those references in Paris, it had been a simple matter to translate them. But who could have ever suspected this? It cast a whole different light on their find in the West Fjord, but just how that light now refracted, he couldn't say. He felt slightly guilty for not telling Serengetti about his meeting with Archer in Paris, but Serengetti would get over it. He always had. One thing was certain. Their workload had just been doubled, along with their security problems. It was clear that AK understood this, and had charged him to handle them.

Larsen felt somewhat guilty as well, as he replied to Archer. The mission he had been given by AK would not make her happy, but he couldn't help that now. He threw his duvet aside and almost ran for the shower. AK had instructed him to take control of the *Nansen-Uemura-3* probe as it made its way to the West Fjord. He was to oversee as well the emplacement of the observatory being carried to the *Nautilus* site by the *Amundsen 1* probe. This was the mission that Archer had looked forward to when they discussed it in Paris, and now it was his. This was going to complicate his sex life, his love life, but there was no other course.

An hour later, Larsen was back in his office in Transpac's rented spaces at Fornebu Technology Park just outside Oslo, as the *NU-3* probe moved south through the Wide Fjord. The *Amundsen 1* probe was just rounding Danes Island in northwest Svalbard, about six hours behind the faster Nansen probe. Larsen absently monitored the visual data coming from *NU-3*, but all it showed was blue water sliding past.

The probes would not arrive in the West Fjord for several hours. Both were being guided by GPS to the exact spot on the face of the earth occupied by Nemo's *Nautilus*. These were coordinates that he himself had supplied to the Directorate programmers. He would not bother to turn on the survey sonar until the unmanned probe arrived in the West Fjord. There was no need to turn it on sooner. At the moment, there was little for him to do. If he had bothered to turn on the side-scan sonar on the *Nansen* probe, however, he would have caught two submarines making their way north and west, around the northwesternmost islands of Svalbard, and into the Greenland Sea.

All things considered, he thought, this mission was becoming almost routine. Even so, he was looking forward to the opportunity to be the first researcher to deploy the brand new *Amundsen* probe. Several hours later, as Larsen attended to other business in his office, an alarm chimed on his console. The *Nansen* probe had arrived in the West Fjord. Instinctively, he switched on the multi-beam sonar and began a routine sweep of the fjord. He could see that the GPS coordinates were only a few hundred meters removed from the location where he and Serengetti had surfaced after their exploration of the *Nautilus*.

Something was not right. The multi-beam was returning nothing to his console. He checked the other numbers on the data strip at the bottom of his console, and every one of them seemed to be returning good data. He returned to the GPS. The lat/lon was now exactly over the spot where the submarine had rested.

The *Nautilus* was gone.

He could feel himself getting hotter, his breathing coming faster. He checked all of the systems again, and then checked them a third time. There was no instrumentation problem. As if to reassure himself that it had not all been a dream, he trained the high resolution camera on the bottom surface and saw the deep impression where the hull had rested. There was no doubt now. Someone had arrived, probably APE, probably within hours after he and Serengetti had left, and raised the *Nautilus* right out from under them. He thought that they must have used some heavy lift salvage ship. But how had they managed to get it on scene so quickly? Further, how did they manage to get away without being discovered by the *Philippe Tailliez*, which he knew was then on patrol just south of Svalbard?

There would be hell to pay for this. It was going to be a very long, very cold winter.

My God, he thought, how could they have been so blind? Larsen searched his screen in vain, as if he could will the boat back into existence. But there was no *Nautilus* to be found. Reluctantly, he wrote three urgent e-posts. The first went to AK, the second to Ellen Archer. The third he held back. Serengetti would still be en route from the Pacific to his apartment on the other side of Oslo. He waited a bit before hitting the send button.

* * *

Kurosawa opened a carved teak humidor in the bottom drawer of his desk and took out a Partagas cigar. He had given up smoking long ago, and kept these Havanas only for important guests, but suddenly he felt an unfamiliar need to celebrate. He had just chaired an executive council meeting discussion of Archer's thrilling data from Bear Island, data obtained within the past twenty-four hours.

His entire staff was now at work on this project. To have discovered Nemo's base in the Arctic was mind-boggling. But to recover statuary thought lost for two millennia or more was almost beyond his most expansive reckonings.

Mission 46. Whoever Nemo had been, besides a geneticist and sea-faring vigilante, he was apparently also a treasure salvager. Kurosawa had a nagging sense that there might be a fourth piece to this puzzle, one just beyond his grasp, but he couldn't put his finger on it, and now it was irrelevant anyway.

Kurosawa was almost ready to reveal to his top deputies that soon they would all travel to Bear Island—possibly in the company of the figurehead Emperor himself! They would survey both the base and its sculpture garden, and—no one but he knew this yet—lament the tragic loss of the *Nautilus* itself to eco-terrorists. As soon as the *Tailliez* had led the *Nautilus* into the North Sea, he would transmit the coordinates of the Bear Island site to Captain Jørriksen, and ask her to lead both subs there immediately. That would be the beginning of the end, or the end of the beginning.

It was all coming together now. He could feel it! It was the best feeling in the world! As he took his first pull on the Partagas, AK thought of another indulgence. He signaled Ms. Higginson, and told her that if she needed to find him, he would be at Rising Sun Mini-Strokes. It was time to conquer Revenge on Fat Boy.

* * *

An hour later, as Kurosawa was celebrating the magnitude of his foresight and —almost as satisfying—the brilliance of his mini-golf game, the *Philippe Tailliez* led the *Nautilus* slowly north out of the Wide Fjord. Soon the two submarines would pass around the northwestern corner of Spitsbergen. Snow was still falling lightly. Jørriksen was thankful that visibility was still close to zero, and that she had the luxury of following the high frequency sonar on board the *Tailliez*. It was time to leave the Arctic. She was glad to be leaving the pack ice. It was time to head south again.

* * *

At Gardermoen, Commander Johansson arrived just in time to connect to Paris. The flight was full and the aisles were crammed with Norwegians escaping for their summer hols in Paris and points south. The icy heat she had felt earlier mutated into professional detachment, as she scanned the passengers with the silently alert eye of a predator. As the steward delivered tea, she found herself squeezing the slice of lemon a bit too long and a bit too hard. A natural hunter since childhood, she planned and enjoyed tracking even more than the inevitable kill, but executed both with equal skill. Her body tensed and relaxed. She was inexplicably nervous.

By the time she had finished her second tea, the confidential personnel file she had requested from a back channel security contact in AK's office had arrived. The file contained, in brief snippets, everything the Directorate knew about one Paolo Raffaele Serengetti.

Paolo Serengetti, Ph.D.
Co-Director, Transnational Polar Archaeological Consultants (Transpac)

1982: Born Paolo Raffaele Serengetti, Metti, Parma, Italy. May 17.

1983: Parents killed by drunk driver while walking infant Paul. Baby thrown thirty meters but survives. Is adopted by parent's close friends, Vincent and Gianna Umana. Family moved to Maine in the United States in 1990.

1991: Gianna Umana dies from a brain tumor.

1998: Completes solo canoe expedition from St. Lawrence Seaway to Cape Chidley, northernmost Labrador. While in Labrador meets 97-year-old Norwegian explorer, Helge Ingstad, who begins his education in both archaeology and Norwegian language.

2000: Sets new world record living undersea (93 days, 6 hours, and 27 minutes), La Chalupa underwater habitat, Key Largo, Florida. Spends three months in Oslo in Norwegian language immersion course.

2001: Enlists in U.S. Coast Guard as Boatswain's Mate, Third Class. Assigned to Polar class icebreaker Polar Sea *in Seattle. Marries Suzanne Rochelle of Seattle, twenty-five-year-old molecular biology graduate student, divorced mother of two: six-year-old Ben and two-year-old Sara, whom he adopts as his own.*

2001-2002: Serves two consecutive Antarctic deployments on board icebreaker Polar Sea. *Awarded U.S. Antarctic Service Medal, Sea Service Ribbon, Meritorious Unit Commendation with Operational "O" device. Classified one-month expedition to Southwest Asia during Terrorism Wars. Awarded Special Operations Service Ribbon.*

2003: Promoted Petty Officer Second Class, transferred to icebreaker Healy, *serves on third deployment to Antarctica; leads shore party to survey ruins, Borchgrevinck 1898 overwintering hut at Cape Adare. Awarded second Special Operations Service Ribbon for second classified Southwest Asia expedition, as well as second Meritorious Unit Commendation. Begins on-line history degree program via Univ. of Washington while in Antarctica.*

2004: Deploys Arctic on board Healy *in support former National Science Foundation survey historical sites Northwest Passage. Awarded Arctic Service Medal, Commandant's Letter of Commendation, Good Conduct Medal.*

2005: Promoted Petty Officer First Class. Given temporary

assignment as interpreter on board barkentine Triumph *for duration special summer cruise to Norwegian archipelago Svalbard. While on deployment, daughter and four first grade classmates killed when estranged boyfriend holds teacher hostage, eventually killing himself as well as teacher. Serengetti re-assigned small boat station near Seattle.*

2006: Bachelor of Arts degree from the University of Washington, major: Scandinavian Studies; minor: history. Application for commission rejected: poor eyesight, bad back.

2007: Moves family Baltimore, joins team fitting out U.S.'s first nuclear Coast Guard icebreaker, Edward H. "Iceberg" Smith. *Awarded Coast Guard Achievement Medal, second Good Conduct Medal.*

2008: Leaves on board Iceberg Smith *for research cruise Wrangel Island, part of joint US-Russia exploration of the wreck of the Soviet research vessel* Chelyuskin, *followed by joint US-Japanese deployment Antarctica for Operation Falling Star, search for Martian meteorites during the winter of 2008-2009. Promoted Chief Petty Officer while on Wrangel Island. Serves as liaison/ translator for Norwegian Rear Admiral Strøm Haugland. Decorated with Commendation Medal. Crosses equator eighth time. While in Antarctica, stepson drowns while on kayak expedition on Mackenzie River in Yukon. Wife files for divorce.*

2009: Leaves active duty with Coast Guard, moves to Norway, begins graduate study Univ. of Oslo. Meets Bjorn Larsen. Introduces Larsen to wife during divorce proceedings. Divorced from wife. Wife marries Larsen. They in turn divorce within two years.

2011: Master's degree in Polar ethnology and archaeology, Univ. of Oslo. Moves Honolulu for doctoral research on human exploration of the Pacific.

2016: Ph.D. from the Univ. of Hawai'i, for dissertation: "Prehistoric basalt mines of the South Pacific as surveyed with element-SAR from space station Inishi-1: Indicators of transitionary post-Lapita migratory routes." Published by Stanford University Press as "Exploring Global Explorers with Space-based Archaeology."

2017: Participates World Heritage Site conference in Havana, Cuba, delivers keynote talk on "The preservation of the Soviet-era mine at Pyramiden, Svalbard." One of twelve participants invited private dinner with 89-year-old Cuban ex-President Fidel Castro.

2018: Moves back to Oslo. With Larsen, forms Transnational Polar Archaeology Consultants (Transpac). Signs agreement with Directorate for Human Exploration in Tokyo for five-year (2018-2022) series of archaeological surveys in polar basin using icebreaker Polar Quest *and submarine* Philippe Tailliez. *Contract now in final year.*

Current Address: Grieg Apartments, Von Øtkens vei, Oslo, Norway.

There was more: a vitae with more publications, reports, invited lectures and all the other dull, self-aggrandizing details of an academic life. There was a small digigraph of him at his desk in Oslo, the corners of his eyes rather downturned. And there were other, medical, details, that she chose to skip over (date of Anthrax vaccination, date of first data chip implant, date of last HIV-3 vaccination, etc., etc.), along with several e-post addresses and his private U.N. mobile number. She wondered what he'd been doing in Southwest Asia during the Terrorism Wars, but knew she had more than enough techniques to get that information out of him if she really wanted it. Johansson closed the file, darkened her console, and rubbed her eyes. Solid service record; good field worker, interesting professional life; tragic personal life. She had read hundreds just like it.

The personal history stood out for her. He had lost not one but two mothers, along with a father. His children had died cruel deaths. Then a divorce. And then Larsen had not hesitated to step in to fill the breach. No wonder he possessed such sad eyes.

She reached up and clicked off her overhead light. Almost subconsciously, she found herself memorizing Serengetti's address in Oslo. More to the point, she now had her own feelings to match with Jørriksen's hunch, a purpose to her hunting: she determined to put her own professional abilities in shadowing, tracking, pursuit and capture to good use.

* * *

Serengetti had turned off the sound alarms on his console, but the blinking light alarms were still active. One of them woke him up as he tried to sleep on his flight to Paris. It was a message from Larsen, and at first Serengetti thought he must be dreaming. How could the *Nautilus* be gone? Like the *Italia*, it was there, then it was gone, vanished into the Arctic mists.

After he read the e-post a second time, he sent a message back to Larsen, but in ten minutes when no reply came back, he shut down his console, removed it from his arm, and put it in his carry-on. It occurred to him that he had not been console-less now for a year or more, and the flesh on his arm where the console had rested was pale and wrinkled. For several minutes his mind went blank, and if he had been able to think of it, he would have recalled that he had endured this same sensation twice before in his life. If he was aware of anything, it was relief that the aircraft cabin was darkened and most of the passengers asleep. Anyone who saw his face would think he had just learned of the death of a close friend.

When his brain started working again, his first thought, incongruously, was of Holland. He thought of some of the paintings he had seen in Amsterdam, classic paintings of the countryside of Holland. In one of those inexpensive museum guidebooks, he had read something that had meant nothing to him then, but came back to him now.

For centuries, the booklet had said, art critics and historians alike had looked at the work of the Dutch masters as true representations of the Dutch landscape. If the cows in the paintings were fat and happy, then the cows that lived in Holland when the painting was composed had all been fat and happy. Then some bright revisionist had gone back to contemporary diaries, and discovered that all the cows of the time had been imported, starving and debilitated, from some diseased port in Russia, Murmansk perhaps, or someplace in the Baltic.

Then the revisionists got to the clouds.

A meteorologist took a look at those famously vast formations of clouds, and concluded that such billowy castles were very impressive physical impossibilities. Clouds existed, of course, but in the real meteorological world such clouds as those rendered by the Dutch masters could not exist. To the meteorologist, it was obvious. The great Dutch masters had never actually seen such clouds. They had simply made them up.

That is what would be whispered about him, Serengetti thought bitterly. He had made the whole thing up, staged it, just as some old-timers still believed about the first landings on the moon. He fingered the small disc of data from the library in his shoulder pocket. If he had been anywhere but on a jet at 30,000 feet he would have pitched it out the window. Who would now believe that the *Nautilus* itself had sat humming on a fjord shallow for 150 years? He had even had a vague but enticing hope that they might be allowed to bring the sub to Oslo, where it could be displayed next to Amundsen's *Gjøa*, Nansen's *Fram*, and Heyerdahl's *Kon-Tiki*. But now it was gone, secreted away into some private transnational collection. Like the clouds painted by a Dutch master, it was a magnificent idea; like a stolen painting, they would never see it again.

Nine: A Victory at Sea

"[The Nautilus] is a world apart, as foreign to terra firma as the planets accompanying this globe around the sun, and we will never benefit from the studies of Saturn's or Jupiter's scientists."

—Jules Verne
Twenty Thousand Leagues Under the Seas, 1870
William Butcher translation (1998)

The *North Sea Avenger* was on patrol less than one hundred nautical miles west of Tromsø, hiding from U.N. patrol vessels. This temporary duty as a freelance killer, under a big contract from APE, would support EM operations for another year. It was clear to Captain Kutepov what APE wanted, but it would be difficult to locate the *Philippe Tailliez* and its unnamed escort without giving away his own position at the same time. It was for that reason that he ordered the *NSA* to switch off its active sonar and steam into a position just south of Spitsbergen, where they would lay to on the surface, watching and listening.

That was hardly the captain's biggest problem. The fuel market at Andreeva Bay had been able to supply them with only two 400mm torpedoes, and one of them was so old he had grave doubts as to its effectiveness. If he was going to execute the contract for APE, he was only going to get one shot at each UNESCO submarine. He would have preferred to put this off until they could re-supply their weaponry with better stuff, but who knew when that would happen? They were lucky to have the two.

As he set their new course, speed, and depth, his X.O., Espadon, was asking why APE cared about a pair of old U.N. subs on patrol way up here?

"Seems they had a little fun with each other earlier this week," said the captain. "The U.N. wants to migrate, and APE wants to find and sell. That makes them enemies."

"Migrate?"

"Yes," said the captain. He repeated the rumor he had heard on one of the green sites that the U.N. wanted to take their command and control operations off planet, leaving the peripherals behind to choke on the foul air created by transnational industries. Everybody knew that the U.N. had been researching migration and exploration sites for five years now, and the new rumor had it that the U.N. was trying to insure that no important genetic or cultural data was left behind. "They've been very quiet about it," said the captain. "But word has been slipping."

"What the hell," said Espadon, who signed on with EM to sink whalers, not cultural resource submarines, and told the captain so. Her politics began and ended with the need she felt to prevent butchers from dragging the living flesh of whales across splintered wooden ramps into two-meter buzz saws.

"Look at it this way," said Kutepov. "If the U.N. does want to go off-planet, they're going to need more nuclear rockets, like the one on the surface of Mars now, and to make more powerful rockets they'll have to do more nuclear tests in the Pacific, as well as more transport and habitat experiments. Well, now they'll have to do their research with two fewer submarines."

The thought that they might be interfering with Pacific nuclear tests changed the complexion of the entire mission for Espadon. Suddenly, she couldn't wait to get into action.

"We'll only get one shot at each of them," reminded Kutepov.

Espadon nodded. "One is all we'll need," she said. "But when we find her, their sonar will light us up like a Christmas tree."

"I know," said the captain with a smile. "It's a good thing the *Philippe Tailliez*, at least, doesn't carry any weapons. The other sub may be just an old hulk, so we'll take the *Tailliez* out first. Once they leave the DMZ around Svalbard, they're fair game."

Of course, thought Espadon, and she let out a breath of relief. She had completely forgotten. They were facing a toothless enemy. The cultural patrol submarines carried scientists instead of weapons, had no countermeasures, and doubtless their sonar was ancient and ineffective. They would catch them on the surface, unarmed, defenseless, and with nowhere to run.

Now she felt even better.

Twenty-four hours later, hidden on the crest of a wide cold thermocline south of the South Cape and north of Bear Island, the *NSA* listened silently as, in the distance, the screw of the *Philippe Tailliez* spun toward their position. Everyone was on their toes now, especially the sonar tech, who was nonetheless having a hard time separating the obvious sounds made by the old and creaky *Philippe Tailliez* from the strange and persistent sonar shadow it seemed to cast about four thousand meters astern.

At first, the tech thought that it must be some kind of sound reflection off the thermocline, but this particular sonar shadow cast by the *Tailliez* seemed to make a unique sound all its own. The tech had never heard anything like it before, so he was having a hard time even finding a description for it. When he reported the shadow to the conn, Kutepov told him that he was probably correct. Most likely it was some kind of reflection off the inversion, or the antique engine of the hulk the *Tailliez* was escorting. Concentrate on the *Tailliez*, Kutepov told him. So he did.

* * *

The *Nautilus* had fallen back, deliberately, and was now more than two nautical miles astern of the *Philippe Tailliez*. As the two submarines navigated down the western coast of Spitsbergen, Jørriksen, ebullient at the continuing success of the mission, had decided to give herself a little sea room in order to see what the *Nautilus* could do. Mystified as to how the boat managed to maintain course and speed with only the tiniest pressure on the antique throttles, she had begun a series of incremental tests of the speed and maneuverability of the submarine.

Controlling the yaw of the massive knife-edged bow also proved to be a challenge. At some speeds and with the trim down in the stern, it seemed to act almost like a surfboard, lifting much of the bulk of the submarine up onto the seas. If she trimmed forward, then the bow sliced downwards into the seas like an Old Norse god, battle-axe held high. Ten fathoms down, the bow knife might actually speed the progress of the submarine through the ocean. Perhaps Nemo had designed it that way, she thought.

It had now been thirty-six hours since they had left the West Fjord, and seventy-two since they first boarded the *Nautilus*. Jørriksen and her skeleton crews on board both subs were exhausted. But the end was in sight. Tokyo had dispatched a new set or orders, and even though Jørriksen was at first irritated that she would not be allowed to lead their two-submarine fleet into a port on the mainland, she was too tired to argue. Bear Island was only a hundred nautical miles south, and following her orders Jørriksen had increased the speed of both subs to eight knots. In less than ten hours, they would arrive at their staging position off the northwest coast of Bear Island.

Just as she was about to ask the Chief to conn the sub while she took a few hours rest, something about the sonar data being patched through to her from the *Tailliez* snapped her to alertness.

"*Tailliez*, conn."

"Go, conn."

"Double check on that anomaly sitting just above the inversion layer, will you?" The Captain gave the sonar tech the range and bearing, about five thousand meters off to the southwest.

"Aye, conn," replied the X.O., Lt. Lindgren, and a moment later the sonar tech had sent a new set of images to Jørriksen.

"Conn, *Tailliez*."

"Go *Tailliez*."

"Nice call, Kaptein. Sonar thinks it's a sub, maybe a *Challenger* Class, trying to hide on the layer."

It was an elementary school trick, thought Jørriksen, the work of an inexperienced captain. Was it shadowing the *Tailliez*, or just passing through on their way to the North Sea from the black market refueling base near Murmansk? Probably stumbled on us by mistake. If they were listening for a clunky diesel, then the high-pitched whirring of the *Nautilus* turbine would hardly register with them. She wondered how Tokyo would react to the knowledge that they had been found. If it was a *Challenger* Class, then it was very likely the same sub responsible for the recent whale-killer sinkings. EM was not known to be able to afford many weapons, so Jørriksen thought it likely that this sub would leave the *Tailliez* alone.

"Keep on him, *Tailliez*. He may be just looking you over."

Even so, Jørriksen kept the *Nautilus* on course, directly in line with the *Tailliez*. Don't do anything to make them think there are two subs here, she thought to herself. Just the old, rusty, harmless *Tailliez* on a walk through the park. Then, perhaps from the feeling of technological superiority engendered by skippering the *Nautilus*, or the duty she felt to protect Nemo's submarine, or from a desire to recapture surging emotions she remembered as a young girl in a movie theater, or from all of these, she allowed herself a brief moment as John Wayne.

"Don't mess with me today, little man," Jørriksen hissed at the sonar image splayed across her console. "That's my sub you're looking at. So don't mess with me today. I'm sitting right fokking behind you."

Just as she was mouthing these words, she heard the excited voice of Lt. Lindgren.

"Conn, *Tailliez*!"

"Go, *Tailliez*."

"Conn, the *Challenger* has flooded her tubes!"

"Bastard!" said Jørriksen.

This was intolerable. Jørriksen had no weaponry, none of the old countermeasures; she was not even on board her own command; and she was being forced to make decisions remotely and nearly blindly, over her console, without direct access to her command team. She punched up the sonar images of the temperature inversion. The anomaly was exactly fifty meters long. It was a *Challenger* Class, alright. Fokking Swedish submarine. And they were coming after the slow and defenseless *Tailliez*. As she studied the new images and tried to conceive of a saving maneuver, she heard the X.O. again. This time Lindgren's voice verged on panic.

"Swim-out!" yelled the X.O. "Torpedo in the water! Shit! Conn, swim-out in the water! Coming hard on the starboard beam. Repeat, torpedo in the water!"

The *Philippe Tailliez* had approximately three minutes to live.

* * *

Kurosawa had not slept this well in months. Moreover, he had enjoyed eight hours of uninterrupted slumber in his own bed, in his own home. As he rose early on the morning of the fifth day—the sun was not yet above the horizon—after the discovery of the *Nautilus*, he paused to enjoy an uncharacteristically large and leisurely breakfast. He even joked with his man-servant. This promised to be a long and extremely satisfying day, and he wanted to enjoy it on a full stomach.

He scanned his morning console traffic, noting the expected e-post from Larsen that the *Nautilus* was gone. He hated lying to his top lieutenants, but there was no other way. Larsen would forgive him, like a good and loyal son. AK was certain of that. After breakfast, still in the darkness, Kurosawa did yet another thing that was out of character. Instead of bicycling straight to his office, he took a short detour and within a few minutes had arrived at the entrance to Rising Sun Mini-Strokes. The previous evening, despite some of the best shot-making of his life, he had been defeated once again by Revenge on Fat Boy. He stood there at the short metal fence, peering over at his nemesis. Then Kurosawa looked over at the dark and empty office, where the racks of colorful balls and rows of neatly arranged putters rested and called out to him. The *Nautilus* would be at sea for half a day or more, Kurosawa thought. No one would ever know if he slipped over the fence, activated his account, and took a few practice shots.

So it was that, for the third time this early morning, Kurosawa found himself bowing slightly toward his blue ball, perched expectantly atop a small tee made from a square patch of rubber. The computer read the bar code on his wing tips and immediately recalculated the angle of the bumpers. But this time, for the very first time, A. Kurosawa correctly surmised the new angles and saw the path clearly toward victory. With a concentration borne of more than four decades of intense academic research, Kurosawa addressed his blue ball, drew back his putter, and executed a smooth and elegant stroke. He watched in growing anticipation as the ball accelerated down several ramps, around a corner, ricocheted off the spinning atom with its exaggerated electron orbits made from clear strips of plastic, and then rolled along a narrow straightaway to the very edge of the tiny round cup.

The ball shivered along the edge for a fraction of a second. Kurosawa held his breath. It seemed to come to perfectly stillness; then it plopped in.

In the insane days that followed, Kurosawa did not forget the thing that happened next. Not only had he himself never sunk this hole-in-one, neither had anyone else, so it came as a complete shock when the spinning plastic mock atom, about the size of a bowling ball, began to turn red and start to emit a sort of strange humming sound. Kurosawa looked around quickly, embarrassed. He raised a single finger to his lips, as if somehow that would make the sound go away. When the humming only increased, and the clear plastic bands began to spin wildly, the Director backed away slowly, then hastily, incongruously clutching his putter for protection. He watched in amazement as the atom shot from the ground like a rocket, attained an altitude of perhaps five hundred meters, and exploded in a shower of red, white, and gold fireworks.

It was several moments before Kurosawa realized that he was actually weeping at this remarkable spectacle, and it was several moments more before he felt the insistent vibration of his console.

He was being hailed, and urgently. When Ms. Higginson patched through the horrific display from the webcams on board the *Nautilus*, Kurosawa's first and only impulse was to think up a lie and think it up quick.

* * *

Serengetti's plane touched down outside of Paris just as Captain Jørriksen, some two thousand kilometers to the north, was swinging the *Nautilus* around and into battle. Serengetti fastened on his console and made his way through the convolutions of Charles de Gaulle. It was the later part of a warm European day, one that would see him at the Verne Archives and end, so he fervently hoped, with him en route to his own bed back in Oslo. He expected to have several hours in the archives before it closed, but he had already decided not to stay overnight. He wanted to be back at Charles de Gaulle for the last flight to Norway at midnight.

He hurried to the Bourse and walked quickly into the Bibliotheque Nationale de France on the rue de Richelieu. He directed his steps to the famous manuscript reading room, a magnificent cavern of cast iron work designed by the architect Henri Labrouste in 1868. Victor Hugo's donation of his private manuscript collection in the 1880s led to a stream of other such author bequests, including, in 1910, those of the family of Jules Verne, who had died at Amiens five years earlier. A handsome young staffer with wavy black hair greeted Serengetti, motioning him toward the guest register. As he signed in, Serengetti could not help but notice that the staffer seemed almost immediately to put his fingers on the box containing ms4.

"There you are," said the young man in French, as he placed the gray archival box on a large smooth wooden table. He handed Serengetti a pair of thin white gloves, explaining as he did so that he would not be allowed to handle the manuscript without them, for body oils were deleterious to old paper. The young man then made an off-hand remark about how it was a good thing that he had not bothered to reshelve the box.

"Gets a lot of looking over, does it?" asked Serengetti.

"Not especially," said the staffer. "But there was a spectacular-looking woman who came in to see it just yesterday."

Serengetti's French was not particularly sharp, but he needed to do no more than scan the densely spaced holograph manuscript. He was looking for a margin note, not something in the text itself. Within twenty minutes he had found it and, before he allowed himself to begin translating, he paused to study the script of Jules Verne. Was it his imagination or were these strokes committed to paper almost violently, with harsh strokes and slashes of emphasis? Leave that to the psycho-historians, he thought. He had enough to worry about.

The note itself was not very long, and he doubted that anyone with merely a passing interest in Verniana would pay much attention to it. It described an expedition to a dormant volcano south of Java, after the hurried abandonment of an expedition base on an Arctic island identified only as "barren." Serengetti recognized the reference immediately. There were a thousand barren islands in the Arctic, but only one that had ever been given that precise name. He got out his stylus and wrote a brief e-post to Larsen, whom he assumed was by now back at Kings Bay. It said merely: "Have lost West Fjord, but gained N at Bear Island. Success! En route Oslo in three hours. At Kings Bay noon tomorrow. PS/Paris."

Before he returned ms4 to its green, acid-free folder and replaced it in the gray archival box, Serengetti allowed himself just a moment to riffle through the remaining pages. Toward the end of the manuscript, he saw an excruciatingly brief question, only six words, clearly written in Verne's hand. Serengetti translated it twice, and then again a third time. The first five words posed no problems. But Serengetti was having trouble with the sixth, in part because he was not certain whether Verne used the verb actively or passively. He was about to ask the young French staffer to offer his translation as well, but thought better of it. As he closed the flap of the gray box, the question rang in his head, over and over and over. The question Verne had asked was this: *Est-ce que Nemo était coincé?* And the best translation Serengetti could come up with was this:

"Was Nemo trapped?"

Serengetti went to the assistant's desk to thank him, and as he did so he was stopped cold by the name he saw written in a small, neat hand several places above his own: Archer, E.

* * *

"Starboard 90°," ordered Lt. Lindgren. "Flank speed. Get us out of here."

One minute later, the sonar tech called out, "Three thousand, three hundred meters and coming on hard."

As the reports and commands filtered onto Jørriksen's console, she listened helplessly. The *Challenger* could fire old NATO Mark 48s; if a 48 was now bearing down on the *Tailliez*, she would not get away. The torpedo had already executed its target acquisition and attack procedure. Even if it somehow missed the *Tailliez*, it would turn and attack again. And it would continue to attack until the *Tailliez* was blown out of the sea.

"Two thousand, five hundred meters, X.O.," called out the sonar tech.

Lindgren said nothing.

"*Tailliez*, conn."

"Go, conn," said Lindgren.

"What's going on with the second fish?"

"Stand by, conn. Sonar, what's going on…

"X.O., sonar."

"Go, sonar."

"Second tube is flooded, but they haven't fired. Two thousand meters now."

"They've got one more tube open, conn," Lindgren said to Jørriksen. "But they haven't fired."

"One thousand, five hundred meters." The torpedo was coming on at more than fifty knots.

They had less than one minute left.

"*Tailliez*, conn," said Jørriksen. She'd be damned if she was going to let her sub go down like this.

"Go, conn."

"Sonar, get me a firing solution!"

Lindgren thought the Captain had gone nuts.

"X.O., sonar. One thousand meters."

"Kaptein, we don't have any bloody weapons…"

"Get it now!"

"Sonar, X.O!"

"Conn, sonar, aye. I'm on it, X.O."

The sonar tech plotted the course and speed of the *Challenger* Class from the *Nautilus*, and fed the data to Jørriksen's console. Then she prayed that her geometry was correct—and that the *Nautilus* was really as fast as she seemed to be. Then she called out: "Five hundred meters."

Frantically, Jørriksen studied the data coming from her sonar tech on the *Tailliez*. She turned the two wheels that trimmed the *Nautilus* and brought the submarine down at the bow. Even as a Norwegian, Jørriksen had to admit her special fondness for the Swedish-built *Näcken* Class. She had herself served as X.O. on a training cruise on board a *Näcken* Class, the *Neptun*.

"X.O., sonar. Four hundred meters."

But she had never been on board one of the smaller, faster *Challenger* Class subs. She would have no remorse over sending this one to the bottom, but she had to get there fast, before they could fire their second swim-out. Why hadn't they fired it already? Probably waiting to enjoy the fireworks from the first one, Jørriksen thought. Or maybe waiting to take a shot at the *Nautilus* itself. "We'll see about that," she said to herself. "By God we will."

"Conn, *Tailliez*. Three hundred meters. Thanks for everything. Godspeed."

But Jørriksen was not listening to the last words of her X.O. Instead she called down to her Chief Engineer in the engine room of the *Nautilus*.

"Engineering, conn," she said steadily.

"Conn, engineering." Jørriksen could hear the excitement in her Chief Engineer's voice. Their blood was up now.

"Chief, I need ramming speed in ten seconds or we're all dead."

"Conn, I don't even know what the speeds *are* on this engine!" yelled the Chief.

"Six seconds, Chief," said Jørriksen. "We're going to ram the *Nautilus* right down their goddamned throat!"

"Captain Jørriksen!" she heard over her console.

"Who is this?" barked Jørriksen.

"Captain, this is Akagi Kurosawa. You are ordered immediately to stand down! I repeat: *stand down!* Under no circumstances are you to endanger the *Nautilus*!" It had been the only lie that Kurosawa had been able to think up quickly. But his frantic call from Tokyo was too late. Ingvill Jørriksen had not spent two decades underwater only to be taken out by a Swedish submarine. She switched off her console. Then she called out to her tiny crew on board the *Nautilus*.

"Ramming speed, now!"

"Hang on!" yelled the Chief. "Three, two, one. *NOW!*"

Jørriksen felt her body jerked backward with a snap she had never experienced on board a submarine. Despite being heavy in the bow, the *Nautilus* almost seemed to leap upward as Jørriksen pushed the throttles all the way forward. As she did so, she resisted a painful need to cover her ears. The shrill whine coming from the engine room was like nothing she had ever heard before.

* * *

On board the *North Sea Avenger*, the sonar tech heard it, too. To him it sounded like the swarming of a million angry bees. Just as he was about to call Captain Kutepov, the sonar tech saw on his screens what appeared to be a seventy-meter-long bullet moving through the water straight for them. His last thought before his instantaneous death was that he had never seen anything move through the ocean so fast.

* * *

The *Nautilus* struck the *Challenger* Class just aft of its sonar dome, piercing the single pressure hull even as the *Nautilus* was still accelerating. Thrown backward when she commenced the attack, Jørriksen was now thrown forward as the *Nautilus* struck, and she felt something crack in her neck as her head struck the top edge of the port lens. Then she heard something about a dud coming over her console. Desperately she willed her mind to clear, just as she realized with consternation that the *Nautilus* was steadily tilting forward. The bow was now down about ten degrees and falling.

The *Nautilus* was sinking.

"Conn! Conn! It never exploded!" screamed Lindgren in delight. "Repeat. They hit us with a dud!"

Jørriksen groaned and somehow forced herself upright. Gingerly she lifted her fingers to her head and felt a gash to her right temple. Blood began dripping into her eye. The *Nautilus* was now down more than twelve degrees in the bow, and Jørriksen found herself again fighting to stand upright. She thought she could hear voices, and realized she was hearing the screams of the submariners on board the *Challenger* Class.

It was only then that Jørriksen realized the full magnitude of the situation. She had not rammed a wooden-hulled, nineteenth-century man of war, but a twenty-first century steel-hulled submarine. Instead of plowing through it, Jørriksen had instead skewered the *Nautilus* to a 200-ton steel anchor. That anchor was now pulling them down, two thousand meters down, down to the bottom of the North Sea. She knew that Jules Verne had written that the *Nautilus* could descend to some ridiculous depth like 16,000 meters—one of her instructors at the old Norwegian sub base at Horten had even made a joke about it—but she wasn't about to gamble the lives of her crew on a fiction. The pressure would flatten the hull of the *Nautilus* before it descended halfway down to the bottom of the North Sea.

"Chief, conn," Jørriksen moaned. "You there, Chief?"

"Aye, conn," said the Chief. "But sweet Christ, I wouldn't recommend we try that little maneuver again."

"Chief, back us out of here."

"All full back, conn. But she's not responding."

Jørriksen heard it, too. They couldn't back off, not while the *Nautilus*' screw was elevated over the surface of the sea, clawing at the air. Jørriksen heard an ominous series of pops and explosions as the *Challenger* Class filled with seawater. Then it began to plummet.

The *Nautilus*, its prey impaled upon its spear, sank too.

* * *

The consciousness that was once the submarine captain Josef Kutepov seemed to float as if weightless. It struggled to connect his thoughts to his eyes and mouth. One eye opened slightly, but his mouth refused to obey the commands of his brain.

A face floated past Kutepov, the face of his sonar man. It drifted on icy water into his field of vision, and he saw that the head had been severed from its body. The sonar man's face possessed a look of wide-eyes wonder, as if this was the first day of school, or summer vacation. Thin clouds of blood trailed from the neck, as if propelling him across his captain's gaze.

Kutepov tried to breathe but his lungs would not work, refusing to suck in. His one open eye saw his executive officer, Espadon, trying to shout an order. All that came out from her wide open mouth was a cloud of deep purple blood. She was shouting at her captain with words of blood.

He had to get back in control of his submarine, but it was impossible to know which direction was up. There was only a bizarre feeling of sliding naked down an endless glacier. Kutepov tried to move but again his body refused to respond. In a fleeting moment of lucidity he remembered that he was Josef Kutepov, submarine captain, reader of great literature, collector of rents. He had been standing near the conn, or was it the 'scope, or the sonar station? A bulkhead had collapsed on him and now compressed his skull against a chart table.

The increasing pressure of the collapsing bulkhead forced the single leg of the chart table through the metal table and against Kutepov's ear. Then into his ear. Then, as he felt himself slide farther down the glacier, the chart table leg cracked his skull. What would come first? Would he freeze, or drown, or be crushed?

The head of his sonar man had floated into the void, and his executive officer screamed at him in saltwater blood. Saltwater blood. Born in saltwater blood; returned to saltwater blood. How long had he been like this? Seconds were as decades, each one longer and so much worse than the one before. The captain lay in silence as the saltwater softly kissed him on his bloodless lips.

A human on the surface of the sea, equipped with average intelligence and a stopwatch, with depth and pressure gauges, could have recorded that the *NSA* had fallen almost a meter per second. A medical doctor could have informed that the captain's neck was snapped at its base and his skull cracked at its apex and punctured above his ear hole. Josef Kutepov had been drowning for ninety-three seconds when the pressure on his lungs reached ten times what he would have felt on them on the surface. Barely twenty seconds of life remained.

Pressure squeezed the final pockets of air from *NSA*, including the one in Kutepov's lungs. As a boy he read a story of the American West: a frontier soldier survived forty years after taking a Sioux arrow to the brain and having his scalp sawed from his living skull by a dull stone blade. As he thought this, the chart table leg transited his brain even as pressure forced the last pocket of air from his lungs.

The consciousness that was Josef Kutepov escaped in that bloodied belch of air, and steadily expanded as it rose toward the surface of the sea. The body that was Josef Kutepov managed to raise a finger in an attempt to retrieve its consciousness, but even that motion was an involuntary motor reflex of a pale-faced corpse.

Muted flickers of light from electronics shorting out briefly lit small areas around the submarine's interior until it, too, died away.

* * *

Serengetti stepped slowly down the steps of the Bibliotheque Nationale and out onto the rue de Richelieu. He needed to sit down but no convenient place presented itself. A million separate thoughts seemed to crash together in his mind. They had lost the *Nautilus*, and for that they would never be forgiven. Worse, while it was still in their hands, he had wasted his time on a fool's errand in Paris. If his return to the Pacific had led to the discovery of Nemo's Arctic base, Serengetti would have considered it worth the pain it caused. Now the *Nautilus* was gone, and Nemo's base, he could only assume, had been located by Ellen Archer a day before Serengetti even suspected its existence.

He couldn't fathom why AK would ask him to look at the Verne Archives when he'd obviously already asked Archer to do the same thing. Perhaps she had screwed up? But that was impossible. Archer never screwed up. So why was he here? Did AK think him not only expendable, but an impediment as well?

Serengetti tried to head in one direction, back to the Bourse, to catch the flight back to Oslo. But almost immediately he walked into a man loading an envelope into an overnight delivery box. He jumped when a construction worker on a scaffold shouted at him, until he realized dully that the man was yelling instead at a co-worker. He wandered toward the Bourse, then past it, even though he knew he had to enter that station in order to return to Charles de Gaulle.

Before he could think through just where he was going, a tall, distinguished-looking man walked toward him, and it became clear that he was on his way to intercept him. Serengetti almost thought that the man had called out his name. But he was still thinking over what he had seen in the guest book, and did not respond. So the man asked after him again.

"Might you be Dr. Paolo Serengetti?"

Serengetti had never heard anyone use his middle name. Not since he was ten years old.

"We met at the conference in Havana, if you recall. Several years ago. You gave an excellent talk."

Havana, thought Serengetti. Yes, Havana. He had indeed been there. But how did this man know his middle name. Serengetti never used that name, ever. Yes, he had been to that conference. But this man's face? He did not remember it. Then again, there were always hundreds of people at those things, and he was terrible with names and faces unless he saw them several times over. Or unless he had a reason to remember them. Like "Archer, E." That was a name scored permanently on the tablets of his memory. Now he would never be able to forget her, even if he wanted to. But not this fellow. This man he did not remember at all. But he was well-dressed, and wore an expensive console.

"Good evening," was all Serengetti could think to say, in French, and it almost sounded as if the words had come from someone else's brain and mouth. He knew he sounded like a fool, but he couldn't really say what he was thinking, which was "Please go away." He was in the middle of an intense concentration on the riddle of the *Nautilus*, and in such a state he had always been able to shut people out.

"*Bon*, Doctor!" the man said. "This is completely unexpected! *Bon! C'est tres bien!* I just wanted to tell you how much I enjoyed your talk." He put his arm through Serengetti's. "Do you have just a moment? Please let me buy you a drink."

Serengetti started to protest, tried to hold onto his thoughts, but the thought of a drink was suddenly attractive. Fill my veins with good wine, he thought. Serengetti felt himself nodding at the man, even as he was utterly disinterested in him, or why he was in Paris. How many times had old colleagues and friends met him in strange places, in bizarre and unexpected locations? You just accepted it. Life was full of mostly happy coincidences like that. Or bourbon, he thought. Why not take the American path to oblivion.

Just as quickly as he had stopped to accept the man's greeting, he found himself walking rapidly again, as the two of them strode away from the Bourse. They walked along the Boulevard Haussmann, then toward the Hôtel Drouot Richelieu, still chatting rapidly about the talk in Havana. Serengetti's mind was beginning to clear when the passed a deep doorway. Finally, Serengetti thought. His thirst was powerful, aching.

It was just then, as he thought they were about to enter the café, that Serengetti saw a woman in jeans and a light jacket approach the darkened doorway. In the split second that followed, he did not know what surprised him more, the identity of the woman, or the dart pistol she pulled from her jacket pocket.

"Step away from him," said Lcdr. Johansson.

For a moment, Serengetti could not figure out whether she was talking to him or to this fellow from the Havana conference. Or how she had gotten here from the *Tailliez*. None of it made any sense.

It was only then that Serengetti felt Havana man's fist close hard around his right upper arm, and he caught a brief flash of silver from the corner of his eye, just before he felt the point of a knife at the base of his neck. Only then did he realize that he had just met an agent of the infamous Artifact Protection Enterprises.

Was this thug after the *Italia*, or the *Nautilus*? Did he know that Serengetti had found one but not the other? Or was he simply an artifact mafioso sent to kill Serengetti and steal his console? Had he known it was their leader, Elgin himself, he might have felt honored that he rated the top man. It didn't matter. At least he now knew that AK had sent Johansson to be his guardian angel. God bless AK. The APE thug was about to get the surprise of his life.

"Now, Dr. Serengetti," the man said pleasantly, twisting the point of the blade ever so slightly. "If you would be so kind as to remove your console and hand it to me. Slowly, please."

Serengetti searched the impassive face of Commander Johansson. But there was no consolation there. She had the dart pistol trained, it seemed, directly at *his* forehead. The thug was incredibly strong, and Serengetti felt growing constriction in his arm. Methodically and almost carelessly, Serengetti unscrewed the three plastic dermal bolts that fixed his console into the cradle implanted into the bones of his left forearm. Have the damn thing, Serengetti thought. The data you want is not there; you should have squeezed my brain.

"I said, step away from him, *now*," Johansson repeated in a soft and even voice, as the last of the bolts came undone. By way of reply the point of the blade made a small incision in Serengetti's neck, and he felt a slight, warm, trickle begin to run down to his shoulder and onto his chest.

"Move along," hissed the APE man, and Serengetti felt the sting of the blade as it probed deeper into his neck. The warm trickle was now a narrow stream, creating a thin red line the length of his tan bush shirt. Even in his rising fear, he could not fail to notice the intense concentration in the wide brown eyes of Commander Johansson as she rocked back and forth on the balls of her feet.

She did not move along.

"*I tre, jef,*" she said, staring at Elgin.

"*To,*" she said steadily, leveling the pistol, and now it was Elgin's turn to be confused. But Serengetti understood. Johansson, a Swede, was speaking in formal Norwegian, as a commissioned officer would speak to a non-com, and using his old rank at that. She was ordering Serengetti to plant his elbow in the thug's gut, when she had counted backwards from three.

"*En,*" Johansson said, and Serengetti aimed low, driving his elbow into the man's groin as Johansson squeezed the trigger. The single dart seemed to come in slow motion directly at Serengetti. For an agonizing moment, he seemed to be perched on the very edge of the world. He felt the knife slice into his neck as the dart passed close by his temple and drove deep into the man's neck. His last thought before he fell was of how he had failed to protect the *Nautilus*, and no wonder. He could not even protect himself.

Then his world went black.

* * *

Kurosawa shouted a few more orders, but no more replies were forthcoming. All he could see was what looked like the *Nautilus*, accelerating at an impossible rate, and ten seconds later, the earsplitting sound of metal shearing metal.

Minutes later, in a cold sweat, he ran into his office. Every screen was dark. The webcams were broadcasting from underwater. Oh my god, he thought, as he realized what this all meant. Instead of sinking the *Nautilus*, the EM sub had been attacked by it. If all three submarines survived this disaster, everything could be compromised. The payment to EM from APE might be traced back to his fingers. The whole line of his life could begin to unravel.

He staggered back to his chair, but missed it and fell instead onto the floor. His staff would be arriving within minutes, he knew. Then they would all know that he had caused this disaster. On his own authority, he had ordered the *Nautilus* out of West Fjord. He had consulted with none of his top deputies, not even Archer, before taking this bold, now catastrophic, action. On his own authority, he had kept the whole operation to himself. Instead of being praised for his foresight, he would now be vilified as the worst of blunderers.

A wave of emotion swept him, and AK lost his equanimity entirely. Sobs welled within him. Hurriedly, before he got sick, he had to hide this evidence of his incompetence. But how? As he vomited, Kurosawa found himself incapable of thinking of anything but his own fractured reputation. Within moments, Archer, along with all of his top assistants, would enter this room and witness the unthinkable magnitude of his catastrophe. He would be ruined, and worse, humiliated. As he stared wildly around his office, hearing the screams of the dying—were they on the *Nautilus* or the EM sub?—hearing Jørriksen vainly shouting orders as she sank in her grave-ship, Kurosawa knew that there were only two things he could do to save himself.

He ran to the private elevator and slammed his hand against the 'down' button. It seemed an eternity before the gleaming wooden door opened, and another before it began its descent to the sub-basement. The elevator door opened once again, this time to reveal a heavy steel security door. Kurosawa swiped his identity badge down the slot of the security console, then allowed his eyes to be scanned. The door opened, and Kurosawa stepped through. Another door like a chain fence required another separate card and another retina scan. Beyond that door was a series of locked file cabinets and secure computer terminals. He went directly to a cabinet at the end of the row, inserted a key, swiped another card, and the top file drawer opened. He took out a folder labeled "Mission 46" and from it removed two smaller folders. One was labeled "Larsen 3" and the other "Archer 6." He replaced the "Mission 46" folder, locked the drawer, and took the two smaller folders to a nearby document shredder. Then he placed the shredded strips into a burn bag. Using his lighter, he lit the contents of the bag. Then he raced back to his office.

There, above the mantel of the unused fireplace, Kurosawa's eyes fell upon the crossed pair of curved, ceremonial samurai blades. This was the most difficult task of all, making the whole episode look like a failed act of bureaucratic hubris, and not an attempt to cover-up his primary mission. But it had to be done. Deliberately, as if in a dream, he walked to the mantel, pulled down one of the blades by its black wooden handle, and retreated to the privacy of his balcony. There he sat down and, equally deliberately, pulled the shirttails from his pants and made the first of four incisions across his belly.

"Bloody Jesus Christ! What in hell is going on? Oh my God!"

Kurosawa heard Archer's voice through his pain. She had entered his office, followed by several others. He heard shouts as their eyes went to the screens, as they tried desperately to reverse events thousands of miles away. Futility. Kurosawa then heard, but from a great distance, someone saying something about an attempted assassination of Serengetti in Paris. That gave him a brief moment of relief. The arc of his failure was not totally complete. Then he heard Archer's voice, suddenly strong and in command: "Contact Lcdr. Johansson. Order her to bring Serengetti in. And find Larsen!" Archer then screamed something unpleasant about how he, Kurosawa, had botched the whole operation in the most—

Sleep then began to come, which was strange, he thought, because he had just awakened.

* * *

As the *Nautilus* settled deeper in the water, Captain Jørriksen ordered the Chief to come to all stop, until a way of extrication came to her. In a few moments, the screw would be submerged, which would provide some traction. She had no idea what the collapse depth of the *Nautilus* might be, but as water surged over the pilothouse and blue sky was replaced by blue water, she knew she would have to act fast if they were to get any help from the *Tailliez*. The *Tailliez* itself would be crushed if it descended much below one hundred and seventy-five meters.

"Conn. Twenty meters and falling rapidly," called out the Chief.

"Aye, Chief," acknowledged Jørriksen, while ripping a small piece of cloth from her shirttail and using it to stem the flow of blood from her temple.

She called out to the X.O.

"*Tailliez*, conn."

"Go, conn. Great work! You really smashed that son of a—"

"*Tailliez*! Prepare for crash dive. All hands prepare for angles and dangles! Come alongside and assist. Repeat, we are going down and require your immediate assistance!"

"Holy Christ!" yelled the Lindgren, spinning the annunciator to flank. "Prepare to come alongside the *Nautilus*. Crash dive!"

"Forty meters, conn."

"Forty meters, aye, Chief."

The *Tailliez* swung around and plunged downward at a ten degree angle. Jørriksen studied her console. The *Tailliez* was not coming on steeply enough, and they had only enough time to try this once.

"*Tailliez*, conn."

"Go, conn."

"I said come alongside! We're down twenty-eight degrees now!"

The *Tailliez* pitched into a steeper dive than the X.O. had ever experienced. Even as she executed these orders, Lindgren realized that the *Tailliez* could do little more than escort the *Nautilus* down to the inevitable break-off point. Or be crushed like an empty soda can.

"Seventy meters, conn. We're down thirty-four degrees. Screw in the water, conn."

"Seventy meters, aye, Chief." Jørriksen studied her console again. Dear God, this had better work. From somewhere forward, she heard what sounded like glass breaking, and the huge, shifting loads of ballast.

"That's it, *Tailliez*!" shouted Jørriksen. "Come alongside." She could now make out the dark form of the *Tailliez* off to the starboard side of the *Nautilus*. The X.O. was having a hell of a time keeping the *Tailliez* pitched so steeply.

"One hundred meters, conn."

"One hundred, aye, Chief. Get ready to back us out of here, full reverse!"

"Aye, conn," sang out the Chief. "Standing by to back us out."

God bless her, thought Jørriksen. Steady as a rock.

"One hundred twenty meters now, conn."

"I'm on it, Chief."

And Jørriksen knew it was now or never.

"*Tailliez*, conn!"

"Go, conn."

"Flood all eight tubes, now!"

Lindgren now knew that the Captain had lost it.

"One hundred forty meters, conn!"

"We don't have any weapons, conn! Even if we did, we could never fire them at point blank—"

"*Tailliez*, conn! Just flood the damn tubes!"

"Conn, aye," said Lindgren, hanging on to the periscope. "Flood all tubes!"

"On my mark," yelled Jørriksen. She prayed that the force of eight slugs of seawater exploding from the *Tailliez's* old torpedo tubes—water slugs that she had only fired previously in training simulations—would dislodge the carcass of the *Challenger* from the bow of the *Nautilus*. It was their only prayer, and it wasn't much of one. "Hit the *Challenger* with water slugs from all eight tubes!"

"Eight tubes, aye, conn," said the X.O., without much hope. "Preparing to fire!"

"One hundred sixty meters, conn!"

"*Tailliez*, fire! Fire all eight tubes!"

"All tubes!" yelled Lindgren. "Fire!"

"Chief," called out Jørriksen. "Full reverse!"

Personnel on both subs heard a dull *swoosh!* as the concussion shuddered the frames of both the *Tailliez* and the *Nautilus*. Swirling bubbles of air blinded Jørriksen's view from the pilothouse. After five seconds, the Captain ordered the *Nautilus's* engine cut, fearing the torque would destroy both of the escaping subs. After a moment, everything was still. Then the silence was broken by the Chief.

"One hundred eighty meters and still falling, conn."

"Goddamnit!" yelled Jørriksen. It hadn't worked. And now she began to hear sharp reports from around the *Nautilus*—or was it the *Tailliez*?—as seams began to groan and split. There was no use in delaying the inevitable.

"*Tailliez*, conn."

"Go, conn."

"That was a nice try, *Tailliez*. Now surface immediately! God bless you *Tailliez*, wherever you're going!"

"Conn," said Lindgren weakly.

"Now!" ordered Jørriksen. "Now—"

"Conn, sonar!"

"Go, sonar."

"She's breaking up, Captain! You did it, Captain! The *Challenger* is breaking up and falling away from the *Nautilus*!"

Quickly Jørriksen scanned her console, and frantically tried to see something, anything. Then unmistakable images were before her. The *Challenger* was falling away, cracking apart and splintering. Huge groaning sounds of air escaping, interspersed with the rat-tat-tat of rivets popping and the terrifying noise of sheet steel buckling, assaulted her ears as the *Challenger* Class fell to the bottom of the North Sea.

"Surface! Surface!" ordered Jørriksen. She heard a final cacophony of wrenching sounds as the *Challenger* Class came apart like a sardine can. The *Nautilus* and the *Tailliez*, she knew, would suffer the same fate if they did not begin to rise immediately. Yet for several long seconds it seemed as if neither of the two surviving submarines would ever rise again. Jørriksen's last view of the

Challenger Class was of a twisted and rent hull spiraling downward. The grinding, gnashing noises began to diminish as the wreck slipped into the darkness. And for the first time in her long career at sea, she felt the unexpected pleasure of vengeance.

"*Mobilis in mobile*," she whispered at the sinking hulk. "Don't ever fokk with my submarine again."

Ten: Barren Island

"...I am dead, sir, as dead as those of your friends reposing six feet below ground!"

—Jules Verne
Twenty Thousand Leagues Under the Seas, 1870
William Butcher translation (1998)

It was 0300 on board the *Polar Quest*, and to Bjorn Larsen, sitting alone in the mess, it seemed as if he was the only person awake on the entire ship. The Chief Steward had wandered sleepily off to his rack, after preparing the breakfast pastries for the oven and leaving a fresh pot of coffee and some cakes on the sideboard. These were usually Larsen's favorite moments on board, halfway through the night, everyone but the mid-watch asleep. Time for reflection on the work of the day just past, planning for the work of the day to come.

But as Larsen cradled an enormous mug of coffee between his thick hands, he felt only an unfamiliar and uncomfortable sense of dread. He stared blankly at the large chart of the North Sea and the polar basin fixed along an entire wall of the mess. No matter where he let his eyes roam, they kept coming back to the triangular island that lay almost in the exact center of the chart.

Bjornøya. Bear Island. The *Quest* would arrive off Bear Island in less than half a day, and then the reckoning would start. It was going to be a tense expedition, and he was not looking forward to it. He thought he might catch some sleep, but just as quickly thought that he wasn't really tired, so he continued to sit. He looked out of the porthole on his left, but could see only a blanket of white fog. He knew that if he went to the bridge he would see the same thing—impenetrable white fog, and the mid-watch monitoring the radar screen and the GPS. It was a calm night, and the *Quest* plowed steadily ahead through quiet waters, a red ship on a white sea. Larsen thought that they might as well be navigating through the clouds of Jupiter, for all one could see out the porthole.

He couldn't think who he was looking forward to seeing less, Ellen Archer or Paolo Serengetti.

* * *

Serengetti awoke in an Oslo hospital, feeling almost fine. Instinctively, he reached his right arm over to his left and felt the reassuring presence of his console. It was only 0300, but already the sun was beginning to rise over the city.

There were just two messages for him, one from AK and one from Bjorn Larsen. Flights to Tromsø and then to Bear Island had been arranged for him for that very morning (that from AK). He was to meet at Gardermoen with AK's staff, all of whom were flying overnight from Tokyo. From Larsen was a short note asking Serengetti to rendezvous with Larsen's survey team at the surface entrance to Nemo's Arctic base on Bear Island. Serengetti couldn't help but note that Larsen passively described this discovery, a momentous find that apparently had been made the previous afternoon, soon after the *Polar Quest* had arrived offshore.

Serengetti lay back heavily, feeling the blood pounding in his head from the effort of sitting up and reviewing his console traffic. None of it mattered, he thought. He found himself suddenly and utterly uninterested in Jules Verne, Captain Nemo, or the *Nautilus*. The submarine was gone, Nemo was an impossible zephyr, and Serengetti was close to concluding (from reading ms4), that even Jules Verne himself had no idea who the Captain was, or had been. All of the expectations that finding the *Nautilus* in the West Fjord had stirred in him were now dead.

But even more than these disappointments, Serengetti found that he was depressed for another reason. With the irrepressible optimism of male ego, he had half expected to find an e-post from Commander Johansson. He now recalled parts of their extended discussion during their long drive from Paris to Oslo, how she lived in Stockholm and kept an office both there and in London. They had many things in common, not least that they were both free agents, at the moment both under contract to AK's Directorate.

Thinking back to the way her eyes occasionally met his as they chatted, Serengetti had hoped that he might find a brief, neutral greeting; *anything* that he might project his hopes onto. Instead there was only empty electronic space. With a sigh he realized that she had just been doing an assigned security job. She had called him "*jef*", so somehow she had learned that in his service days he had been an enlisted sailor. Though his service time was long past, he realized that it was too much to hope that an officer would be interested in him. It was an old prejudice, he knew, an awareness shared by all the enlisted in every service in every country in every century. No academic degree in the world trumped the lack of a commission.

He lay awake in his bed, almost desperate to get away from this place and walk the streets of Oslo. Laying about, immobilized, was torture. As the outlines of the buildings beyond his window began to sharpen, he found himself trying to tie together some of the scattered threads of the past days. But he had always found it difficult to think clearly when he was not in motion. If he could just walk, his thinking would begin to clear. He forced himself out of bed and walked to the window. Nothing stirred in the streets below, just as when he had looked at Oslo from his computer screen at Wellman Station. When was that? It seemed like a long time ago, yet it was only five days. Five days!

It occurred to him that in all the rush to get back to Oslo, and then the flights to and from Paris, that he'd never had a chance to access the Fiorelli Archives, to check whether or not anyone had ever excavated Scillus. Almost out of boredom, he began to surf the Glöbnet archaeology databases on his console. He went to the ancient Greek d-base, and absently typed in *ANABASIS*.

The d-base returned three results. One was the full text of Xenophon's history; another, a short biography of everything known about Xenophon himself. But it was the third link that caught Serengetti's interest. For the first time since he had seen the volume in the library of the *Nautilus*, he read the translation of that one word, "Anabasis." For reasons he could not understand, the simple words conveyed a special meaning and power for him.

"Anabasis" meant "the march up country."

"The March Up Country," Serengetti repeated aloud. It gave connotations of both exertion and promise. The absence of Darwin in the library of the *Nautilus* now seemed to make some sense to him. If Nemo was a half man, half spirit, then he might be locked in some kind of eternal struggle with a set of perverse Gods. He would have resented to the point of hatred any implication arising from the work of Darwin that life existed simply to reproduce itself, with no essential difference between a conscious man and an insensate parameceum. Yet, like Ahab, Nemo behaved like a man whose whole system of belief has left him bereft, adrift, without the kinds of earthly moorings enjoyed by someone like Bjorn Larsen. Philosophical corridors in Serengetti's mind opened and closed. Did he dare go in? Did he dare stay out?

Perhaps Nemo's expedition, whatever its purpose might have been, was not so mysterious after all, Serengetti thought—searching for the little lower layer. What if, by the time he had finished his voyaging, he discovered instead that his Gods were all dead, their temples in ruins, and no one was left to accept his offerings or answer his prayers?

* * *

Serengetti had a whole day to himself before the flight to Tromsø and the sea voyage on *Polar Quest* to Bear Island. He took a solar taxi to Nordstrand, from where he walked the few blocks to his small home overlooking the eastern edge of Oslo fjord. By now he was tired, having been awake since 0300, but fought off a desire to slip within the duvet of his bed. Instead, he walked into the largest room in the small home, his study, past the framed print of Frits Thaulow's "Watermill," and connected a cable from his console to a plug in his reading chair. In a moment, the four-meter wall screen began to glow.

He searched quickly, for he didn't have much time. He entered the word "Scillus" into the d-base and waited. Occasionally, as was his wont, he spoke aloud to the information as it came back to him. The Fiorelli Archives had no record of an excavation at Scillus, but did have more than twenty excavation reports about the famous site nearby.

That site was none other than Olympia itself, arena of the original Games. The French archaeologist Blouet had excavated the Temple of Zeus as early as 1829, and the great German archaeologist, Ernst Curtius, cleared the entire sacred precinct between 1875 and 1881. Using exploratory trenches cut across the site, Curtius bounded the great stadium itself. The Germans began a restoration of the stadium in the 1930s, work interrupted by the Second World War. Not until the 1960s, nearly a century after Curtius first worked the site, was the entire original Olympic stadium cleared and partially restored.

The problems that had confronted Curtius were almost insurmountable. At one point or another, every archaeologist experiences a moment of recognition when it becomes clear that excavations do not reveal the ancient world. Instead, they are the start of a puzzle, even a game, to understand all of the transformations wrought by time and people and environment that separate the ancient world from our own. As he cut his trenches and exposed an enormous ruin of collapsed Doric columns, Curtius understood that he was not uncovering ancient Olympia, but the barest remnants of that enormous stadium complex built almost 4,000 years earlier. The famous statue of Zeus that loomed over it, one of the wonders of the ancient world, had vanished long ago.

The reports Serengetti now scanned on his wall screen contained less of Olympia itself, and more of the periodic and almost complete destruction of the site over time. When the gods at last fell, they fell hard and heavy. A Christian Roman emperor, Valentinian III, ordered Olympia leveled in 426 C.E. as a place of pagan worship. The statues of Zeus and Hera, Hermes and Apollo, all were shattered under hammer blows. Earthquakes further demolished the arena in 522 and 551. Silt from the Alpheus River and mudslides from the nearby mountain of Cronos then buried the whole, toppled mass. What Curtius uncovered more than a thousand years later was only the faintest shadow of what it had once been.

Yet that shadow was in itself magnificent. Serengetti noted with interest that, even now, archaeological work continued there. No wonder Xenophon's Scillus had been ignored, he thought. Curtius and the Germans who followed him had had more than enough on their hands with Olympia. The only record of work at Scillus, Serengetti found at last, was a brief note from a German survey team in the late 1950s. The presumed site of Xenophon's estate, the note read, was five kilometers south of the site of the stadium, and was either buried under at least five meters of soil, or had been paved over during the construction of a postwar highway.

Serengetti looked up from his console to see the first vehicles of the morning making deliveries to bakeries, shops, and restaurants. Was the sketch map he had located within the *Anabasis* Xenophon's estate at Scillus?

If Nemo had visited the site, Serengetti concluded that he must have done so at some point after 426 and before 522. And if he had recorded his observations of it within the endpapers of a nineteenth-century copy of the *Anabasis,* he was not sketching a map but attempting to recall two distant yet distinct memories. One memory derived from his visit to the site of his home as it looked in ruins, one thousand, five hundred years ago.

And the other memory of that same place? Serengetti tried to imagine it, but of course could not. Archaeologists studied the dead, and suffered as a result in their relations with the living. How could he know how glorious Scillis had appeared, with flax being sown in the fields below and the scent of lemon trees filling the porch, when the scattered papers and histories lay unfinished on Xenophon's great desk, and his wife and children were at play in the setting sun?

What Serengetti did know was this. This other memory, of a living Scillus, was a thousand years older than the first. His uncertainty now vanished. He now believed that the avenger known as Captain Nemo had been offered a new chance every few generations to transform human society, only to fail each time. Nemo had been mobile in a mobile element, alright. But that mobile element was not water. It was time.

* * *

Serengetti met up with some of AK's lower level staffers at Gardermoen, and by the time he reached Bear Island the next day, he had learned the rough outlines of all that had transpired since he left for Paris. Over some very good coffee in a Gardermoen café—how luxurious to simply sit in a café and enjoy a coffee!—the staffers treated him as a minor figure in the drama. It soon became clear to them that he could not advance their careers, so for the most part they ignored him. He sat by himself on the flight to Tromsø, somewhat lost in thought, and troubled by all that he did not know about the classical world. He found himself suddenly missing Johansson.

Serengetti's helicopter reached Bear Island two hours later than scheduled. It was immediately obvious that this isolated and fogbound weather station had been transformed into the center of UNESCO activity. Security was tighter than he had ever seen it. Most of the staffers were kept offshore on board the *Polar Quest*, and for several hours Serengetti himself had been forced to cool his heels in the mess, making idle conversation with the Chief Steward and the First Mate. There was talk that both AK and the Emperor were now being shown the base, and no one would be allowed ashore until the ceremony had concluded.

When Serengetti innocently asked "what ceremony?" he was told that AK, Larsen, and Archer were receiving the UNESCO Medal, the highest award for service to cultural programs of the U.N., for discovering the *Nautilus* and the base on Bear Island. Serengetti took his mug and wandered outside to the bow and stood there for the longest time, leaning on his elbows and warming himself with his coffee. He wondered what decoration they were going to give them all for nearly destroying the *Nautilus*.

He reached into his coat to the tiny shoulder pocket of his bush shirt. There he had stowed the tiny disc containing his brief digital video clip of the library. It was, so he still believed, the only evidence left that the library had not been an illusion, not a cloud painted by Rembrandt.

It didn't matter. He knew, or thought he did, all he was ever going to know from that library. As usual in archaeology, there were too many questions and not enough data to begin to answer even half of them. And this bizarre archaeology of the *Nautilus*? He had learned everything and somehow it seemed like nothing. It was very strange.

He turned the disc over slowly in his hand, watching it catch the dim northern sun. Then he pitched it into the sea.

* * *

When he finally got ashore, he was met by Larsen.

"Nice medal."

Larsen was almost going to say "*jo*" but thought better of it. It wasn't the moment for kidding, and, he thought, it probably never would be again. He was direct instead. "Just hold your jaw," he said, using the Norwegian phrase for 'shut up.' "We have to talk."

Larsen escorted him away from the small knot of staffers, toward the entrance of Nemo's Arctic base. He spoke quietly and rapidly the whole way. As Serengetti listened, growing increasingly incredulous, he thought that AK had won after all, and had to marvel at the old man's foresight. When he heard what Archer had discovered inside the base, he had a sudden and unexpected feeling of guilt. It was only natural for an archaeologist to feel possessive about a major find, but he knew he had not found this site first. If only by a day or so, Ellen Archer had found it first, with a little help from the Viking standing next to him.

Then Larsen told him about many of the inner parts of the saga, those messy parts of which the lower level staffers knew nothing. After Serengetti nodded that, yes, he would keep his mouth shut, Larsen told him of AK's attempted suicide, along with the reasons for it, his intense shame at putting the *Nautilus* at risk in order to preserve it. Even Archer herself, who had found AK half dead on his balcony, and who had then performed some quite heroic field surgery, even she had been forbidden from revealing anything about the incident.

"You know," said Serengetti. "At this point I could really care less about AK. He almost sank the *Nautilus*, to say nothing of what he put the *Tailliez*, Jørriksen, and her whole crew through in the bargain. Screw AK."

"That's why I had to stop you before you go down there," said Larsen evenly. He hadn't worked with Serengetti for almost ten years for nothing. "You have to keep your big goddamn mouth shut down there. AK is hanging by a thread, and one bad move will send him over the edge."

"You see this?" said Serengetti, pulling back both his Arctic hood and the collar of his sweatshirt. "AK's not the only one hanging by a fucking thread."

"Look," said Larsen, "Ellen and AK are both well aware of what you did for the Directorate."

"I did nothing for AK and Ellen. Or the damned Directorate. I did it for you and me." And, he could have added, for someone whose identity he was just that much closer to knowing.

"There'll be time for other fights," Larsen said as they reached the hidden entrance to the submarine base. "But that time is not today."

"OK, OK," said Serengetti stiffly. "Let's get this over with."

They descended through the narrow entrance, which looked almost as if it had been designed deliberately to imitate the entrance to an abandoned mine. When he reached the landing and looked out over the long cavern to behold those two magnificent submarines, Serengetti had to fight to control his emotions.

The high-speed torpedo hit had impacted just aft of the *Tailliez's* conning tower, creating an enormous dent in the hull. A series of ugly gashes ran down the length of the knife-edge of the *Nautilus*. It was now perfectly obvious what a horrendous battle it had been, and the toll it had taken on both machines. It had taken an extraordinary level of heroic work by the Jørriksen and her crew to bring these submarines in.

"Good God," Serengetti breathed.

"I know," said Larsen. "I feel the same way. It was a huge mistake."

Mistake, thought Serengetti. Mistake! It was a fiasco. But before he could think very much about it, he felt the massive male presence next to him. Deliberately, Larsen stood too close, leaning into Serengetti's space. Serengetti had always felt reassured by Larsen's presence; now he felt oppressed. Serengetti nodded in the direction of Ellen Archer, who was at that moment standing on the deck of the *Nautilus*, in the middle of a small circle of very important people, preparing to hand them off to a staffer for a brief tour of the interior. "Oh, that," Larsen said, and for the first time since his reunion with Serengetti, the self-assurance fled from his face. "You shouldn't really feel badly about that. Instead, you should feel sorry for me!"

They talked like that for awhile, for the moment neither one really believing what the other was saying, but realizing that such things had to be said. At some point, and some time soon, they would have to work together again. But their relationship had suffered a serious blow, and it would never recover fully.

* * *

As they stood with their elbows leaning on the railing, Serengetti's eyes were drawn to the spectacle of a sizeable team of researchers, dressed in survival suits, sloshing in water up to their waists. They were clustered at the far end of the cavern, and for the first time Serengetti saw the semi-circular array of classical statues, a pantheon of the gods of the ancient world. And the thought that came into his head was so penetrating, and so clear, that he felt at once that it must be true. In that instant, everything came together in his mind. Then he smiled a sad smile. He smiled both for what he knew, and for all he would never know.

As he watched those world-class scholars and technicians at work, he suddenly felt renewed and alive. There was so very much that he knew so very little about. On the flight from Tromsø he had toyed with the idea of leaving fieldwork and trying his hand at university teaching. Someone had told him that an archaeology professorship might be available at Uppsala. He had found himself wondering how he would adapt to a sedentary life of lecturing to bright eighteen-year-olds at a staid old Swedish university. Now he realized how ridiculous the thought was and dismissed the idea out of hand. Highly specialized researchers tend to become too comfortable with their blinding knowledge of a single narrow subject. That narrow brilliance now struck Serengetti as universal ignorance. Five lifetimes would not suffice to fill in all the yawning gaps in his knowledge.

He knew nothing of physics, little of engine mechanics, had forgotten most of his global navigation. The ancient world, as he had learned so sharply in the library of the *Nautilus*, was almost completely dark to him. He was filled with a new enthusiasm for all the things he would now turn his attention to. He had been only once to Rome, had never visited Persepolis. He couldn't speak Malay, and had never drifted the Bay of Bengal on a raft made from bamboo. Darius I was as mysterious to him as the moons of Jupiter. Perhaps he would take up a new dig. And now he thought he knew where he wanted to go.

For this sudden awareness, he had the anonymous avenger to thank. Captain No One, whoever he was, wherever he was, had revealed to him the depths of his ignorance, and that knowledge was greater than any treasure on the bottom of the sea. There was so much to learn, and death could come in an instant. There so little time left!

Serengetti was lost in his reverie when Ellen Archer drew alongside. In the midst of his sudden renewal, all he could think was, My god, how impossibly beautiful this woman was, in the strange unbalanced way her face seemed to radiate light. Her intelligence intensified her sensuality a hundredfold. He tried not to be too obvious as he stole a glance at her hand slipping around Larsen's arm.

"AK wants to see the both of you."

They descended the few steps onto a ramp that led around the back wall of the cavern. They passed the place where the statues were arrayed, and there the three of them paused, while Archer tossed off a few confident instructions to the survey team. Then she turned back to Larsen and Serengetti.

"These statues were all sculpted in the "austere" style," Archer said, almost lecturing. "Pre-Hellenistic, dating to about the mid-fifth century, B.C.E. We've been able to identify all of them except one."

Serengetti was impressed yet again by the depths of her intelligence. How could one person be so well-trained? He noticed that the statues still retained traces of the paint they had originally possessed. The features on the familiar faces, with this unfamiliar coloring, seemed almost to glow back at him.

"The statue in the center is Zeus," Archer continued. "As best as we've been able to determine, it's an original Phidias, the same sculptor who created the chryselephantine Zeus at Olympia. And there is Hermes, carrying the young Dionysus. And Hera, and Apollo. There are two statues that we believe represent historical figures. One is almost certainly Socrates. As for the other, we aren't sure, so for now we are simply calling him 'The Stranger.'"

Serengetti separated himself from the knot of specialists, who had by then recommenced an argument over the arrangement of the statuary. One of them thought that the array was similar to the Greek gallery at the British Museum, another was equally certain that it imitated the entrance to a classical Roman amphitheater outside of Tunis. Everyone had their own hypothesis, and each was convinced his or her personal interpretation was the correct one. Serengetti stepped lightly over the railing and into the icy water. He sloshed over to the far end of the Pantheon, to study the face of the statue that the experts had identified only as The Stranger.

"Only the survey teams are allowed in the water," Archer called after him, but he wasn't listening. Serengetti stared at the young, beautiful, androgynous face for a few seconds, until Archer called out to him again.

"Doctor," she said impatiently. "The Director wants to see you in the library, immediately."

But still Serengetti stood there, gazing at the eyes, trying to see into the mind of a born revolutionary, until he realized with a start that he and The Stranger were approximately the same height. And that made him take a step back. He had a feeling that he had now met the man he wanted to meet. He had no desire to meet with AK.

As they took their leave of the specialists, Archer offered her opinion that Nemo must now be considered to be the greatest collector of the world's cultural heritage who ever lived.

"He wasn't collecting," said Serengetti evenly.

The specialists suddenly stopped arguing. Nobody contradicted Ellen Archer like that. They waited expectantly for Serengetti to finish his thought, while Serengetti wished he had kept his mouth shut.

"What do mean, he wasn't collecting?" Archer said, with more than a slight edge in her voice. "What is all this? If he wasn't collecting, just what in hell was he doing?"

Serengetti suddenly felt all of the specialists staring at him, and felt the blood rushing to his face. He could feel it beating against the stitches in his neck. He looked back at the statue of The Stranger, almost as if searching for an ally. But he found no comfort in the vacant, infinite, eyes.

"He was worshipping."

They all looked at him rather blankly, and just as quickly went back to their measurements and conversations. Archer exhaled deeply, and Larsen nudged him sharply with an elbow, as if to say, 'knock that stuff off!'

Then they headed off toward the *Nautilus*.

* * *

Serengetti entered the *Nautilus* for the second time, this time from the top hatch aft of the platform where Pierre Aronnax had smoked his daily cigar. As he descended the gangway, he heard several hushed conversations, all going on at once. One was in Norwegian and he recognized Jørriksen. The Captain was still reeling from her dressing down by Kurosawa, and as Serengetti listened, he heard equal expressions of anger and remorse.

Another conversation, this one in Australian-accented English, was the unmistakable sound of Archer. She was telling some international dilettante on the UNESCO Board about her research in Moscow that had pinpointed the *Nautilus* in the West Fjord, and her work in the Verne Archives that had led them all to this base. As Serengetti passed out of earshot, he thought he heard Archer ask the board member if he thought that the Emperor might be persuaded to write a Foreword to her soon-to-be released book about the discovery.

As Serengetti passed down the track-lit passageway, past the still-locked galley door, past the crew cabins, he heard the growing sounds of another animated conversation. This one was being conducted in very formal Nipponese, and it was coming from the library.

As he reached the hatchway leading into the library, Serengetti paused and drew back stiffly. Kurosawa was giving the Emperor a private tour of the *Nautilus*. As he listened from the passageway, he heard Kurosawa explaining how Nemo's library had the potential to revolutionize our understanding of human development and how fortunate it had not all been lost in the criminal attack by the EM submarine. Serengetti's Nipponese was extremely limited, but he caught several of the phrases. The word 'greatest' was getting a lot of work. 'Greatest addition to our knowledge in a century and a half,' was one. Another was 'greatest technological breakthrough.' AK was no doubt shaking the Emperor down for more funding, thought

Serengetti. Was it his imagination, or did it seem as if the Emperor thought that this discovery might be *too much* of a breakthrough?

But it wasn't only the presence of the Emperor that drew Serengetti up short. Only now could he see firsthand the shattered condition of the library itself. The attack on the EM sub, and the thirty-degree descent as the *Nautilus* was pulled under, had all but turned the library upside down. At such a calamitous pitch, the shelving, the bars of which he had retracted when he touched the Poe volume—and had not known how to return to their original protective position—had been unable to retain its contents. The result was total chaos. The formal arrangement of the library had been destroyed. Books had been tossed from their shelves with such force that hardly a single volume remained in its original place. He saw three of Scott's novels standing alone on a top shelf. The great green carpet was almost completely obscured by a tsunami of books.

No one but Kurosawa and the Emperor had been allowed to view this part of the *Nautilus* until this moment. Nothing had been disturbed, and Kurosawa was telling the Emperor that nothing would be disturbed until they could return the contents of the library to their original places.

It was then that AK noticed Serengetti for the first time.

"Ah, Dr. Serengetti," said Kurosawa, switching to English. "Please join us."

Serengetti stepped tentatively into the library, making certain not to step on any of the hundreds of volumes scattered across the green carpet. He bowed deeply to the Emperor, who nodded in return.

"I was just telling His Imperial Majesty about your initial work in this room," said Kurosawa. To their surprise, Kurosawa was interrupted by the Emperor.

"Even given the unfortunate events of the past few days," the Emperor began. Serengetti thought he could almost feel AK wince at that. They never should have removed the *Nautilus* from the West Fjord, and even the Emperor knew it. "I have confidence that we shall ultimately find a way to retrieve the vital secrets of this vast collection."

Serengetti bowed deeply in reply. One did not speak to the Emperor. One only listened attentively and bowed in reply. AK motioned in an irritated manner for a staff photographer to join them in the library. But as the man entered with his tiny digigraph recorder, the Emperor waved him away.

"No," said the Emperor curtly. "No digigraphs. Not now."

AK seemed to seethe with indignation, but held himself in check.

And as quickly as that, the Emperor left the library, where a staff retainer waited to escort him down the passageway, up the gangway, and out of the *Nautilus*. When the Emperor had gone, Serengetti and Kurosawa both straightened and turned to face each other directly for the very first time. For so many years he had been so completely in thrall to AK's dominating voice and commanding presence on the giant conference room screens, that Serengetti was now surprised to discover himself a full head taller than the Director.

"Now, Paul," Kurosawa began, and Serengetti was surprised at how quickly AK dropped the extreme formality he had displayed for the Emperor. "How are you feeling? I heard you had quite a terrible time in Paris. We have a lot of work in front of us. Our first job is to recreate this library from your data. I want copies of all of your data discs from the survey of the library turned over to my library working group before you return to Oslo."

So that was it, Serengetti thought. Hand over the tapes. Serengetti was profoundly conflicted. AK wanted someone else to handle the analysis of the library. He paused, looking around at the mess. Mentally, he was already replacing books to their proper places. He saw the empty shelves where the science series had stood, then the poetry shelves, even the place where Nemo kept his copy of *The Count of Monte Cristo*, and the first edition of Poe's *Tales of the Grotesque and Arabesque*, the volume that contained "The Descent into the Maelstrøm." Then Serengetti noticed a dark stain on dark green carpet. They had smashed his bottle of brandy.

AK had shown no remorse. Not even a glimmer of appreciation for what he and Larsen had accomplished. Nor, Serengetti thought in passing, not even a hint of further survey work with the *Tailliez,* if they somehow managed to get her repaired. It occurred to him then that AK considered him a screw-up. Worse, he thought, after letting the disc with the library data they now needed slip through his fingers, AK would be correct. He had no hard data to offer AK, only feelings and surmises based on, what? An old map and an archaeologist's intuition? It was nothing. Still, AK hadn't even offered to let Serengetti lead the team that would put the library back together. Well, Serengetti thought, I might as well confirm his worst fears.

"I'm sorry," Serengetti lied at last. "We used all the data discs in the study. I never filmed the library."

* * *

"But surely you recall the general arrangement of the books?" Kurosawa said sharply. "You're telling me that you spent almost an hour in this room and never recorded a single *thing?!*"

Serengetti drew back. He had never heard AK so much as raise his voice. Even Kurosawa seemed surprised at his own reaction. He seemed to realize that the others on the *Nautilus* might hear his brief outburst, so he quickly controlled his anger. Serengetti thought that he might have painfully strained the sutures in his belly. Actaully, Kurosawa cared not a whit for pristine library and felt nothing but immense relief that the whole badly-bungled mission had not crashed on his head. It might still, and his lost chance at a digigraph with the Emperor was a clear signal that the higher echelons were not pleased. Still, he had to play the part, and he knew how to play it. Quickly he softened both his voice and his tone. It was absolutely vital that he be certain that Serengetti knew nothing. There were only so many times you could kill someone unsuccessfully.

Serengetti looked around again. He saw where the copy of *A Journey in Brazil* had fallen. How long, he wondered, would it take AK's bibliophiles to realize that that book should not be here. His eyes were drawn toward that telltale depression in the couch.

"A lot has happened since we were on board," said Serengetti, remembering now the thrill of the discovery, a thrill that was now a distant memory. "The details are a bit fuzzy."

His most vivid memory from the previous three days was of a knife slicing his neck. What could anyone expect? The hell with the disc. He had done more than his share for the damned Directorate.

But Kurosawa, he could now see plainly, was controlling himself only with considerable effort.

"But I seem to remember," Serengetti began. Kurosawa's eyes almost shined expectantly. "I seem to remember that this bottle of brandy was only half full."

"Yes, yes," AK said rapidly. "But the books. The books! Do you recall *anything*, anything *specifically*, about the books?" Did this fellow know something? Or did he not?

Serengetti looked around once again, as AK looked at him expectantly.

"I'm sorry," Serengetti said at last. "I don't remember."

Kurosawa was almost trembling. Just as Serengetti thought AK would explode in anger, the old man's pinched face hardened, his shoulders squared, and a look of resignation came over him. At least it looked like resignation to Serengetti. Perhaps it was something else. For his part, AK looked closely at Serengetti for a long moment, then stormed out of the library.

Once beyond Serengetti's vision, Kurosawa slowed his gait and let out an enormous sigh of relief. He was now convinced that Serengetti knew nothing, suspected nothing, and had uncovered nothing. AK allowed himself his first smile in days. At least in this one particular he had succeeded. He had picked the right person for the job after all.

* * *

Serengetti remained behind, alone in the middle of the great wreck of the library. Behind him, he heard Kurosawa barking out a rapid series of instructions. The entire forward half of the *Nautilus*, the Director ordered, from the library bulkhead to the bow, was now officially off limits. No one was allowed in or out with his express written permission.

Serengetti gently lifted a leg and stepped over a series of piles of books, until he had arrived in the corner of the library where he had first noticed that clear and singular depression in the couch. Intently, he scanned the hundreds of volumes on the couch and the floor, searching for something.

Then he saw it.

He bent down slowly, and reached out to put his hand on Nemo's copy of the *Anabasis*. Still here, he thought. And maybe *he* is still here, somewhere.

For a moment, Serengetti had a notion to place the *Anabasis* in one of the deep wide pockets of his Arctic jacket. Then he had a crazy thought that perhaps, as in a secure archive, Nemo might be ahead of him, and might have placed a bug in every one of the books in this private library. If he tried to walk out with it, he imagined an alarm going off, lights flashing, security arriving, the whole scene. Why compound the incompetence of throwing away the disc with thievery of the *Anabasis*?

Serengetti looked rapidly through the book, and shivered as he read the words once again: *"At this moment, brothers, we have no other possession save arms and valour. If we keep our arms, we imagine that we can make use of our valour as well, but if we give them up, we will certainly lose our lives. We should not give up the only possessions we have. Instead, we should battle the King for his."*

He paused to contemplate the sketch map. He turned it over and looked again on the mysterious equations. Where are you right now, Captain? he wondered. AK found your submarine, but he didn't find you. And perhaps he never shall. Kurosawa had retrieved the artifact, but not the mind behind it. And in archaeology, that equation ultimately equaled failure.

Carefully, Serengetti lifted the book from its place on the deck of the library. He searched the shelf behind the depression until he found the ever-so-slight stratchings he was looking for. He started to replace the *Anabasis* but then he stopped. He couldn't bring the whole library back, nor the disc he had pitched into the sea. But at least he could try to somehow salvage their meaning. He looked around to make sure no one was watching, then slipped the small volume into his Arctic jacket. Soon, he thought, he would begin his own march up country.

Then he followed Kurosawa out.

* * *

An hour later, they had all made their way back through the cave to the surface, where the VIPs were being loaded onto a Super Puma helo for the short flight back to the *Polar Quest*. The *Quest*, moored off the southeastern coast in anticipation of a heavy swell from the northwest, was delivering them all to Tromsø, where they would go their separate ways. Serengetti had hoped to catch the first ride back to the icebreaker, but Kurosawa asked him to stay behind to make room for another of AK's very important people. It was impossible not to notice that neither Larsen nor Archer had been asked to give up their seats. At least Larsen had winked at him before escorting Archer to the helo. Serengetti walked away from the helicopter as the rotors began to spin, and decided to hike across the northern edge of the island to the ruins of the old mining dock at Tunheim. From there he could board one of the *Polar Quest's* small boats and ride through the heavy chop back to the icebreaker.

A heavy mist was drawing down upon Bear Island, so he opened the three dimensional orienteering programme on his console and set the alarm to tell him when he was within two kilometers of the old Norwegian radio station. He double-checked his .357. He threw his daypack over his shoulder, and set off.

Bastards, he thought. The *Nautilus* was only half of Verne's secret. The other half, the most important part, was still out there, almost certainly walking somewhere on the earth at this very moment. Serengetti imagined a distinguished, aloof graybeard, tucked up in some mud hut in Tanzania, or hauling in sheet, part of the crew of an Arab dhow in the gulf. Or perhaps brooding amongst the ruins on the hill above Olympia. Or maybe, he thought, suddenly looking over his shoulder, somewhere on this island, hidden in the fog. He had a ridiculous premonition that perhaps Nemo was pursuing him, rather than the other way around. Maybe he had meant the *Nautilus* to be a museum to his expeditions. That's how they should have left it.

Maybe they already knew. AK had certainly shown himself to be far ahead of Serengetti at every step. No doubt he had the library figured out already, and was simply testing Serengetti. The Directorate was set to announce the discovery of the *Nautlius* over the Glöbnet later that very day. He had overheard AK's staffers whispering that the Director had authorized Archer and Larsen to write a popular book about the discovery. The staffers had talked about how much the North American rights would bring in, how much the advance might be. One of them had wondered aloud whether Archer would agree to share credit with anyone for the discovery; the other staffer had then asked, "Didn't you know about those two?" Then there were indecipherable whispers about an intense tryst. When they'd started to jabber about who might play Larsen in the inevitable movie, Serengetti had asked the steward for another small bottle of wine and wistfully unscrewed the metal cap.

Serengetti had to force himself to remember that, after all, he *worked* for Kurosawa. At least, he owed the existence of much of his career, of his office at Wellman Station, and of his cabin on board the *Philippe Tailliez*, to AK's Directorate. The *Nautilus* was the price of his career. Now that it had been taken from him, he tried to force himself to believe that it did not matter.

He consoled himself by arguing that momentous archaeological discoveries were inevitably subsumed by politics. And if he was to be honest with himself, the implications of the discovery went far beyond archaeology, beyond politics, into realms he knew nothing about. He couldn't really blame them for putting others in charge of the sub, even if it brought up the acid in his stomach to think about it. He was a field scientist, not a bureaucrat or a politician, much less a supernaturalist.

Yet, as the shadowy outlines of the old radio station started to come into focus, thoughts of the graybeard would not go away. He had long ago promised himself that he would never go back to the Pacific. Yet he now felt certain, though he could not explain why, that the other half of the secret existed there, more than halfway around the world from the ground upon which he now stood. Perhaps, while Scandinavia slept through a long winter, he would slip away.

But that was ridiculous, he thought. He was completely and utterly powerless. Hadn't it taken Nemo 20,000 lifetimes—or perhaps 20,000 leagues under the seas?—to learn that lesson? As he walked, the mist turned to a light snow. Winter was coming on fast. It was time to head south. He suddenly wanted nothing more than to return to his apartment in Oslo and hide for a few weeks. Maybe hike up to a *hytte* in the mountains where no electricity could reach him.

If he could find any consolation as he walked around a shallow still pond, it was that no one had come out of this mess looking good. As he well knew from his service days, medals were given to fuck-ups and chicken-shits as often as heroes. The flunkies from AK's office had even let slip a rumor that AK himself was in danger of being removed. It wouldn't happen immediately, of course. It hardly ever did. The only one he felt truly sorry for was Jørriksen. After all, she had just been following orders. And if she had violated those orders by attacking the *Challenger* Class, what was she supposed to have done? Stand by and watch as the *Tailliez* was sent to the bottom? Yet she had looked positively miserable on board the *Nautilus*. The only moment she had brightened was when she caught sight of him, and he had returned her shrug with a glance that said 'We'll find each other in Oslo later.'

No, they would take their sweet time before they dropped the ax. It was even likely that nothing drastic would happen. The only people outside of AK's Directorate who had seen the *Nautilus* with their own eyes were the Captain and possibly the XO of the *Challenger* Class. And they were now entombed at the bottom of the North Sea.

That is what would come of this whole affair, Serengetti decided finally. Nothing. There would be no recriminations, no one would lose their job, everybody would be decorated, and everything would go on as before. Except that the *Phillippe Tailliez* had suffered enough damage from the high speed torpedo hit that the bureaucrats in Tokyo would now have their justification to send the boat once and for all to the wreckers.

And that would be the end for him, too.

Epilogue: E6

Early Autumn

"On its surface immoral rights can still be claimed, men can fight each other, devour each other, and carry out all the world's atrocities. But thirty feet below the surface their power ceases, their influence fades, their authority disappears. Ah, sir, live in the heart of the sea!"

—Jules Verne
Twenty Thousand Leagues Under the Seas, 1870
William Butcher translation (1998)

On the afternoon of his first Friday back in his Oslo apartment overlooking the fjord, there was a knock on Serengetti's door. Looking through the privacy hole, he was surprised to see Lcdr. Johansson waiting impatiently on the other side. He opened the door, and for the very first time since he had first seen her, on board the *Tailliez's* z-boat, she smiled at him.

"Commander?"

"It's Karenna," she said, without anything in the way of an introduction. "C'mon. Let's go. You look like you need to get away for a few days. I thought we would drive to Stockholm for the weekend."

Serengetti felt conflicted. As Johansson looked over his shoulder and into his apartment, he thought that perhaps AK somehow knew that Serengetti had stolen a volume from the *Nautilus* library, and had sent Johansson to get it back. When it seemed clear that she really did just want to visit him, Serengetti felt awkward for another, more mundane reason.

Earlier that day he had put his ancient 2009 BMW in the garage for a long overdue tune-up and oil change. He had been avoiding this step for months because the carbon fee for his old car was absurdly high. When he told her this she said, "My car is downstairs. Remember, my job has been to follow you and keep you alive for the past few days. If it had been up to me, the Directorate would have been forced to give you a new car by now."

Fifteen minutes later, they were at the curb in front of his apartment building. Johansson walked around a bright yellow Saab solar convertible, and threw herself into the driver's seat.

"A bit flashy for a global security agent, isn't it?" Serengetti asked as he placed his overnight bag in the boot.

"I spend enough of my time driving around in gray sedans trying to protect little lost boys like you," she said without any edge in her voice at all. "So when I'm home, I like to enjoy myself."

"Did you grow up in Stockholm?"

"No. I grew up in western Sweden and have lived in the capital for ten years now. We're spending the weekend at my place there."

Her directness was staggering. No hand-wringing, no hesitation—direct action. Serengetti enjoyed the flush of blood to his crotch.

For Scandinavia, the late August weather could not have been better. It was a warm afternoon, with barely a cloud in the sky, and none expected for three days, an almost unheard of forecast. He found himself once again fascinated by Karenna Johansson, by her hair, her voice, her breasts, even by her whiny solar car and the music she listened to. A small prism hung by a string from the mirror, catching and refracting the bright afternoon sunlight as it twirled.

It was warm enough that Johansson had the convertible top down. They left Oslo on the E6 and, with the early northern autumn streaming past, drove along the fjord for a hundred kilometers until they reached Sweden. They talked and laughed about everything except the events that had brought them together. For the first time in days he felt the heavy weight he carried from Bear Island leaving his mind. The bright red barns that seemed almost to decorate the western Swedish farmlands through which they sped at 150 kilometers an hour became the subject of animated discussion.

"You can tell in a minute that the Norse who worked these lands would have been entirely comfortable with the land they found in New England. The two are almost identical," said Serengetti.

"Exactly," said Johansson. "More true than you know. These are my home lands."

A few hours later, about halfway between Oslo and Stockholm, along the almost deserted Route 47 between Vänersborg and Falköping, Johansson suddenly turned left onto a road that led from the open farmlands into an extended patch of forest. The maneuver was executed so abruptly that for a brief expectant moment Serengetti thought that perhaps she was searching for a private patch of forest where they could make love.

Instead, she spun the Saab to a stop near a small wooden building and jumped out, and she invited him to join her. When he did, she took his hand and led him into the small open building. In the center of the one-room building was a gravel floor. In the middle of the floor stood a solid pillar of stone nearly two meters tall. On the stone, more than a thousand years ago, someone had carved the story of a Norseman who gave up his lands in the surrounding area to become a Viking and voyage west in search of new and better lands. Serengetti moved his fingers over the incisions in the rock as Johansson effortlessly translated the Runic inscriptions.

Instantly he understood. This was the story of her family, set in stone over a millennia ago. She had driven this way deliberately, in order to share her family history with him, inviting him into her private world. She was also showing him the source of her limitless self-confidence. Like the old American revolutionary rattlesnake flag, everything about this site screamed out: "I know who I am, so don't tread on me." And that thought, one he had seen so recently expressed on board the *Nautilus*, brought him up short.

"*Nemo me impune lacessit*," Serengetti said softly. He wondered what it was like to have an anchor like this, a solid mooring for your very existence on the planet. The earth could orbit the sun a half a million times, and still the testament to your history would endure. What must it be like to know with absolute assurance just who you are and what you are about?

"What's that?" she said.

"Nothing," Serengetti said. "Just a phrase."

For a moment he thought she would kiss him, or was about to tell him something, or ask him something, but instead she merely led him back to the Saab, and they sped off toward Falköping. They talked about where they might have dinner in Stockholm, since they would arrive rather late. They made plans to visit the museums near the Strand the next day, and visit the bookshops near the Sergelstorg.

Beyond Jönköping, they picked up the E4 to Stockholm. Johansson stopped a short distance beyond Jönköping at a small station on the edge of Lake Vättern to give the Saab a quick 15 minute charge for the last stretch to Stockholm. Serengetti went into the station store to get them each a coffee. Halfway to the door he stopped and looked across the lake, to the lights of the giant windmills on the island of Visingsö as they winked slowly on and off. The night was coming on utterly calm and clear, and he inhaled deeply, feeling a sort of peace.

It was almost time for the station to close, and as he entered the store, a wrinkled old Swede behind the counter was speaking in German to a German customer in front of Serengetti. When Serengetti reached the counter, he asked in Norwegian to pay for both the charge and the coffee. The old Swede nodded, and immediately switched to Norwegian. But when he said something in dialect that Serengetti didn't understand, Serengetti switched reluctantly to English, and the old man switched along with him. They chatted about the local area, with the old man pointing out some of the tourist sites he should be sure to see.

Finally Serengetti begged off, politely telling him that they were headed for a weekend in Stockholm. The old man nodded as if he had heard similar responses a thousand times over. When Johansson entered the store to pay for the charge, Serengetti handed her a coffee and told her he had taken care of it. As they walked out, Serengetti heard the old man say something in that same impenetrable dialect, but since his thoughts were now all on Johansson, he merely nodded and followed her out.

"What on earth did he mean by that?" Johansson asked, a few moments after they had resumed speeding toward Stockholm on the E4.

"What do you mean?"

"The storekeeper. He said to you: 'Where is the King tonight?'"

Serengetti froze. "Are you sure that's what he said?"

"I'm sure of it. He obviously learned his Norwegian in the far north. His accent is very heavy, almost like Old Norse."

"Stop the car," he said suddenly.

"Why?"

"Just stop the car!"

When they had rolled to a stop, he jumped over the door of the yellow convertible and began to sprint back to the station. Within a hundred meters he was out of breath, and stood gasping for air along the side of the road, as Johansson backed the Saab up to him. He looked up at the stars overhead, then down at the station in the far distance. He watched in the darkness as the lights of the station were turned off one by one. It was no use. For a brief moment he'd had a piece of the answer. For a brief moment, he could see a new heaven and a new earth. But then it was gone. He knew then that if they went back, the old man would be gone.

He looked back at Johansson, solid-as-a-thousand-year-old-rock Karenna Johansson. She must be wondering if I am nuts, he thought. But she had never known what it was like to try to survive this life without a single strong mooring. To learn that zephyrs are alive, and find oneself in the midst of an invisible global revolution. Then a thought registered in his brain. Karenna Johansson was a Viking.

"Case of mistaken identity," he said.

"Really," she said evenly.

"Let's go," he said. "We'll miss dinner."

She looked him over, as if deciding something for herself. Then she put the Saab in gear, and they drove away.

Acknowledgments

Nautilus: a modern sequel to 20,000 Leagues Under the Sea, is extrapolated in part from years of experiences during archaeological expeditions to islands in the Arctic and the Pacific, from dives to manned undersea research stations in the Caribbean and on board a nuclear submarine in the Atlantic, combined with other wonderful years as a museum, library, and archives rat. The novel's projection of state-of-the-art remote sensing techniques onto archaeological sites in the near-future is one I believe is coming much more rapidly than even I would have imagined when I wrote the first draft of the first chapter in the summer of 1996. Since then, its imaginary world where archaeologists on satellite-guided submarines, conning autonomous undersea vehicles and establishing remote-control outposts on islands in the polar regions, to discover the greatest secret in the history of global exploration, well, it all seems, today, like every day adventure fiction rather than futuristic science fiction.

I owe much in this book's development to the Oxford University Press William Butcher translation and annotation of *Twenty Thousand Leagues Under the Seas* by Jules Verne published in 1998. An earlier edition, introduced by Ray Bradbury, has been a constant dog-eared companion in my library since boyhood. A Harvard University translation of *Anabasis* really exists, but was translated into English by Carleton L. Brownson and revised by John Dillery (Cambridge, Mass: Harvard University Press 1998 (1922)), not Caldwell. The latter is a tribute to a dear professor from my undergraduate days at the University of Rhode Island, who passed away in 1997.

Another lifelong mentor from those days was Prof. Wynne Caldwell, who read each early draft of the manuscript and continued for many years to act as my literary guide through an increasingly disturbed universe. My close friend from our Washington, D.C. archives rat days, Brendan McNally, kept me up on Euro-gossip over the years and inspired me with his own successful march to the novelist's summit. Two other close colleagues, Bill Thomas at Montclair State University and Susan Barr of Riksantikvaren in Oslo, Norway, read and made insightful suggestions to the first draft, Susan on the Arctic and Bill on the Pacific. Still a fourth colleague, J. Michael Lennon, formerly of Wilkes University, took it from there, slogging uphill through a dozen drafts while constantly sharpening my focus even as he expanded my literary horizons. Without the aid and comfort of these friends, I would not have finished this work in anything close to the story you read now. My wife—best friend, closest companion, and gentle critic—has endured innumerable drafts as well, and helped refine my understanding of the science laboratory. To her this novel is lovingly dedicated. That said, I hold them responsible for no errors, omissions, statements or misstatements of facts or opinions.

In fact, the close student of Arctic and Polynesian exploration will have fun trying to figure which places and references are real, and which imaginary. Literature, I believe, should provide a both a distraction from the everyday, and an alternative to it. My experiences as a field archaeologist in Svalbard are some of the most highly treasured moments of my existence on this planet. It is perhaps the Arctic's geography—so different from the sandy scrub pine forests of my native Massachusetts—that has given to me its powerful sense of being another world, a place of infinite possibility, almost like another planet. It is where, in the end, I would have no trouble believing that an explorer might find the wreck of the *Nautilus*.

A final note: My pseudonym, Pete Shaw, derives from Scottish ancestors, Peter McLachlan (1834-1907), a young Irish railway plate layer who, while working on the Great North of Scotland Railway in